PENGUIN BOOKS

THEIR *Greatest* STRENGTH

GREATEST LOVE SERIES BOOK 5

About The Author

Hannah is an Amazon top 50 bestselling author from Canada. Obsessed with swoon-worthy romance, she decided to take a leap and try her hand at creating stories that will have you fanning your face and giggling in the most embarrassing way possible. Hopefully, that's exactly what her stories have done!

Hannah loves to hear from her readers and can be reached on any of her social media accounts.

Instagram: Hannahcowanauthor
Facebook: Hannah Cowan Author
Facebook Group: Hannah's Hotties
Youtube: Hannah Cowan Author
Website: www.hannahcowanauthor.com

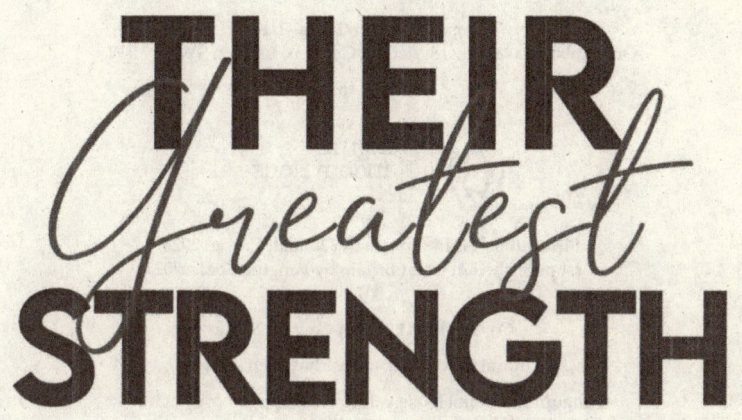

THEIR Greatest STRENGTH

GREATEST LOVE SERIES BOOK 5

HANNAH COWAN

PENGUIN BOOKS

PENGUIN BOOKS

UK | USA | Canada | Ireland | Australia
India | New Zealand | South Africa

Penguin Books is part of the Penguin Random House group of companies
whose addresses can be found at global.penguinrandomhouse.com

Penguin Random House UK,
One Embassy Gardens, 8 Viaduct Gardens, London SW11 7BW

penguin.co.uk

First published in Canada by Hannah Cowan 2025
First published in Great Britain by Penguin Books 2025
001

Copyright © Hannah Cowan, 2025

The moral right of the author has been asserted

Penguin Random House values and supports copyright.
Copyright fuels creativity, encourages diverse voices, promotes freedom
of expression and supports a vibrant culture. Thank you for purchasing
an authorized edition of this book and for respecting intellectual property
laws by not reproducing, scanning or distributing any part of it by any
means without permission. You are supporting authors and enabling
Penguin Random House to continue to publish books for everyone.
No part of this book may be used or reproduced in any manner for the
purpose of training artificial intelligence technologies or systems. In accordance
with Article 4(3) of the DSM Directive 2019/790, Penguin Random House
expressly reserves this work from the text and data mining exception

Editing and proofreading by Sandra @oneloveediting
Interior illustrations by Jordan Burns @joburns.reads
Printed and bound in Great Britain by Clays Ltd, Elcograf S.p.A.

The authorized representative in the EEA is Penguin Random House Ireland,
Morrison Chambers, 32 Nassau Street, Dublin D02 YH68

A CIP catalogue record for this book is available from the British Library

ISBN: 978-1-405-97876-7

Penguin Random House is committed to a sustainable future
for our business, our readers and our planet. This book is made from
Forest Stewardship Council® certified paper.

Also By Hannah

Swift Hat-Trick trilogy

Lucky Hit
Between Periods
Blissful Hook
Overtime
Vital Blindside

Greatest Love series

Her Greatest Mistake
Her Greatest Adventure
His Greatest Muse
His Greatest Treasure
Their Greatest Strength

Cherry Peak series

Strung Along
Catching Sparks
Chasing Home
Stealing Sunshine

Amateurs In Love duet

Craving The Player
Taming The Player

Standalones

Snow Harm, No Foul
Till cupid do us part

Family Trees
CHARACTER ORIGINS

SWIFT HAT-TRICK TRILOGY

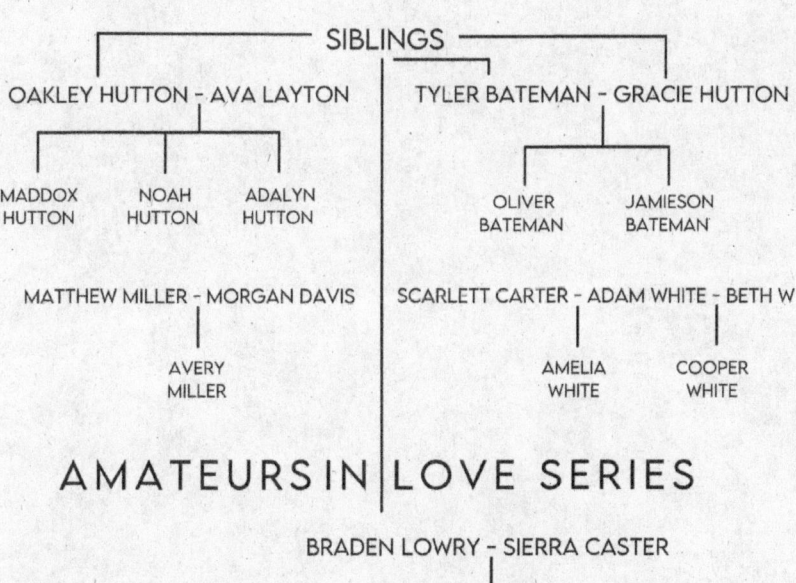

AMATEURS IN LOVE SERIES

BC PYTHONS
Important Names

GRAHAM WARREN	OWNER
RILEY TANNER	COACH
JAXON HAYES	QB
JAMIE BATEMAN	WR
CHASE HUDSON	WR
ZACH MERCER	DT

Enchanted (Taylor's Version) — Taylor Swift ★	4:45
Love Me Land — Zara Larsson	2:40
A Girl's Love — Mitchell Tenpenny	4:44
Pieces (Hushed) — Andrew Belle	3:19
2 Hands — Tate McCrae	3:02
jealousy, jealousy — Olivia Rodrigo	4:08
Lover (First Dance Remix) — Taylor Swift	3:53
Finally // beautiful stranger — Halsey ★	3:41
Turning Page — Sleeping At Last	4:16
Kiss Me — Ed Sheeran	4:41
How You Get The Girl (Taylor's Version) — Taylor Swift	2:37
We Found Love — Rihanna, Calvin Harris	3:35
Love — Lana Del Ray ★	4:33
Take on the World — You Me At Six	4:31
fOoL fOr YoU — ZAYN	3:22
Light Me Up — Ingrid Michaelson ★	4:08

Disclaimer

This story centres around the CFL instead of the NFL. The CFL shares many similarities to the NFL, but there are a few key differences. For the sake of this story, Jamie makes more than the current highest-paid player in the CFL. It is not an accurate representation of the real world. And yes, there really are only three downs in Canadian football.

Please beware of some sensitive topics in this story. These sensitive topics include: parental abandonment, mention of alcohol and drug abuse, mention of an overdose, and past death of a parent.

Please read at your own discretion.

If you haven't subscribed to my website or joined my Facebook group, now is the time!

www.hannahcowanauthor.com
Hannah's Hotties on FB

1

Blakely

My ass is numb from sitting in my chair all day. The tightness between my shoulders is impossible to roll out as I lean over my desk and stare at the time on the corner of the computer monitor.

4:53. Only seven more minutes until I can get the hell out of this prison and back home. I take the next customer off hold and speak into my headpiece.

"Thank you for calling Wavelink. My name is Blakely. What can I do for you today?" I ask, reading off the script that's become imprinted in my mind.

There's a very loud, very male huff. "Finally! I've been on hold for twenty minutes. Do you people just sit around doing nothing all day?"

I smile tightly despite nobody being here to see it. I'm in a tiny cubicle surrounded by fifteen other tech support workers, and not a single one of us gives a shit about the other. We're all here for a paycheque and nothing more.

"I'm sorry, sir. What can I help you with today?"

"Do you not talk to one another over there? I've already explained this issue to three other people before you!"

"I'm sorry. Can you just repeat the issue one last time?"

Or, depending on your attitude, I can wait until you've explained it and send you to yet another worker to do it again.

"My bill is completely wrong! I've been charged three times more than I have been the last several months. I'm not paying this!"

"I understand. Can you give me your account number, please?"

He rattles it off, and I quickly type it in before opening his last five phone bills. Despite only being on a call, I swear I can feel the dude breathing down my neck as I scroll through them.

"Have you been keeping track of your bills, sir?" I ask.

"Of course I have. What type of person do you think I am? Do you think I'm dumb?" he attacks.

I inhale, letting his anger roll off my back. "No. I'm just asking because your last bill was only twenty dollars higher than the previous four, and I'm seeing that you've added on another phone to your plan."

"I added another phone but didn't agree to a price raise!"

"You added an additional phone plan to your account. Every phone has its own charges, so it wasn't possible for you to stay at the same price," I explain, hoping I don't sound as shocked by his stupidity as I feel.

Even after doing this job for three months, it never fails to surprise me how assuming some people are. And just downright rude.

News flash: if you expect help from someone, you should at least try to keep your asshole comments to yourself until after you've gotten it.

"You're kidding me. Why wasn't I told this when I added another phone?"

You absolutely were. "I'm not sure, sir. But there isn't anything I can do to lower your bill for the past month as the charges were what they were estimated to be. The only thing I can offer is to remove the additional phone if you don't want to pay extra in the upcoming months."

"No!" he screams into the phone. "I need the second phone! If I didn't, I wouldn't have added it. God! Do you know how to listen at all, or are you deaf as well as stupid?"

4:59.

I'm burning with rage both inside and out. Reminding myself that this is just part of the job isn't working this time. Maybe it's my lack of sleep last night from taking care of a sick teenager or, honestly, just a lack of patience for men who don't understand how to treat people—women specifically—with respect.

I show up to do the same job as thousands of other people, and I'm good at it. Even though I constantly feel like I'm wasting my days away slouched over a computer desk with the same rehearsed speech on my tongue, I continue to show up because I need the money. Still, there's only so much a person can take, and three months of this has worn me very thin.

I'm not lesser than anyone because of my job or my gender, and I'm really, really fucking tired of feeling like I'm a piece of trash they're shoving to the bottom of a garbage bin. I may need this job, but I've never wanted it. If it weren't for needing to put food on the table for my brother, I wouldn't be here at all.

With a white-knuckled grip on my computer mouse, I watch the time change on the monitor and let loose.

"You know what? The fact you didn't even think for two seconds that you'd have to pay for another phone plan makes *you* the stupid one. And I mean that in a really offensive way. Come on, you have to pay for everything in this economy! Why would you ever get a phone plan for free? Are you the freaking owner of the company? Or are you just like the other millions of people in the world who believe that you deserve whatever you desire on a silver platter? Wake up, buddy! Because I can promise you that the world really isn't all that great or kind and that spending your time yelling at me won't change that. Now, pay your goddamn bill and decide if you want me to just delete your account so you'll never have to pay another bill to us ever again!"

I widen my eyes as my breath saws in and out of my lungs. Staring at the sheet of paper taped to the side of my cubicle with the reminder of every call being recorded, I debate backtracking and apologizing for everything I've said.

I don't. I won't.

Someone shuts a file cabinet door, and it's so quiet in the office that you can hear it rattle. If someone dropped a pen on the carpet, I'd bet everyone from a floor up could hear it.

The customer doesn't say anything, but as the busy line light continues to flash, I know he hasn't hung up. I release my hold on the desk and press my fingers to my brow.

"Look—"

"Enjoy your last day of pay. I'm going to be calling your superiors the moment I hang up on you to make sure he starts hiring more competent employees!"

Thank God I didn't apologize to this man.

I curl my fingers into a fist and lean over my desk to the point I'm nearly falling out of my chair. "Oh, you can get fucked, asshole!"

Hanging up on the call, I bring my fist down hard on the desk, making it shake with the force. The gasps that fill the office try to bring me down to a normal level of realization, but I ignore them and fall back into my chair, head shaking. With a push of my leg, I spin myself away from the computer.

I'm not expecting to come face to face with my boss.

Arms crossed and scowl prominent, he stares me down from the entrance to my cubicle. His eyes are so angry that one look at him has my stomach turning and my bag already in my hand.

There's nothing personal on my desk besides one framed photo, so I shove it inside my bag and stand, refusing to hunch from shame.

"For the record, he was a douchebag," I mutter.

The guy doesn't so much as soften his glare slightly. "HR will contact you."

"Great."

He doesn't give me extra room me to pass, so I make sure my shoulder makes contact with his and keep my nose turned up to the sky.

Then, I walk out of this building while ignoring the icy dread of not having a plan for what to do next.

"It's okay. That place wasn't good enough for you, anyway," Nate says, his cheek pressed into his pillow.

For being only fifteen, my brother is smarter than most people double his age and has such a calm and understanding view of the world. I always said that's why I was born with such a short temper. We had to even each other out somehow.

I press the back of my hand to his forehead and frown at how hot it is. "I'll figure something else out for work."

"You know, I have enough money saved to buy my own uniform this year. It's not that much, is it?"

Lying is easier than telling him just how expensive it is to outfit a teenager for minor football and afford everything else that comes along with the season.

"No. You're not buying anything."

He pushes himself up onto his elbow and frowns at me. "What's the point of me working if I can't help out around here?"

"It's not your job to take care of us. Your money is for you to have. Buy yourself something nice or save it. It doesn't matter what you do with it as long as you aren't using it on things that are my responsibility to provide. I'm your guardian, Nathan. That's that."

I stand from the bed and cross the small apartment to the kitchen before starting to heat up some soup in the microwave. The backs of my eyes prickle, but I refuse to cry. I've figured out how to fix worse problems than I'm facing right now.

Ever since our mother left on my eighteenth birthday, five years ago now, I've been taking care of Nathan as I would a son more than a little brother. That's meant working shitty jobs during any hours of the day and night and scraping together pennies to keep this apartment over our heads and cheap food on the table.

We've hardly made it these last five years despite my shrinking belief that if I only give it a little more time, everything will end up working itself out. If anything, it's only grown harder to keep going.

Between unpaid rent that I've had to beg the owner of the building for yet another extension on, the costs for Nate's football this season, and the power bill that's been rolled over for a second month, I feel like I'm drowning just thinking about having to find a new job.

"You're too stubborn," Nate says.

His voice has me turning from where the bowl spins in the microwave. Sweat drips down along his temples as he leans against the wall. It's been the year for the flu, and we've both had it one too many times at this point.

"And you're not supposed to be walking around. Go lie back down, and I'll be there in a second."

"I'm sick, not dead. I can microwave my own soup."

"Practice starts next week, Nate. You're not missing your first day of school either, so you need to get better quickly. That starts with resting and letting me feed you."

I pull open the cupboard above the microwave and stare at the empty shelves once stocked with medication. The bottle I finished this morning sits on the countertop as a reminder that I forgot to pick some more up on my way home.

"How are you feeling now? Have you thrown up since this morning? Once I get you into bed with some food, I'll make a trip to the store to pick up some more medicine," I ramble, pulling the microwave door open.

The bowl is blistering hot when I grab it, and I curse while setting it on the counter, the soup nearly sloshing over the rim. Steam swirls into the air, and I'm quick to take the sleeve of crackers I left out earlier and pull a few free to crunch into the soup. I dig a spoon into his dinner and swirl it around.

"I can live without more meds, Blake. Stay home and watch TV with me tonight. I made sure not to get ahead in our show while you were gone today," he says, discreetly trying to bribe me.

I smile at that and use my shirt sleeves to protect my fingers while carrying the bowl to him. "We can watch an episode when I get home."

"You promise?"

"I promise."

We walk together to the only bedroom in the apartment, and I let him enter first.

While we've been here since before Mom left, it's only been the last few years that Nate's had a room to himself. He's fifteen and needs his own space. Some privacy. Before the shift, we shared the pull-out couch in the living room. While we might not be financially thriving right now, this is the best option I can give him. It works for now.

Nate flips the light on and tosses himself onto the messy bed. Once upon a time, the comforter was covered in little footballs, but those have long since faded, leaving brown splotches amongst the blue.

I focus on the trophies on his dresser and find reassurance in my choice to keep him in football regardless of the cost.

"Come on, get under the blankets," I order, placing the soup on the nightstand.

His textbooks and pencils clutter the small desk on the other side of his room, but otherwise, he's kept the space clean and tidy. Laundry is in the bin, and dirty dishes are in the sink.

He groans while yanking the blanket over his long legs and propping himself against his pillow. His stomach growls when I move the bowl of hot soup to his waiting hands.

I exhale, brushing his hair away from his sweaty forehead. It's too long, but I know he likes it this way. With his deep brown eyes, strong nose and jaw, and a love for the world that doesn't seem well-deserved, he reminds me of our dad in too many ways to count.

Yet, I swear that every day he becomes a little bit more like him than the last.

Watching him grow into a good man is all I want. If I can help him get there, I'll know that it was all worth it. That's why I push myself the way that I do.

Always for my little brother and the life I yearn for him to have.

2

Jamie

I don't know where I got my charm from.

My father's idea of flirting comes in the form of caveman grunts and threatening glares, and my brother . . . well, let's just say that the apple didn't fall far from the tree.

It could be a natural-born gift, and I was the only one in three Bateman men who was blessed with it. Yeah, that sounds about right.

"With the season over the halfway mark now, can you tell me what your main focus is when it comes to improving your game for the last half?"

The blonde bombshell of a reporter along today's sidelines extends her small microphone in my direction, waiting for a reply. I flash a lopsided grin and use the microphone as an excuse to lean closer. With my mouth hovering over it, I brush the back of her hand with my knuckles.

"Are you hinting at my game needing to be improved, Jas? Because I can assure you that it's still as good as it's always been," I tease.

The apples of her cheeks burn bright beneath her makeup as she shoves my arm. "That's not what I meant, Jamieson, and you know it."

"It's Jamie, babe," I remind her.

"You're a flirt, *Jamie*. Now, answer my question before my boss replaces me with Edgar again."

I suck air through my teeth and give her hand a final touch before backing up. "Not being able to see your beautiful face on the sideline every practice would be a crime."

"So, let's try this again. With the season over the halfway mark now, can you tell me what your main focus is when it comes to improving your game for the last half?"

Pawing at my jersey, I peel it up my chest to wipe at the sweat sticking to my throat. The final week of the August heat is in full swing, and our two-hour practice only finished a handful of minutes ago.

Jas's eyes wander to my abdomen, wide and hot, and I swallow a knowing laugh before answering her question correctly this time.

"I've been working a lot with our receivers coach on my footwork and timing to make sure I'm where I need to be more often for our QB. That's definitely been a big focus for me this year."

I'm the top-paid wide receiver in the CFL, but that doesn't mean shit if I'm not fast enough to beat out a solid defense and get a ball in my hands. I've lost track of how many extra hours I've put in the last few months, striving to be better.

"Have you noticed a difference so far? Has your chemistry with Jaxon Hayes changed this season? It appears that he's searching for you more often than he maybe previously would have."

Releasing my jersey, I absorb the question and think twice about my answer. Media training has been a blessing when it comes to pain-in-the-ass reporters, but sometimes, I'd love to be as honest as I want with the good ones. Censoring myself for the good of the team is more difficult than one would think, even if I don't have anything necessarily bad to say.

It doesn't help when we keep getting asked the same questions. That's if more than the same two reporters come to talk to us. It's like the Pythons have been shoved to the bottom of the Must Interview list the past two seasons.

"Been watching me often, Jas?"

She blinks and snaps her eyes up my body to my face. They tighten at the corners. "Everyone has. Your new contract sent the fans a bit haywire. There's a spotlight on you right now."

"There already was. Now, everyone just has another reason to stare besides my outrageous talent."

"I guess we'll see during Saturday's game. Are you excited to face Edmonton?" she asks, trying to keep control of the interview.

"I'm ready. The team's ready."

"So are we. Thank you for taking the time today, and good luck Saturday."

I tip my chin and wink before leaving her at the sideline and jogging away from the other reporter hounding Zach Mercer, our best defensive tackle. Back when I first joined the team, we didn't allow on-field interviews before, after, or during practices, but Coach has been as pressured from upstairs about the media as the players have been.

We're supposed to be focused, not eyeing the cameras at the sidelines. But according to the owner of the BC Pythons, we're not involved enough. We've dropped down the list of in-demand teams with potential players, fans, and the media. Considering our rebuild team status, nobody gives two flying shits about us. We're to do everything we can to change that as soon as possible, and that goes beyond playing better.

Personally, I just don't have the time for them. If I'm not playing, I'm at the gym or with my family. The media has never been a priority for me, regardless of how much I love to see my handsome face onscreen.

"Bateman!" Jaxon Hayes, my QB, uses his scorning father shout to grab my attention from where he's avoiding the media down the field. "Over the shoulder!"

There's no point in going to meet him. Instead, I fit my

helmet back over my head and go to my starting mark. Coach is watching alongside the reporters when I get into position, stressfully pulling at the end of his mustache. A beat later, his whistle blows, and I'm moving.

Hayes lets the football loose in a perfect spiral that I track as I take off down the field. I pump my legs beneath me as I steady my breaths and smack my gloved hands together. Adrenaline burns my blood as I take the curve of my route and snatch the ball from the air, cradling it in my hands.

"Show-off!" Chase Hudson, my favourite wide receiver besides myself, yells before booing like an ass.

He's standing beside Jaxon, pointing accusingly at me as I jog over to them, panting. The running felt good an hour ago. Now, not so much.

"I wasn't showing off, Chase. I'm just that much better than you," I say through a toothy grin.

Sweat glistens off his dark skin as he rolls his brown eyes at me. "In your fucking dreams."

"Figured we should give them something to gawk at while they're here. Maybe they'll give you a spot on their lame podcasts with that catch," Jaxon huffs out.

Our QB grabs the ball from my hands and grips it tight in his. Standing two inches taller than me at six two, he runs a hand through his sandy-blond hair and nudges his chin toward the sidelines where the reporters linger.

"It's such a waste of time doing interviews. What did she ask you about, anyway?"

Coach negotiated for the hours during which the media should be allowed on the field but was only given so much leeway. So, now they show up in pairs whenever the hell they want to, and we're forced to entertain them. It's been taxing on the team.

I steal a glance at Coach when he glares down at his clipboard and stalks in the opposite direction of the reporter heading his way. It'll be a tense locker room in a few minutes, and that's not my favourite environment by a long shot.

"She wanted to talk about you, actually," I say, propping my hands on my hips. "Our chemistry and the shock of my contract."

Hayes scowls. "They make it seem like I hated you last season."

Chase barks a laugh. "In reality, you're just a grumpy motherfucker and used to take that attitude on the field with you."

Jaxon launches the football down the field and into the arms of a running back lingering near Coach after being done with his interview.

"Fuck off."

I pull my helmet off and shake my hair out, droplets of sweat flinging. Jaxon shoves me aside and leads us down the field toward the entrance to the stadium.

"Hey, you're better now. That's what counts," I offer.

Chase blows a kiss at the receiver coach as we pass. "You're still an asshole, Jax, but at least you drop the hole for game day."

"Nothing like the Pythons' QB dropping his hole on the sidelines." I let loose a loud laugh, leaning into Chase's side. "Maybe that's why we've been punished with the media. We're cleaning up your filthy messes."

Jaxon curses us out and jogs away. We run after him, both of us laughing too hard to stand properly. A loud, intimidating-as-hell voice cuts through our laughter.

"Bateman! Get back here, will you?"

Chase sucks in a sharp breath, glancing over his shoulder. "The fuck did you do, J?"

"Other than flirt with the pretty reporter? Nothing."

"Of course you did," Jaxon grumbles. "You know Coach's got eyes in the back of his head."

I shift my body to face the players on the team heading our way. "It was harmless! There's no rule about not flirting that I know of."

"Ready to get spanked, Bateman?" Zach asks mid-stride, his long blond hair tied in a bun behind his head.

"I've always liked a bit of spanking."

He barks a laugh and passes me with a smack on my ass. "Make sure you let Graham Warren know that."

"Wait, you're talking—"

"About the owner? Yup. He joined Coach a couple'a minutes ago."

"Shit," I curse before pivoting and taking off back down the field.

For Coach to be staying after practice is saying something. He's not the type to stay longer than necessary, and after getting to know him over the last three years, I can safely say that he would have told the owner of the team exactly that if it weren't for something non-negotiable.

I've never met a guy so desperate to leave once time is up than Coach. I always wondered if he had a wife at home or something, but there's never been a ring on his finger.

Graham Warren, the owner of the BC Pythons football team, looks exactly how one would imagine a forty-five-year-old white dude with more money than I'd ever know what to do with. He's shorter than me for a change, with silver hair cropped short and Botox keeping his frown lines from becoming permanent.

Standing rigid on a football field in a full navy suit and glossy black shoes, he stares at me with expectance. Like he's already prepared for me to agree to whatever it is he's planning on asking me.

I clear my throat, smoothing a hand down the front of my jersey. "What's up?"

Coach tugs at his mustache, checking me over. For someone in their mid-thirties, he looks as young as I do. And his casual clothes make him stand out beside Graham. He looks a bit more human.

"You looked good out there today," he tells me.

Suspicion ripples through me. "Yeah? My releases were a bit lagged."

"Slightly. But I'm not concerned."

"Thanks. Were you down watching practice today?" I ask Graham, searching for the reason he's here but not trying to be obvious about it.

"No. I came down a few moments ago and wanted to catch you before you left."

"You're just in time, then."

Coach taps his clipboard to his thigh and turns to Graham. "Do you want to go up to your office to talk about this?"

"That might be best," Graham agrees, focusing on me.

Even with my bulk, the way he's looking in my direction has me feeling like a kid again.

I hang behind the two men the entire way through the field and into the stadium. Coach attempts to create conversation in the elevator, but I'm not up for chatting, and neither is Graham.

Once we step into the large office, I work to keep my limbs loose despite their desire to tighten up. "Alright. Let's hear it."

Graham Warren unbuttons his suit jacket and sits behind his desk, swallowing the chair with his huge frame. From what I know about him, he never played football and was handed his father's Pythons legacy when he passed a few years back, but with his intimidating-as-fuck height and hulk shoulders, he'd have been useful on D.

"I'll keep this short, Jamieson. Have you ever considered getting married?"

3

Jamie

"Come again?" I ask, positive that I've heard him wrong.

Graham doesn't so much as blink before repeating, "Have you ever considered getting married?"

Coach leans against the closed door and blows out a breath, his nose pinched between two fingers. Something unsettling churns in my gut.

"Uh, yeah, I guess. In like ten years from now. I'd have to have a girlfriend before considering that type of decision," I say cautiously.

Graham props his elbows on the glossy wood desk and clasps his fingers. "What are your thoughts on marriage for business?"

"Like for a work visa?"

It's not completely unheard of for international players to marry for work visas. But I'm Canadian, and unless they're wanting me to marry a man, I don't think I'm on the right track here. I wouldn't have necessarily said no to marrying a guy, though—

"No. Not a visa. For the team itself," he says, interrupting my train of thought.

I furrow my brows. "I'm confused."

Coach steps up beside me and pats my back, providing a bit of stability in a sea of confusion.

"You don't have to do this, Bateman," he mutters.

"He's right. You don't. But the entire Pythons team would be in your debt if you did," Graham adds.

I blink rapidly and sit in one of the plush chairs across from his desk with my knees parted wide. "Back up. You still haven't even told me what it is exactly that you need from me."

"I'm sure that you're aware of the empty stands at our home games and the lack of media interest," Graham says.

"I think the entire country is aware of that."

His jaw tightens at that answer. "Yes, it would seem so. Which is why I'm even entertaining this idea enough to bring it up."

I wait for him to continue, unsure of what will come out of my mouth if I open it. Coach seems to be doing the same thing.

"I've had an . . . idea brought to my attention by a few members of the organization. And we've all decided that you are the best player we have who can help us turn it into something that could potentially change things for everyone."

"They want you to marry a fan, Jamieson," Coach declares, cutting to the chase.

Crickets.

I lean back into the chair and cross my arms, huffing a laugh. "And that's supposed to fix things for us? A marriage between me and someone nobody knows? I don't mean any offense here, but do we really expect anyone to fall for that?"

"Do you spend a lot of time on social media, Jamieson? Honestly, I don't. But there is an entire team of people in this organization who know more about it than we could ever imagine. They've laid it all out for me, and I believe them. This is the easiest and fastest way to start a change here, and I'm only asking you to give it a chance. If you can't, I will find someone else who will, and we can forget I even brought it up," Graham says, his voice tight with restraint.

I scrub a hand down my face. "How would it even work? Are you planning on just picking some girl off the street and dropping her off at a church for me?"

Coach stifles a rough laugh while Graham reels backward, his features twisting with revulsion.

It's the latter who speaks first, disgusted. "No. Of course not. We were planning on leaving the choice of who up to you. All you'd have to do is bring whomever it is to meet with me first."

"So you can what, vet her?" I laugh, distraught, as I look back at Coach. "You don't think this is a good idea too, right?"

He keeps his expression closed off. "It isn't up to me."

"It's not like I have a contact list full of football fans that I can just call up one by one until we find someone suitable enough. And even if I did, how am I supposed to explain this? I mean, come on! I'm supposed to just get married to someone out of the blue? My fans won't buy it."

My phone doesn't have a single contact saved outside of my family and close friends. When I sleep with someone, I don't keep their number. Most of the time, I can even get away with whoever it is I take to bed not knowing who I am. It's always been easier that way. There isn't anyone to call on for this.

"I think you could convince them. That would be the entire point of this. The marriage would be certified to keep the truth behind the intent from coming out, but what you decide to do behind closed doors is up to you and the woman you decide to marry. Of course, we have a list of rules, but they're mainly for security purposes. It would only be for two, maybe three months, and then we would help with the divorce. You'll have our entire legal team at your disposal to ensure an easy transition both before and after this agreement," Graham explains.

While my head is spinning, I manage to ask, "So, you think that after the divorce, the team won't just fall right back to where we are now?"

"No. I don't. With big enough headlines, you will help put us back on the map. The stands will fill, we'll gain traction on social media, and jersey sales will increase. You won't be able to walk around Vancouver without seeing a handful of fans wearing your name and number, Jamieson. That's a promise I can make to you right now. This will work, and we'll have you to thank for it."

"This is insane," I declare on an exhale.

"It's not a situation I expected us to find ourselves in, and I had to insist both legal and PR let me handle this conversation on my own to not overwhelm you. I fear this may be our last hope before we're forced to find other ways to cut costs and find revenue to keep going."

Fuck.

"It's that bad?"

He keeps his confident stance, but I swear I can see some worry slash across his face. "I have investors and a board of directors to answer to."

"Again, no offense, but why should I agree to this? You can't punish me for saying no."

Graham cocks an eyebrow, appearing almost surprised by the question. Like he wasn't expecting me to know how to barter. "What do you want in return?"

"I'm not sure what's on the table."

"Your contract has already been taken care of."

I swallow, running through options in my head. I've never been much for money. It doesn't drive me or even give me surface-level happiness. The most important thing to me is my family. Everything I've done has been to make them proud. With a Vancouver Warriors legacy hockey star as a father, my choosing football instead of what was expected of me has always lingered in the back of my mind.

"What about a limited-edition jersey release? A collaboration between the Pythons and the Warriors," I blurt out.

There may as well be dollar signs flashing in Graham's eyes now. "For what?"

"A Hutton hockey jersey with both the Pythons and Warriors

on the front. No number. Call it a legacy edition, I don't know. But, yeah, I think that's my condition. I'll do this for you, and you'll make the jersey happen for me."

"You've got a deal," he declares.

"It's that easy?"

Coach chuckles. "You didn't ask for enough, Jamie."

"I don't need more than that," I say, jostling a shoulder.

I'm not sure I've ever seen Graham smile, but the slight twitch of his lips is close enough.

"You'll get more from this agreement regardless. I'll make the jersey happen, and in addition to that, you'll get to be the one to help the team. Your name will be everywhere."

"How long do I have to find someone?" I ask, feeling doubt wiggle into my chest.

I'm not doubtful that I can pull this off for the team. I know I can if I can find someone to help me. This will be a very insufferable few months if I can't enter into this sham of a wedding with someone I like or enjoy being around.

Then, there's my family. Shit, my brother is getting married next month to the woman he's loved for decades, and here I am, considering announcing a marriage of my own with a potential stranger.

The owner of the BC Pythons puts the full weight of his stare on me, but I don't buckle beneath it. "How long do you need?"

"Three weeks. I'll find someone, and you can meet her, but I need to at least get to know a few things about her first. I'm not marrying a complete stranger, and I'm damn sure not doing it before my brother's wedding."

"I'll accept that."

"We need to talk about what his obligations are while in this marriage, Graham. Don't be coy," Coach grunts.

His support comforts me, even if I should be worried that I didn't think to bring that up myself.

Graham stares at him and then me, tipping his chin. "This will be a PR stunt, Jamieson. We would need you to be completely on board with attending public events, posting on social media, and speaking of your new wife in interviews with the media. The aim is to create buzz. To bring new and old eyes to the team and its players with a story of an unlikely romance between one of the league's best players and an ordinary woman. If all goes according to plan, the public will fall in love with the story you create."

I lean over my legs and dig my elbows into my knees. "And my sponsorships won't be negatively affected by this?"

"We'll ensure that doesn't happen," he swears.

"Well, shit, guys." I huff out a laugh. "And I don't suppose either of you have any ideas of where to start looking for a wife?"

Coach barks a laugh. "Not unless you want to spend a few nights in a sports bar or outside of the game Saturday."

"I haven't been to a sports bar since college."

"You'll figure it out, Jamieson," Graham says.

I knock my knuckles against the edge of his desk. "You might as well call me Jamie at this point. Considering everything you're asking me to do, I'd assume that makes us friends."

Under normal circumstances, I wouldn't think about talking to the man in control of my entire career with such nonchalance, but like I mentioned, this should make us friends. I'm taking a giant risk for him and this club, and I think that earns me some points.

It doesn't help that I'm fully aware of how heavy my contract was. I cost this organization a shit ton of money, and while it might not be fair, I do feel like I owe them this. It's only three months of my life. I'm young and have much more time left. It could be worse.

They could be choosing someone for me. Someone I might hate and dread spending however many months with. At least I'm in control of this choice. And they did give me the chance to turn them down and leave it up to another player to deal with, not to mention my impromptu demand.

"Why didn't you ask Jaxon or any of the other guys to do this instead?"

"We're interested in it being you," Graham answers.

"Okay, but why? Jaxon's more popular."

Coach is reluctant to meet my curious gaze, and I grow more confused.

Graham isn't as reluctant to look at me, but I suppose that comes from being such an intimidating mofo. I doubt he gets nervous about saying anything to anyone.

"Jaxon is more popular on the team but not in the country. You're Tyler Bateman's son and the cousin of both Maddox and Noah Hutton. You have the connections and the fans at the ready to come running once the news breaks of this new relationship."

I sniff. It's not the first time I've been used to get something from my family. When you grow up with one of the most successful hockey players in the NHL as a father and then alongside a cousin like Maddox Hutton, who soared even higher in the professional hockey league, you learn to accept that sometimes, people only want to know you to meet someone else.

My parents knew I'd choose football from a young age, but everyone else . . . I think they wished I'd followed in the hockey footsteps that had been laid for me to follow. Maybe that's why Graham agreed so easily to my offer. All men at the level he's at are focused on one thing. Money. I've promised him that twice over.

Oliver, my older brother, didn't choose either sport. Instead, he opted for a life as a firefighter, and he's never regretted that. Not once. We're similar in that way. There's no way I'd have chosen anything other than football, regardless of what anyone else in my family had done.

Noah Hutton, Maddox's younger brother, didn't choose hockey either. He chose music and is now one of the most successful artists in the world, selling out stadiums left and right, including the one I'm in right now.

If it were possible to bond with a man as cold and vicious as Noah, he would have been my top choice with everything we have in common.

Letting loose a soft laugh, I wink at Graham. "Using me for my family name. How very social climber of you."

"If I had another option as good as this one..."

I shake my head at my boss, keeping an easy smile in place. "Nah. I get it. And I'll do it."

"Thank you. You're doing a lot for the entire organization, Jamie," Graham says, relaxing slightly in his chair.

"You got it. I'm a team player."

"I expect updates from both of you," Coach barks, slipping into a dad role effortlessly. "And this isn't to take precedence over the game itself. Jamieson is my player before anything else."

Graham stands and holds the edge of his desk, keeping Coach in his sights. "Of course. We are nothing without the game."

"Glad we got that sorted, then."

"I guess I'll start looking for a wife now, then, huh?" I ask, breaking up their showdown.

Coach huffs a breath and starts for the office door. I linger, waiting for Graham to dismiss me first. As much as I want to get out of here and shed this dirty gear, I was raised around men like Graham Warren and know better than to leave without confirmation that we're finished.

"Yes. And keep me posted. I trust you'll handle this quickly and subtly."

It's almost a threat.

"You got it."

Graham lifts a hand toward the door, where Coach is lingering with a scowl. "We're done for now, then."

I take my leave eagerly and follow Coach out of the office. It's not until we step into the elevator that he speaks.

"You should have told him no."

Leaning back against the side of the elevator, I cock my head at him. "We both know that wasn't really an option. If I had said no, he could have just found a way to make me do it anyway. Plus, I still got something out of it."

Maddox was in this position years ago in a move orchestrated by his old hockey team, the Vancouver Warriors. Only instead of a wife, he was forced to enter a fake dating arrangement with his childhood sweetheart to hide a scandal. I know all about the illusion of being able to say no when, in reality, the moment you do, you're told that *yes*, you *are*.

At least the asshole was allowed to fake date her instead of getting very legally married. Even if he would have secretly loved marrying his now wife that much earlier.

"What are you planning on doing? Going onto the street and holding a sign that says, 'I'm looking for a wife, any takers'?" Coach grunts.

I laugh, watching the doors open to expose the hallway leading to the dressing room.

"No, Coach. We both know I'm more of a waiting for a treasure chest to wash ashore type of guy."

4

Blakely

WALKS HAVE ALWAYS HELPED CLEAR MY HEAD. I MAY NOT BE ONE for normal exercise, but there's something about a silent walk in a softly lit neighbourhood that soothes me. The calmness of the evening, the chirping of grasshoppers in overgrown grass, and the drone of cars in the distance. It's the time I take to just be.

To feel like myself again instead of a failing mother figure and the person whom I'd hoped I'd be by now. It's only been one day since I lost my job, and I'm already tempted to pull my hair out. If I don't find another soon . . .

I kick a rock with the toe of my old sneaker and stretch my fingers at my sides, as if I'll be able to run them through the air that's felt too suffocating the past few years.

I've never been down this street before. It's a new neighbourhood, and as I stroll down the sidewalk, it becomes clearer and clearer that I don't belong here.

The houses have tripled in size since I crossed the street a minute ago, and with that, so has the cost of the shiny cars in the driveways. Convertibles, tinted SUVs, and luxury imports with the logos from TV.

I stumble on the perfectly smooth sidewalk when I reach a

house that might as well have been plucked from the pages of a home design magazine.

Two storeys high with a covered porch, black wood accents, white brick siding, and wide-paned windows, it's . . . gorgeous. A house like one that I *did* cut out of a home magazine and glued onto my dream board.

The landscaping is perfect, all deep green grass and tall hedges for privacy. There are tiny rocks lining the edges of the sidewalk leading to the porch before splitting to surround trimmed shrubs. It would look even better with some flowers, but with fall coming soon, there wouldn't be a point in adding any.

Not that it matters, Blakely.

I tuck my hair behind my ear and realize I've stopped directly in front of the house to stare like a creep. But that realization doesn't have me continuing on my way like it should.

Something draws me closer to this specific place. Like there's an invisible hand shoving at my back, I leap forward a step past the hedges. My shoe scuffs the sidewalk, and my heart pounds hard and quick.

"Oh, you're such an idiot," I whisper to myself.

My throat constricts when I get far enough up the sidewalk to realize that the black front door with a gorgeous golden handle is open. It's odd, considering the lack of vehicles on the long driveway. They could be parked in the three-car garage, but what if the owner isn't home and someone's broken in?

I pat my pocket where my phone rests and slowly continue up the sidewalk. Sure, it would be really stupid for someone to rob a house like this when the sun hasn't even fully set yet, but I know better than anyone that when you're desperate enough for something, the time of day doesn't matter. You'll make it work no matter what.

With slow steps, I make my way onto the porch, only an arm's length from the open door. It's silent inside, even after I knock my knuckles against the door and wait.

"Hello? Is anyone home?" I call.

This is so stupid. And reckless. Nate will tear my ear off about this the minute I go home, but my damn conscience won't let me turn away now. The chance something could be wrong is enough to keep me from running off.

Holding my breath, I push open the door and move inside. "Hello?"

Still nothing.

I suck in a sharp breath at the interior of the home. The door is still open behind me as I drift through the entrance and gawk at the crown moulding, the black accents that have been carried in from outside, and the perfectly coordinated furniture.

Directly to the left of the entrance is a sunken living room with a U-shaped sectional, a real brick fireplace, and a massive flat-screen that must have cost thousands of dollars. It opens into a luxury kitchen with every high-end appliance known to man and an island fitted with six bar stools.

There are clothes strewn all over the living room. I make out a pair of boxer shorts with . . . eggplants all over them on the back of a white armchair? And are there really three gaming consoles hooked up to the TV? Who needs that many?

Growing distracted, I hurry to the row of consoles. My frown is solid as the desire to be able to give even just one to Nathan swallows me. He gave up asking for one by the fourth Christmas in a row I just couldn't make it work.

There was never any rudeness from him when one didn't show up because that's not who Nate is. He's sweet and understanding above all else. But that didn't mean I hadn't wished and wished that I could have given him one.

Crouching in front of the row of them, I look around the room for any sign of another person. Unless the clothes are a sign of a robbery or, shit, even a murder, I don't think anything went on here. It seems more likely that the owner of this home just forgot to close the door all the way.

The first game console is plugged into the back of the TV, and while I've never hooked one up before, I know it wouldn't be that hard to tug at the cords and run out of here with it . . .

I hesitate with my fingers brushing the top of it, a war of good and bad raging in my head. Whoever owns these is clearly well enough off that they could simply buy another one to replace this, but they shouldn't have to.

I'm not the type of person to steal, but . . . *fuck*, I'm desperate. Desperate for just one thing to give Nathan. Sure, he could buy one on his own, but all I've ever wanted is to provide for him, and to see the look on his face when I show up with this? Especially after the week he's had with the flu?

Reaching up, I pull the connecting cord from the TV, my mind made up. Fuck guilt. The saying is "eat the rich" for a reason.

"Would you like some help with that? Or if you're interested, I have a huge stack of games you can steal while you're at it."

I jump at the deep voice and gasp while falling backward onto my ass. The floor is hard enough that the impact rattles my bones as I look in the direction of the man and tense.

"Who are you?" I attack, crab crawling backward before pushing to my feet.

Shit. This is so my karma for attempting to steal.

This guy is not who I was expecting to own a place like this. Not because he doesn't look like he could be successful, but because he doesn't seem to want to skin me alive for sneaking into his house and attempting to steal from him.

The smirk on his plump lips and humour in the steel blue of his eyes throws me for a loop. This isn't an overly funny situation, and I'm certainly not feeling very at ease about it. I've just been caught stealing from a stranger. It's a surprise I haven't torn out of this place yet.

I definitely should when I realize that he's currently half-naked. Wearing only a pair of low-riding grey sweatpants and a backward baseball cap, he leans against the wall with his arms crossed. And by arms, I really mean tree trunks. Christ alive, they could be as thick as my thighs, and I've always been heavier-set.

Clearly, he's some sort of gym buff. First, the arms, and now, a stomach fit with flexing abdominal muscles and a deep-cut V leading to the waist of his sweatpants.

I snap my eyes up to his face again and scowl. While he might not have abs up here, it's still a struggle not to get distracted by the sharp lines of his jaw or the strong nose that leads up to eyebrows that may be better kept than mine.

He's too good-looking to also be so well-built. Any guy who's hot both above and below the shoulders either has an incredibly small dick or an arrogance that already has me pushing to my feet, prepared to leave at the drop of a hat.

As if hearing my thoughts, he reaches up to press his hat further onto his head, causing the curling blond hairs beneath it to splay out.

"I live here. Who are you?"

Fuck. Even his voice is hot. All low and husky with a slight smoothness that I wouldn't doubt has led several females to his bed.

"I'm nobody."

He cocks his head slightly, eyes scrolling up and down my body. When he meets my stare again, his mouth lifts in a half smile.

"You're not a nobody."

"To you, I am," I argue.

"Currently, yeah. But I'd prefer to put a name to the face of the woman robbing me."

"Too bad."

His laugh is just as husky as his voice. "Would it gain me any points if I said that it's a pretty face?"

"It would actually make you lose points."

"Shit. You play hardball."

"You have no idea," I say with a huff.

He pushes off the wall and takes three steps toward me, careful to leave double that still between us. "I'd like to get one."

"Get what?"

"An idea. And a name. Anything, really."

"Don't you think you're being a bit desperate? Did you forget already that I was *just* trying to steal from you?"

His eyes crinkle at the corners as his laugh grows louder. "I can't say that anyone has ever called me desperate before, but if that's what it takes to get me what I want, then so be it."

I blink at him, a brow arching. "And what you want is my name?"

"Yeah, Bandit. I want your name."

"Don't call me that. We're so not on pet name status yet."

"Yet?" he asks, his smirk returning as he takes another two steps closer.

I narrow my eyes and glance at the front door, looking for an escape route just in case. When I look back at him, his smirk has morphed into a frown.

"I'm not going to hurt you," he clarifies, and I think I hear genuine sadness in his tone.

"You can't expect me to know that or to believe it. I don't know you."

"You could just as well hurt me if that's the basis we're using."

I fold my arms over my chest, forming a barrier between us. "You're also a man. And you're much bigger than me."

"You've got a point there. But I don't have any plans to hurt you. You're safe here."

"Safe," I echo, biting at the inside of my cheek. "From what, exactly?"

"From whatever it is you think I'm going to do that has you looking like if I take one more step in your direction, I'm going to end up with scratch marks all over my face."

"I was going to give you at least two steps before I did that, but if you insist on one." I shrug.

This feels a bit too much like flirting for me. Every word is just slipping out of my mouth without any thought. That sort of ease around a stranger isn't normal, and it's a sign that I need to leave now. Not to mention that Nate will be wondering where I've wandered off to if I'm not home soon, and the last thing I need to be doing is admitting that I almost stole something for him.

"I'm Jamie. J to my friends," the owner of the house reveals, offering me his hand. "We can pretend to shake hands if you want."

I simply stare at his hand, taken aback by how massive it is. Even without the lights on in the living room, I can make out the thick calluses on his palm, revealing that he must use his hands for work.

"Nice to meet you, Jamie, but I'm still not giving you my name. Now, unless you're planning on calling the cops on me, I need to leave."

Interest flares in his eyes. "Maybe I am. Why, do you have someone waiting for you at home?"

"You could say that."

He hums, and my pulse spikes at the way his gaze sharpens, as if he's already preparing to uncover the truth I'm hiding.

"If you're not going to give me your name, at least give me the first letter."

"Do you swear not to call the cops on me?" I barter.

"If I were going to, I would have the moment I saw you sneaking through my living room."

I blanch. "You saw me come inside?"

He winks. "I heard you yelling outside but didn't come downstairs until you passed the couch."

"Why didn't you stop me?"

"You looked so focused I figured I'd see what it was you wanted to take from me. I wasn't expecting the Xbox, though. There are more expensive things in this house than that."

I tug at the hem of my old shirt, suddenly more aware of how

I look amongst everything around me. There's a pasta sauce stain on this shirt and a rip in the ankle of my leggings, for crying out loud. My hair hasn't been washed in a few days in an attempt to keep the water bill down, and my shoes are one walk away from falling apart.

I'm sure I look pathetic in a house like this. Like a beggar desperate for something to pawn off for a few hundred bucks.

"I wasn't going to sell it. I didn't even come inside to steal from you. Your door was open, and I thought someone else might have broken in or worse," I mutter, too embarrassed to look at him. Instead, I focus on the path to the front door.

"You can have it," he offers quickly, and I realize that he's moved forward a step.

I shake my head, already moving down into the sunken part of the living room. It's easier to go this way than to pass by him and risk being touched. He might think he doesn't look like a threat, but as a woman who grew up in a run-down neighbourhood without the protection of anyone but myself, I know better than to let my guard down. Even if something in my gut tells me I can take this one at his word.

Jamie watches me move with a frown but doesn't chase after me. The relief of that is instant.

"I don't want it. It was a mistake to try and take it, and I'm sorry," I apologize, hoping it will help extinguish the embarrassment I feel.

He pulls his hat off his head and runs long fingers through his hair. "Can I drive you home?"

And show him where I live? Not a chance.

"No."

"So, you're just leaving now?"

I'm out of the living room by the time I hear him coming up behind me. The door is still open, and for a moment, I grow jealous at the knowledge. The fact this neighbourhood is safe enough that Jamie isn't the least bit worried about not double-checking that he locked it the moment he got home feels . . . unfair.

I've been woken up to the sound of my doorknob being jiggled from the outside too many times not to check the lock a minimum of ten times before going to bed every night.

"I shouldn't have been here in the first place. I'm sorry again," I mutter before slipping outside.

The air is still warm, but the breeze has cooled slightly. It's silent on the street as I rush down the porch steps and wrap my arms around my front.

"You chose this house out of all the others in this neighbourhood," Jamie calls from behind me. "Why do you think that was?"

I don't risk looking back and instead pass the tall hedges before answering him.

"It was the only place with an open door."

5

Jamie

"I THINK I FELL IN LOVE LAST NIGHT."

Mom almost drops the coffee pot in her lap. "I'm sorry, what did you just say?"

I shift my weight on the patio chair and sigh against the homemade cookie I'm hovering near my mouth. "I think I fell in love with my robber."

"Your *robber*?" she echoes. The coffee pot clunks on the table before blue eyes the same shade as mine narrow into slits. "Are you trying to give me a heart attack, Jamieson?"

"No, Ma. I'm just being honest, and I don't have anyone else to tell this to."

"Perhaps your brother? I was absolutely not prepared for that. Not from you."

She sits across from me, her stare gentling when I don't backpedal. I'd have grown defensive if there was any part of me that thought she was wrong for being so surprised.

I doubt this is what she was expecting us to be talking about during one of our morning coffee dates. I've been so busy the past week with training that this is the first time I could make the trip over to my parents' place. They'll be at my game Saturday, but there's never much time to chat then. Especially about topics like this.

"Maybe love is stretching it a bit," I admit.

"A bit or a lot?"

"Whatever is halfway between those options."

"Oh, Jamie," she says with a sigh.

I take the coffee pot and fill my mug to the rim before taking a long pull of the bitter liquid. My tongue burns while I decide to dump even more word vomit onto her.

"When I said robber, I didn't mean it literally. She was more like a bandit in training."

Mom props her cheek in her tiny palm. She was always a dainty woman, but as she's aged, she's shrunk even smaller. The platinum-blonde hair I've seen on her head since my childhood is still intact, without even a strand of gray appearing. It wouldn't surprise me if she's been dyeing it in secret all these years and lying about it.

"Continue, then. I fear I won't be able to move on with my day without knowing all the details."

"Well, are you wanting an entire recount of my evening or just the good parts?"

Her smile is bemused. "I'm always up for an hour-by-hour breakdown of your day, sweetheart."

"Okay, maybe not hour by hour. Don't be so needy, Ma," I chastise with a cluck of my tongue.

"Have I ever told you that you're too much like me?"

I huff a laugh, leaning back in my chair. "Only a million times."

"Good. Just making sure."

"Anyway," I drawl, crossing my arms. "I had just finished up in the gym when I heard someone shouting inside—"

"What do you mean 'inside'? Did you leave the front door open *again*?"

I hold out a hand before she can give me another lecture. "Maybe, but I swear I thought I'd closed it this time."

It's only happened a handful of times since I moved into my new place, as if that makes it any better.

"Jamieson, you can't be leaving your front door open! How many deer do you have to have wander inside and scare you half to death before you realize that? And for God's sake, you were robbed!"

Her cheeks have flushed with worry and anger, her firm mom gaze unwavering. I wiggle beneath it, still incapable of ignoring how well it works to make you uncomfortable.

"That only happened once, but I see where you're coming from. I wasn't exactly expecting to be robbed when I forgot to shut the door last night. The neighbourhood has a gate with a code, Ma." I blink, curiosity blooming. "Wait, do you think she knows one of my neighbours, then?"

"Who, Jamie? You've got to slow down here."

"My robber. Do you think she knows one of my neighbours? How else would she have gotten in?"

Mom rubs her lips together. "What happened? Because if she robbed you, the police need to be involved. It doesn't matter whether she knows someone in the neighbourhood or not."

"She didn't *actually* rob me. That's why I'm calling her a bandit in training. When I caught her in my living room, she was mortified to see that I was there. I even offered my Xbox to her after, but she refused to take it. That's not very robber-like, right?"

"Oh, honey. Did we shelter you a bit too much when you were growing up?"

I take a bite of the soft cookie and chew to keep from laughing at the question. We were absolutely not sheltered growing up. Not when Dad and my uncle Oakley were constantly in the spotlight, and we were exposed to nosy reporters and news articles.

My cousins and I grew up knowing that our actions were being watched and that we had to always be careful. That doesn't necessarily mean that we weren't up to some crazy shit in our teen years, but we had to be sneaky about it.

Dad never wore a mask in front of us either. He was his blunt, grumpy, sailor-mouthed self every single day of our lives. Mom even contemplating that we were sheltered is laughable.

"You did not shelter us. And I know I sound like an idiot right now, but there was *something* about this girl. I believed her when she said she didn't come inside to steal from me but because she was worried something had happened to me. Doesn't it say a lot about her that she went inside a stranger's house just to see if they were okay?"

"If she was telling the truth, then yes, it does."

"She was."

She nods. "Okay, let's say she was being honest. Did you get her name? Did she seem to know yours? What exactly happened?"

My stomach drops, the same reminders that have plagued me since last night making another appearance. "No. I didn't get her name. Even when I asked for it, she wouldn't give it to me. And as far as I could tell, she had no idea who I was. When I caught her in the living room, she looked like she was expecting me to storm over and curb stomp her or something. I didn't want to scare her, so I didn't push too hard. We talked for a few minutes while she rejected all my efforts to get to know her, and then she left."

"So, she thought someone might be in trouble when she saw the door open, then she went inside and tried to take your Xbox? Then you caught her, and you talked for a few minutes before she left?" Mom asks.

"When you say it like that, it sounds ridiculous."

Reaching across the table, she pats my hand. It's not a pity gesture but a genuine one that she's done a million times over the past twenty-three years of my life.

"Nothing that brings such strong feelings out of us is ridiculous. I'm just trying to piece together the whole story," she explains gently.

"That's all there is to the story. It's nothing crazy. I just . . . felt something when I was talking to her. Maybe I'm losing it."

Because surely there's no way I *actually* wanted the bandit to stay for another few hours just so I could learn a bit more about her.

Maybe it was how beautiful she was that had me all tangled up. It isn't normal for someone who looked like her to just show up randomly in my living room on a Wednesday night.

I've been with my fair share of women, but not even one of them has been able to hook me as quickly as my bandit did. Her chestnut hair was short and wavy, framing her narrow jaw and cheeks. Matched with her green eyes, naturally pouty lips, and a sharp tongue that lashed out without hesitation, I was more than intrigued.

The distance she kept between us and the worry in her eyes with every step I took toward her was concerning. I've always been a pretty protective person, and this stranger, a woman I've never seen before and worry I never will again, had me curious enough to contemplate asking for answers I had no right to have.

Even wearing ripped leggings, a dirty shirt, and her unabashedly bad attitude, I wasn't turned away. That says more than I can explain to my mom right now. My desire to learn about her isn't something even I can comprehend right now.

All I know is that I want to see her again. As ridiculous as that seems.

"You're not crazy, Jamie. I'm proud to have raised a son who is so in tune with his emotions," Mom says.

I can't help myself when I grin and ask, "Are you finally admitting that I'm your favourite son?"

"No. But you and Oliver have very different and just as special qualities that make you incredible men."

"Boo," I mutter before taking another sip of my coffee and taking another cookie from the plate.

She shakes her head, smiling slightly. "I'm very happy that you feel comfortable enough with me to tell me these things, sweetheart. I'm always going to be here for you, no matter what it is you're going through."

"Thanks, Mom."

"Of course. Are you going to try and find this woman?"

I arch a brow, tapping my mug. "You don't think that's creepy?"

"No. It actually sounds like something a younger version of me would have done."

"So, what was with all the questions? I thought you were thinking that I was just a weirdo for even contemplating being enthralled by a stranger!" I accuse, pointing my chocolate chip cookie at her.

She tucks a strand of blonde hair behind her ear and curls her mouth into a sly smile. "I'm your mother. Of course, I'm going to get all the facts before adding my opinion. You've always been more like me than your father, and this is absolutely something I would have done. Nothing is ever too far-fetched for you and me, especially not this."

I blow out a breath of relief before reality sets back in. "I have no idea how or where to find her, though."

"Considering how you met, I want to say that fate might intervene again sometime."

"So, I just have to wait until then?"

"Don't pout, Jamieson. Wait, or don't. Just make sure you know the risks with trying to find her with more . . . unconventional ways."

"Like hiring a PI?"

She laughs and steals my cookie. "Exactly like that."

Waiting doesn't sound that terrible. I've never been in a rush to find a girlfriend or— *Shit*. I'm supposed to get married in a few weeks.

Suddenly, sitting here with my mother is the last place I want to be. Maybe I could just tell her the truth. It's not like she'll share it with anyone.

Only my father and brother, all my aunts and uncles and cousins.

I blanch, my skin growing cold and clammy.

"Are you okay?" she asks, leaning forward and peering at me.

Clearing my throat, I stand. "I've remembered that I have a meeting this afternoon."

"Oh! Well, I won't keep you, then. Can I send you with the extra cookies?"

"Dad won't want them?"

"He's cut out sweets again. Says he's losing his abs with all my baking recently."

I bark a laugh. "He lost those years ago."

"Don't tell him that."

"You have my word.'

"Is that a yes, then?" she asks hopefully.

"It's always a yes."

Her eyes light up as she moves quickly, the plate of cookies held to her chest. We step in from the patio, and she searches through the kitchen for a container.

"Call your father today, okay? He's going to be pissed that he missed you this morning," she says while dumping all the cookies into a Tupperware.

I lean a hip to the counter and shove down my guilt for the last few minutes I'm here. "One of these days, he's going to have to retire for real and stop spending his afternoons at WIT."

White Ice Training is a hockey training facility that one of my dad's best friends owns. He's still as busy as ever and will continue to be that way forever at this rate.

"I think we both know that won't be for a while yet. He doesn't know the meaning of relaxation."

"Book a spa trip with his credit card and pack his bags. He won't have a choice then."

Mom pops on the lid of the container and hands it to me, her expression warm. "Maybe I'll do that after Oliver and Avery's wedding."

"There's less than three weeks to go now."

"It's finally time for you boys," she murmurs before sniffling. "First, I watched my brother's children fall in love and get married, and now I get to watch you and Oliver do the same."

I take her into my arms as she cries, not having the heart to tell her that for now, the focus should stay on Oliver.

When she watches me get married for the first time, it'll be nothing but a sham, and if she ever learned the truth, it would break her heart.

6

Blakely

I triple-check the sum in my bank account before putting my phone away and tightening my hold on the shoebox. The clearance tag on the shelf is bright yellow, but I stare at it one last time, making sure I grabbed the right shoes.

With Nate at football practice this afternoon and then work at the video game shop, I knew I wasn't going to get a better chance than this one to sneak away and pick him up the shoes he's been eyeing for months now. They've never gone on sale before, so when I saw the flyer in the mailbox with these exact cleats circled last week, I found a way to make the discounted price work.

Sure, I could use the money on something more important. There's always a cost that I could prioritize over a pair of fancy cleats, and I have been doing that. For months, I've passed on new clothes or a book that caught my eye on the shelf at the grocery store. My makeup is expired, and I've cut my lotion bottle in half to get all the remaining product out. Nathan has been using the same football gear for the past two years, and with how fast he's growing, I don't know if I'll be able to make it another without upgrading.

His passion for football will be what gets him out of our tiny apartment that I'm on the brink of losing. He's made for the big leagues, and with his drive and passion for the sport, I know he'll get there one day. My only job as his guardian is to give him everything he needs to succeed while loving him along the way. And after the events of last night, I've been thinking about that a lot more. I don't want to have to steal things to make him happy. I'm going to do it the right way.

That's why I'm here in this store today, prepared to use ninety percent of this week's grocery money on a pair of shoes.

Keeping my stride confident, I move through the aisle of sports gear while pricing out the things I need to replace for Nathan. It's busy in here today, and I'm one more bump from a stranger away from snapping at the one closest to me.

"No, he went that way. Why would he be at the tills?" a teenage girl snaps while shoving at another girl's back. The name on the jersey she's wearing looks familiar, but I can't place it.

It's a football jersey. I don't own one myself, but I've washed too many of Nate's not to recognize one when I see it.

The girl's friend doesn't appear to believe her. "Did you see him go that way, or are you just guessing?"

"I don't know! I'm just guessing because that's where everyone else has gone. Duh."

"Fine! But if you're wrong, I'm so going to cry."

The girls hold hands while slipping around a tall man also in a green jersey and racing to the back of the store. I carry on toward the tills, realizing the crowd has slimmed over here.

Whoever everyone seems to be here to see isn't on this side of the store. I release a thankful sigh and make my way to the first empty register.

"Hi!" The cashier's smile is genuine as she waits for me to hand over the shoebox.

I smile back. "Hey."

"You chose a busy day to come do some shopping."

"Yeah, I noticed that. Is there some sort of signing or something going on?"

The woman behind the register looks young, maybe a year or two younger than me, and is wearing another one of those orange jerseys. The logo on the front is the BC Pythons, Nate's favourite CFL team.

She takes the box from me and scans the barcode before moving it to the other side of the till. "It's not really a signing. A player from the Pythons showed up about an hour ago to sign some of his shoes." Eyes widening, she lifts the shoebox up between us and taps the name and number on the side of it. "Oh, wow. This is actually who I'm talking about. You should totally go get these shoes signed after you finish paying!"

I double blink. "You mean number seventy-seven is here? Right now?"

She nods furiously. "I think he'd prefer us to call him by his name, but seventy-seven works too."

I've never been able to remember all the players' names that Nate loves. It's much easier to focus on the numbers instead of matching both. But Bateman would make sense. That's the name on the back of all the jerseys I've seen while I've been here.

"I do think I'll get these signed after. Thank you," I say.

"No worries. I'd hate for you to miss out on such a great opportunity. I'm going to try and get him to sign my jersey!"

"Is he a nice guy?" I ask, pulling my bank card out from behind my phone case.

She finalizes inputting the shoes with a nod. "Not only nice, but he's *so* good-looking. I started sweating so bad when he got here that I had to sneak away and reapply my deodorant. There's just something about a man in a backward hat, you know?"

Oh, I know.

A rush of shivers travels down my spine. It's like I can almost feel Jamie's eyes on me again. That lightning-blue gaze that attempted to peel me apart layer by layer.

"Oh, I'm sorry. I've been gushing. You probably just want to pay and get out of here. The total for the shoes is one hundred and fifty-seven dollars and twelve cents. You're paying with debit?"

My stomach shrivels. "How much did you say?"

"One hundred and fifty-seven dollars and twelve cents."

"What about the sale? Is that with the discount?"

She purses her lips and looks at the screen beside her. Another customer joins us, pretending to be busy looking at the socks on the hooks beside the register as they wait behind me.

"I don't see a sale here. As far as I know, that ended yesterday."

"Yesterday?" I ask, my voice cracking. "No, I put the date in my calendar and everything. It ends tomorrow."

"I'm sorry. It was yesterday."

The sting behind my eyes is instant. My throat tightens, making it hard to speak. "Are you positive?"

"Do you want me to call my manager? I can have him check and confirm, just in case," she offers softly.

I press my hand to my chest and stare at the box, something cracking behind my ribs. The eighty dollars I had saved was already a lot, but I was willing to sacrifice a few things to be able to afford it. This would be almost double that, and I don't . . . I don't know if I can make that work right now. Not with me being between jobs.

The cashier's gasp doesn't faze me. I curl my fingers in my shirt and swallow, hoping the other customer has decided to find another register instead of watching me right now.

"I'll pass on these—"

"There you are, babe. I was starting to think you got lost. Had me looking all over the place for you," a familiar voice drawls.

There's no way he's here right now. Not while I'm about to embarrass myself.

I squeeze my eyes shut, but his presence lingers, pressing into my side. The smooth scent of expensive cologne floats toward me, and then a very large, very warm hand is touching my spine.

Hot air curls around my ear, forcing another shiver down my body. "It's a goddamn pleasure to see you again, Bandit. Now, play along for me, yeah?"

Pulling my stare from the shoebox, I swing it past the shocked cashier and to those same lightning-blue eyes I was thinking about minutes ago. The calmness in them is like a balm to the madness in my brain, and like a fool, I let it relax me for just a second.

Jamie looks from me to the box of shoes at the register and does a piss-poor job of hiding a smirk. With a flick of his tongue over his bottom lip, he slides his hand up to my shoulder blade and flashes the cashier his bank card.

"I don't know why you insist on buying these when I have a million pairs at home, but if it makes you happy, we'll add another one to the collection," he says, his voice a low rumble.

"You have them at home?" I whisper, trying to piece together what's happening right now.

"Of course I do. They're mine. How did you forget?"

My thoughts lag. "Yours?"

Jamie chuckles as he twists his body until he's nearly wrapped around my side. My arm hangs limp at my side, knuckles grazing the thick muscle in his thigh.

"Mmhmm, just like you, baby," he murmurs lovingly while tapping his card to the debit machine.

I don't have the confidence to look at where I can feel the cashier gawking at me. There's no part of me that wants to know what she's thinking. If I did, I'd feel even shittier about myself, no doubt about it.

This man, this *stranger*, has just swooped in and not only saved me from the embarrassment of being the person who has to admit they can't afford something that so many others can but has also played it off like we're together. Romantically.

The transaction goes through with a loud beep, and then the

cashier is handing him a receipt that he tucks into his front pocket alongside his card. He spreads his fingers over my shoulder and runs his nails over the thin material of my shirt.

"You didn't mention that you were dating Jamieson Bateman while I was gushing about him! That's so seriously cool," the cashier says, sounding a bit winded as she glances between the two of us, then focuses on him. "Can you sign my jersey? If you have the time, of course. I'm a huge fan."

Without stepping away from me, Jamie—*Jamieson*—flashes a dimpled grin at her. "Do you have a pen?"

She whips one out from the waistband of her leggings and all but shoves it into his hand before turning to show us the name and number on the back of her jersey. The same number that's on the shoebox that I snatch from the register.

Jamie is quick with his signature, and a beat later, the cashier is spinning back around, her grin wide enough it must hurt.

"Thank you!" she squeals.

"No worries."

"Could you sign something for me too?" another customer asks.

A third joins the mix, and I realize quickly that the crowd is starting to grow. "Me too!"

This time, they're too far away for Jamie to stay close. His eyes focus on me for a few seconds before he almost reluctantly pulls away to face the fan.

With his attention spread between everyone around us, I escape. The shoebox feels heavier than it did before as I hug it against my chest and rush out of the store. It's all very thiefy, but despite my antics last night, that's not who I am.

The sun is hot when I step outside, but it's better than burning alive in Jamie's vicinity. Every step I take away from the store loosens the chains wrapped around my throat until, finally, I can get a full breath in.

He didn't have to buy these shoes for me. I almost wish he

hadn't. If I didn't know that this was the only way for Nate to have them, I would have left them there.

"Bandit!"

His voice hits me, and a beat later, I'm increasing my pace.

"I know you can hear me! Just wait up for a second. Please," Jamie begs before footsteps start pounding the pavement.

"My name isn't Bandit!" I yell back, unable to help myself.

"So, tell me what it is. I'm desperate here. And slow down, I had practice today already!"

"Aren't you supposed to be some fancy football player? How are you winded?"

"So, you do know who I am after all."

I can just hear how wide his smug grin must be.

"Only because I had your name shoved in my face so many times in that store," I toss back.

He blows out a laugh, sounding far closer than he was a second ago. His cologne hits me first, and then his bicep brushes my shoulder.

I refuse to look at him and keep my eyes trained on the pedestrians crossing the street ahead of us.

"You know more about me than I do about you. How about we change that?"

"How about you stop following me like a weirdo instead," I suggest.

He doesn't get offended by my rudeness. "I wasn't expecting to see you in there. Wasn't expecting to see you at all without a lot of effort, to be honest. But I'm happy I did."

Coming to a sudden stop, I plant my feet on the concrete and pin him beneath narrowed eyes. He realizes that I've stopped walking half a second after and does the same. When he looks back at me, I stomp down on the part of me that screams about how attractive this man is.

I thought having to stare at him half-naked in his house was the worst possible thing for me, but today, right now, I'm not faring much better.

He's wearing the same baseball hat as last night, keeping it fixed backward, but instead of sweatpants, he's in a pair of above-the-knee, olive-green shorts. They're short enough that I can make out the bottom of his thick hamstrings and the bulging muscles in his calves as he stands in front of me. They're criminally sexy. Maybe even more so than his abs.

Maybe.

I jab a finger into the air and hope I don't look as flushed as I feel. "Don't say stuff like that."

"Stuff like what? I'm a very honest guy. It's impossible for me not to tell someone how I'm feeling," he admits.

"Well, stop. You don't even know me. While I appreciate you saving me from embarrassment back there, it doesn't make us friends."

"What would, then?" he asks without a hint of hesitation.

"I don't understand you."

"What's there to understand other than that I want to get to know you?"

"Stop saying stuff like that!"

The corner of his mouth quirks. "Does it make you uncomfortable?"

"Is this charity or something?" I accuse.

His smile falls. "Charity for what?"

"You caught me trying to steal from you, and now I can't even afford a pair of shoes? I didn't need you to butt in and buy them for me either. I've never taken a handout in my life, and I don't plan on making a habit of it now."

We've stopped in the middle of the sidewalk. It's beyond awkward when people begin to pass us with odd, curious looks. Either they recognize him and don't understand why he's dealing with a crazy chick on the street yelling at him, or they're just judging our conversation. Either way, it doesn't help my emotional turmoil right now.

Jamie slides his hands into his pockets and rolls his bottom lip into his mouth. "You're not charity, Bandit. I didn't think that last night, and I don't today. The only thing I've been thinking these past few minutes is how grateful I feel to have seen you again. And I know that sounds like a line, but it's not."

Keeping my chin high, I ask, "I'm just supposed to believe that?"

"I'd like it if you did, but I don't expect you to. I'm just a random guy."

"That's not a very convincing sentiment."

"Do you want me to stand here and convince you?"

"No."

"Then let's spend our time doing something else. If I were to ask to drive you home, would you let me?"

"No. But, as a thank you for the shoes, you can walk with me."

"Deal."

My eyebrows jump in disbelief. "You don't want to think about that for a minute? I could have us walking for three hours."

"That's three hours I'll have to convince you to say yes to my proposal. I wouldn't turn that down."

"What proposal?"

He winks before finding a spot at my side again and tilting his head down to look at me. "We'll talk on the way."

7
Jamie

I still don't know her name.

And it's not like that's the only thing I don't know. It's just one of many questions I have. Where does she live, why did she walk instead of drive when it's hot enough that my thighs are probably burning in the sun, and who was she buying those shoes for?

With a glance down at her feet, I confirm that there's no chance she's a men's size eight. They're incredibly small, and considering the flopping sole at the back of her old sneaker, I can't see her choosing a pair of cleats for a replacement.

Whoever she was getting them for is lucky. I don't say this because I'm the face of the shoes, but they're pretty great. They're the ones I wear on the field for every practice and game.

I move to her left side when we reach the street and stay close enough that our arms continuously brush. Every touch sends sparks through my limb as I search her face for any sign that she feels the same thing, but I'm met with a wall of cool nothingness.

If anything, her lack of visible reaction only makes me want to step up my game and draw one out of her.

"Are you going to tell me about this proposal yet, or are we going to be walking in silence the entire time?" she asks stiffly.

"I was waiting for you to make the first move, Bandit."

"My name is not Bandit," she reminds me sternly.

"Tell me what it is, then."

"What do you plan on doing once you have it?"

I steady her with a hand to her back when a guy on a bike rips up beside us, nearly crashing into her. With a glare at his back, I say, "Nothing you don't want me to."

Despite shrugging out of my hold, she flicks a look up at me. "Blakely."

"Blakely," I repeat, rolling it around in my mouth, tasting it. "I like it."

"Oh, thank God. I was worried you wouldn't and I'd have to change it," she deadpans.

I choke on a laugh, staring down at her with interest I don't bother hiding. The tip of her nose is red, and for a second, I swear I can make out the slightest curve of her lips before they're flat again.

"So, I've got a proposal for you, Blakely."

"And what is that?"

The group of people in front of us has stalled at the crosswalk up ahead, and we bypass them completely when Blakely turns right, leading us away from them. My brows tug inward at the new direction.

While I may have been born and raised in Vancouver, there are plenty of spots I haven't explored yet. The upcoming neighbourhood is one of them. It's silent over here, like the noise from a few steps back has hit a wall and died out completely.

On instinct, I crowd her even more, keeping on the outside of the sidewalk. If she notices, she doesn't mention it.

"I'll be blunt here, Blakely. I need a wife."

Her head whips in my direction, and I bite back a smile at her bewildered expression. I've apparently made a habit of surprising people today because that's exactly how Mom looked at me this morning.

"You need a wife?"

"Yes. It's a long story."

"So get to telling it."

I ignore my damp palms and play it cool. "It's for the Pythons. They're looking for a bit of a scandal to boost sales, and I've been asked to get married to a fan."

"Okay, first of all, I'm not a fan. And second, I'm no genius, but I'm pretty sure you shouldn't be telling me all that."

She has a point, but I risk it anyway. "Explain the shoes, then. You just so happened to be buying a pair of cleats with my name and number on their box only a day after breaking into my place?"

I know she isn't a fan. If she were, she'd be the worst one I've ever met, considering how rude she's been to me. But I'm not about to turn down a chance to tease her.

Her nostrils flare as she clenches her jaw, avoiding looking at me. "The shoes are for my brother. And if I'd known they were yours, maybe I'd have insisted he ask for a different pair."

"Ouch, Bandit. That shit hurts right here." I hit the centre of my chest.

"As if."

Reaching for her hand, I give it a loose tug. She turns to me, staring down at our hands before pulling free of the hold and crossing her arms.

"I know you're not a fan," I clarify, bending the brim of my hat. "That's what makes you perfect for this role. Not to mention, there's little chance of you falling for me. Am I right?"

Honestly, it's not that great that she isn't a fan. Graham expects me to find one, which means if by some shot I got her to agree to this, I'd have to teach her enough to impress him come meeting time.

"There's *zero* chance of it."

"Okay, I wouldn't say that. I am quite charming when I want to be."

"You can be as charming as you please, but that doesn't mean I'll fall for you."

I ignore the part of me that searches for the thrill of proving myself. "Fair enough. So, what do you say?"

"No." She spins away from me and starts down the sidewalk.

"Thank you. You have no idea how grateful I am—" I double blink at where she used to stand. "Wait, no? Why not?"

"You're asking me to marry you, Jamie. We're strangers."

Jogging to catch up with her, I let my determination take the reins. "We don't have to be strangers. I told the owner of the team that I need three weeks before I marry anyone for this specific reason. We can use it to get to know one another."

"And then what? We get married? For how long? And what would that even mean? This is insane."

"Stop walking and I can answer all of your questions," I plead.

Surprisingly, she does. With her eyelids blinking heavily, she stares up at me in waiting. I can still feel the burn of the hand that finds her curved, jutted hip.

The neighbourhood behind her is in terrible shape. Buildings with graffiti and peeling siding, gaping cracks in the sidewalk, and overgrown lawns are everywhere. The abundance of chain-linked front yards fit with weeds crawling up through the metal and the beaten-down vehicles lining the curbs spark alarm in my mind.

Blakely doesn't seem bothered by our surroundings, and that may be even more concerning.

"Are we almost at your place?" I ask before she can speak.

She tongues her cheek. "Yeah, but this is as far as I want you to come."

"What are you talking about?"

"I'm not stupid enough to bring a guy I barely know to my house."

"You shouldn't be walking by yourself in this neighbourhood."

She leans back on her heel, eyes flashing. "Don't. I'm perfectly capable of taking care of myself, pretty boy."

"You think I'm pretty?"

"I'm going to leave," she threatens, voice tight.

"Okay, I'm sorry. Don't go."

Her scowl smooths out. "Give me answers, Jamieson."

"Jamie. Call me Jamie."

"Fine. Give me answers, *Jamie*."

I shift my weight to my other leg and keep her in my gaze. "We would get married in three weeks, once my brother's wedding has passed. There are some people I have to introduce you to first, and you could get more answers from them. We'd have the best lawyers out there to make sure there would be no problems when the time comes for a divorce. There would be PR responsibilities and things we'd have to do to please management."

"I still don't understand why this is necessary in the first place. Is the public going to believe that you've suddenly gotten married? Have you dated that much?"

"It's necessary because the team is struggling. At least half of our stands are empty when we play, and we've become the team that no reporter wants to take the trip to interview. I'm not a huge fan of this either, but if it means that I can keep playing the sport that I love, then I'm prepared to do it. I know you don't share that loyalty, but I'm asking you to please consider what it would mean if you agreed to help.

"We *are* strangers, and I know all of this sounds weird as hell. Yes, I've dated my fair share of women, but that doesn't mean I can find just anyone and convince the country that we're in love. But I think I could do that with you."

She flicks her eyes between mine, rolling her lips. "What's so special about me? I'm just some girl who you found snooping in your living room. I don't think that would be a very convincing leading line to the public."

I chuckle, rubbing the back of my neck while opting out of telling her that from what I've gathered already, she's not just some girl.

"Yeah, maybe not. But I still want it to be you. You'd keep me on my toes, and when I think of finding someone to marry, that's a quality I'd like them to have. I think we could pull it off, Blakely."

"I don't want to sound like a total bitch, but what would I get from this arrangement? Other than my privacy being taken away to be made into a pretty little wife for a player on the BC Pythons."

"What do you want from it? I have several things I could give you in return for your help. Money isn't an issue for me, and you've seen my place, so you know space isn't either."

Her eyes grow wide, worry deepening the green. "You'd want me to live with you?"

"Yes. My wife would live with me, wouldn't she?"

"I mean, I guess. I wouldn't be your real wife, though."

I move closer to her, testing if she'll leap back like she did in my house. Other than the brief stiffening of her shoulders, she doesn't retreat.

"That's the thing, Blakely. On paper, you *would* be my real wife. If we didn't live together, it wouldn't be too hard for someone to discredit us."

Her throat strains with a swallow. "I need to think about it."

"How long do you need?"

"I don't know. A few days, maybe? A week?" she rambles, heaving in a breath.

Pushing her right now will do more damage than good. Strangers or not, that much is obvious. This is a lot to dump on someone.

"How about I give you my number, then? Give me a call or send a text when you have an answer for me," I suggest.

Her eyes fall to watch as I pull my phone out of my pocket and jot my number into the notes for her to copy.

"I don't like calling anyone," she mumbles.

"Text me, then. Anytime. Just please don't ghost me."

"You're not going to ask for my number so you can make sure I don't?"

I shake my head. "I don't want to pressure you with this decision. It's not something simple."

Her entire demeanour softens, and I mentally raise a fist in celebration. "Thank you."

"You're welcome."

She pulls a phone out of her jeans pocket and taps the cracked screen before putting my number in. "I meant what I said about you not walking me to my place."

"Is this your way of telling me to go away?" I ask, still totally into the way she seems to have no filter around me.

It's refreshing as shit.

"I mean, if you want to stand here in the street after I leave, then that's your prerogative. But I'll be going to my place alone."

"And you'll text me, right? Regardless of if it's a yes or no. Although, I'd much prefer yes."

"I'll text."

"Then I'll go."

And the next time I'm here, I won't be leaving without calling her my fiancée.

8

Blakely

"I'm sorry to let you know that we won't be moving forward with your application at this time. Please do try again in the new year when we have more spots to fill."

"Alright. Thank you for your time," I say, putting every ounce of strength I have into not sobbing.

"Have a great day, Blakely."

"You too."

When the call ends, I brace a hand on the countertop and drop my head. It's been over a week since I lost my job, and this is yet another rejection. I thought I had a fighting chance with this last one, but I guess I just didn't have what they were wanting.

My heart is heavy in my chest as I shut my eyes, refusing to cry over this. I've always been able to find my way out of a dark spot, and I plan on doing that again. The path out is just a whole lot harder to find this time, my guiding light dim.

"Is everything okay?"

Pasting on a smile, I turn to face Nate. He's dressed for practice, looking older than he is with his hair pushed back and eyes bright with anticipation. Another wave of emotion crashes into me, this one harsher, crueller.

"Everything's great. Are you ready to go?"

He doesn't move a muscle as he takes me in. "What happened?"

"Nothing you need to worry about. I have something to give you before we leave." I spin away and press my thumb into the corner of my eye to make sure it's dry.

"It's not my birthday."

"It doesn't have to be a special occasion for me to give you a gift."

"Alright," he relents, suspicion still heavy in his voice.

I shoved his new cleats in the front closet behind the mop bucket, knowing that he wouldn't find them there. The last time Nate mopped the floor, he left it so wet that the linoleum started to peel.

It's been hard keeping them a secret, but I wanted to wait until his next practice came around first. He'll want to wear them as soon as he sees the box. And after today, I think I need to give them to him just as much as he deserves to receive them. Especially after he made it through his first week of school with only a few complaints.

School has never been easy for him, and I was expecting the worst. I always told him that while he can't start the fights, he can always end them, but he's still maturing and, with that, still putting on muscle.

Last year, he was picked on quite often, and I watched as it tore him down peg by peg. My only hope for this school year is to see him without a frown when he gets home at the end of every day.

"Go sit on the couch and cover your eyes. No peeking!" I order, moving toward the closet.

He obeys with a wave of his hand, so I grab the box from the exact spot I left it and join him in the living room portion of the apartment. It's just one open space with the addition of the single bedroom and bathroom, but at least the pull-out couch helps break it up a bit.

"Okay, you can open your eyes now."

"It better not be a snake," he warns before staring at the box.

I let loose a quiet laugh. "It's not a snake."

"Holy shit!"

I stumble back a step when he shoots off the couch and takes the box from me. With his height in comparison to mine, he dwarfs me as he yanks me into his arms for a hug, squishing the box between us.

Mouthing curling into a soft smile, I hug him back. "I'll take this as you liking them?"

"Like them? I love them! These are top-of-the-line, Lake! How did you manage to get them?"

Breaking away from me, he gapes down at the writing on the lid. With a flick of his wrist, he has the shoes revealed. White with orange details, they look worth the price, even if it still makes me want to throw up at how much they cost.

It helps that I wasn't the one that paid. But only partially. Once I remember that the man who tapped his card at the store is still waiting for an answer as to whether I'll become his fake wife, my stomach sours once again.

There are far worse things to be, but I still haven't decided if I want my first and maybe only marriage to be a sham, even if it won't be for forever.

Divorce isn't just a possibility. It's the only path ahead for us. If I go along with this, I'll be divorced before I'm twenty-five.

"That's not important. What is is that you like them. That's all I want," I say.

"Bateman wasn't my favourite player on the Pythons last year, but you should see him move this season! You blink and he's already in the end zone!" he gushes, picking a shoe up and lifting it in front of his face.

I play with the ends of my ponytail, growing antsy. "He's that good?"

"He's a beast. I want to be as fast as him one day."

Oh, I'm sure Jamie would *love* hearing that.

"What else do you know about him?"

Nate glances at me, eyes wide and bubbling with excitement. "Are you interested in ball now? Is that part of the reason you got me these?"

"Slow down, buddy. That's not what I said."

"You've never asked about players before. I remember you telling me once that my football talk was making your brain melt out of your ears."

"Okay, that was one time. And I only said that because I was on a phone call when you were giving me a rundown."

He sits back on the couch and hikes his socks up before readying the cleat. His foot slides in easily before he starts lacing it up.

"Whatever, sis. That's not the point. I just wanna know why you're asking about them now."

"One of the Pythons players was at the store when I got those shoes. My interest was piqued, that's all," I say, choosing my words carefully.

Nate freezes. "What? Who?"

Shrugging a shoulder, I try playing it off. "That Bateman guy."

"What?" he shouts, shoe forgotten and falling to the floor with a clunk. "You're not being serious."

"It was only a brief encounter."

"You *met* him? Why didn't you mention this to me before? What the hell, Lake! Did you talk? Did you tell him about me?" he rambles, looking like he might burst if I don't watch what I say.

"Slow down. It wasn't like I went there planning on meeting him. It just happened."

He shakes his head, huffing a breath while picking the cleat up off the floor. "You don't meet your brother's favourite football player and not get him a signature or something! Or at least ask for a picture! Oh, my God, I've failed my teachings with you."

It's hard to keep a straight face as I pat his shoulder. "I'm so sorry to have not pounced on a stranger for you."

He blows out a heavy exhale, looking away from me. "Thank you, but I can't forgive you yet."

"I don't know how I'll go on."

"Don't be sarcastic right now! This is so not the time," he sasses, darting his eyes back to mine.

"How about you just thank me for the shoes, and we move on? Maybe you'll find it in your heart to forgive my lack of sports star etiquette after practice."

His expression softens with appreciation. "Thank you. Really, these are incredible. The best gift I've ever gotten."

"Even if I did fumble the ball with the player?"

"Hey, that was the right way to use that. Maybe you are learning. I'll be able to make a football fan out of you one day."

I roll my eyes and pass him the second cleat, watching as he holds them close to his chest. "Get to it, superstar. If we miss the bus, you're piggybacking me all the way to the field."

He doesn't need any further motivation, and two minutes later, I'm handing him his bag, and we're rushing out the door.

"I'm really close to being able to afford a car, you know?" he asks when I shut the door behind us. "What do you think of a truck? Not a fancy one, but like an old, reliable one?"

With my key in my hand, I spin to lock the door.

At the sight of the piece of paper taped onto it . . . My legs threaten to give out.

Eviction Notice.

Nate comes up behind me, easily peering over my shoulder before I have a chance to rip the paper off the door.

"What's the hell is that? Are we—"

Snatching the notice, I crumble it into a ball, but not before he reads the writing on it. "It's nothing."

"Yes, it is. Don't lie to me. I'm not a kid anymore."

"You *are* a kid, Nathan. And you will be a kid to me forever," I snap, my voice cracking on the last word as I toss the crumbled paper onto the floor.

The hall is shrinking around me, the walls brushing up against my arms as a sharp sensation of failure stabs me deep in the belly. Suddenly, the dark spot is more like a pit of tar dragging me deeper and deeper until I'm breathing and seeing black.

"Hey, it's okay, Lake," Nate murmurs, touching my arm. "We'll figure it out."

I don't have it in me to tell him he's wrong. "We better go."

"Are you sure? We don't have to go. Maybe we should stay and talk about this instead."

"No. Your practice is important. I'll figure this out afterward."

"How much does the landlord need? How far behind are we? I told you that I have money saved. Let me help."

We're only one of six apartments on this floor, and with how paper-thin the walls are, I know everyone who's home can hear every word we're saying. It shouldn't be embarrassing, considering where we live, but after what happened with the shoes last week on top of this, my give-no-shit attitude is starting to crumble. I don't know how much more I can take right now.

Facing my baby brother, I keep my expression stern, hoping it'll drive home my words. "I'll take care of it. I know you want to help, but it's not your place. You were just telling me about the truck you want. Let's go back to that, okay?"

"I'm not going to pretend everything is fine, Blakely. That worked when I was twelve, but it won't work now. I'll leave it until after practice, but that's it," he says, as stubborn as me.

"Fine," I relent, ruffling his hair. "Now, can we please go?"

"Do you promise that we'll talk about it? If not tonight, then tomorrow?"

My throat is sticky when I say, "Yes."

And fifteen minutes later, when we're sitting on the dirty bus, his clunky football bag bumping against my knees in the small area between our seats, I send a text that I've been avoiding for a week.

> Me: Hi. It's Blakely. Can we meet to talk?

9

Jamie

I'VE BEEN TRYING TO GET JAXON OUT OF MY HOUSE FOR THIRTY-FIVE minutes. For a guy who claims to hate personal contact outside of football, he's certainly hanging out with me a lot. Sprawled out on my couch with his legs spread wide, he looks like he's planning on camping out there for another few hours at least.

It's not happening. Not today of all days.

After waiting a week, my beautiful bandit finally reached out to me yesterday. It was only a request to meet up, but a win is a win in my mind. I've got the confidence to know that I'll be able to convince her to agree to my proposal by the end of our conversation.

"I have plans, Jax. You can leave any minute now," I say.

"What plans?"

Walking up behind the couch, I grab a chunk of his hair and reef on it. When he tosses his head back to glare at me, I point toward the door.

"The kind that don't involve your snoopy ass."

"I thought we were best friends."

I brace my hand on the back of the couch and jump over it before bouncing onto the cushion beside him. With a kick of my foot, I have his leg pushed away from where he had it spread-eagle.

"You are, and that means when I tell you to leave because I have plans, you should listen."

"I want to know what you were talking to Graham and Coach about in the exec office first. You've been oddly zip-lipped all week."

"What do you mean oddly? As if I'm such a blabbermouth."

He rolls the back of his head along the couch, brow lifted in question. "Fuck off. Just tell me what happened, and then I'll leave you to your *plans*."

"Why are you saying 'plans' like that? I really do have plans."

"Plans with your hand don't count as plans."

"Stop saying plans so much. Christ, it's giving me the shivers."

His laugh is low, almost rough-sounding. "Only if you tell me what happened the other day."

I groan, folding my hands behind my head and letting my elbows bang into his cheek before he grumpily shifts over. "They needed help with something for the team."

"Okay, and?"

"And that's all. Now, get your ass up off the couch. I'll walk you out."

"You're joking me, Bateman," he says, not moving an inch.

While I'm pretty strong, I don't know if I'll be able to lift the goliath that is Jaxon Hayes and carry him through my house. I may have more bulk, but he's got a few inches on me.

"You've gotta keep your mouth shut about this, Jax. It's not public knowledge, and if it ever gets that way, the entire organization is in deep shit," I warn.

His expression sobers as he leans forward, completely zoned in. "What's going on?"

I explain it with as little detail as possible, making sure to keep Blakeley's name out of it for now. Until I get a for sure answer from her, I'm keeping her part in this close to my chest.

Jaxon is pacing on the carpet by the time I finish. "You believe that'll work?"

"I've got no other choice than to believe it."

"I knew shit was bad, but I didn't think it was this bad. You're going to get married for the team? For real?"

"Is it that surprising?"

He scratches his jaw. "Don't you want to get married for real someday? To someone you love?"

"Well, yeah. But I didn't expect it to happen for a while yet. I've got the time to find something real after this is over and done with. Why? Is that something you're focused on in your life?"

I can't tell whether his scoff is from annoyance or a way to cover his embarrassment. Either way, I'm not going to push to find out.

"No. I just thought that you'd care about that."

"'Cause I'm so romantic?"

"You're the most stand-up guy I know. Figured love would be on your to-do list."

"The only things on my to-do list right now are to find a wife before Graham finds me some stranger ready to fill the position and to bring the Grey Cup home."

"So far, you're oh for two."

I roll my eyes. "Thanks for the reminder."

"I guess I should leave now before you attempt to toss me over your shoulder and injure the both of us," he mutters.

I clap. "Finally, you're getting it. I'll even walk you out."

"With your outstanding manners, finding a wife should be a walk in the park."

Leading him back through my living room toward the front door, I sneak a look at the Xbox beneath the TV. I haven't used it since I found Blakely yanking at the cords, almost like I didn't want to replace her fingerprints with mine.

Okay, that was a creepy way of phrasing that.

I'll be keeping that one to myself when she gets here tonight.

"Thanks, buddy," I say, giving him a smack on the back.

He slips his sneakers on and steps onto the porch, throwing me one last look. "Enjoy your plans tonight. Don't stay up too late. Gotta be at the stadium early."

"Game day. Yeah, I'll make sure I'm tucked in early, Dad."

"Good. We need to keep the momentum up. The last two wins have taken some of the pressure off, and I'm enjoying it. Coach didn't chew my ear off last week, so I made it home before midnight."

Two back-to-back wins isn't usually much to celebrate. However, with any team as . . . weak as ours, we take what we can get and use it to grow the confidence of the newer players. The last time we were close to clinching a third win in a row, Jax threw a party at his place that grew wild enough to summon the cops. We were up into the early morning getting reamed out by Coach and lost our next game.

I'm going to take a shot in the dark and assume that's why he hasn't decided to do it again.

"I'll do my best, QB. You know I've got you," I remind him.

He tips his chin and knocks his knuckles on the doorframe. "Yeah, I know it. I'll see you tomorrow."

"Drive safe."

With a backward wave, he cuts across my grass to where the flashy McLaren sits on the driveway like a trophy on the wrong shelf. The guy chooses to live in a shack in the mountains but drives a luxury sports car, whereas I'm the opposite.

He unlocks it and goes to open the driver's door when he pauses. I hover in the entry and try to make out the figure strolling up past my driveway.

Jaxon doesn't hide his staring, and once I see the flash of chestnut hair beneath a deep purple beanie, I lurch forward a step.

"Get in your car, Jaxon!" I holler.

His smirk is positively wicked when he looks at me while popping open his door. "See you tomorrow, Bateman!"

Blakely heads up my sidewalk at a slow pace with her head cocked, watching him leave. Only when he's out of the driveway and speeding down the street does she look in my direction.

"A friend of yours?" she asks.

I'm too busy staring at her to reply.

I've never been one to wear beanies, but one look at her in one and you can consider me a big fan. Somehow, it fits her perfectly and highlights the sharp angles of her cheekbones.

In a pair of jeans and a thin coat bulging at the pockets from where she has her hands tucked away, she lingers at the bottom of the porch steps.

"A friend and a teammate. That was Jaxon Hayes, the Pythons' quarterback," I explain.

Only a slight glimmer of recognition sparks in her eyes. "Right. The name sounds familiar."

"You'll need football lessons if you agree to be my wife," I tease, testing her reaction.

I need to know how hard it's going to be to convince her, after all.

She swallows and leans past my bicep to see into the house. "Are you going to ask me to come in, or are we having this conversation on your front porch?"

"Shit, right. Come in. I promise I'm not usually a bad host."

I move out of the way, and she passes me with a whole lot of confidence. While she slips out of her shoes, I close the door.

"Do you remember the way to the living room?"

She blinks up at me, unimpressed with the question. "No. I wasn't exactly memorizing the layout of your house when I was here last."

"Feel free to do that this time. You know, for when you move in."

"Let's go to the kitchen. Do you have a dining table or somewhere we can sit and talk properly?"

I roll my lips and leave the teasing for another time. "Yeah, follow me."

As the silence grows, I start wishing I'd put some music on or something.

"Did you have a good week?" I ask gently, stepping into the dining room and automatically pulling a seat out for her.

She eyes the chair and then me, almost like she doesn't understand why I'd do that for her. After a few seconds, she takes it, sitting stiffly.

"Do you want the honest answer or the pretty one?"

Playing it safe, I choose the seat across from her. "Always the honest one."

"My week was terrible."

"What can I do to help?"

She blinks slowly, shifting as if I've made her uncomfortable with my question. "You know why I'm here, Jamie. There's no need for the whole caring act."

"It's not an act, and I don't know the specifics of why you're here. You could have planned to rob me a second time and just needed an in."

"I think we've already established that I'm a pretty shitty burglar. My criminal days are behind me."

Propping an elbow on the table, I rest my chin on my knuckles. "While we're on the topic of criminal activity, I've been wondering how you got past the gate outside. You've done it twice now."

"The one at the end of the road? It was open."

"Both times?"

She jostles a shoulder. "Yes."

"Oh, boy, my mom will have a total fit if she finds out about that," I mutter.

"She's protective?"

My smile is instant at the mention of her. "Yeah, you could say that. Maybe more dramatic than protective, though."

"You sound close." It's a blunt answer. Closed off.

I lean forward in my chair and search her face for the reaction she's trying to hide but fail to distinguish it. She's too good at pretending not to care.

Why? What happened to make her so closed off?

I'm too stubborn to let it go, promising myself to find the answers to my questions.

"Are you close with your mother?" I ask.

"No, I'm not. She's been out of my life for a while now." She grits her teeth and glares down at the table. "If I agreed to marry you, I would move in here, right?"

Straight to business, then.

"I think that would be best. Obviously, you'd have your own room. There are four, so you can choose whichever one you want. My home gym is in the basement, and the backyard has a pool."

"I wouldn't have to sleep in your room?"

"Absolutely not. I'd never make you do that," I answer honestly.

She plays with the sleeve of her jacket, avoiding my eyes. "I mentioned before that I have a brother. He's fifteen. Sixteen in four months. If I moved in, he would need to come with me."

I bite my tongue when questions load themselves on it. I've got to watch myself with Blakely. At least right now. She's like a deer hiding in the trees, knowing a hunter is on her tail. One snap of a twig and she'll be gone.

If I ask one wrong question, I can forget about her being my wife.

With a half smile, I say, "That's fine. I have the space."

"Nathan's a good kid, I swear. He's incredibly smart and doesn't stay out late or party. Football keeps him busy, so you probably won't even notice he's here," she rambles, twisting the sleeve of her jacket tighter in a move I'm starting to assume means she's nervous.

I file away the football information for a later time.

"Hey, you don't have to convince me. If you say he's a good kid, then I'll choose to believe you. I'm asking a lot from you here. The least I can do is let your brother have a place to stay. What else do you need from me?"

Pain travels across her features, and I scoot my chair closer to the table on instinct. She doesn't notice.

"I'm between jobs right now, so I can't exactly help with the mortgage or anything. If you make a tab for me while we're staying here, I'll make sure to pay you back once I find something."

"Not happening. You don't pay a damn dime the entire time you're my wife, Blakely. That's one of my rules. I've got the mortgage, the groceries. Hell, you can drive one of my cars anytime you need to leave. Just let me know what bills you have, and I'll make sure they're taken care of while you're here," I say, almost offended that she thought for even half a second that she'd need to pay me back for anything.

Almost, because like she told me before, she's just not the type of person to take handouts. And while that isn't what this is, I can understand why she'd connect those dots.

"I'm not a charity case. I might not have the money now, but I will eventually," she presses.

"If you want to collect a *pay Jamie back stash*, go for it. But just know that I won't take a single cent of it come divorce time. My wife won't pay for anything essential. Providing for you is my job, and it's what I want to do."

"This isn't the 1800s. Women can provide for their families nowadays."

A smirk curls my lips. "My woman won't need to provide for me. I have more money than I know what to do with, and it will only continue to grow as long as I'm playing football. You want to go out and buy yourself a new pair of shoes? Use your own money or use mine. But when it comes to the roof over your head and the food in the fridge, that's on me, Bandit."

Her cheeks flush. "I'm not your woman. Not for real."

"Maybe not. But every time we leave this house, I'll be treating you like it. If you agree to marrying me, of course."

When she releases a loose exhale, I know there's a real chance of her saying yes. And that . . . that's the most exciting thing to happen to me in a really long time.

10

Blakely

JAMIESON BATEMAN IS TOO SLICK FOR HIS OWN GOOD.

It doesn't seem to matter that agreeing to this could end terribly because the moment he started spouting off about taking care of me and accepting Nate, I melted into mush.

I'm one strong-ass bitch when it comes to almost anything in any given situation, but apparently, all it takes is one hot guy with a six-pack and flexing biceps to offer to house and feed me, and I'm ready to give my hand in marriage.

Embarrassing as it may be, I'm desperate enough not to wind up living on the street that I can't even be all that mad at myself.

"What can I get you?" said hot guy asks, leaning a forearm against the open fridge door and peering inside.

It's one of those two-door, stainless steel ones with a bottom pull-out freezer and an ice machine. On the appliance sexiness scale, it's slamming against the end with a flashing red light.

"I'll just have water."

"Water? You sure? I've got plenty to drink in here. There's pretty much every type of pop and a few kinds of juice. My niece has a habit of drinking sugar like water whenever she comes to visit, so I keep pretty stocked up on the stuff."

"Are you using your niece as a scapegoat? I didn't think

professional athletes were supposed to drink so many sugary drinks."

He turns in my direction and winks before lifting the hem of his shirt up to expose his stomach. The grooved muscles flex and strain, keeping my eyes occupied.

"Don't worry about my sugar intake, Bandit. I work hard in the gym to burn off my drink choices."

I yank my eyes up and away from his abs and narrow them on his smirk. "Put your abs away before I leave."

The shirt drops instantly, and then he's reaching into the fridge. Cans and bottles clink and clang as I sit perched at the kitchen island and wait.

"Coke or strawberry and kiwi juice?" he asks, facing me with two different cans in his hands.

"Water."

"Water wasn't an option." With that statement, he shuts the fridge door and joins me at the island. "Coke or juice?"

"Have anything stronger?" I ask, eyeing the cans.

He chuckles, bracing his arms on the island. "Yeah, I've got stronger. What's your liquor of choice? You didn't drive here, right?"

"Whiskey. And no, I don't drive."

He heads for the cabinet above the fridge. "You don't drive at all?"

"No. I was never taught," I admit, my cheeks burning as I wait for his judgment.

Only it doesn't come.

"Well, lucky for you, your future husband is a great driver. Sounds like we'll be having lessons a few times a week from now on."

"Has anyone ever told you that you're too confident?"

"No. Usually, confidence is a good thing." With a fat-bottomed bottle of whiskey in his hand, he meets my watchful gaze. "Are you a neat, on the rocks, or a mix type of whiskey drinker?"

"You don't have a guess?"

His grin is dimpled. "Of course I do. I'm trying to be a gentleman, though."

"Try me. I promise not to deduct gentleman points this time."

"So generous," he purrs.

"I'm waiting."

"Alright, maybe not *that* generous. I'm going to guess on the rocks. Straight whiskey goes right to your head and makes your guard slip. You need ice to water it down a bit."

Turns out that I don't need the whiskey for that at all. Jamie's worse for my walls than any hard liquor could be.

"I do take it on the rocks, but only because if I drink it straight, I'll wind up punching you in the dick instead of agreeing to your proposal, and I can't afford to be sued right now," I mutter.

"You'd be the first woman to punch my dick. We're just collecting firsts at this point, you and me," he teases, already filling a short glass with ice and then pouring too much whiskey into it.

"I can't say that I thought the idea of a broken penis would be entertaining to you."

"Penis is such a middle school term, Blakely. I let dick go because you're being so sweet today, but I prefer cock."

My stomach jumps, skin growing clammy. "We're not playing the name game right now. Especially not about that."

"Don't go shy on me now. I'm having fun," he half pleads, half teases.

"Something tells me that you'd be able to find the fun in any situation."

His eyes sparkle, the blue almost blinding, as he offers me my glass of whiskey and pours a can of Coke into his. I wrap a warm palm around the chilled drink and slide it across the island.

"I try not to take things too seriously most of the time, but I'm like an onion, baby. I have layers. Serious situations call for fitting reactions," he drawls before lifting his drink to his lips and taking a strong pull.

I glide my fingertip along the dewy side of my glass, the wires in my brain close to crossing. "Is this marriage one of those serious situations?"

"That's the most serious one I've got." He sets his drink down and returns to his bar stool beside me. I'm too curious to keep from glancing at him, so I give in, finding him completely zoned in on me. "Look, I want to do this right. It's not ideal, but I think we could both benefit from it. I've already laid it out for you, and depending on how it goes if you agree to meet with the owner of the Pythons, I'm sure we'd be able to pull off everything that we need to."

"I'm not in a position right now to turn you down, Jamie. Your offer is the best one I have, so yeah, depending on how this meeting goes, I'll do it."

It's easy to speak those words, and I take that as a sign from the universe that maybe I'm not going to regret this. That after we're finished with this and the divorce papers are signed, I'll be able to move on with my life as though it never happened in the first place.

Jamie's mouth curves as he reaches for my wrist. It's only a friendly squeeze of his fingers, but I jerk back and away on instinct, folding my hands in my lap.

He follows my movements with curious eyes before blinking up at me. "We'll have to work on that, too, if we want this to be believable."

"I just don't know you," I defend myself.

"I get it. And we have the time to learn about one another. That's one of the reasons I demanded a couple of weeks before getting married."

I nod, wetting my dry lips. "What are the other reasons?"

"My brother's getting married in two weeks, and I wasn't about to take the spotlight from him for a fake one of my own. He deserves the moment with his soon-to-be wife."

"The niece you mentioned, is she his daughter?"

"Stepdaughter, if we're being specific. If we're not, then yes, she is. Her name's Nova, and she's sweet enough to give you a toothache from being near her. My brother, Oliver, was into her mom, Avery, for years before they got together, but the timing was never right. A year ago, that changed, and they're finally tying the knot," he explains lightly, a genuine happiness floating in his tone.

I take a sip of my drink and try to relax into the ease of this conversation. Finding a man to have a real, genuine conversation with is nearly impossible in the world right now unless they're wanting to sleep with you. So, yeah, I think I'm going to take advantage of how open and genuine this one appears to be without the promise of sex lingering above us. He might be getting my hand in marriage at the end of this meeting, but there's something about Jamie that tells me that isn't playing a part in why he's being the way he is with me right now.

"Are you the older or younger brother?" I ask.

"Younger."

"You and Nate have that in common."

"Don't forget about our shared love of football. Speaking of, what position does he play? Does he have a favourite team?"

"You just want to know how to win him over."

"Damn right I do. Now that I've won you over, he's next on the list."

I keep my expression flat when my lips try to twitch. "You haven't won me."

When he scoots his stool over an inch in my direction, I hold my breath. His knee presses against mine, and . . . I guess that's alright.

Jamie leans an elbow on the island and props his cheek in a massive hand, his grin teasing and bright. "But I could. If I wanted to."

I scoff to cover the embers popping in my belly. "In your dreams, Pretty Boy."

"You keep calling me pretty, Blakely. It's getting to my head."

I make a show of looking him over. "Yeah, I can see that."

"Shit, you're going to keep me young these next few months."

"How old are you, anyway?"

"Nuh-uh. If you want me to answer another question, you need to answer mine. Starting with what position your brother plays."

I take another sip of the cool whiskey before answering. "Wide receiver."

"Yeah?" he asks, a quiet eagerness threading through his tone. "Does he have a favourite team?"

"The Pythons. We were born and raised in Vancouver, and our dad loved them."

He nods, seeming to understand what I'm saying without needing clarification. My father isn't a topic I feel like talking about now, if ever, and I can appreciate someone who doesn't push on sensitive topics.

"My family weren't huge football fans. More of a hockey-loving bunch."

"Honestly, I've never been able to understand football, so you have your work cut out for you. Nate's tried to teach me a million times."

"I'm not worried," he declares slyly.

"Well, I am. You said they wanted you to marry a fan, right? How am I supposed to pretend to be one during this meeting with your bosses?"

"They're not going to hand you a pop quiz, Bandit. I have a game tomorrow, and then I'll get something set up and let you know. Are you good for this weekend?"

The scent of whiskey travels through the space between us, mild and muted, weakened by the cologne that's hanging on to his T-shirt. I get the urge to lean in to smell the fabric and quickly decide this is a great moment to leave.

"This weekend is fine. Nate has practice on Sunday, but I'm free Saturday," I say haphazardly.

It's not like I have work or anything anymore.

Fuck, that burns.

"I'm twenty-three, to answer your earlier question." Jamie slides off his stool and hovers a hand over my back while we retreat through the kitchen. "Are you taking the bus back?"

"I was. Were you planning on offering me another ride?"

"Would you have agreed or told me to get screwed?" he teases.

I nip at the inside of my cheek and turn my head so he can't see my mouth curl at the corner. "Look at you learning."

"Might as well mark me down with honours, Blakely. You're my new favourite subject."

11

Jamie

I HAND THE BALL OFF TO THE REF AND TUG AT THE BOTTOM OF MY jersey. Another first down, and I'm buzzing while shoulder bumping Chase. He's too zoned in to the game to notice me as Jax and the defense take position for the next play.

It's the best reaction he could have. If Jaxon can't get the ball to me, Chase is who I want to take the touchdown.

We part, going to separate sides of the zone. The team sets up, and I pull in calm, slow breaths, flexing my toes in my cleats and fingers in my gloves. The linebacker across from me licks his lips, and I toss him a wink, unbothered by the intimidation. Soon enough, he'll be chasing after me.

The snap comes quickly. I'm already moving, feet digging into the turf. Mr. Dry Lips mirrors me, his shoulders back and gaze intense.

I explode into action, cutting hard to the outside. Jax is rolling right, searching through the moving bodies in front of him. He's patient and calm. It's what makes him the best QB in the league, and right now, he's waiting for me to get clear.

Throwing a quick jab step to the inside, I watch for the moment the defender loses me and push my legs harder, leaving him a step behind. The ball is already sailing through the cooling evening air when I turn my head to track it. My pace is fast enough that for half a second, I worry whether I'll be able to stop once I've slid into the end zone or if I'll ram face first into the barriers.

The crowd screams, and I bundle the noise up, shovelling it down into my chest. My cleats rip into the turf as I clear yard after yard until, finally, the ball drops.

I catch it in one hand before cradling it into my chest at the same moment the defender dives for me. He misses, only succeeding in making me stumble slightly.

Once I've gained my balance, I'm gone again. One defender has a bit of an angle to attempt to take me down, but I cut back inside, leaving him flailing. The end zone opens up in front of me, and I cross the line untouched, pumping the ball into the air.

Chase and the closest players to me run up as I cradle my invisible bow and shoot an arrow straight at Jaxon. The fans roar when he points back at me and mouths, "All you."

It's a tradition that started at the beginning of this season, and while the media doesn't give a shit about the team, they do get quite a kick out of our little bromance. *Jaxison* is our supposed couple name.

I head to the sidelines and get a slap on the back from Coach.

"Good job out there, Bateman. Eyes open and legs loose," he says with a dip of his chin.

"Thanks, Coach. Jax found me easily."

Taking a seat on the bench, I turn away the jacket offered to me and lean forward, eyes on the Edmonton QB as their offense sets up. It's growing colder after sunset now, but we're a far way off from the frozen October nights I'm craving.

Jaxon drops down beside me and squirts water onto his face. "Three in a row."

"Don't jinx it," I warn.

Odds are we won't be on the field again tonight. Not unless the other team can somehow pull off a miracle and double their thirteen points to reach our thirty-one with only a minute left on the clock.

"Think we've got a chance this season? Beat the odds and all that?" he asks, his gaze glued to the rival QB when he passes the ball off for a run play.

His question floats into the air without a response from me. We're both too focused on what's happening now to bother with talk.

Our defense is hungry tonight. Famished, even.

Zach Mercer may very well be taking the title of best defensive tackle in the league by the end of the season. Watching his eyes gloss over as he tears through the other team's offense is both terrifying and exciting.

But it's nothing compared to the sight of him spotting the running back, who's mistakenly landed himself in his direct path and barrelling into him. He goes down with what appears to be minimal effort on Zach's part. Our defensive tackle bares his teeth at the running back and pounds his chest, towering over him.

When the crowd grows in volume, I laugh in disbelief because Zach's hand isn't empty.

"Crazy fucker just recovered another fumble," Jax notes before standing and shifting to talk with Coach about what his plan is for our next play.

I almost feel bad for Edmonton. Getting whooped by a team estimated to finish the season third from last place isn't a confidence booster.

At the same time, I'm selfish enough to be grateful for the monster win. Especially when I know that I'll be telling Blakely all about it once this game is over and she arrives.

My hair is still wet from my post-game shower when I walk Blakely out of the elevator and down the hall to Graham's office.

She's put on a brave face, but I caught the slight tremble of her hands when she grabbed the railing in the elevator. I know nothing will happen to her where we're going, but she doesn't share that confidence, and I don't expect her to.

We're about to enter a room full of businessmen who she's never met before. I'm desensitized to these situations because of the way I was raised and how many times I've been in this exact same spot, whereas most people are and should be wary. My dad didn't stop insisting on joining me in business meetings until my second season for this very reason.

You never know if someone with more power than you is going to flex it and force you into a situation you're not comfortable being in. I know myself well enough now to be able to recognize when I'm uncomfortable with agreeing just because I'm being pressured to, but I had to get pushed around a few times to be able to find that confidence.

I'd offer Blakely my hand if I didn't think she would bite it clean off.

For now, I'll offer her my words and hope that they have the same supportive payoff as a physical touch would.

"The guys in there are probably more scared of you than you are of them," I offer, keeping my words light.

"If you're trying to compare a room full of men to a bear I've stumbled upon in the woods, I'm sorry to say that I'd rather choose the bear."

"So would I," I admit.

She looks over at me, biting at the inside of her cheek. I point at the office at the end of the hall and risk leaning closer.

"I remember a few years back, my mom got all my female cousins bear spray for Christmas and told them to always keep it with them. My uncles took over the tradition and get replacements for them every year. None of my cousins have ever had to use theirs, but it was never really for bears. So, yeah, I'd choose the animal over the man any day," I explain, lowering my tone. "Doesn't matter my size or position on this team. They're freaky to me too."

Her features soften. "If your cousins used bear spray on someone, they'd be charged."

I curl my fingers, nails scraping my palm as I avoid touching her. "One of us would be catching a charge regardless, Bandit. Them or me. It would be picking and choosing at that point."

Blakely stares at me in silence for a moment, her lips parting on a puffed exhale. Some colour returns to her cheeks for the first time tonight, and that has my chest puffing a smidge, proud that I was able to help even a little.

"You're a good cousin, Jamie," she murmurs.

"One day, I'll prove that I'm more than that. But I'll take it. Thank you."

She nods slightly. "Will this meeting take long? I haven't told Nate about any of this yet. I'm hoping that after this, I'll be able to. He's not usually up too late. Even on Saturdays."

"No. I'll make sure it's right to the point. We'll get you home quick," I swear.

The toes of her simple black flats scuff the floor as she taps it and adjusts her dark-washed jeans. "You're going to offer to drive me home again, aren't you?"

Dropping my head an inch, I lean in close enough to catch a whiff of vanilla. I capture her eyes in an easy stare and grin.

"Yeah, I'm going to offer to drive you home. Gonna keep asking until you agree."

I half expect her to turn me down. Instead, she proves once again that over the course of this marriage, I'm going to be kept on my toes.

"We'll see."

I'm left standing in the hallway, watching as she pulls her shoulders back and struts the rest of the way to the office door. With a glance over her shoulder, she has me laughing.

"Are you coming? You're not off to a great start, Pretty Boy," she says flippantly.

I raise a hand to my chest and hold it there in case she uses whatever voodoo magic she's tapped into to demand my heart leap through its cage and into her palm.

"Do you take apologies in the form of words or sacrifices?"

"Surely that would depend on the sacrifice."

"What type do you prefer? The fluffy bunny kind or the bloody heart kind?"

She rolls her eyes, a muscle in her cheek twitching. "Are those my only two options?"

"Give me another one."

We're stalled in front of the office, but I don't have it in me to stop this conversation in exchange for a stuffy business meeting. Not until I have to make that call.

"Fine," she says, tilting her head like she's deep in thought. "How about a year's supply of tea? Or a public declaration of undying loyalty? I could accept skywriting as well."

I smirk, leaning on my back foot. "Skywriting, huh? Well, as long as you're not asking for much."

She shrugs, her coy attitude back in full swing. "Bunnies are cute, and bloody hearts are messy. Tea is practical. And skywriting? Timeless."

I store that info away. "What's your favourite kind of tea?"

"Peppermint. I hate ginger."

"And no coffee?"

"Are you keeping a list of answers to all of these questions somewhere?" she counters.

I tap my temple. "It's all up here, baby. In a very organized filing cabinet with your name on it."

"Don't call me baby."

"Why? Is it making you fall for me already?"

She huffs, turning to give me her back. I chuckle while eating the space between us with long strides. When I reach her, I brace a hand on the wall beside the door, bracketing her with my chest while not touching her directly. We're a foot from the door now; every second we stay like this is another that we risk being ripped open. I'm all for seizing the opportunity to show everyone how well we're already doing together, but Blakely . . .

She's breathing heavily, her arms flat at her sides. I'm a bastard because instead of stepping back to give her space, I dip my head just enough that I can catch that vanilla scent again.

"For the benefit of our agreement, I recommend acting like you are," I rasp, clenching my jaw to keep from rubbing my cheek against her hair like a dog. "Or like you could. You might not be a mega fan, but I'll convince them that I can make you one if they pick up on anything. All you have to do is pretend that you can stand to be this close to me long enough to make this work."

Her green eyes are deep and guarded when she slowly turns her head and stares up at me. I almost reach for my chest again. Not out of fear of her commanding my heart to fall into her hand, but that I'll end up ripping it out myself and gifting it to her.

"Thank you for making it easy, Pretty Boy."

12

Blakely

THE DOOR OPENS AS I FINALLY GET THE WORDS OUT, LEAVING JAMIE no time to reply to them. It's a blessing, really.

I shouldn't have said anything at all. The last thing he needs is more confidence or any sort of hint that I'm beginning to enjoy his company. No, I'm not falling for him, but friendship doesn't seem too far in the distance, and I fear that's as scary as love.

Having him directly at my back does make it easier to face the man now in front of me. From the three-piece suit to the glistening silver Rolex on his watch, he screams wealth in a way I'll never be able to truly comprehend.

"Blakely, I assume?" he asks, peering down his nose at me. Not in a rude way, just . . . like he knows he's got an advantage over me.

I refuse to look weak in front of him or any one of the men coming after him as I tilt my head back and answer, "Yes. And you are?"

Jamie leaves his position at my back, settling at my side instead. I feel the ghost of his palm as he hovers it over my back, not making contact.

"This is Briggs. He's the lawyer I told you about."

Right. If only I remembered a single thing from the summary

Jamie gave me in the elevator on the way up here. My skull is full of hot air right now, not a lick of knowledge to be found.

"It's nice to meet you," I manage to say.

The lawyer shifts out of the doorway and gestures for us to come inside. "Likewise. Come in, everyone is here and ready for discussion."

"PR is here?" Jamie asks, hovering in place.

His hand makes contact with my back, and I suck in a breath at the blistering heat coming from it.

Briggs nods sharply. "Everyone is here that you insisted be."

"Why PR?" It's out before I can zip my lips shut.

"You need to know everything required of you before you sign off on this. From today to our wedding and afterward. I don't want any surprises for either of us," Jamie says, a sharp edge to the words. A warning, maybe.

If it is one, Briggs reads it loud and clear. "We hear you."

Jamie flashes a smile. "Perfect."

I follow his lead, putting all my limited trust in the hope that he won't turn out to be a piece of shit after all.

We enter the office, and I'm immediately hit with a sharp sense of inferiority. I've never been around so many different successful men before. It's like being suspended above a tank of piranhas and hoping that the rope around your waist doesn't snap.

The bulky man behind the massive desk must be Graham Warren, while the leaner one resting his back against it looks too much like a coach to be anyone else. It's not even the windbreaker with the BC Pythons logo on it, but just an overall aura. Like he's the guy who's capable of demanding a team with not only power and success but respect.

Then, there's Briggs and a—woman.

Naturally, I drink in her presence and take it as a good sign. She appears completely calm and collected, lounging on the white leather couch with one leg slung over the other beneath a slim-fitting pencil skirt. Her pink blouse is professional but still cute, and her bright red hair is swept back into a professional bun that draws attention to her plump cheeks and lips lined with a soft blush colour.

She adjusts her position on the couch and offers me a warm smile. "Hi, Blakely. Since nobody else has decided to do it, I'll introduce myself to you first. I'm Sadie, and I'm so happy to meet you. Thank you for taking the time to come down here tonight."

"It's nice to meet you too, Sadie."

"Sadie's the one with all the answers," Jamie chimes in. "And she's the nicest one in this room. Other than myself, of course. But you already knew that."

Sadie looks to the other men. "Cocky as he is, he's not wrong. The others will be on their best behaviour. Right, Graham?"

The man behind the desk clears his throat and fixes his gaze on me while moving his hand around the room. "I'm Graham Warren, the owner of the Pythons. In front of me is Coach Riley Tanner and, obviously, the team's lawyer, Briggs Porter."

"Briggs has been in contact with the best family lawyer in the province to organize all the paperwork for today and has also put together an NDA and contract with the information that we'll be discussing in this meeting," Sadie says, patting the empty couch cushion beside her.

Jamie inches away as if to encourage me to go. I jump at the chance to be closer to the only other woman in the room and sit beside her. In my old jeans and last unstained shirt, I try not to pay too much attention to how incredible she looks and the way it must make me look even sloppier.

When I risk a look up in Jamie's direction, he's smiling confidently at me. Aware of everyone watching us, I lift the corner of my mouth slightly and look to the last spot left on the couch. It's a signal to take it, but he hesitates. I realize a second later that he's become fixated on my mouth.

"The plan for today is to go over all of the contracts and upcoming obligations for the both of you, and we'll run a background check before sending final copies of everything for signature," Briggs explains.

A background check seems reasonable, but still. It's freaky knowing these strangers are going to be combing through my history, even if I know there isn't anything there for them to find unless they dive deeper than basic knowledge.

"How in-depth will this check be?" I ask, feigning ease.

Jamie sits beside me, his previous daze broken and focus back on the situation at hand. I don't think about it again as Graham leans forward in his chair and taps the bottoms of his clasped hands on the desk.

"It will be intensive. We won't take any chances with anything coming out in the press once the marriage is official. So, if you have anything you'd like to disclose before that happens, now would be a good time."

From the corner of my eye, I catch the tightening of Jamie's jaw before he speaks. "Is my trust in her not enough? She's my choice. Do you really need to go digging into her past? I'm not going to make her tell all of you anything that isn't your business."

My heart swells, forcing my chest to expand around it. Appreciation blows on the ember of friendship that's already begun to grow, expanding its flame until I'm left with no choice but to consider this man an ally. A friend.

I shove any tingle of anxiousness to the back of my hand and drop my hand to his knee. To everyone else, it probably looks romantic. But it's a sign of appreciation. A thank you that I hope he understands.

The loose shorts he's wearing only reach the middle of his thighs, leaving the rest of his legs bare. I seemed to have forgotten that fact when I reached for his knee. It's warm and speckled with coarse hair that scrapes at my palm. Still, I don't pull back.

I'm glad for that when a beat later, Jamie's hand engulfs

mine, squeezing gently while his thumb glides over my knuckles.

Curious, I stare down at the hold. I expected his palm to be sweaty, but it's only warmth and a grounding steadiness that I feel. Unlike the last few times I've let a man hold my hand, there isn't a nipping at my gut telling me that something's off.

My intuition is one of my strongest attributes. It's kept me from my fair share of bad situations, especially with men. I'm picky with the company I keep for good reason. If something doesn't feel right, I'm always out of there sooner rather than later.

With Jamie, I've yet to feel the need to run.

Sadie speaks up from my side, her voice understanding yet still strong. "I understand how invasive it can feel. We appreciate you agreeing to help the team with this, and you have my word that everything we learn will be kept quiet. It's for security purposes only."

"Run one on me too," Jamie says, the demand obvious.

Graham shakes his head. "We already have one."

"It wouldn't be for you. Run a new one and give it to Blakely."

I suck in a sharp breath. "I don't need your background on a piece of paper."

"It's only fair." His grip on my hand grows firmer as he narrows his stare on Briggs. "Can you just do it, please? I think it's the least demanding thing in this entire agreement."

"It'll be done. We'll get it added to the final contract come signing time," Graham says, his gaze curious and heavy as it hangs over me.

It would be so easy to defend myself and tell them all that I had nothing to do with Jamie's call. Maybe when I was younger, I'd have bowed under the pressure to find any opportunity to make these people like me. *Maybe*.

The person I am now and have been for the last five years doesn't give a shit what these people think of me.

"Should we start looking through the fine print, then?" Sadie asks.

It's the break in conversation that we need. Everyone is quick to agree, and a few minutes later, I have a thick stack of papers in my hands and a highlighter I'm meant to use on anything I don't like.

We've only made it to the third page when Jamie clears his throat and highlights the line about the proposed wedding and announcement dates.

"You want to leak the wedding to the media the day of? When are we announcing the engagement?"

"The engagement will be announced publicly a week before the wedding. And leaking it makes it more authentic. One public announcement is more than enough in only a couple of weeks of time. Anything more than that and it will appear unauthentic. You won't have to entertain anyone during the wedding or afterward. Security will be tight, we'll make sure of that," Graham explains, voice rigid.

"It will only be our families in attendance, right? I don't want a big wedding," I add.

My first wedding won't be a real one, and I don't want it to ruin my expectations of my second. If I'm going to do this, it's not going to be anything overly special. I won't be able to deal with the disappointment of my real wedding never living up to the fake one.

Jamie grips his pen in his left hand and scribbles along the side of his contract. *Keep the wedding small.*

"As long as we can have a heavy spread of photos for the press, small is fine," Graham agrees.

We work through the next few pages before Jamie starts reading a paragraph he's highlighted.

"'The Parties agree that, for the duration of the marriage, Party A shall reside with Party B at a mutually agreed-upon residence, and both Parties shall make reasonable efforts to maintain the appearance of a cohabiting marital relationship in accordance with the agreed publicity arrangements.'" He wets his lips and scribbles along the margins again. "I don't want it in the contract that Blakely has to live with me. If she wants to leave at any time, she can do as she pleases while still fulfilling her side of the agreement."

Nobody speaks for a moment, and I stiffen.

"If you don't live together, it will spark questions," Sadie cautions.

He doesn't back down. "Let them question, then. It'll only give them more stories to write about us. Isn't that what you want?"

Graham's nostrils flare. I think I enjoy knowing that Jamie isn't intimidated by him enough to allow them to potentially take advantage of either of us.

"Fine. Once the paperwork is filed and you are husband and wife, you are not obligated to share a residence. However, you do need to do everything in your power to appear as though you do."

"Done." Jamie goes back to reading.

For the next hour, we don't move from the couch. It lasts longer than I anticipated, and every minute that passed had me twitching to grab my phone to check on Nate. If Jamie hadn't been the one interrupting every five minutes with a change to the contract, we'd have been out far earlier.

It's impossible to be frustrated with him for that, though.

Especially when he ushers me out of the office and down the elevator again once we've finished.

"I'm so sorry, Bandit. I didn't think it would take so long," he mutters, exhaustion thick in his voice.

"It's okay. There are no surprises in the contract now."

"Yeah, at the cost of your entire night."

I lean my back against the elevator wall and check my phone for any messages or missed calls. There isn't even one.

"Aren't you tired? You played today, right?"

"You didn't watch?"

"I wouldn't have known what was going on."

He braces his hands on the railing and hums. "Teaching you football is number one on my to-do list. You're about to be seeing a lot of the sport these next couple of months."

"You told them not to ask whether or not I was a fan, didn't you?" I ask, my gut telling me that the answer is yes. It was from the moment I realized nobody had brought up my knowledge or lack thereof.

His grin is wide and knowing. "I might have given them a bit of a rundown before you arrived. Sue me."

I swallow, copying his stance and feeling the cool gold bars in my hands. "Thank you for everything you did back there. Not just for the fan thing."

"I'm pretty much your fiancé now, Blakely. In two weeks, I'll be your husband. I was just doing what a husband should."

"Do you still want to drive me home tonight?" I blurt out.

His eyes grow wide. "I do. You're going to let me see where you live now? Is this a fiancé perk that I didn't know I was getting tonight?"

"Don't get ahead of yourself. You'll still be dropping me off on the corner."

"I should have known." He blows out a soft laugh.

I cock a brow. "Is that still a yes, or have you changed your mind?"

"For you, I'll hog every corner in the neighbourhood."

13

Jamie

My older brother is a grumpy shit most of the time, but he has moments when he checks that part of his personality and welcomes a lighter vibe. Usually, that's only when we're around Mom, his fiancée, or he's got his daughter in his arms.

I've never seen him as happy as he is with his new family. The one he found when he was certain he'd be spending the rest of his life with only a scowl to keep him company.

It's wild how fast life can change. One minute, you're laughing while your teenage brother chases you around your childhood home with an electric fly swatter because you wrote *I like boobs* on his favourite hat, and the next, you're laughing with every male relative you have in a party bus for his bachelor party ten years later.

"There better not be any strippers, Jamie. Braxton already threatened to have me sleep in Hades' doghouse if I stepped foot into a club," my cousin Maddox grunts.

His brother, Noah, doesn't threaten me with words. Instead, he glowers at me with the strength of a thousand suns, daring me to bring him anywhere close to a woman that isn't his Tinsley. I toss him a wink and keep a wide berth while moving around him to the seat on Maddox's other side.

That guy could cut through the trunk of a tree with his glare alone. I'd blame the whole rock star thing if he hadn't been so ruthless from the moment I met him as an infant.

"Addie suggested strippers. She thought it would be fun," Cooper chimes in.

The oldest of the group, Cooper, is not blood-related to any of us. His involvement in our group comes from his parents' friendship with ours. He grew up with us and may as well be blood at this point. He, Maddox, and Braxton, Maddox's wife, were the closest out of everyone growing up.

Now, he's married to Maddox's younger sister, and they have an adorable baby girl.

"Adalyn's opinion of fun needs to be studied," Maddox notes. "She's not one to be trusted with this sort of thing."

Oliver, the husband-to-be, rests an arm along the back of the opposite leather couch. "Avery had to talk her out of hiring their own strippers for the bachelorette party. We all need to be prepared to find half-naked cops in my living room when we get back in case she didn't heed the warnings."

"Not happening," Noah states coolly.

He reaches up to untie the bandana from where it holds his long black hair back and wraps it around his knuckles instead, rubbing it back and forth.

The collection of face tattoos he's sporting nowadays is intimidating as fuck, but the one at his temple is my favourite simply because I know the meaning behind it. Tinsley has one to match.

Her younger brother is here too, and that's an odd change. Easton is the second youngest member of our little family, but he's finally old enough to be able to go out with us now.

The kid is only two years younger than me, but compared to Cooper's thirty-three, he's just a baby. We both are, I guess.

Easton has always preferred Noah's company, so it wasn't surprising when he piled on the bus and went right to his side. He shares quite a few of Noah's personality traits, including the dark shadow that lingers over his bluntly spoken words and lack of funny bone.

"If there were going to be strippers at your house tonight, they would be firefighters, not cops," Cooper tells Oliver.

Maddox chuffs a laugh while the bus takes a right turn through traffic. "Are you not giving her enough strip shows in your gear, Olliepop?"

"I'm not talking about our sex life with you assholes," my brother grunts.

I abandon the conversation for now and reach for the cooler sandwiched between me and Cooper. The array of Jell-O shots that the girls made us have been stacked in containers.

"Oh, fuck off, Jamie," Maddox says, scraping a hand down over his bearded jaw. "I'm too old for Jell-O shots."

I roll my eyes and start handing them out to everyone. "Nobody is too old for shots. I don't hear Cooper complaining."

"Are you hinting that I'm extra old?" he asks, already taking the lid off his plastic shot glass.

Noah's glaring at his, his top lip curling in disgust. I ignore him, having seen him pound back bowls of the stuff when we were younger.

My brother squishes the sides of his shot and jiggles the contents into his open mouth. I copy him and immediately taste how much vodka the women used.

"Shit, they must have dumped the entire bottle in," I hiss, shaking my head as my throat burns.

Cooper laughs, finished with his shot. "Did you expect them to measure properly?"

"I don't think Braxton has *ever* used a measuring cup in the kitchen. She's a measure with your heart type of woman," Maddox puts in, wincing when he takes his shot.

What type of woman is Blakely? The follow the recipe type or one that measures with her heart? I already know she wouldn't be using vodka, that's for sure. These shots would be ten times stronger with whiskey or maybe even tequila.

A week after going over the contract and dropping her at the corner of her neighbourhood and I'm itching to see her again. Contact has been brief between us, but I haven't stopped reminding her that I'm here.

Once Oliver's wedding has come and gone, it'll be our turn. She'll be my wife, and that's a crazy reminder.

"Is your food at least seasoned, then? I've been trying to help Addie with that, but she's adamant that pepper is enough for almost everything," Cooper muses.

Maddox snorts. "Yeah, not surprising. She used to offer to help with breakfast back when we were kids, and everything would be so bland that Dad started slipping us those tiny salt packets to use when she wasn't looking. Sorry to say that's a you problem now."

"Seasonless food is more than worth it to be with her," Cooper declares, squishing his second shot.

Oliver brushes the comment off and stares at me. "Adorable. But where are we even going right now, Jamie? What's the plan?"

"Oh, we have a crazy one for tonight to celebrate your last night as an unmarried man. I've booked us three glorious hours of paintballing before we hit our reservation at the best Mexican restaurant in town that just so happens to also be your favourite."

None of us have been paintballing in at least five years. Oliver got banned from the last venue after he shot our team leader four times in the groin when he tried saying that our dad was an overpaid, overrated bench warmer throughout his career. The ban has long since been lifted, but I played it safe and chose a different spot in case the same guy is working there tonight.

"You're going to give Noah a paintball gun?" Cooper asks, glancing between me and Noah.

"Won't be a problem because I call dibs him on my team."

Noah lounges back on the seat, his arms crossed and legs spread wide enough that the rips in his jeans grow in size.

"If I were going to injure you, I would have done it when you came home from Europe married to my sister. Not at a bachelor party years later," he drones.

Oliver hides a laugh behind a cough. "From what we heard, Maddox took care of that."

"His punch was weak," Noah rebuttals.

His older brother scowls. "You weren't even there to see it."

"His nose didn't break. Nothing did."

I pick up another shot and toss it back while they bicker. Oliver looks at me and signals for another one, and I give him a blue one.

He leans toward me, lowering his voice with taking his lid off. "Thank you for setting this up, Jamie. Means a lot to me."

"You got it, big bro. Would have appreciated a bit more guidance on your part with what you wanted, but I think I made it work. How are you feeling? You're getting fucking married in three days."

His entire expression shifts, becoming so much lighter as the brown in his eyes warms. "The waiting is killing me. I need her to be my wife more than I need to breathe. I've been thinking about seeing her walk down the aisle and just—it nearly kills me. Her and Nova, man. They're everything."

"Love looks good on you. So does fatherhood."

"Crazy to think that I'm a dad now. Even more than a husband. Nova feels like mine too. It doesn't matter that her blood isn't mine. She's my daughter where it counts."

Emotion builds in my throat, and I cough to clear it before I get choked up. I grab the back of his head and bring our temples together for a beat.

"You deserve all of this."

"Yeah, I'm starting to believe that."

"I hate to break up the moment, but where did you book this paintball at?" Maddox cuts in.

I release Oliver and turn my body to follow his stare out the tinted glass. The name of the venue is right, but the stickers on the windows look completely wrong. Splatter Studio is there in big painted letters above the door . . . yet the vibe is very wrong for what I was expecting.

"Did you look at the website for this place before booking?" Cooper asks, always the calmest person in any room.

"Of course I did." *Not.*

I made an online reservation on the way to my post-game interviews weeks ago. It's a miracle that I could even do that with cameras flashing in my eyes.

"It sounds like a paintball place," Oliver says, trying to ease our growing worry.

Maddox shakes his head, amusement curving his lips. "Cream Filling can sound like a donut shop while also being a porn studio."

"Who the fuck is naming a donut shop Cream Filling?" I choke out.

Maddox shakes his head. "I don't know! You're the one who booked us a paintball afternoon in a place with flower and heart stickers all over the window."

"It's purse painting," Noah grunts.

Cooper clears his throat. "What?"

"That's what you do here. You paint purses."

We turn to look at him now. The rock star's got his chipped phone screen turned toward us, displaying a part of Splatter Studio's website that I didn't look at.

The photos of painted purses draw a laugh from deep in my chest. Oliver joins me a beat later, and then the bus is full of rough male laughter.

I guess Blakely will be getting her first gift from me sooner than expected.

14

Jamie

THE GUYS ARE GRUNTING AND GROWLING WITH EFFORT AS IF I HAD taken them to a CrossFit gym instead of a purse painting class.

I'm one more snarl from Noah away from starting to colour his tattoos in with paint to distract him. The last thing we need tonight is to get arrested because he's tossed his hideous purse through a window.

I don't know how I would explain that to my brother's soon-to-be wife when she came to pick us up in the morning.

"Do you know who you're giving these to?"

The old woman standing at the front of the room has stopped drifting between us and offering her help and suggestions. After she told Easton that his purse would look better with other colours besides black and he stared at her blankly for three minutes straight, she's kept her distance.

Her question now is awkward and forced, like she just can't stand the silence anymore.

"My daughter," Oliver says, smiling loosely from the alcohol in his system. The paintbrush in his hand is crusted halfway down the handle with blue paint.

Cooper, the literal art professor, has made this project his bitch. He's shown all of us up and then some. There are patterns and blended colours on both sides of the bag that look like they should belong on a canvas instead.

"My wife. But I have a feeling she'll insist we keep it for our baby girl."

"How much did Cooper pay you to take us here instead of the paintball place, Jamie? Look how much better he's done than all of us," Maddox complains, furiously dabbing the tip of his brush against the side of his purse.

"I didn't pay him anything."

"Can confirm that he didn't pay," I note, turning back to my project.

Maybe I went a little overboard with the designs on my purse. I was fully in the zone for at least half an hour. The material of the bag is a soft beige leather, and now it's covered in little black robber masks and game controllers.

I swirl my paintbrush in the cloudy cup of water and tilt my head at the purse, squinting to see if you can tell that the controllers are controllers and not fat lumps of coal.

"What's with the black masks and smudges?" Maddox asks while leaning over my shoulder, the vodka from the Jell-O shots we brought in with us strong on his breath.

I whip my head to glare at him and hover the wet tip of the brush an inch from his deep green button-up. "They're not smudges, asshole."

"Look like smudges to me," Noah mutters.

"Your purse is literally smeared with red. Is it supposed to be blood? Are you a full-blown psychopath now or something?" I retort.

He bares his teeth and chomps the air. "Make sure to keep your doors locked at night. You never know what could crawl inside when you're sleeping."

"I like the red," Cooper says, inspecting Noah's purse.

I roll my eyes at him and take another shot. "Your opinion doesn't count because you're still trying to earn forgiveness."

Noah drops his brush into his cup of water and leans back in his chair, the hint of a smirk appearing. "My forgiveness can't be bought. It would be pointless for Cooper to try."

"Exactly," his brother-in-law states while using a knuckle to push his glasses up his nose.

Maddox goes back to his seat and starts blowing on his purse. "Mine can be bought. Just FYI."

"What could you possibly need, Money Bags?" Oliver grunts, lips stained blue from the shots he's taken.

"I love when you call me that. It makes me feel superior."

"He's just jealous that you don't have to run through burning buildings every day for a living," I say, wiping my hands on the piece of paper towel we were each given.

My fingers are overly sensitive, but then again, I think that's just all of me. The vodka has gone right to my head the way it has the rest of the guys, minus Noah. He's as sober as a judge.

Maddox shrugs. "Should have chosen something less life-threatening, then. Like a bus driver or teacher."

"Teacher was already taken," Oliver mutters.

I couldn't imagine my brother as a teacher, regardless. He'd wind up quitting midday at the first hint of a teenage spat in his classroom.

Maddox replies with a quick tease, and I tune them out, attention drifting to my phone. There are no new texts from Blakely. It's not shocking. It seems to take me reaching out first for us to talk, and I don't mind putting the effort in. We're closer than we were a couple of weeks ago, but there's still a lot to learn about one another. I don't see that stopping anytime soon.

> Me: Do you like purses?

I send the text and leave my phone on the table while drying my paintbrush. Our craft instructor is lingering near the front of the room, so I lift my hand like a student to grab her attention.

She looks to me with suspicion in her gaze. "You don't have to lift your hand to ask a question."

I grin wide. "I figured it was more polite than screaming across the room."

"Then I suppose a thank you is only fitting."

"Nah, I don't need one of those. I do, however, need to know how long these purses will take to dry. We have dinner plans in half an hour."

"Usually, they dry quite quickly with the paint we use. I do suggest leaving them here overnight and having them shipped out in the morning, or if you wanted to stop back in tomorrow, we could have them ready for you."

"Are they okay to take tonight if we can't wait? I've got plans of surprising someone with it after dinner."

I can feel my brother's attention shift from his conversation with the other guys to me.

The instructor rolls her thin lips for a moment. "Yes. Just beware of the risk of smudging or chipping. You're planning on carrying these around with you all night?"

I wink at her. "Yeah, why not? Men can use purses too."

"I'll leave mine here," Cooper says.

Oliver agrees with him while everyone else decides to take their purses home with them.

Blakely probably has her fair share of purses, so it's not like she'll actually use this one or anything. It'll sit on a shelf or hide in the back of her closet. The only thing I hope is that she sees it and feels appreciated in some way.

My phone buzzes on the tabletop, and I leap on it before anyone else can.

> Bandit: I guess. Why? Do you?

> Me: I have a man purse.

> Me: The kind that you wear across your chest.

Where else am I supposed to keep my wallet and phone? In the back pocket of my jeans, where they constantly dig into my ass every time I sit down?

> Bandit: I should have known you wore a murse.

> Me: Be nice to your fiancé.

> Bandit: I don't see a ring on my finger.

My laugh is so loud I'm sure the entire street can hear it. I look up from my phone to find everyone waiting for me, standing by the door with their purses in their hands.

Oliver's brow is lifted in a silent question that I ignore while facing the woman and asking, "So, where do I pay?"

"Are you sure this is where you want to be dropped off?" the Uber driver asks once he's pulled off the main road.

Even with my stomach full of the best tacos and salsa money can buy, the tequila from the four margaritas I had hasn't settled well. Mixed with the amount of vodka I drank during painting, and it's created quite a volatile mix that has the world spinning around me.

"Yep! Thanks, man."

My hand slips off the handle when I try to open the door. I attempt it again and manage to hang on tight this time. The SUV is stuffy despite the large size, and I eagerly stumble out onto the sidewalk with my purse in tow.

Oliver insisted I let the party bus drive me home the way it is everyone else, but if I'd agreed, they would have found out about Blakely. It isn't time for that yet. I can't risk anyone knowing about this before her brother does.

And that's something she hasn't taken care of as of now.

I suck in a deep breath and crinkle my nose at the polluted

smell. Garbage and exhaust don't help a sensitive stomach much more than another few shots would.

Stumbling slightly, I look around the neighbourhood, trying to make note of the way it looks in the dark. I'm an idiot sometimes, including right now. My wallet's in the purse I'm planning on handing off to Blakely, stocked with cash, all of my bank cards, and ID. I don't have anything on me that I could use to defend myself other than my sluggish limbs, so really, I'm a prime victim for a robbing once again.

Despite all of that, a cab isn't my next call.

I put my phone on speaker and let the dialling noise fill the empty street as I sit on the curb and bend over my knees. The purse hangs between them, safeguarded as best I can manage.

"Jamie?"

I'm positive that I'm grinning. I just can't feel it. "Hey, Bandit."

"Do you know what time it is?" she asks, voice raspy.

"Yeah. It's past my bedtime, but I don't have practice tomorrow, so it's okay."

"Should I be worried about you right now?"

"I'm perfectly fine. But if you insist on worrying, I won't complain," I tease, the slur in my voice more prominent than I thought.

"Are you drunk right now?"

Seems she caught that.

"It was Ollie's bachelor party tonight."

"Right."

"I got you something."

A pause on the line. "At a bachelor party? It better not be a stripper's thong."

"It's not a thong."

"Alright, good—"

"It's a pair of briefs, actually."

"I'm hanging up now."

My heart rate speeds up. "I'm kidding! We didn't even go to a strip club. I'm not really into that kind of thing."

"You're not into staring at naked women?"

"Of course I am. Just not like that," I argue.

"What did you do tonight, then?"

"How about you come to our curb so we can talk properly?" I ask, shutting my eyes for a quick minute.

There's a slam nearby, and I open my eyes immediately to stare into the dark street. When nothing pops out from behind the dumpster, I slowly drop my shoulders.

"Or better yet, tell me where to go, and I'll come to you," I offer.

"Are you actually on our curb right now?" she asks, sounding airy. Like she's tired.

Is it really that late?

Wait. She said *our* curb.

I'm pretty sure I'm smiling again. "I wanted to see you and give you this present."

"Why did you get me a present, Jamieson?"

"Oooooh, *Jamieson*. So fancy, Blakely," I tease, my tongue rolling funny.

"Fine. You won."

Hushed voices sound, and then a door closes near where she is. I turn my body to face the direction she always goes when we part ways and keep my phone cradled in my palm.

Minutes pass as I wait, the line staying silent but the call still there. Like a reminder that while she isn't saying anything, we're still connected.

"You're ridiculous, Pretty Boy," she shouts from the road, her figure shadowed but obvious.

I stumble to my feet, swaying as I wave and put my phone in my pocket. "You came."

"You asked me to."

"I'm happy to see you."

"Don't get romantic. We're not married yet," she grumbles.

Her sweatshirt and sweatpants are a few sizes too big and hang off her shoulders and bunch at her ankles. She's hidden her hair beneath a beanie again, and her skin is bare, shiny, almost like she used some kind of cream on it before coming downstairs.

"Is this permission to be romantic once we *are* married?" I counter.

"You're like a puppy who hasn't been walked in a week."

I lean forward on the balls of my feet, fighting for my balance. "Can I lick your face?"

Her cheeks turn red, so much so that I notice in the dark and with no hair free to hide them. "Oh, my God. No, you can't. I'll call you a cab."

"Not yet. I haven't given you your present yet."

A hiccup punches up my throat as I fall back on my heels and wipe the sweat from my forehead. It's a million degrees outside right now, and I have too many clothes on.

With a huff, I reach behind my head to pull my shirt off, swapping the purse between my hands so I can free my sleeve. When I uncurl my fingers, the shirt falls to the dirty street. The lack of fabric on my torso feels fucking great.

"Why did you do that?" Blakely asks, eyes flying to the sky.

"Was hot." I lift the painted purse between us. "This is for you."

Slowly, she lowers her gaze. I flex my abs, but she skips them entirely, only focusing on the bag.

Suddenly, I'm nervous, even with the alcohol in my veins.

"Is that a purse?"

"Yes. We painted them tonight. Look, I put little masks on it for my bandit wife. And these look like splotches, but they're supposed to be controllers. You know, for the Xbox you tried to steal from me," I explain, rambling without any hope of slowing my words.

"This is why you asked about the purse thing."

"Mmhmm. I wanted you to have it. It's an engagement present."

It wasn't cheap, at least. I don't know how much you're supposed to spend on a pre-wedding gift—or if those are even a thing since I didn't ask any of the married guys tonight—but I must be at least halfway there. If not, I can always get something else . . .

"I didn't need any gifts," she mutters, fisting her hands against her stomach.

I swallow. "I know. It's still for you. I know you might not want to use it, but there's nobody else I wanted to give it to. Plus, I've painted it especially for only you. Too late to change my mind now."

She studies the purse. Her mouth is twisted as she nips at the inside of her cheek and continues to hesitate to grab the purse. I'm buzzing. Every moment it takes her to move is another I start to grow more antsy.

Finally, when I'm on the verge of taking her hand and forcing it around the handle, she lifts her eyes. They lock on mine, unmoving and warm.

"If you don't mind sleeping on the couch, you can crash at my place for the night."

The offer is there and gone so fast I stand frozen in shock, unsure if I heard her correctly.

"What?"

She flattens her mouth and blinks twice. "You can crash on my couch. If that's something pretty boys do."

"It's something this one does."

I know I seem overeager, and to be honest, I couldn't care less. I'm not wasting this chance.

15

Blakely

I KNEW HE WAS OUT WITH HIS BROTHER TONIGHT. NOT BECAUSE I care that much about what he does in his personal life, but because in the few texts we sent this week, he mentioned it more than once. I didn't know about the purses, though.

It is nice to see how deeply he cares for his brother. Or, really, his entire family. There's a connection he has with them that I admire. It's loyalty and love in the purest form. The same emotions that I feel for Nate.

My stomach tightens as I keep Jamie's heavy arm around my shoulders and help him up the stairs. The apartment is on the third floor, and I've never wished we had an elevator more.

"Do you eat rocks for breakfast?" I ask between rough breaths.

He leans his head against mine and heaves himself up another few steps. "I prefer bricks. Crunchier."

"Do you ever stop joking around?"

"Does it bother you when I do it?"

I grip the railing and cringe at how slick my palm is as it slides down with every step I take. Jamie yawns in my ear and stumbles hard enough that my side hits the railing.

I hiss in pain and grit my teeth, keeping us moving.

"I'm sorry," Jamie slurs, reaching his arm around both of us to rub at my side. "Did I hurt you?"

My cheeks thump with a blush as he palms my side and his forearm pushes into my chest. His eyes are glassy but innocent, which is the only reason I haven't let go of him and watched him tumble down three flights of stairs.

Carefully, I release the railing and take his hand from where it's gently massaging the soreness away. He continues to watch me while I remove his arm and leave it lying limp at his side.

"I'm okay," I say. "It was just a bump."

"Promise?"

"I promise."

"Did I wake you up?"

I guide us up the final step and into the hall. "No. I was already awake."

"Sweet. I just didn't want to go home without seeing my fiancée first."

On instinct, I look at the doors we pass, making sure they're shut. There are some nosey and not-so-great people in this place, and I don't trust that they won't try something if they see him here and recognize who he is.

My heart thumps harder and harder as we close in on my apartment. Nate was heading to bed when I left, so he shouldn't be up to see Jamie come in. Still, it wouldn't be the first time he's changed his mind and decided to stay up on the couch for another few hours.

"Is fiancée going to be the new bandit?" I ask, keeping my voice hushed.

"Mm, I was thinking of skipping the whole fiancée thing and going with wife instead."

I ignore the jump of my pulse and lean him against the wall. My keys dig into my palm as I unlock the door and toe it open.

"Nate's sleeping, so try and be as quiet as you can," I whisper, dropping his arm back over my shoulder.

He nods once, making sure it's dramatic as fuck. "Got it."

With my heel, I close the door behind us. It's easier not to look at him for a reaction when he takes his time inspecting the place in the dark. Instead of dwelling on whether he thinks I live in a dumpster compared to his big fancy home, I turn my focus on getting him to the couch.

It's already pulled out and dressed in sheets and a blanket. The ones that haven't been washed in a week . . .

"I'll change the sheets for you. Just sit for now and try not to make any noise. The walls are thin," I ramble, on edge and growing more nervous the longer he's here.

He furrows his brows, not giving me a vocal reply as he looks around the apartment. The shoes that he kicks off his feet are probably worth more than all the furniture in this place, and the polo shirt he left on the filthy street had one of those fancy logos on the upper-right corner that may as well be a big fat dollar sign.

I've never allowed anyone to make me feel small, but right now, even without him trying, I can't help but wish I just had *more*. More money and space and someplace that I'm proud to show off.

Instead, I have a single pull-out couch that counts as my bedroom and a bathroom that most definitely is sprouting mould.

He smooths his hand across the thick sheets and offers me a simple but kind smile. "Don't change the sheets. But if you have an extra blanket, I wouldn't mind using that. I might freeze on the ground without one."

"The ground?"

"Did you think I was going to take your bed from you?"

"I'm offering it to you."

It must have been the fact it was already made up prior to his arrival that clued him in to it being where I sleep at night. Embarrassing as it may be, there's clearly no hiding that.

He uses a two-handed grip on the thin mattress to lower himself to the ground. "Too late."

"You're going to sleep on the floor in those clothes?"

His laugh is like a gentle stroke of a hand up my back. Warm and reassuring. "I could strip completely, if you prefer?"

At least I'd have a good view before I shut my eyes.

"I'll get you a blanket," I mutter before leaving him there.

Keeping my steps as muted as possible, I peek into Nate's room and sigh at the sight of him splayed out in the bed, the blanket tangled around his legs. He snores softly, relaxed and completely unaware that his favourite football player is about to sleep on his living room floor.

I close the door and snag a blanket from the small linen closet. It's nowhere near big enough to properly cover a man as big as Jamie, but it'll have to do for tonight. At least it's clean.

When I get back to the living room, he's already lying on the ground with an arm folded behind his head. I step around him and hold out the blanket.

"It's not too late to get a cab home," I mutter when he takes the blanket and drapes it over his legs.

"Nah. Already comfortable here."

I lay my hands in my lap and perch on the edge of the bed. "Alright."

"Unless you want me to go. If you're not comfortable with me staying the night—"

"No. It's not that. I'm just overthinking," I admit heavily.

"Overthinking what?"

Frustration bubbles up inside of me. I scoot back onto the bed and angrily kick my feet beneath the covers. Glaring at the bumpy ceiling, I take the risk of opening up a bit to him.

"That you're lying down there grossed out and judging my home. It's not much, but it's what I've got."

He's silent for a beat. It's a long enough pause for me to contemplate suffocating myself with my pillow.

"I'm not much for judging, Bandit. I've been to my fair share of designer houses all over the world, and very few of them felt like homes more than they did a boring display of wealth."

I pull the blanket up over my mouth and shut my eyes. "You don't have to say that to make me feel better."

"I'm not. Husband's honour."

"Like I said before, I don't even have a ring yet."

"No, but you do have a purse."

I'm grateful for the darkness and the blanket that keeps him from seeing the smile that peels my lips apart. It feels like a secret.

"Thank you, by the way."

"You're welcome."

"If you don't sneak out at the break of dawn, Nate will see you when he wakes up."

He scoffs. "You're not a bad hookup. I'll be here. He needs to learn about what's happening."

"What are we even supposed to tell him? The truth or the lie?"

"What do you want to tell him?"

I want to sneak a look down at where he lies on the ground, but it's so silent he'd hear me moving around and tease me about staring.

"We both signed an NDA. Wouldn't telling him the truth be breaking it?"

"Not if nobody found out that we did."

I contemplate that, knowing he's right. "Nathan's too smart to fall for a lie."

"So we tell him the truth," he declares, sounding like he's on the brink of passing out on me.

"That . . . I'd appreciate that, Jamie."

He yawns and then groans while moving around on the ground. "It's my pleasure."

Without a second thought, I slide the pillow out from under my head and hang it over the edge of the bed.

"Here. I have an extra one," I lie.

He takes it from me and shifts again. "I have the sweetest wife."

"Good night, Pretty Boy," I say with a roll of my eyes.

"Sweet dreams, Bandit."

Even with the mattress beneath my head, it's better than the floor. I don't want to be in trouble for putting the Pythons' star wide receiver in such terrible sleeping conditions. If he pulled his back out and couldn't play, the fans would be outside with pitchforks.

That's why I offered him my only pillow.

Totally.

"Um. What's going on here?"

I roll from my side to my back and wince at the sharp pain in my neck. It's bright as shit in here too. When I open my eyes, I immediately cover them with my arm before freezing, realizing who spoke.

"Morning, Nate," I say, fully aware that the moment I put my arm down, I'm going to see my brother gaping at the man on the floor. "How did you sleep?"

"Looks pretty well rested to me," Jamie rasps.

I press my arm harder into my eyes when his husky tone fills the room, and a shiver travels down my spine.

"You—You're Jamieson Bateman. You're the best wide receiver in the CFL. This is *my* house. My living room—Jamieson Bateman is in my living room! How? And why? What? Did you . . . Is this why the door was unlocked this morning?"

There's a record scratch in my ears. I drop my arm to the couch and push up to stare at Nate. "The door was unlocked?"

He doesn't stop staring at the floor. "Yeah. I locked it before I noticed *this*."

"I don't leave the door unlocked," I mutter.

But he's right. I don't remember locking it behind us or double-checking before I fell asleep. That hasn't ever happened.

"Can we talk about this later?" He holds a hand to the one side of his mouth in a pitiful attempt to hide what he's saying from Jamie and hisses, "When we don't have football royalty in our living room."

I groan, rubbing my eyes. "Don't flatter him. I'll never hear the end of it."

Nate gawks at me like I've grown a second head before going back to Jamie. "I'm so sorry. She's very uncultured in the world of football."

"Nate," I warn.

"It's okay. We still have time to teach her," Jamie says, the tease in his tone just for me. "It's nice to meet you, man."

"It's nice to meet you too!" Nate clears his throat and deepens his tone, shoulders rolling back. "I mean, yeah, it's cool."

I drop my gaze to Jamie for the first time this morning, trying to get a feel for what he's thinking about my brother. His loose grin settles me somewhat.

"How long have you been up?" I ask my brother.

"Only a few minutes."

"Did you sleep well?" It's painfully obvious that I'm just trying to busy myself with pointless questions right now.

Jamie leans against the mattress and drops his shoulder to look at me, reading me to filth. "I slept like a baby, Blakely. Thank you for asking."

It was stupid to hope that he'd wake up looking like a goblin. One sweep of my eyes over his perfectly sleep-rustled hair is enough to have me contemplating hiding beneath my blanket before he can get a good look at my messiness.

"Your sister tells me that you play ball?" Jamie says, releasing my eyes and looking forward at Nate. He stretches his arm across his chest, the bare curves of his shoulders flexing above the mattress with the effort.

Of course he's still shirtless. Would it have really been that hard for a raccoon to have crawled into the apartment and brought him his shirt back from the street while we slept? I'm going to have every single inch of his torso burned into my memory at this rate.

Nate's eyes nearly pop out of his skull. "Yes! I'm a wide receiver."

"That's my man. It's the best position to play."

"Exactly!"

Jamie stands and twists to crack his back before offering my brother his fist to pound. "You hungry?"

Nate jumps at the opportunity, a toothy grin spreading his lips as their knuckles bump.

"Nate's always hungry," I drawl, craning my neck back to look up at my *fiancé*.

Jamie rolls his lip between his teeth and offers me a hand. "And you? Care to join me for breakfast, Bandit?"

There's only one answer to his question.

"As if I have a choice."

16

Jamie

I'M THE TYPE OF GUY WHO USUALLY ORDERS MEALS IN, EVEN IF I CAN cook pretty much anything if I have a recipe to follow. My ma made sure that Ollie and I were capable in the kitchen and would always remind us that women don't appreciate men who don't know how to cook. I took that shit to heart and would go so far as to practice making her favourite meals whenever I had the time.

This morning, I was planning on showing off my skills to Blakely and her brother, but one look in the fridge and I knew that wasn't going to happen.

I might be a smart guy, but I know my limits. Creating an edible meal out of a bottle of mustard, a few slices of processed cheese, and a tomato that's completely deflated on the bottom is more of a challenge than I'm up for this early.

"Here, scroll through this and let me know what tickles your fancy," I say once I've pulled the menu up for Lucy's Diner on my phone.

"Sweet!" Nate snatches it from my hand and hunkers down at the kitchen table.

Leaning with her back to the counter, Blakely doesn't look

excited at all, and that doesn't sit well with me. It's too early for her to be so in her head.

"If you're going to tell me that you don't eat breakfast, you should know that I'm a huge breakfast advocate," I tease her.

She chomps down on her bottom lip, avoiding eye contact. "We don't usually have the money to order food. I'm not sure that's the best way to spend it right now."

"Did you forget what we spoke about before signing the paperwork?" I ask, taking a single step toward her. "Because I remember telling you that you aren't spending a dime on anything for the duration of our marriage."

Her eyes dart to where Nate's sitting, still enthralled with my phone, before bringing them up to snare mine with unease.

"We're not married yet."

Her favourite reminder falls on deaf ears. "A technicality that won't count for much longer."

She doesn't duck away when I risk another couple of steps closer. Her head falls back to keep our eyes connected, and I force myself to stop when there's only a foot between us.

"I've been taking care of him since I was eighteen," she reveals softly. "Everything we have, I've worked hard for."

She's twenty-three now. That's a long time to be carrying everything herself.

"Letting someone else help from time to time isn't going to take that away," I murmur.

"Maybe not."

"It's only breakfast. We can start easy."

She releases a breath. "Fine."

"Hey, Nate, can you order for your sister too?" I ask without looking away from her.

Her hands are linked at her belly the way she seems to do when she seeks comfort. Setting my hand atop hers comes naturally. It feels right to lean forward and bring my lips to the top of her head, leaving them there for a few moments.

She inhales sharply and remains still, not pulling away and slapping me for overstepping.

"Got it! Still like french toast with Nutella, Lake?" Nate asks.

Blakely settles a hand on my chest, poised like she's going to push me. Then she freezes. I bite back a smirk when she lowers her gaze to where we touch, cheeks blazing.

It wouldn't take much effort to glide her hand a few inches down to the muscles I love teasing her with. With how fierce her touch burns my skin, I may not survive that, though.

"Loosen up a bit, Bandit. I've got you," I whisper before stepping back, forcing her hand to fall.

She clears her throat and turns to face her brother. "Yeah, Nate. I do."

Not wanting to continue to crowd her, I join Nate at the table, sitting across from him. He finally looks up and cocks his head at his sister when she takes the spot between us.

"Are you feeling okay? You're really red."

"I'm just thinking about how we're going to explain everything to you," she says.

"Yeah, I was wondering that too. Just figured you'd wait until we were eating."

"It's probably better to just get it done with sooner rather than later. Is everything added to the order?" I ask.

"Yep. Here you go. I've already put our address in too."

"Thanks, buddy."

He hands over the phone, and I add my breakfast to the cart before scrolling through what he's chosen. It's a bit slim and lacking the protein I'd recommend for a kid his age, but today isn't about all that shit.

A couple of minutes later, the food is ordered and I'm setting my phone down on the table. Blakely watches me, her features tight and leg bouncing beneath the table.

"How about I start?" I offer, cutting through the tension.

Nate nods eagerly. "I'm listening."

I meet Blakely's nervous stare and attempt to calm her with a half smile. "Your sister is doing me a massive favour, Nate. But I need you to promise the both of us that you won't share what we tell you before we spill the beans."

"And we really mean that. You can't tell a soul what you learn today. Not your friends or teammates. Not even a stranger. This is serious, but I just don't want to lie to you," Blakely says sternly, no room for discussion in her voice.

Nate furrows his brows slightly. "Okay, now I'm getting worried."

"It's nothing bad. Just super secret. If anyone outside of this room found out about this, there would be major repercussions," I explain.

"I won't tell anyone. I promise."

"Swear it, Nathan," Blakely urges, her hand palm up and hovering above the table.

He copies her, and before I know it, they're spitting on each other's hands and shaking.

My brows shoot to my hairline while my dick twitches in my wrinkled slacks at how confident and unbothered she is shaking a spit-slicked palm.

"It's sworn, Lake," Nate says before wiping his hand on his PJ pants.

Blakely does the same with her sweatpants and sneaks a look at me that she tries to play off by staring just past my head.

I want to ask her when they started doing that handshake. For now, it gets scrawled on my growing To Learn About Blakely list.

"Before you freak out about anything, you have to hear us out to the very end," she warns Nate.

He's adorably eager as he nods quickly. "Okay."

Blakely and I share a look before she gives me the go-ahead to speak first. I throw caution to the wind and get right to the point.

"I'm going to marry your sister, Nate."

THEIR GREATEST STRENGTH

BY THE TIME breakfast arrives half an hour later, Nate still hasn't said a word. I didn't hold back with my explanation, and while I thought that was the right choice, maybe it wasn't . . .

Blakely passes him a couple of syrup packs, looking worried at his silence. It could just be that he's in shock. That would be the best-case scenario.

If he told her he didn't approve of what we're doing, I know that would kill a part of her. I'd wind up never playing another CFL game after telling Graham to rip up our paperwork so she didn't have to ruin her relationship with her brother over this.

"You're freaking me out, Nate," she says once he's cut into his stack of pancakes.

I spread salt over my scrambled eggs and mush my avocado onto the toast while glancing between the two of them.

"*I'm* freaking *you* out? It's the other way around!" Nate shouts, breaking out of his shocked state. He lifts his syrupy fork to point at his sister. "You knew about this when you got me those shoes and didn't say anything."

"Is that what you're the most upset about?" she asks cautiously.

Nate rolls his eyes. "I'm not even upset, Lake. I just wish you had told me earlier."

"That's it?"

"Do you want me to be angry with you for marrying my favourite football player like *ever*?"

"It isn't a real marriage," she blurts out.

He looks to me. "You said there would be a wedding."

"There will be. It will be real in the eyes of everyone but those of us who know the truth."

Blakely taps her fork to the side of her plate. "You'll be at the wedding, right, Nate? I only agreed to doing a small ceremony, but I want you there."

"Hell yeah, I'll be there. Real or not, you're getting married."

She visibly relaxes, and seeing her loosen up helps me do the same. It's a good sign. A promising one.

"And you're okay with moving into my place?" I ask Nate.

His eyes bulge at the reminder of the topic I breezed over earlier. "Yes! Totally cool with that. When are we doing that, exactly? Because the eviction notice said we only have—"

"Nathan!" Blakely explodes, fear written across her face as clear as I've ever seen it on anyone.

Worry gnaws at me. "Eviction notice?"

Blakely pushes away from the table and wraps an arm around her middle. "Not everything has to be public knowledge."

"It's not public! It's just Jamie," Nate defends.

I stand and face Blakely, leaning a hand against the table. "I'm your fiancé. If you're in trouble, I want to help."

She avoids looking at me, and I don't say anything about it. Don't tease her or make a lame joke. Odds are that right now, she'd kick me out if I did.

"Blakely doesn't like letting other people help with anything. I've been asking to use my savings to pay for my football, but she refuses," Nate explains.

I shake my head. "I'll be paying for all of that now."

She glares at him and then me, her mouth parted around silent words before snapping shut.

"How long do you need to pack your stuff?" I ask.

A smile spreads slowly over Nate's face. "Are you saying that we can move in soon?"

It's Blakely that I focus on, even as she tries to pretend neither her brother nor I are here right now. I get her reaction completely. While Nate was only trying to help, having me know something as sensitive as them being kicked out of this place has made her put her walls up. Maybe she expected me to judge her the way she feared I would last night, or it's just taken her by surprise. Either way, I'm trying my best not to show too much of a reaction to it, even if I'm crawling out of my skin with worry.

I meet Nate's waiting eyes and put on a relaxed front. "Today, preferably. If your sister is okay with that."

"Today?" she guffaws, hands now on her hips.

"Do you want to stay longer? I have my brother's wedding in three days and a game Saturday, but we could make it work for Sunday if you'd prefer."

Nate deflates, and Blakely notices immediately. Her inhale is deep, sounding like it's almost painful.

After what feels like forever, she looks at me. The war in her eyes puts me in motion.

Shoving my hesitation down, I make the decision for her and hope to God I haven't made the wrong one or overstepped in a way that's going to set me back a couple of weeks of progress.

"You got a bag, Bandit? We're getting out of here."

Her shoulders droop, relief travelling across her features. I feel real fucking good getting that reaction from her. It's almost like I can read her just as well as she can read me.

She's had to carry a heavy load on her shoulders for years, having to be the one to make the hard decisions. I think she might enjoy handing that responsibility over to someone else from time to time.

"Yeah, Jamie. I have a bag." She focuses on where Nate's bouncing in place. "We both do."

17

Blakely

WAKING UP IN A NEW PLACE HASN'T GOTTEN ANY EASIER BY DAY three.

It has less to do with the abundance of space in the room I chose and the soft king bed inside it and more with the lack of neighbourhood noises that I'm used to waking me in the middle of the night.

I've tried my best to let go of the fears that I grew to have in our last place, but with my several trips to the front and back doors to ensure they're locked and moments spent in Nate's doorway watching him sleep, I'm failing.

Every night, I'm up for hours. Only when I'm too exhausted for my body to stay alert do I finally pass out.

Jamie keeps his distance once I disappear into the bedroom, not so much as stepping foot on our side of the hall. I know that because I spent the first night with my back to my door, listening for a creak in the floors, and the second a bit further away on the rug beside the bed.

It's ridiculous, considering I let him sleep on the floor right beside me a few nights ago. That should have permanently engrained in me that he's safe and I'm not in danger around him. For a normal person, it would have.

It would seem that I'm far from normal.

More like severely untrusting and fit with half a decade's worth of abandonment issues.

The lack of sleep is wearing on me now. The weight seated on my eyelids makes it hard to see anything on the TV besides blurs of bright colours. With the soft couch beneath me and the fuzzy blanket tucked around my feet, I know it's only a matter of time before I pass out from exhaustion.

"Blakely."

I answer with a hum, prying my eyes open. The brightness on the screen in front of me makes them burn as I blink away the tears that appear.

"You should go to bed. The couch isn't all that great for sleeping."

Jamie crouches in front of me and adjusts the blanket on my lower half, hiking it higher. He glances at the TV and chuckles.

"Did you notice that you're watching cartoons?"

It's early enough in the morning that it would make sense. "I wasn't really watching them."

"I know. You're passing out instead. Is there something wrong with your bed? Or the room? I can swap you if you're having trouble sleeping where you are."

"It's not the room or the bed."

"But it's something, right?"

With my vision free of tears, I stare at him and feel in real time as my mouth dries bit by bit.

It's like opening a magazine to find a male model poised on the pages. Hair gelled back and face clean-shaven, Jamie stands to his full height and adjusts the sleeves of his suit jacket. The dusty-rose colour could be tacky on the wrong person, but he pulls it off with ease. His suit pants cup the thick muscles of his thighs, hardly restrained within the straight material. There's no tie, and I think that fits him better than wearing one would.

The flexing of his fingers when he tucks one beneath the collar of his white dress shirt and tugs is dirty as fuck. Veins on a man's hands are sexy on a good day, but toss in my sleepiness and the entire playboy in a suit thing he's got going on, and I'm pretty much panting.

"Bandit?"

I cough, words getting caught in the knot in my throat. He drops to a crouch again and smooths his hand over my blanket-covered knee. The concern written over every inch of his face nearly does me in.

Not only is he really, really fucking hot, but he's also one of the nicest men I've ever met. And I'm supposed to marry him next week?

Fuck. My. Life.

"Hey, breathe. I've got you, yeah?" he soothes, thumb stroking the curve of my knee.

I squeeze my eyes shut and focus on not leaning into his crowding body. "I'm good. Just tired."

"I know. How about you take my bed while I'm gone? It's bigger than the one you have."

My refusal is immediate. "I'll be fine here."

"I'll be back late tonight. I'm already late, and my brother's going to chew my ear off if I don't get out of here in the next thirty seconds. But just think about it. I'll arm the alarm system when I leave, so just try and get some sleep."

I rest my cheek against the back of the couch and nod. "Have fun, Jamie. I'm good here."

He furrows his brows, not looking as though he believes a word I'm saying. His watch pings, and he sighs while reading the notification that appears.

The depth in his brown eyes is staggering when they flick up from the watch. "The fridge is full. If you need anything, I'll have my phone on me. The ceremony is only an hour, and then—"

"I'm more than capable of taking care of myself, Jamie," I interrupt before he can go full caregiver on me.

After Nate's and my first night here, I thought Jamie would

relax a bit, but if anything, he's growing more anxious. Like he's scared I'm going to decide I'm not happy here and take off. At least before the wedding.

There's a lot of trust in this agreement on both sides. I'm trusting that he's not going to turn into an absolute psycho, and he's trusting that I'm not going to be a runaway bride and jeopardize his entire career.

He blows out a long breath. "I know you are. I'm just . . . You're my friend, and I want to make sure you're taken care of."

You're my friend.

I squeeze his hand, letting those words sink in. "Go. Send me a picture of you dancing later."

"So you can imagine you're there with me?" he teases, his grin crooked.

"Obviously."

Laughing loosely, he plants a kiss on my head and stands. The shoulders of his suit jacket pull taut when he rolls them and starts backing out of the room.

"The first time we dance together at a wedding, it'll be ours, Bandit."

"Guess I should warn you that I'm a terrible dancer, then."

"Even better. I've got two left feet."

I roll my lips before saying, "Don't be late for your brother's wedding. Go."

"Take a nap in my bed."

"I don't nap."

"Have you ever just tried doing it?"

He's nearly out of sight when I flip him off.

"Only as many times as you've tried telling yourself not to stare into the mirror every time you pass one."

His smirk is the last thing I see.

"Touché, baby. Touché."

Jamie

Oliver's possibly the chillest groom in history.

He's as focused as I am on game day. The only time his calm exterior shook was when Mom came into the dressing room sobbing. She buried her face in his chest and cried long enough that my dad had to come and soothe her.

I took over when Dad moved to Oliver and pulled him in for a hug with softly spoken words exchanged between them. All I caught was a simple *I'm proud of you.*

Mom's walking down the aisle with Oliver now, their arms linked and her hand gripping him tight.

I'm a step behind with little Nova, the maid of honour, watching as my big brother kisses Mom on the cheek and takes his spot at the altar.

He's standing tall and proud, not the least bothered by the eyes on him for the first time in his life. While he never loved attention growing up and straight up detested it in his adulthood, right now, I know he's not paying a single person around him any attention.

The only person he cares about is the woman a few paces behind me, hidden out of sight in her father's arms. Avery, my soon-to-be sister-in-law, has been a member of our family for decades. Today only signifies the official marking of her place in our lives as my brother's wife.

If I hadn't already witnessed real, soul-altering love from my parents, I'd have found it in my brother's eyes every time he spots Avery. Whether it's in a crowded room or somewhere with only them and me, it's so potent that I'd have to be clinically blind not to see it.

And then there's Nova.

The adorable little girl who isn't all that little anymore with the flowers in her hair and a long, deep green dress that swishes over the grass. She's a spitting image of her mother with blonde hair, blue eyes, and the tiniest button nose in existence. After a sudden growth spurt, she's teetering on being taller than Avery soon.

"Uncle J! You'll make sure I don't trip on my dress, right?" she asks, bouncing in the sparkly Crocs she's hiding beneath her dress.

"Oh, I've got you, Nova-Bug," I swear.

She hugs my waist and squeezes tight. "Thank you. I want to make sure this is the best day for Mom and Ollie."

I won't lie and say there's not a part of me that wishes my brother could hear her call him Dad. Her birth father already stole that title, even if he isn't worthy of it and my brother is.

Maybe one day, she'll switch it up and surprise him.

"Oh, it already is, honey. Ollie's been waiting for this day for years."

Nova peers up at me with wide, hopeful eyes. "For us?"

Careful not to wreck her hair, I palm the back of her head softly and nod. "Yeah, Nova. He's been waiting for the both of you his entire life."

Shit, that chokes me up. Sniffing hard, I wet my lips and release my niece.

The wedding coordinator urges us to get back into our spot at the front of the wedding line, and a beat later, Addie is sneaking up on my other side.

I grin at her, noting the dark green dress that matches Nova's. My cousin flashes a soft smile.

"You ready to hand your brother off?" she asks.

"Were you?"

"There was nothing to hand off when Maddox got married. He'd been Braxton's since they were kids."

"I guess it's the same for me," I admit, recalling the first time I caught Oliver staring at Avery back before I knew girls and guys could even like each other like that. "Our brothers seemed to have things figured out long before we did."

She laughs brightly and steals a glance back at where Cooper's lined up waiting for her.

"I had a disadvantage. My husband was completely off-limits until I was an adult."

"Was he worth the wait?"

Bringing her crystal-blue stare back to me, she squeezes my arm. "The best things are always worth waiting for, Jamie."

"Okay, it's time. Everyone get in line with your partners. Wait for my signal and keep your pace slow. Don't rush," the planner demands, strolling past me to fuss with Noah again.

I think a piece of him died being shoved into a pink suit. Even if it's a nice shade and not anything over-the-top, he'd have preferred black like his soul. I don't want to know what Tinsley had to do to get him dressed this morning.

"Ready, Nova-Bug?" I ask, offering her my arm.

She takes it eagerly, her grin toothy and bright. "Ready, Uncle J."

We're the first to go, and I guide Nova the first few steps before she grows more comfortable with the attention that falls on us. I wink at my uncle Oakley when he gives me a thumbs-up and waves at Nova.

Dad's sitting in the front row beside Mom and across the aisle from Avery's mom. The tissues in Mom's hand are crumpled as she wipes beneath her eyes and puts a hand on her heart. The pride and happiness in her watery gaze is enough to have me looking away and blinking up at the sky.

Only when I'm nearly in front of my brother do I look straight ahead again. I almost wish I didn't when the glassy look in my brother's eyes threatens to ruin me.

Releasing Nova, I let her have him first. She runs right into his chest and clings onto him with a strength that doesn't seem natural for such a tiny thing. Oliver holds her even tighter and kisses the side of her head over and over again.

"Love you, peanut," he breathes out.

"I love you too, Ollie."

I look away from them long enough to catch a tear falling from my dad's eye. Chomping down on my tongue to keep from cursing, I face forward again before I have a complete breakdown.

My brother's waiting gaze doesn't help at all.

I wait for Nova to step to the side and then yank him into my arms. He slaps my back and squeezes tight as my shoulders shake.

It's a bomb of emotions going off in my chest.

"I'm so proud of you, Oliver. So fucking happy. You got the girl after all."

"I got more than one."

"That little girl adores you."

Pulling back, Oliver keeps his hands on my arms and drops his voice nice and low. "There's another baby on the way, J."

I laugh, a fierce wave of happiness slamming into me as the news settles. "Of course there is."

He smiles and pats my arm as we quickly collect ourselves. Maddox and Braxton are close now, and I take my spot beside my brother before I delay anything.

Cooper and Adalyn are next, then Noah and Tinsley. The final groomsman and bridesmaid to make their way down are Easton and Amelia, the youngest of the entire group.

They're also the only two people in our friend group that can't stand each other. Amelia is Cooper's seventeen-year-old sister, and she's, well, she's Easton's female equivalent.

I thought the whole sassy behaviour and winding up in trouble was a phase, but it's been four years since she started acting out, and it's only gotten worse.

Her dark green dress has been hemmed shorter than the rest of the bridesmaids and looks like she stapled tulle onto it .
. .

The music changes, and everyone stands, their attention

zeroing in on where my sister-in-law comes into view. I swallow the emotion in my throat and peek at my brother.

His awestruck expression only grows in intensity when he whispers, "Fuck me."

Avery is so focused on him that for a moment, I worry she'll trip on her long dress and fall. It's like their eyes have become so locked that even if the world were burning, they couldn't look to see.

A sharp sensation tries to dig through my happy haze. The reminder that when I'm in my brother's shoes, my bride won't love me in the way I'm witnessing right now. I won't have the weight of my family's support and approval like Oliver does with Avery.

It will be a media circus, one designed for the benefit of everyone but me and Blakely.

With a jerk of my head, I toss those thoughts far away and focus on my brother, his beautiful wife and daughter, and the life he's about to make with them.

18

Jamie

It's two in the morning when I make it home, bumping into the front door and grunting like an animal. I nearly forget to turn off the alarm before going inside and sagging against the wall.

My head is spinning from the alcohol I've consumed, and my shirt is only half-buttoned. I'm still not sure how I made it into an Uber and away from the venue once the media arrived.

Fucking reporters were everywhere. My eyes are still sore from the burn of camera flashes that attacked at the end of the night. At least my brother was already gone by then.

The media wasn't even there for him. From the shouts and number of fans chasing the reporters' tails as I was diving into the SUV, it's safe to say they were there for Noah. Who knows how they found the location of the wedding with how well it was kept hidden, but they wasted their time.

My cousin was gone three hours into the reception.

Shit, my head hurts.

It's too hard to kick my shoes off, so I keep them on as I sway down the hall to the kitchen. I'm starving, even if I did pound back at least an eighth of the buffet and dessert table. My workout tomorrow is going to be intense.

It's dark in every room of the house that I pass. When I trip into the kitchen, I flail and slap a hand to the light switch. With it lit up, I have to blink to soothe the sting in my eyes and immediately head to the fridge.

My stomach grumbles again while I scour my eyes over the fridge's contents and squint at a clear-wrapped plate. The food on it isn't anything I cooked. At least, I don't remember cooking it.

No. I've never made . . . chicken pot pie?

My stomach growls again, fiercer this time. I snake the plate and go to tear the wrapping off when I see the Post-it note on top.

In case you come home hungry. It's no burger, but it should help soak up the booze. And if you're sober, I don't care. Eat it anyway.

Night,

Blakely

My grin is lopsided as hell, but goddamn, I think my almost wife is starting to warm up to me. Never thought she'd be the type of woman to write cute notes on home-cooked meals, but I think I love being surprised by her.

After folding the note and putting it in my pocket, I tear the wrapping off before putting the dish in the microwave. Once it's started to spin and heat up, I fill a glass with tap water and gulp it down.

My agent called me a few times tonight, but I didn't answer. Rude as hell for him to call during my brother's wedding. I don't care if it's an emergency. When I'm with my family, I'm not up for business talk.

Sighing, I pull my phone out and struggle with the passcode before opening the missed texts.

> The Agent: I have an update on your upcoming marriage arrangement. Call me when you can please.

> The Agent: Can you step away from the wedding? Just want to touch base.

> The Agent: I'll pop it in here then. The engagement announcement is expected on Friday before the game. There's a pass for Blakely. Please make sure she's in attendance. Enjoy the wedding tonight, Jamie.

The microwave beeps as my stomach flops around like a fish. I knew it was only a matter of time, considering the wedding is set for next weekend, but it's suddenly very real. Once we announce an engagement and our plans for a wedding, there won't be any hiding away.

The game is about to start, and we have no option but to win.

Tony is a great agent. He likes to give me my space to figure things out on my own before getting involved. My dad helped me hire him before I was drafted, and with how picky the old man was, it's no surprise that I wound up with a good guy on my side.

When Tony wasn't against this idea of marriage, I took that as an extra good sign. He's supposed to be helping coordinate with a wedding planner for Blakely, and while I haven't heard anything about it from her, I don't think that's odd. She hasn't seemed overly eager to plan anything. I don't blame her for that. This isn't a real wedding despite the legality of it.

I lean over the counter and shovel back the pot pie she made me, filling my booze-heavy stomach with something to soak it up. The flavours that hit my tongue have me speeding up my bites, desperate for more. Somehow, she got the crispiest shell without drying the shit out of the chicken. The filling is good enough I'd eat it on its own.

When it's gone, I stare at my empty plate in shock.

Disappointment strikes harder when I put the plate into the dishwasher and go to my bedroom. Pretty sure I forgot to turn the light off, but fuck it. My feet are killing me, and now I'm in a food coma so intense I'm genuinely considering whether I'll be able to get up for practice tomorrow afternoon.

The stairs seem to go on forever as I lean against the railing and slump my way up them—

"Fuck," I grunt, nearly missing a step and stubbing my toe.

Wincing at my outburst, I open my bedroom door and step inside. It's dark in here, but the moon leaks in through the sliding glass patio door, so at least I can see where I'm going.

Then again, if I do stub my toe a second time, maybe Blakely can bandage me up.

With a groan, I shrug off my suit jacket and unzip the fly of my pants. The cuffs on my shirt are tight, so those go next—

I come to a jerky stop at the edge of my bed. I'm pretty sure I didn't pile pillows under my duvet when I left this morning, but there's most definitely a lump there right now. A human-sized-and-shaped lump.

I steady myself with a hand on the mattress and lean over the body. It moves with deep, steady breaths, and as I get closer, I can make out brown hair splayed all over my pillow and usually tight features completely relaxed. Brown brows flat, pink lips parted slightly, and lashes fluttering.

Blakely.

Blakely is in my bed.

Blakely is in my bed sleeping.

She's got the covers up and tucked beneath her chin, her fingers gripping onto it for dear life even in sleep. Like she's scared someone will try and take them from her.

My muscles loosen as I bring a knuckle to the curve of her ear and nudge a few strands of hair behind it. She doesn't so much as twitch, completely shut off to the world.

I'm happy she's fallen asleep. I know she's been up late since she moved in. She might think that she's quiet while pacing up and down the hallway or that I can't sense her sitting behind her bedroom door when she thinks I've gone to bed.

I won't tell her differently.

Her finding my bedroom—my *bed*—somewhere safe enough to fall asleep is dangerous to a guy like me.

The type who falls in love easily and without restraint. I'm the guy who banters with a woman for a few hours and asks, "What are we?" It's easy to fuck around and keep things surface-level with someone who doesn't tickle that special space in your chest upon first meeting. You put on a smirk and cage your heart for a few hours, reminding yourself that this isn't the one.

The first time I met Blakely, I felt that tickle.

But the Blakely from that first night is somehow so different from this one.

There are so many pieces of her that I'm trying to fit together into one beautiful picture. Just when I think I've figured them all out, she goes and throws in another, like leaving me dinner on the off chance I went to the fridge when I got home.

I like to joke around, but with her, I have wondered if it could potentially lead to more than that. And that's exactly why I need this wedding to come as soon as possible. Every single piece of her that I've seen has intensified that tickle.

Maybe if I'm reminded of why we're doing this, it won't feel so much like playing house and more like what it's supposed to be. A business transaction that ended up budding into a friendship along the way.

It would never turn into anything other than with Blakely. Entertaining the idea of any variation of a future with her when I know she's unavailable will only hurt me in the long run.

Without stripping further, I turn and leave the room, content to sleep just about anywhere else.

IT'S BARELY daybreak when I thump my fist against the door of my brother's hotel suite. I'm still in my wrinkled suit and haven't so much as brushed my teeth. I stink like booze and a long night of overthinking.

The hotel manager gave me a weird look when I passed him

on my way up here, and I didn't have it in me to try and convince him that I'm not always this weathered.

I woke this morning in the hall outside of my room and booked ass here. With my head a bit clearer, I knew I needed to warn my brother about the news breaking tomorrow. It's not an ideal bomb to drop the day after *his* wedding, but it's that or I keep it inside for the next few months.

Footsteps stomp behind the door before it's whipped open. Oliver's scowl is in its proper place when he glares at me.

"Did you miss the memo where it's the day after my wedding? You're not supposed to bug me today," he grunts.

The up-and-down look he gives me is enough of a sign that I look as bad as I suspected. Oh well, he can deal with it.

"Sorry, that rule doesn't apply to me. This is an emergency. Now, scoot and let me in," I say, trying to weasel my body between his and the speck of a gap available for me to enter the suite.

He sets a hand on my shoulder and gives me a light shove backward. "What's wrong with you?"

Out in the open like this, I can't exactly confide in him. There's too much at stake if the wrong person is too close.

"Oh, you know. Nothing much."

"Don't play with me today, Jamieson."

I attempt to look past him into the suite at where Avery sits watching us, but he takes a step in front of me and scowls.

"I don't want to talk about it in the hall, Oliver. Let me in so nobody else hears this," I plead, dropping my voice in the hope that he can sense my desperation.

"Keep your eyes off my wife," he warns before finally letting me in.

While he shuts the door behind us, I head right for his wife, knowing she's the only one who can convince my stubborn-as-a-mule brother to do something he doesn't want to. And right now, that's talking to me when he so obviously has other plans.

I flop down on the bed beside her and open my mouth to speak when Oliver snorts.

"Wouldn't sit there if I were you. Honeymoon and all."

Once I realize what he's talking about, I hop right back off the mattress with my nose crinkled.

"Fuck off, Oliver. I knew it smelled like sex in here."

"I'm going to the bathroom while you boys talk," Avery mutters, her cheeks red as she watches her husband.

He doesn't bother pretending he's not hating every inch of distance between them as he gawks at her. "We won't be long."

"We might be," I say.

Avery slips off the bed, and I contemplate pleading with her to stay and help calm her brother when he inevitably freaks out at my news.

"Eyes off my wife, asshole."

I laugh, batting my lashes at him. The post-wedding bliss must be chafing a bit. "Call her your wife again. I don't think you've said it enough yet."

"I'll call her my wife anytime I want to. Now, tell me what it is you need so I can get back in bed with her."

My laugh dies, all my humour replaced with nerves as I blurt out, "I'm engaged."

He stares at me blankly, not believing me.

"I'm not lying. Hand to God," I add weakly.

"We're not religious."

I stifle a sigh. "Okay, hand to the fucking sun, then. I don't know. I'm not lying."

"Since fucking when are you engaged? To who?" he asks sharply, his stare blazing.

"I met her a couple of weeks ago. Nice girl."

What the fuck? *Nice girl* is the last way I'd choose to describe Blakely. It's way too plain for her. Bordering on insulting.

"A nice girl? She's a nice girl? You asked someone to marry you, and the best you can do is say she's a nice girl?"

"Okay, she's a nice, gorgeous girl. Better? Fuck, don't bust my balls right now."

"You came here, Jamie. I'll bust your balls if I fucking want to because what the fuck did you do? You're not the marriage type. And you're surely not the asking a nice girl to marry you out of the blue type. Has Mom met her? Dad? I damn well haven't. You've gotten one too many concussions. I knew you should have stopped playing football."

Jesus. I don't know what's more hurtful, the fact he doesn't think I'm the marriage type of guy or that I'm doing this because I've hit my head a few too many times. Just because I haven't stayed celibate for years doesn't mean I'm not interested in the idea of marriage. Just never expected it to happen already.

I hold my hands out in front of me and shake my head, feeling the colour and heat leach from my face. "Slow down. First, I've only had three concussions. And second, no. Nobody's met her but me. But that doesn't mean anything. We're getting married, and that's that. I just wanted you to know before the news went live tomorrow."

Oliver balks, turning more green than pale. "The news?"

"Yeah. I'm announcing it tomorrow. It's happening."

"No. It's not. Call it off right now. I'll have Dad come over so we can talk about it together," he declares, already hunting for what I assume is his phone.

I grab his wrist and tug. "No. You're not calling Dad. I'm not telling them yet."

I will once I have to. When they won't have the chance to convince me to change my mind.

"What?" he shouts, eyes bugging out of his skull.

"Don't yell!"

"You've lost your mind."

"No, I haven't. You and I both know if I tell them, they'll convince me not to do this the same way that you are right now."

"If you want me to do anything other than convince you not

to do this, then you need to tell me everything. You might be able to bluff your ass off to anyone else, Mom included, but I'm not falling for it. Tell me what the fuck is going on, Jamieson, or I swear I'm going to call Mom and Dad and get them to come here right now."

The bathroom door squeaks open as Avery slips out and comes to Oliver's side, worry obvious in her expression as they hold eye contact.

Fuck. I knew he wouldn't be easy to convince, but I'd hoped it wouldn't be this bad. He's not the gossip type, and we're brothers, but lying to our parents is bad enough when I'm doing it, but both of us? If our parents found out, it would kill them.

I collapse on the small couch across the room and swallow a thousand refusals before speaking. "Fine. But nobody learns about this. Not even our parents."

"Fine."

And for yet another time, I let the truth free.

19

Blakely

"Tomorrow? What do you mean we have to announce the engagement tomorrow? And why do you look so terrible?"

"I'm surprised they waited this long. We don't have a choice now. A Friday night home game is the opportunity they want to capitalize on."

Jamie ignores my last comment and shakes out his messy hair as if that'll help any.

He's still in the suit he went to the wedding in, only now it's wrinkled, the buttons mismatched, and sleeves rolled nearly to his elbows. There's a dark shadow across his jaw and a bleakness to his usually vibrant blue eyes that makes my stomach twitch with unease. The smell of alcohol that's wafting off him is strong enough to reach from the doorway of my room to my bed.

Crossing my legs beneath the heavy comforter, I lean forward and fold my hands in my lap. Is it okay for me to ask what he was doing all night? Should it matter?

I roll my lips. "Are you okay?"

He pauses, as if surprised by my question. With a shoulder against the doorframe, he lifts the corner of his mouth.

"Yeah, Bandit. I just watched my brother get married to the woman of his dreams. What's there to be upset about?"

"You can be happy for him and be upset about something else at the same time."

"It's just the hangover. You don't have to worry about me," he says softly.

Yeah, well, I am. And it's all your fault.

"What time is the game tomorrow?" I ask, deciding to drop it to avoid looking too invested.

If he doesn't want to tell me what's upsetting him, then there isn't anything I can do about it. If I keep digging . . . what happens if I don't want to stop?

"Kickoff is at seven. I'll be there a few hours early, and you and Nate will come closer to the game. It shouldn't interfere with school."

"I assume we have tickets already?"

His grin is smug. "Not tickets. *Passes*, Blakely. Get with it."

"And do you have these *passes* for me?"

"Nah. I'll grab them after practice today. For right now, we need to focus on getting you and Nate game-ready. Think he'd be up to rooting through my old jerseys?"

A loud thump in the hallway has Jamie lunging out of the room. Even looking like he's been out at a bar crawl all night, he's alert, his reflexes sharp.

"Jesus, Nate. You scared the hell out of me," he pants.

"Did you say I could look through your old jerseys? And that we get to watch the game tomorrow on the *field*?" Nate rambles, exposing his eavesdropping.

I swallow a laugh and lie back in bed, tucking the chilled covers beneath my chin. It was only a couple of hours ago that I snuck out of Jamie's bed and into this one. God, how mortifying would it have been if he'd come home and seen me sleeping in his bed?

I'd only meant to stay there for a little while. He wasn't home, and I knew he wouldn't be for hours. It's my fault for not napping like he suggested and instead forced myself to the brink of passing out at the kitchen table after dinner. My bed wasn't working, so on a whim, I went to his.

I fell asleep in only a few minutes, surrounded by dark sheets, expensive cologne, and a deep sense of safety.

Fuck, it was so creepy of me to go in there. He may have offered his bed to me, but he could have just not thought I'd use it. Like one of those offers you only make to avoid feeling bad while hoping it's never taken.

With a sigh, I think back to the glass patio door and the glimmer of backyard lights on the walls of his bedroom. If I hadn't been so exhausted, I'd have gone outside to lie on the grass and count the stars without wondering if I was going to be accosted by someone. With the tall fence around me, I'd have felt safe the same way I do in this house.

"Are you coming, Blakely?"

I blink, focusing on Nathan as he stands beside the bed. Jamie is a few paces back, watching us while pretending not to.

"Yeah, give me a minute to get dressed. We don't have too much time this morning, Nate. You've got school in an hour," I remind him.

Nate beams at me, more excited than ever. "Yeah, yeah, I know! We'll wait in the hall."

I ignore the soft expression on Jamie's face and slip out of bed, grateful for the flannel pyjama pants I slipped on when I got back to my room. If he knew I wore only an oversized shirt and panties in his bed, he'd be unbearable.

Right now, I doubt he even wants to look at me. I'm not a pretty sleeper, so combine the mess that is my hair with ratty old PJs, and I'm sure he's trying to hold back from tearing out of here in disgust.

I move a little faster now, pulling some clothes out of my old bag sitting atop the gorgeous white wood dresser.

"You can unpack, you know. You're going to be here for a while," Jamie notes.

Nate hovers beside him by the door, frowning at the bag as if he's just now realized that I haven't taken my clothes out of it. He's been unpacked from the hour after we got here the first day. That's just how he is, though.

When I'm bursting with fear and doubt, he's calm and sure. This move was easy for him while terrifying for me.

"I'll do it soon," I mutter.

Jamie doesn't push it further. "Alright."

Lifting my clothes in front of me, I arch a brow at the two guys. "If you wouldn't mind?"

"Right. We'll be in the hall," Jamie blurts, walking backward out of the room and taking Nate with him.

Once they're both gone, I shut the door and take my clothes to the ensuite. A few minutes later, I'm watching Nate root through a giant bin of old football jerseys with wide, wild eyes. There must be at least fifty of them, all of which have apparently been worn before.

I'm not sure if that's cool or disgusting.

"Are you sure I can choose any of them?" Nate asks, finally pausing his search with a white-knuckled grip on an orange jersey.

Jamie nods from his spot beside me, his hands tucked in his pockets and posture loose. "Yeah, buddy. All they do is sit in this bin now."

"I choose this one, then."

Nate stands and yanks the jersey over his head before tugging it the rest of the way down. It's a few sizes too big, but from the cheek-splitting grin on his face, it's obvious he doesn't care one bit.

"Do you want to wash it first, Nate?" I ask carefully.

"Shit, do you think I put all my sweaty gear into bins to save for later? Have a little faith in me, Bandit," Jamie jokes through a low laugh. "They've all been washed."

I glare at him. "How am I supposed to know that?"

"You've spent too much time with dirty boys."

"Lake doesn't even spend time with boys," Nate pipes in, staring down at the front of his chosen jersey.

I huff, palming my hips. "I'm going to glue your mouth shut, Nathan."

"It's okay, Nate. I'm the only boy she needs now, right?"

My brother pauses his fanboying over the jersey and inspects Jamie, something passing between them that I can't grab onto.

Nate shimmies his shoulders in his new jersey and passes us, heading for the door. "Yeah. You are getting married, after all."

"Do we start a countdown now or something? To make it more official?" Jamie asks, his brows dancing.

"You haven't been counting down already?" I ask.

Nate laughs at my question before leaving, apparently done with our little closet hangout. He's probably going to stare at himself in the bathroom mirror for the next hour.

Jamie watches him leave and then turns his body to face me fully, the weight of his full attention smacking into me face first. Handsome in a reckless yet charming way, he's the perfect example of an up-to-no-good playboy. The exact type of guy I never think twice about.

It's becoming a bit harder to stick to that habit.

"One week tomorrow, baby," he purrs, his voice so soft the words kiss my cheeks.

I move closer, hovering only a few inches from his front. He tracks the movement with a coy smile, light dancing in his eyes for the first time today.

"For tomorrow . . ." I start, my fingers tingling as I raise them to rest on his bicep. His tongue slips past his lips to swipe along them as he stays still, aside from the muscles beneath my fingers that flex. "It's our first night out together. As an engaged couple."

"That's right."

"So, we need to act the part."

He sways closer, the heat from his body curling around mine and urging me to lean forward just a little more. My hold on his arm has grown stronger, wider as my fingers spread and glide around the thick muscle.

"I'm listening," he rasps.

"You can touch me."

It's out there before I can take it back. I don't say another word, waiting and waiting . . .

I'm not sure what I was expecting. A hand in mine or another kiss on my head, maybe.

The firm pressure of his hand on my waist as he hitches me forward to rest against his body is almost as surprising as the one that cups my jaw and tips my head back.

I suck in a breath and go lax in his hold, a blast of comfort settling deep in my chest.

"Like this?" he asks lowly, his tone rough.

Jesus, when did his eyes get so blue? Even with his pupils swelling, they're so vibrant, like the kind of sky you get lost in, the kind that promises warmth after years of frigid winter. And I'm not sure I'm ready for that, but here he is—offering it anyway.

His thumb moves, stroking the skin so close to my mouth that if I turned into his palm, I'd be able to taste him. A shiver starts at the top of my spine and grows in intensity when I refuse to let it travel further.

"Blakely?"

I look at him through my lashes and press the hand not holding him against my thigh, not surprised by the wet heat of my palm.

"Yes. That's good," I whisper.

"Can I try something else?"

My stomach explodes. "Like what?"

"Just tell me to stop at any time," he murmurs.

His fingertips slip behind my skull, kneading my scalp as he guides my head back further. Heart racing, I give in to my desire to touch him more and reach desperately for his hip, as if that will help stabilize me.

Instead, it only intensifies our connection and has me pressing further into his body. He's just so warm and steady. I don't jerk back when he lowers his head and brings his mouth so, so close to my nose.

My nails slip beneath his shirt to scrape at the bare skin above the band of his jeans, and I swear I hear a low groan slip up his throat. It's gone before I can be sure.

I'm prepared for him to kiss me. It would be the next step, especially if we're supposed to put on an act for the world tomorrow, right? I can kiss him like this and do it again tomorrow, just as practice. It's simple. Meaningless. Exactly the way I like it.

But no. His lips don't touch mine.

They brush my cheek instead, far enough away from my mouth that when I sigh, I know he doesn't feel the hot puff of my breath.

He's in front of me and then gone in the span of a blink. The pink tint of his cheeks slowly fades as he smiles, a dimple popping.

"Was that okay?"

I drop my hands instantly and stumble backward, putting distance between us. I'm so hot, so tense, it's like I've just been dipped in hot wax and yanked back out.

"It was fine. If you're wondering if you can do it tomorrow, then yes," I answer him, trying to keep my tone as distant as possible.

I don't think he believes me, but he lets it go. The closet is crowded, even without Nate in here with us, and I need to get out.

"Come on. I already have a jersey for you," he says, recognizing my habit of retreating.

"The ones in the bin don't work?"

"No. My wife isn't going to be wearing an old jersey with grass stains."

"I thought you washed them."

His laugh is a welcome sound. Almost like a reset button.

"I have. But some stains don't come out no matter how much time we spend scrubbing them."

Our eyes catch and hold, the real meaning behind his statement in the open for me to catch. I nod and follow him out of the closet.

I'VE WATCHED FOOTBALL BEFORE. *Obviously*. Nathan's been playing since he was six years old, and I've been in attendance of at least half of his games.

I know what a touchdown is and that there are three downs. Although, that's only in the CFL as Nathan so dutifully told me on the way to the stadium.

He tried to give me a bucketload of pointers in the cab, and I'm proud to say that I remember at least ten percent of them. Jamie absolutely put him up to the quick tutor session, and I'm a bit spiteful of that. He should have sat me down and taught me himself. Win or lose tonight, he isn't getting off without being bugged about it.

A cool breeze rips through the field, and I tug at the sleeves of my shirt to cover my hands. The game hasn't started yet, and I'm already freezing. It's not like it's in the negatives yet, but with only a long-sleeve shirt on beneath the thin jersey Jamie gave me, I'm a bit underdressed. Nathan was smart enough to put a hoodie on beneath his jersey, at least.

The chill I'm feeling could be from more than the temperature, though.

Jamie's coach is already out, along with at least a dozen unfamiliar faces, all of whom haven't hidden their curiosity about my brother's and my presence. My skin has been itching for the last half hour that we've been here, standing well enough behind the team's staff to avoid getting in the way.

Nathan's having the time of his life, not sharing my anxiousness. He's been smiling and waving at the members of the team huddling around and shouting directions.

We didn't arrive early enough to catch warm-ups, and I know that disappointed him a bit. However, he has spent quite a few minutes gawking at the cheerleaders across the field. One even gave him a wiggling finger wave after a short cheer, and he got so nervous he blushed.

Restrained chaos is the best way to describe what it's like on the sidelines. Every minute that ticks toward the players coming out, the stands become fuller, the hum of conversation growing in volume. The coaching staff for both teams seem to become antsier, and the people running along the sidelines with cameras keep swaying our way, like they're debating coming over and asking who the hell we are.

The name and number on the back of our jerseys are impossible to miss, but throw in the dual black sevens Nathan demanded we paint on our cheeks, and there's no mistake about who we're here for.

In only a few hours, our lives are going to be very different. I'm not a public person, but that won't matter. While my background is clean enough for the team to agree to me being involved, that doesn't mean it's not still smudged with a bit of dirt. Nothing about my life growing up is pretty, and knowing that there isn't anything I can do to keep it a secret has made me uncomfortable. I just have to push past it and try not to spend too much energy worrying about what other people are going to think.

If Jamie doesn't care, why should it matter if other people do?

Nathan elbows me in the side, and I jerk away, hissing, "What was that for?"

His eyes dart to the left over and over until finally, I follow them and realize Coach Tanner is coming over. My stomach tightens as I keep my expression flat, collected.

"Blakely," the older man says, tipping his chin. He looks to my brother. "And Nathan, right?"

He's in the same team jacket he was wearing in the owner's office the night I met him, but this time, he's added a matching hat and holds a clipboard against his chest.

"Yeah. Y-yes. I'm Nathan. It's so awesome to meet you, Coach," Nathan stammers, shooting his hand out.

The coach takes it, shaking it firmly. "You too. I hope you're not too uncomfortable over here. The team will be coming out any minute now, but we don't have chairs or anything."

"Do people not stand over here during games?" I ask, glancing at the lack of other non-Pythons team members on the sidelines.

"Down on the field? No."

"But we're allowed to?"

It sounds ridiculous. I get the whole needing to make a statement thing, but for such a big field, there isn't all that much room for an audience down here. Getting in the way of staff or players isn't an ideal situation for me.

The coach levels me an understanding look. "I wouldn't expect to be down here for many more games. Just make it past this one, and I'm sure you'll be up in the stands for the rest of them."

"That's reassuring."

"You're needed down here to grab wandering eyes, specifically the media's. Just try not to distract Jamie. I need him in the game and not chasing your attention."

"I don't think that will be a problem," I reveal with a scoffed laugh.

He doesn't look as sure. "Wouldn't put money down on that. Anyway, the team's coming out in a minute. Just . . ." The smile he gives me is more of an awkward grimace. "Just stay in the open but not in my way."

"Stay visible but not too visible. Got it."

With another dip of his chin, he pats my brother's arm and then heads back to where he came from.

Nate's awestruck voice fills the space around us. "We just met Riley Tanner."

"You did. I've already met him," I tease.

He bumps my shoulder. "This is insane, Lake. Like, the most insane thing that's ever happened to me."

I put my arm around his shoulders and lean against him, grateful that he's here with me today. For support, but more importantly, this entire experience. Never in a million years did I think I'd be able to give him a night on the Pythons' sidelines or a meeting with their head coach.

That itself is worth everything I'm doing.

20

Blakely

Honestly, I'm glad I didn't wear a sweater.

Once the music ramps up in the stadium and the cheerleaders line up along the entrance of the tunnel, I'm sweating. A video starts on the jumbotron, but I don't look away from the tunnel, counting down the seconds in my head as I wait for Jamie to appear.

Nathan's vibrating beside me, his focus on every inch of the show being put on. This is his future; I feel it deep down in my soul.

Someone in a Pythons jersey runs down the path created by the cheerleaders with a giant orange and black flag in his hands. The open-mouthed Python on the flag ripples as it catches a small breeze.

A deep voice rings out through the stadium, and my pulse kicks up a notch. I don't know what to do with my hands, so I fold my arms. It doesn't feel right, so I drop them and press my palms to my thighs. That still isn't right, but I don't switch it up. If I keep twitching, the only headline coming out about me and Jamie is that he chose a weirdo to be his wife.

Keep it cool, Blakely.

"Oh, God," I breathe out when smoke fills the air beside the first set of cheerleaders and bodies start appearing from the tunnel.

We didn't go over anything. Didn't plan how we'd do this—and we're *so* screwed. It's going to be terrible and awkward. I'll never get over the embarrassment.

Nathan steps into my space and takes my hand while waving his other one. I squeeze the shit out of his fingers and keep my eyes trained on the players emerging.

Jamie's second out of the tunnel.

Even with a helmet and bulky equipment on, I know it's him. The tall length of his body, flexing fingers at his sides, and the hand that goes up to wave at the crowd screams Jamie.

He only confirms my suspicions when he skips down the field and lifts both arms into the air in a *louder* motion. I nip at the inside of my cheek and watch him holler into the stadium, his white teeth flashing behind the bars of his helmet.

I think that'll be it. That he'll put on a bit of a show and then go to the bench with his team. Oh, am I ever wrong. Instead of doing that, he turns and jogs right for me.

My breath stalls in my throat. The gasps from the fans behind me are so loud they echo in my ears. Nate tightens his hold on my hand as if to calm me down, and I don't have the heart to tell him it isn't working.

Jamie takes his helmet off, leaving it banging against his thigh as he slows his pace, getting closer and closer. His gaze is electric as he looks at me and grins so damn wide that some of my nerves dissipate.

With his football gear, he towers over me. His normally wide shoulders are bigger, and with the short sleeves of his jersey, those thick biceps corded with never-ending muscle are exposed, rippling with every brief stretch. It's outright arm porn, and I'm struggling to catch my breath in front of him right now.

I've heard of a puck bunny, but is there an equivalent term for football? A ball chaser? Fuck it, the only balls I'd ever contemplate chasing are Jamie's, and even then, I'd prefer not to do any literal chasing. Or have anything to do with balls.

"Smile at me, Bandit," he says, voice low as he moves in close. "And please hug me back, or this is going to look really awkward."

Warm, strong arms slip around my body, folding me against a firm chest. I release a tight breath and slowly wind my arms around Jamie, feeling the padding beneath his jersey and the scrape of the fabric against my palms.

It's hard to tune out the cheers and bright flashes of cameras around us. Even with my eyes shut, I can see every white light and hear the various reactions from the fans.

Jamie palms my lower back with the gloved hand not holding his helmet, and I move, bringing my face to his chest. I'm hidden here, only growing more so when he adjusts his position and guards me with his arms. Something hot and sharp digs into my chest, and I squeeze my eyes tighter against the burn.

I'm protected. Even if just for as long as I'm right here.

"Good luck, Jamie," I whisper.

His hold tightens, hand wandering up my spine to press me closer. "With you here? I'll play the best I ever have."

I can't tell if he's teasing or not, so I just assume he is.

He slowly releases me, moving carefully enough that I have time to prepare myself for reality again before it smacks me in the face.

Keeping his head dipped, he brings his mouth to my ear, softly breathing on the shell. "I'm going to kiss your cheek again, and if you're feeling frisky, you can smack my ass when I turn away."

The tease in his voice has me snorting a laugh. He grins against my cheek before pressing his lips to it, lingering there for a few moments.

Once he's stepped away, I ignore the sudden change in temperature and watch as he fist bumps Nate.

"Keep your sister safe for me, buddy. And don't forget to have fun," he tells him.

Nate nods firmly. "You got it."

Jamie rubs a hand over Nate's hair and offers me a quirked, goading smile. His brows bounce around, and I follow my gut, waiting for him to spin around before acting.

"Go show off, Pretty Boy," I call while whipping a hand out and smacking his ass.

The immediate recoil is far more attractive than I was anticipating, but it has nothing on the wink Jamie shoots my way on his way to his team. The finger he keeps pointed at me with every single step draws even more attention to us.

It's another claiming. And for the first time since I agreed to this, I'm starting to really believe that we can pull this off.

And by the time Jamie and the team set up for another play in the second quarter, I'm still fairly confident in that statement. He's gotten three touchdowns so far, and while I was expecting some sort of big production when he scored, he's kept his reactions pretty plain. Nate, along with the entire stadium, was weirdly silent when he celebrated his latest touchdown with a simple hip-swinging dance.

To me, it looked fine. But Nathan pointed out that I only felt that way because I'd never seen his usual celebration. Whatever that means.

"I wonder if something's wrong with him," Nate mumbles, eyeing whom I've learned is the quarterback when he sets up on the field.

Jamie finishes talking to another member of their team and then tucks his mouthguard in while taking his position. Bending forward, he claps his hands between his thighs and points at the player opposing him. When he turns his hand upside down and makes a walking motion with two of his fingers, it's obvious to everyone that he's goading him.

"He looks fine to me, Nate," I muse.

"Maybe he's feeling sore or something. He's never so boring when he scores a TD."

"Dancing is boring?"

Nate huffs. "It is compared to what he usually does."

"Okay, and what does he usually do?"

"Shh, they're about to start the play."

I bite my tongue, letting it go. Nate's completely zoned in to the action, waiting and waiting . . . before whooping loudly. The noise hits me, and I'm instantly on high alert, narrowing my eyes on the players separating on the field.

The quarterback is retreating with the ball in his hands, his head on a swivel as he searches for someone to pass to. Nate lurches forward a step when the football cuts through the air in a perfect spiral, aimed right for Jamie.

My fiancé is already moving. He cuts through a circle of players and spins, evading the same one who he was taunting and continuing to sprint alongside the ball.

I hold still, a wince building in preparation for seeing him get plowed down. The last thing I want is for him to get hurt, and that's the thing with football. It's always a possibility.

Free healthcare in Canada is the biggest benefit we've had with Nate's love of the sport. The number of cuts and broken bones he's had would have bankrupted us without it.

With my hand gripping my shoulder, I wait and watch. Then, the crowd is erupting at the same time I am. I jump when Jamie slips past the closest player and leaps off his feet to snatch the ball and tuck it close before speeding off down the field.

He's incredibly fast. For someone his height and with his bulk, it doesn't seem like he should be able to move that fast. But he's left everyone in the dust.

Nate clutches my arm, silently watching Jamie get closer to the end zone by the second. The coach has moved closer to the lines along the edge of the field, his clipboard held as tight as Jamie's holding the ball.

It all happens so fast.

One second, Jamie is still sprinting, and the next, he's crossing into the end zone and smashing the ball on the turf. The fans scream while the cheerleaders dance and chant, their pompoms swooshing. Nate's cheering into his domed hands, and the staff near us are clapping.

It's chaos. Even without the score being close and this being a deciding touchdown, the celebration is incredible.

"He's amazing!" Nate shouts, looking up at me with stars in his eyes. "I can't believe we were here to see that!"

"Yeah, he's pretty good." I bump our shoulders and keep Jamie in my sights.

With a blown kiss to the crowd, he leaves the ball where it lies on the turf and starts back our way. Instead of doing the same dance as earlier in the game, he changes course completely and doesn't come the entire distance to the sidelines.

Nathan's excitement is potent in the space around us, and even without him telling me what Jamie's doing, I piece it together myself.

Jamie stops in the centre of the field and stares at me. Despite the distance between us, his eyes are so bright, alive with adrenaline and a love for this sport. They hook mine, and I keep still, afraid that if I move, the moment will end.

Shouts from those behind and around us make my ears throb as Jamie stretches his arms in front of him and shoots an invisible arrow at me.

"Point at him, Lake," Nathan whisper hisses.

I don't question the order, pointing at the proud football player. *My friend.* The man who's shown me more kindness than anyone else ever has.

He grins and mouths the words *for you.*

The crowd erupts beyond any level I've heard yet tonight, and if it weren't for the security that's surrounded us in the past few moments and the swarm of reporters, I'd be looking into a camera right now.

That's what I'm supposed to want. It points to us doing a

good job and is a whole lot safer than wishing I could cut across the field and tell him that despite my lack of knowledge and passion for this sport, I'm proud of him.

Especially when we only have a few more months of this. Then . . . then there will be someone else on the sidelines catching his invisible arrows.

21

Jamie

POST-GAME MEDIA ISN'T MY FAVOURITE WAY TO CELEBRATE A WIN. It's always the same old questions and blank expressions in the crowd of reporters. They usually want to be there as much as the players do, and that makes for a very boring, very tiring event.

Tonight, though, the atmosphere is a little different.

Coach didn't give me five minutes after I'd hopped into the shower before telling me I was set to go out to answer questions. Or spill the news, more like.

He went to find Blakely next. And after I'd spent the entire trip from the field to the locker room worrying that she'd gotten lost or swallowed up by clusters of strangers, I was grateful that he chose to do that. Not being able to be out there with her to guide her inside was frustrating. It didn't feel right to leave her and Nate on their own.

My shorts and sweatshirt are a nice break from the weight of shoulder pads and a tight jersey as I step up onto the platform and take a seat at the table. More cameras than usual flash, and Jaxon takes the chair beside me with Zach on his other side.

The team is as curious as the media is, but they didn't get a single answer out of me in the locker room. I told those nosey fuckers to tune in tonight instead.

It's almost like the Pythons invited every single media outlet in Vancouver and from two provinces over to be here tonight. There are so many faces I've never seen and names on badges that otherwise wouldn't be here or care about post-game interviews.

Coach steps inside through the main door and leans against the wall away from the media, offering me a head nod that I hope means he's found Blakely and brought her into the lounge. Graham didn't exactly give me a step by step for tonight, but he did lay out some ideas. Specifically, making a scene during the game and during this upcoming interview session.

The details were and will be all me. I just have to hope that I don't upset Blakely with them.

Sadie, leading the interviews as usual, gives the go-ahead to one of the news reporters from the middle of the seats.

"Jamie, incredible performance tonight. How does it feel to secure the win, and what do you think made the difference out there on the field?"

I fold my hands on the table and lean toward the microphone. "It feels great. We were hungry tonight, and we capitalized on the loose defense. What more can you ask for?"

"Jaxon, you and Jamie seemed to have great chemistry on the field tonight. How important is having that connection, not just in the game but off the field too?" a familiar face from *Sports Weekly* asks.

I know even before Jax opens his mouth that this is the moment that changes everything. He's the only player on the team who knows what Graham asked me to do, and the asshole's been chomping at the bit to be involved. This is his chance, and he won't miss it. Especially not once he receives an approving nod from Sadie.

"Oh, the connection's crucial. Jamie and I are practically telepathic at this point. But honestly, I think his real inspiration tonight was having Blakely on the sidelines. The guy's been floating on air ever since she showed up in his life. I mean, I've never seen him this focused—or distracted." He turns in his chair, smirking at me. "Care to explain what's going on to everyone?"

Mumbled voices grow in volume throughout the room, recorders lifting with a vigour that wasn't there after our last game. Interest gleams in the eyes of those who are itching to get the newest scoop out to the public first.

I give them all a wide grin. "I suppose I can answer a few questions about my fiancée, for those curious."

Whispers grow from the less-sports-focused media until suddenly, they're pushing to the front of the room. I'm relieved that Blakely isn't with me to deal with those who would have bypassed me completely to get to her first if she were.

Sadie, expecting this, is quick to hop onto the stage and wave a hand through the air to draw everyone's attention.

"Alright. We'll take two questions for tonight. The rest of you can keep an eye on social media for more information."

"Was it Blakely on the sidelines with the team tonight? This is such big and surprising news. Why announce it now? The season is in full swing!" a woman shouts, elbowing her way to the front of the stage.

Her press badge hangs around her neck, telling me she's from the *Vancouver Pulse*, a rag site that was responsible for posting a shirtless photo of Addie online a year back. It took Maddox three days and a few thousand dollars to get it taken down, but his sister doesn't know that.

I force my annoyance with her presence to the back of my head and keep my grin strong.

"Yes, it was her. And why not now? Blakely isn't the type of woman you have and don't try to lock down. I'm proud to have her and am done hiding that from everyone like we've been doing for the last few months."

"I can only imagine the reactions from your fans once the news breaks. Are you excited for them to meet her? Or, more importantly, is Blakely ready to be in the spotlight? Especially after this long without it."

The question comes from another woman, and the guy beside her scowls. His badge is a familiar one, and I know he doesn't give a shit about any of this. He's here for football, and that's that.

Sorry, man.

"Blakely has nerves of steel. She's one of the strongest people I've ever met. So, yeah, while she might not be ready per se, nobody really is. That doesn't mean she won't be able to handle it. As for the fans, her being one was how we met, so I think they'll get along just fine."

"Can you tell us more about that meeting? Was it really a classic fan-meets-player moment like you're making it seem?"

I don't catch who asked that, but I answer regardless.

"Yeah, it was. The entire time, all I was thinking is that this girl has no idea she's about to change my life. It wasn't flashy or planned, but it was . . . perfect. Just meant to be, you know?"

The words are a lie, but the heat in my chest as I recall our real meeting is the furthest thing from it.

Sadie cuts in again, keeping control of the room. "Okay, that's the end of those questions. If anyone has anything else to ask about the game, do that now before we're finished for the night."

I lean back in my chair and glance at my teammates. Jaxon is as smug as I expected him to be, but Zach looks almost . . . soft. Like he's read too far into my words. As the only guy in our friend group who's in a relationship, it isn't surprising that he's able to see right through me.

Coach is still leaning back against the wall. He offers me a tight-lipped smile before the next question comes for Zach.

I know I've done well, but there's still this stupid twisting sensation in my side that tells another story. It's hard to be happy with nailing these questions when I know that my answers are going to be the ones my family sees when this story breaks.

While I managed to sneak a warning phone call to my parents this morning, their reactions have stuck with me all day.

"You haven't been to the house in over two weeks, Jamieson," Mom scolds through the phone.

"I've been busy, Ma. You know how it is."

"Hmm. You always make the time for us."

Dad huffs a laugh. "Just try to come by soon, or your mother will be at your front door any day now."

Stomping down on my nerves, I reply, "I was planning on coming by tomorrow. I've got some news, and I know once it breaks, you'll have questions that are better to ask in person."

"What are you talking about? Just tell me now," Mom urges gently.

My throat is sticky. "I'm getting married."

"One day? Yes, I always figured you would, honey."

"No. I'm getting *married*, Mom. Next weekend."

The following pause is so silent that my dad's cough makes me flinch. It's Mom who recovers first.

"You're not even dating anyone. Wait, is this the woman who robbed you?"

"What do you mean, 'robbed him'?" Dad barks.

Mom sighs. "I'll explain it to you after, Ty."

"Yes, Ma, it is. Her name is Blakely, and I'm marrying her. I want you to meet her officially before the wedding."

"Well, that's generous of you," Dad grunts, his frustration leaking through the phone. "We wouldn't want to have not met your bride one single time before you married her."

"Don't be like that, Dad. It's all just happened so fast."

"Why are you making this decision already? Are you in trouble? If you are, we can help," Mom offers quickly, worrying the way she's always done when it comes to Oliver and me.

"I'm not in trouble."

"Does Oliver know about this?" Dad asks.

"He does."

"We're the last to know, then."

Mom's voice is too soft when she says, "I'm sorry for our reactions. You're just my baby, Jamie. Always. And I worry about your gentle heart. Some people take advantage of those who care too much."

I didn't stay on the phone for much longer after that. It's no secret that I've got a heart double the size it should be. I've never considered that a weakness, though. Not before I was asked to do this, and not now.

If I hadn't told my mom about Blakely weeks ago, there's a chance she wouldn't have immediately thought the worst when I told her about the wedding. There's no going back now, though, and honestly, I'm glad I vented to someone about it then.

As the reporters gather away from the stage, signalling the end of the interview, I'm quick to pat my friends on their backs and hop off the stage. I'm not overly interested in chatting with anyone in this room right now.

Coach must read that on my face because he lets me pass without a word. I'll tell him how much I appreciate that on practice Tuesday.

It's cooler and quieter in the family lounge. I'm antsy to see Blakely, and once I find her and Nate inspecting the Pythons logo on the wall, I take a deep breath.

"Well, if it isn't my two favourite people in my favourite place," I drawl on my way to them.

Nate spins first, his grin immediate. Blakely follows suit, but her smile is much softer, calmer. I'd take any smile from her right now as a good sign, but a kind, genuine one is even better.

"You were incredible! Four touchdowns!" Nate exclaims.

I offer him my fist to punch, and he slams his against it harder than I expected. "Thanks, buddy. You and your sister must be good luck charms or something."

"Do you need good luck charms?" Blakely asks.

"Not usually. But having one as beautiful as you on the sidelines didn't hurt."

Her smile slips briefly as she evades her eyes, staring at the door I just came through. "Is that what you told everyone in there?"

"Amongst other things. Are you ready?"

"Everyone knows?"

I slowly take her hand in mine, interlocking our fingers. The shake in hers has me squeezing tighter. The family waiting room is empty by now, and in any other circumstance, tonight would have been a good time and place for Blakely to meet a few of the other wives and friends, but with how nervous she is right now, empty is better.

She's already taking in a lot right now.

"They know enough. The rest will come out tomorrow."

"If they're mean, I'll protect you, Lake," Nate declares, punching the inside of his hand.

"That's a good man, Nate. We won't be speaking with anyone tonight, though. Just leaving the stadium together."

"As a family, right? A collective front?" Nate asks.

Blakely stares up at me, a silent plea in her eyes for me not to tell him otherwise. I tug her close and brush my mouth over her temple, breathing her in. We're as alone in this place as we'll ever be from here on out, but I don't touch her for anyone other than me.

"From here on out, we are family," I declare.

Nate tries to hide his reaction to the words, but his grin is too wide for that. Hell, I think mine might be too.

22

Blakely

When Jamie said that the rest of the information about our engagement was still to be revealed, I wasn't sure what that really meant. He spoke to the media for a while after his game, and I was selfishly hoping that almost everything had already been explained.

I was very wrong.

My social media presence is fairly minimal. It's not very fulfilling sharing photos of crowded streets or a selfie in the broken mirror in our old apartment bathroom online, so I've simply avoided it altogether. Today, as Jamie sits across me at the kitchen table and posts the photo of us Sadie instructed him to, I'm grateful that I've avoided the online world.

His cool five hundred thousand followers react instantly, and I'm so stiff, so stone-like, that I'm worried I'll break and crumble if I so much as lean a hand on the table.

"This is the easy part, Bandit," he murmurs.

"The easy part? You think having half a million people comment on our relationship is easy?"

He curls the corner of his mouth. "I like when you call it a relationship, wife."

I roll my eyes as I let go of the tiniest bit of tension. "Don't tease me right now. This is serious. They're going to hate me."

"Why? There's nothing to hate. We look great in the picture, and the whole fan-meets-her-hero narrative is going to kill."

"Did you actually say that you're my hero? Because I swear—"

I reach out to snag his phone, but he holds it to his chest before I can, mischief lighting his eyes. "No, I didn't. But maybe I should have."

"At least they chose the photo with my face hidden."

It's a good photo. At least it is if you don't know that I was only hiding my face in his chest because I was freaking out inside and the position was calming amongst the madness of the game.

He sobers slightly. "They won't all be like that. This is just the beginning. Our engagement photos will be published online too. Which, speaking of, are still scheduled for tomorrow."

"I know. Your agent was very thorough with his info dump."

Including the location and when the stylists would be arriving to get me ready. It's not enough that I'm being dressed by a stranger. A second one will be here to do my hair and makeup as well. I've never had any of those things done for me before, and my nerves are more from fear of winding up looking like a version of myself I'll never be able to replicate on my own than they are anything else.

"Good. I don't want you to be surprised by anything."

"Do you prefer hydrangeas or roses?"

Jamie scrunches his brows but goes with it. "Roses."

"White or yellow?"

"Whichever you prefer."

"Silk or satin?"

"Are you just trying to get away with not making any wedding decisions, Blakely?" he asks coyly.

I cradle my forearm on the edge of the table. "It isn't fair that the bride should have to choose everything for a wedding. It's not the Stone Age."

"You're right."

"I know I am. So, silk or satin?"

"I'll choose the fabric, but you're in charge of the colours. I've always been shit at that stuff," he barters.

I take in the smoothness of his features and hold his warm gaze. Jamie has to be the easiest-going guy out there, and I'm learning quickly that I don't hate that as much as I thought I would.

While he's not someone you can walk all over, he's also not the type of guy who turns everything into an argument. When I ask his opinion on something, he gives it while simultaneously not pushing one way or another. There's room for discussion on everything, and he'll sit and listen to my points without judgment or urging me to move quicker.

It's a far sexier habit than him barking orders and relying on me to make all the decisions that neither of us wants to.

"That's fine. There aren't many choices we have to make since we're not doing a reception. Only the flowers and decorations for the ceremony. Specifically, flower arrangements and fabric for the bows on the chairs," I explain.

"Tony explained it well, then?"

"He did."

Jamie nods before taking a drink from his tall glass of orange juice. His top lip is shiny when he says, "I told my parents about the wedding yesterday before the game and said we'd come over today so you could meet them beforehand."

I sit with that, letting it hit me fully. Once it does, I'm panicking all over again. My nerves are completely shot after yesterday, and now this? It's a miracle I manage to keep my tongue from lashing out.

"You could have run that by me first," I bite out.

He grows still, glass in his hand. "I know. I'm sorry. I've been struggling with blindsiding them, and I offered without thinking about how it would affect you."

"What exactly did you tell them?"

"That I met a special girl and decided to marry her."

My pulse throbs in my neck. "And did they believe you?"

"Not yet."

Not yet.

I stare down at the plate of crepes in front of me and frown when my appetite makes no sign of appearing. Other than the burgers Nate asked if we could get on the way home from the game last night, I haven't eaten. The crepes were quick and easy to make while Jamie set the table and attempted to wake Nate up.

My little brother refused, leaving Jamie and me alone for breakfast.

I'll admit that it's gotten easier to be around Jamie. He gives me my space and doesn't push me too much unless, with the help of his apparent superpowers, he can read me well enough to be sure that I'll let it slide. Things have gotten . . . comfortable recently. I don't mind him hanging out around me or having random conversations about stupid, pointless things, and we're not even married yet.

"What time are we supposed to be there?" I ask tightly, not letting him off too easily, even if I can't fault him for wanting to warn his parents about this.

One of the things I've learned about him is that his family is an important part of his life. I can't imagine that lying to them would be easy. It wouldn't have even been possible for me to do it to Nate.

"If Mom had it her way, she'd have had us there from the moment we woke up." I must look straight terrified at the idea of that because he quickly adds, "I talked her down to after lunch. Figured it would be less overwhelming if we didn't have to have a sit down at the table with nowhere for us to run."

Nodding, I swallow and watch as he nervously digs his fork into the middle of his pile of crepes.

"Is Nate allowed to come?"

"He's allowed to come anywhere, anytime. Always, Bandit."

I flash a soft smile. "Thank you."

"You don't have to thank me for that."

"I already did."

"It wouldn't kill you to let me win from time to time, you know?"

"Where's the fun in losing?" I ask.

With a loud laugh, his eyes crinkle at the corners. It's a good look on him. The best, actually. Being able to feel and accept such an open happiness is special.

Once he's quieted, he scoots his chair forward and taps a finger to the side of his glass. "I've been meaning to ask you about the cooking you do. First, there was the pot pie in the fridge and then the homemade lasagne the other night, and now crepes for breakfast. Maybe I'm just reading into it, but I'm starting to think that you like to feed people."

"Is there a question somewhere in there?"

"Alright, Ms. Hardball. Do you have a passion for cooking?" he asks pointedly.

"Yeah, I do. Even went to college for a few months to try and get my degree for it," I reveal.

His surprise is obvious, taking over every inch of his face. "What? Why only a few months?"

"That's all the time I had. I dropped out to take care of Nathan."

Suddenly, the air around me burns to breathe in. An ache so jarringly sharp cuts right between my ribs, and I push my chair away from the table before standing.

Jamie watches me prepare to run away, a sad glimmer in his eyes that hurts worse than the pain in my chest. I don't want his pity. Not now, not ever.

"I have to get ready to meet your parents. If you leave the dishes, I'll get to them before we leave," I ramble.

He stares at me in silence for a moment before nodding once. I get a few steps from the table when his voice cuts through the dining room, carving words that I've needed to hear for years into my heart.

"You have nothing to be ashamed of, Blakely. Not everyone has the ability to put others in front of themselves. Especially when what you have to give up is a part of who you are."

Tears blur my vision the entire way up to my room.

I PICK at the hole in the knee of my jeans and cringe, knowing that in only a couple of minutes, I'll be introducing myself to Jamie's parents looking like I couldn't be bothered to dress up.

In reality, this is an occasion that I would have put a shit ton of effort into. I've outgrown my dressier clothes and figured that yoga pants were even worse than ripped jeans. At least I remembered to grab my work blouses from our old apartment before they were lost forever.

We've yet to go back there, but I'm positive the locks have been changed and the things we didn't bring with us have been taken to the dumpster. It's terrifying to remember that once my time is done with Jamie, I need to find us somewhere else to live. We don't have anywhere waiting for us.

"Are you sure that your parents like blueberries, Jamie?" Nate asks from the back seat of the SUV.

I still can't get over the sharp scent of real leather mixed with Jamie's cologne. The heated seats curve around my body, and the screen on the console is massive. Like a small TV, just without the unlimited movies and shows. His music is playing on it now, and while I may be naïve to the interiors of expensive vehicles, I do know music. And the song he's playing is "Golden Girl" by Noah Hutton, one I've had on my phone for a while.

Jamie uses the buttons on the steering wheel to lower the volume and glances at my brother through the rear-view mirror.

"My entire family loves anything berry flavoured, buddy. Why are you stressing?"

"Well, because we made blueberry tarts. I wanted to double-check."

He softly jostles the platter of berry-filled desserts on his lap. We rushed to make them after he woke up this morning, but I think they turned out okay. I'd have preferred raspberry, but the only fruit in the fridge were blueberries, so we made do. There was no way I was risking showing up not only looking like a slob but without a dessert to offer.

It could just be my nerves making me feel like this, but I've worried myself to death thinking that they'll take one look at me and disapprove. Our marriage isn't real, but having to spend the next few months knowing that Jamie's parents hate me would kill me slowly.

I don't need their approval; I just stupidly want it.

"They'll love them. My mom's been on a baking kick recently, and she'll probably end up asking for the recipe," Jamie says with a flick of his eyes across the console.

I turn my head and thank him with a stiff nod.

"Is that your house?" Nate gasps.

Jamie chuckles low in his throat. "My parents' house, yeah."

"It's . . . woah."

I think I'm going to be sick.

"Did your parents win the lottery or something?" I whisper, watching as the tall house at the top of the hill expands in size the closer we get.

"Not exactly."

"So, what, they're CEOs of some multibillion-dollar company, then? Because that house is not normal. I thought yours was too much, but this? I'm not dressed for this place," I blurt out, cupping my knee in a tight hold.

The driveway at the top of the hill flattens out, leading to three garage doors. Six peaks extend from the roof, and the front entrance has a rounded cover, protecting it from the elements. If we weren't heading into the middle of fall, I'm sure the massive lawn would be bright green, and the hedges would be springing with flowers.

"Did you not tell your sister anything about me, Nate?" Jamie asks, parking the SUV beside another similar one on the driveway. "Aren't I your favourite player in the history of ever?"

Nate scoots closer to the front and pokes him. "Hey! Don't blame me. Isn't it your job to brag about yourself?"

Oh, he has been. He just decided to leave out everything about his family.

Jamie turns the engine off and twists in his seat to face us. Humour lines his expression, but he doesn't laugh like I expect. He's too zoned in, taking my lack of knowledge as an opportunity to teach me.

"A job I've failed but will fix right now. Starting with no, my parents didn't win the lottery. My dad was in the NHL for a long time and built my mom her dream house before retiring at forty. My ma owns a non-profit ballet studio that gives lessons to those who can't afford them."

I grab onto the last bit of his explanation. "Why did she choose to do that?"

"I bet if you asked her that, she'd love to tell you all about it."

"Is that my segue, then? Asking about why she cares about poor people?"

Jamie chokes on air, bewildered. I clamp my lips shut and let my brother try to pat Jamie's back from the seat behind him. It doesn't work, and instead, Nate just slaps at Jamie like he's got a limp wrist.

"Jesus, Bandit. You fucking kill me sometimes," Jamie wheezes.

My cheeks flush. "I wasn't trying to kill you."

"I'd suggest maybe not wording it like that if you do choose to ask her about it."

As if I'll be risking mentioning that at all ever again.

"Should we go in now?" I ask, desperate to get out of this vehicle.

He turns it off and snags his keys from the cup holder. "Of course we can. But let me open the door for you in case we already have an audience."

I don't argue because he's right. This isn't a hug on the sidelines at a football game. We're about to introduce our relationship to his parents. The two people who know him best.

With my hands in my lap, I wait for him to get out and round the hood. Nate follows suit once Jamie pauses at my door and quickly opens it up.

He offers me his hand, and I stare at it for a beat before taking it. It's steady and warm, the way it always is.

With a backward shove, I close the door behind me and go to head for the house when suddenly, Jamie's closing in. Lips parting on a silent question, I'm unable to evade him as he crushes his chest against mine and lifts our hands to his sternum.

I can feel Nate's eyes on us. Who knows if Jamie's parents are watching too. That doesn't make me pull away from him the way it would have weeks ago.

His attention is so fierce, the kind that makes you feel like the only person in the entire world who matters to someone. Like you always have every ounce of their focus.

The constant glide of his thumb over my knuckles is just another reminder that he's as aware of every point of contact as I am.

Leaning down, he lowers his voice. "There's something I want to give you before we go inside."

"Another gift?"

"In a way."

I hold still in waiting. It's almost impossible to see him

moving, but I feel the shift of his thigh against mine and the pull of the tight muscles in his chest as he digs into his pocket.

When he glides something cool down my ring finger, I trap a breath in my throat and slowly, carefully, drop my eyes to my hand.

The size of the square diamond on the silver band is . . . is hard to believe. It's surrounded by so many smaller ones that glitter just as bright. Dreaming of an engagement ring was never something I did. I didn't have any idea of what I would want when that time came, yet this isn't what I would have expected in a million years. Even from a ring that I'll be returning.

"Do you like it? I would have had it for you at the game, but it wasn't ready yet," he murmurs.

"It's stunning, Jamie. It's too much. I'm not the girl for this—"

His voice is strong despite staying muted as he cuts me off. "Don't finish that sentence. This ring is yours, and it's not too much. You've got it backward, Blakely. You deserve something bigger and brighter, but this one will have to do for now."

Will have to do?

"I'm not your real wife," I argue weakly.

"Tell me what's wrong. What are you thinking in that head of yours that's making you feel like I should have gotten you some flimsy, fake ring from the dollar store?"

It's not the time to be dealing with this, yet that doesn't make the insecurities that have been building and building go away. I have to deal with the wreckage they've caused, even if I risk doing it with an audience.

"Look at how I'm dressed and how my hair is styled and the lack of makeup. I don't look like the fiancée of a sports star and certainly not like I fit into a neighbourhood and house like this one. I'm the girl who you'd expect to be escorted away from somewhere like this. From a guy like you," I say, fighting against the urge to let my voice wobble with emotion.

One blink and he's released my hand. A rough, callused palm

smooths over my jaw instead, tilting my head back in a way that forces our eyes to hold.

"If you don't tell me to step away, I'm going to kiss you right now," he rasps, such a confident determination in his gaze.

It cuts right through me. "Why?"

"Because I'm hoping it will help convince you that you're the opposite of everything you just told me. If I wanted to find someone who wore designer dresses, dyed their hair blonde every few weeks in the salon, and wore makeup all the time, I would have."

"And you think us kissing will help convince me of that?"

His small smile wavers. "Well, that, and it would start our performance today off with one hell of a bang."

He's still holding my face, and once I realize I've been leaning into him this entire time, I still don't stop. It feels like it would be harder to break away than continue to sway forward.

Am I really going to let him kiss me right now? I guess it has to happen eventually. Nobody will believe that we're in love if we don't kiss. Do I really want our first one to be at the aisle during our wedding ceremony?

The soft, reassuring press of his thumb to the middle of my chin is comforting and warm, and I'd be lying if I said it didn't also make my toes curl ever so slightly in my shoes.

I part my lips and then wet them, hoping he can read my acceptance in the action. By the subtle flare of his pupils as he watches my tongue glide across the bottom one, I know he has.

Holding my breath, I start lowering my lashes and wait for him to make the move—

"Uncle J!"

The high-pitched squeal is a shock to my system. I stumble back and hide my reaction to the sudden bite of cold against the cheek just cradled in his hand.

"Uncle J! Were you just about to kiss each other?"

Jamie clears his throat and opens his arms to the girl now

launching herself at him. He bundles her in a hug and mouths an apology to me.

I shake my head at him, not needing an apology, before turning in search of Nate. He's leaning against the side of the house, his phone in his hand but attention on us now, if it were ever anywhere else at all.

"Hi! I'm Nova. Who are you?" the girl asks, standing in front of me with Jamie at her back.

Her blonde hair is braided in two halves down her scalp, and her yellow overalls are just the slightest bit too big for her. Freckles are splattered across the middle of her face, making her look a bit younger than I'd bet she is.

"I'm Blakely. It's nice to meet you, Nova," I say.

She grins wide. "Why were you about to kiss my uncle?"

Jamie chuckles, palming her shoulder. "Blakely is my fiancée. We're getting married next weekend."

"Oh! That's fun. Will it be like Mom and Ollie's wedding?"

"Kind of. Not quite as big, though. Only my favourite people are invited."

Her eyes widen. "That means me, right?"

"Sure does. You're my absolute favourite."

"Who are you? Are you another favourite person?" Nova asks Nate, finally spotting him.

My brother slides his phone into his pocket and introduces himself with a welcoming smile. "I hope so. I'm Blakely's brother, Nathan. You can call me Nate."

"Awesome."

Jamie takes my hand again, rubbing the band of my engagement ring with the tip of his thumb. "Is everyone ready for us inside, Nova?"

"Yep. We got bored of watching you through the window upstairs, so I came down to see what was taking so long."

I nip at the inside of my cheek, debating whether I should look up to see if they're still there.

"Well, we're coming inside now. Want to lead the way for us?" Jamie asks his niece.

"Sure!"

She skips in front of us, and Nate sneaks ahead, not appearing nervous to meet Jamie's family. I wish I shared the same confidence.

Jamie all but suction cups himself to me, offering a silent support that I'm over pretending not to want. My grip grows tight on his hand as I straighten my shoulders, silently slipping my mask of bravery back on.

23

Jamie

My mom all but falls face first onto the porch when I open the door. She stabilizes herself with a hand to my shoulder and beams up at me, feigning innocence.

"Oh, hi, sweetheart," she blubbers, gathering me in her arms for a hug. "I didn't know you were here yet."

Appearing over her shoulder in the hall, Oliver snorts. "Don't lie, Mom."

"What happened to your sense of loyalty, Oliver?" she chides, releasing me with a pat on the back.

My brother ignores her question and slaps my arm in hello. "Nice of you to finally join us and return my daughter."

"Your daughter came to get me because she loves me. Don't be so jealous. Green isn't your colour."

"Not jealous, asshole."

"If anyone should be jealous, it's me. The moment either of you are around, *my* daughter seems to forget I exist," Avery chimes in, curling immediately into Oliver's side.

He would glue her to his side if it were socially acceptable and Avery wouldn't threaten his untimely death daily with how often he'd annoy her.

They look good together, though. Happy and in love in a way

that I know my brother doubted he'd ever want to be if it weren't with her.

I wink at Avery, keeping my hold on my fiancée firm and supportive amongst the chaos that's already erupting.

"Mom, this is Blakely. She's going to marry Uncle J," Nova announces, stepping in front of her parents with her hands on her hips.

Mom's already looking at Blakely, bright blue eyes bouncing over every inch of my fiancée as if she's searching for hints as to who she is on the inside without having to ask. It's a harmless action, but my protectiveness of Blakely spikes, encouraging me to act.

I take our connected hands and bring them to my mouth before releasing her and curling an arm around her back. She fits into my side with ease, but the muscles in her back are tense with nerves.

Dad settles beside Mom, his brown brows low over a dark stare. More like Oliver than he is me, he's blunt and grumpy, while Mom is bright and cheery.

With a backward glance, I find Nathan a few steps behind me and tip my head, silently telling him to come closer. He's the picture of overwhelmed but has opted to try and fade into the background instead of asking for support.

Fuck, thinking of that kid upset tears me up.

"So, before everyone starts asking the millions of questions I know are coming, I want you to officially meet Blakely, my fiancée, and her brother, Nathan," I say, putting more emphasis on the titles as if that'll help point out how little I want to hear any arguments on any of this. Spreading my fingers out along Blakely's side, I hold her closer to me and add, "Blakely, Nathan, this is my mom, Gracie, my dad, Tyler, my brother, Oliver, and his wife, Avery. You've already met Nova."

"It's nice to meet you," Nate says, speaking first.

It takes me a beat to notice the way he's shifted to stand at Blakely's other side, a stone sentinel at the ready.

Nobody here is going to hurt her, regardless of how confused and concerned they are about what's happening, but seeing him protect his sister only makes me respect him more. He's young in age, not maturity.

"Thank you for welcoming us into your home," Blakely says, back to the woman I met all those weeks ago in my living room. "It's beautiful."

It's awkward, more like. She doesn't know that my parents are aware of how we met. They're not judgmental people, just protective. I have to hope they don't treat her any differently because they're privy to information they never needed to know in the first place.

Dad rubs a hand down Mom's arm and offers Blakely a sincere smile the way I was hoping he would. As intimidating as his towering height, dark-as-night, silver-streaked hair, and deep brown stare are, he can be a total softie.

The recognition in his expression isn't obvious to those who don't know him as well as we do. I see it all as he tries to dive inside Blakely's head, searching for the reason behind the mask she's been wearing less and less around me but has slipped on today. A façade of wholeness and the lack of weight that's been slowly crushing her shoulders.

Dad sees all of that because he was in her shoes once upon a time. Only instead of needing to be strong for a brother, it was his mother he was taking care of while silently suffocating inside.

"Thank you. Come in, we don't bite," he says.

Nova peers up at him. "That's a weird saying, G-Pa."

"What's weird about it?" he asks.

"Why would we bite her?"

"It's just something someone says to be reassuring. Like double-checking locks on the doors before going to bed, it just makes you feel safe," Nate tells her gently.

I don't know whether to scream or start to cry because that was the first thing that came to his mind. I'll be changing that. By the time this marriage is over, neither he nor Blakely will fear anything again.

"Exactly," Dad notes, nudging Mom to guide us all inside the house.

"We brought some dessert. Jamie said you were berry fans, and I don't like showing up somewhere empty-handed," Blakely rambles, waving to the platter of tarts in Nate's hands. "I didn't have a chance to try them before we left home, but Jamie did sneak one and said they're pretty good."

Mom snaps out of whatever worried haze she was just in and focuses on the dessert. When she smiles at Blakely, it's warm and open, relaxing me a bit.

"That was very kind of you. I attempted tarts a little while ago but couldn't quite get the filling right. Do you have a specific recipe that you follow?"

"I do. If you want, I can write it down for you?"

Mom nods enthusiastically. "I'd love that. I have a pen and paper in the den."

The tension drains from Blakely's muscles beneath my fingers. I release a tight breath. Mom snags her hand and pulls her from me before taking Nate's as well. Nova clutches her mom's fingers, and then every one of them is rushing away.

"I need your help with something, Jamie," Dad says once they've disappeared.

Oliver cocks a brow. "Am I allowed to come, or am I supposed to follow my wife?"

"Considering you knew about Blakely before I did, you've already got a head start," Dad grunts.

I smirk. "You heard him. Go away."

"I'm going to eat all of the tarts and leave the both of you nothing but crumbs."

"Have at it. Your mom has been feeding me enough baked goods lately," Dad says.

Oliver glares at the both of us before all but stomping away.

It's a valiant effort on his part, acting like he would rather be here than wherever it is his wife has wandered off to.

"What do you need my help with?" I ask, slipping my hands into my pockets.

"Nothing. I just figured you'd rather talk without Oliver around."

I snort a laugh. "Fair enough. Outside?"

"Sure."

We step onto the back porch a couple of minutes later. I take a seat on the long bench beneath the kitchen window, Dad following my lead.

"You're going to give your mother a heart attack, Jamie" is what he says first.

"Jeez. No easing into it, huh?"

"Is that what you've been doing? Easing into it?"

Alright, fair enough. "Mom seems okay now."

"She's trying to be polite. We all are."

I swipe a hand through my hair, messing it up. "You don't need to pretend with me or with Blakely. Doing that will only make her feel more uncomfortable. She can tell when someone's putting on an act."

"Actors recognize actors, Jamie."

"What is that supposed to mean?" I snip, my cool slipping.

Dad's eyes widen at my outburst, a hand lifting in surrender. "I'm sorry. That's not how I meant it to come out."

"How did you mean it? Because I didn't come here to have Blakely put under a microscope. I came here because as my parents, I figured you deserved to meet my future wife before my wedding day. Please don't make me regret that."

"We're just worried about you, Jamie. You've always been an act first and think second type of person, but this? We had a wedding invitation slipped in the *mailbox*. Are you sure that you understand the magnitude of what you're going to be doing? Marriage isn't anything to be taken lightly. It's a forever thing. Have we not shown you that over the years?"

"Of course you have. Shit, Dad. I've been surrounded by marriages my entire life. I get it. I do. Your worries aren't necessary. I'm marrying Blakely because I want to."

My stomach burns, the lining disintegrating with every half-truth I tell. It's wrong not to just blurt out the truth to him. He'd understand. Out of everyone in my life, he would get it the most. The pressure to make my team proud and be the guy who can get the job done. I just can't put him in a position to lie to Mom, and if they both know the truth . . . It's too big of a risk with the closeness of our family.

He's not believing a word I'm saying, though. Not even one.

"Your mom won't let it go. Especially not when you confirmed that Blakely tried to rob you. Want to get into that? Because I'm pretty sure that's called some shit like Stockholm syndrome," he mutters.

"That's when you fall in love with someone who's kidnapped you or something. I'm not holding her against her will. Sheesh."

"Fuck, fine. I just think that this is . . . odd."

"It's a story to tell. She wasn't in my house with the purpose of robbing me, anyway. It just happened."

"She just *happened* to try robbing you?"

"Fuck, Dad. Can you just forget that I even shared that to begin with? Blakely will be mortified if she hears anything about it. She's still nervous to this day to touch certain things in the house because of what she did."

He sighs, leaning further against the back of the bench. "Just promise me that you're at least signing a prenup. Not because I think poorly of her, but because it's important for everyone to have entering into a marriage. Especially someone like you."

"Already done. She's not after my money, though. Just so you know. I think that's the last thing she'd take from me."

"What makes you so sure of that?" he asks, not coming off as abrasive, just purely curious.

"How easy was it for you to take money from those in your life when you were my age, Dad?"

He pauses, digesting the question. The memories of his past surface in his gaze before he blinks them away.

"I didn't want to assume anything about her. I've always hated when people did that with me."

"If you give her a chance, I think she'll surprise you. The two of you would get along."

Pinching the bridge of his nose, he turns his head, focusing on me. "This marriage is a fucking sham, Jamie. You don't have to tell me the truth, but I know you better than you think I do."

"Believe what you want—"

He clears his throat pointedly. "I wasn't done. I'm just telling you how it's most likely going to be here, and I guarantee your mother is going to be in the same boat as me. However, if you say Blakely's good people, then I'll respect that, and I know everyone else will too. You're a grown man, and your choices are your own. However, I am going to tell you to be careful. Whatever you're doing here has the chance of turning sour."

"Isn't that risk there with everything?"

He chuckles, patting my shoulder. "Yeah, it is. I'm just speaking from my own experiences here a bit. Your mom worked real fucking hard to get me to open up, and there were times where it was the last thing I wanted to do. If Blakely is anything like me, it won't be easy for you."

None of this is news to me. Blakely isn't an easy woman, but I've never wanted easy less than I have with her. Fake or not, she's one week away from being my wife, and I have the next two months to break down the walls my dad's describing.

The challenge doesn't scare me.

It excites me.

24

Blakely

MY MOM IS THE COMPLETE OPPOSITE OF GRACIE BATEMAN.

Nate and I were raised with the knowledge that our existence was a burden. The money it took to pay for groceries, the roof over our heads, and clothes on our backs was a nuisance. I heard several times over the course of my life that it would have been easier if she only had to take care of herself and not two children who were never quite grateful enough for her *sacrifices*.

Dad was always the one who tucked us in at night and made sure our supper was heated the entire way through when Mom left it out for us to serve ourselves. He tried his best to pick up the slack. To this day, I'm positive that if it weren't for us, he'd never have stayed with Mom. He was the glue keeping our family together, and once he passed, that glue dried up, and the two halves fell apart.

I'm only grateful that Nate was young enough when she left to not have bonded much with her. He missed her the first few months after she left and wouldn't sleep anywhere but beside me for several more after that. Then, he started growing up too fast.

I blame our mother for many, many things, but the most

important is the loss of Nate's childhood. Ten years old is too young to have to be without a father and a mother.

Being here in this house with a family who bursts with love and appreciation for one another has been hard for me to witness. They haven't had to do anything more than offer hugs and smiles and kindness, but it's been more than enough.

From the moment I met Jamie, it was painfully obvious that he was raised well. Not only with respect and love but also support and guidance. There's a light inside of him that shines from the deepest crevice of his soul. Every day I spend with him, he tries to draw something similar out of me, and I'm growing to hate my inability to flash him with a bright light even once.

It's obvious that his mom doesn't trust me, yet she hasn't treated me any differently than I'd suspect she would if she did. There's something incredible about that.

"So, I guess I'll just come out and ask," she starts, palming the mug of coffee in her lap. I hold my breath. "How much of the wedding has been planned so far? Do you have a dress? Flowers? Avery runs a flower shop, and I'm sure she wouldn't mind helping."

Those weren't the questions I was expecting at all.

Releasing my breath, I tuck my leg further beneath my body. "I'm nearly done. Tony got us in touch with a planner, and we've made a lot of progress. I haven't gotten a dress yet, and we decided on roses, but if you all think there's something better—"

"Roses are beautiful. Don't feel pressured to include me. I'm sure whichever shop you choose will do an amazing job," Avery says gently.

Nova watches while Nate peels the foil from his tart before picking up one of her own and copying him.

She grins at it and then says, "My mom's shop is the best. You should use her flowers. I'll help and make them extra beautiful for Uncle J."

"If you're available, Avery. I'm sure Jamie would love you to be involved," I tell her.

Flowers don't matter to me. We could not have any, and it wouldn't be the end of the world. In the grand scheme of things, they'll die faster than our marriage will.

Excitement sparks in her eyes. "Absolutely. If you give me your number before you leave today, we can chat about them a bit more."

Gracie doesn't bother hiding how pleased she is by what just happened. In fact, I think it only makes her more confident to keep pushing.

"What about a dress?"

"I was just going to order something online."

Her gasp is dramatic as fuck, which I think might fit her. It's very Jamie-like. His mom is a perfect example of a tiny woman with an attitude meant for someone double her size.

"How will you know how you like the dress if you don't try it on first?"

"I think they have websites now that let you upload a photo of yourself so you can virtually try it on," Avery says, offering me a sympathetic smile.

I nod, pretending like I know all about those websites. "Exactly. It's just easier for me that way."

"Half the fun of planning a wedding is choosing a dress. I spent hours holding my phone in the shop for Avery's mom on FaceTime so she could see her in every dress she was trying on. We cried on and off for days afterward," Gracie says, her eyes watering.

Avery leans into her mother-in-law's side for support but keeps her encouraging stare fixed on me. "If you choose to go in somewhere, we'd love to come. As long as that's something you and your family would be okay with. I know how moms can be with this sort of thing."

"A mom won't be an issue. Ours doesn't even know about the wedding and isn't invited."

I stiffen, Nate's comment falling into the room with the

weight of a cement block. The impact slams full force into my chest, making it hard to breathe.

In the blink of an eye, Gracie's on high alert, her body nearly slipping off the edge of the couch as she leans as close to us as possible without standing.

The pity twisting her expression is what I was trying to avoid. What I *always* try to avoid. Having them learn about this so soon . . . on a first meeting?

It's mortifying.

"I'm sorry. I shouldn't have said anything," Avery apologizes quickly, guilt dripping off the words.

Nate sets a hand on my knee in a silent apology, and I fake a smile for him, not wanting him to feel bad for what he said. It's not his fault. I can't blame him for being honest, even if it exposed more than I was ready to right now.

The burn of Gracie's eyes on my face forces me to meet her stare. All signs of pity are gone, replaced with a steadying offer of support that shocks me. Maybe it shouldn't, considering the son she raised.

"My dad didn't come to Mom and Ollie's wedding and doesn't see me a lot anymore, but we still had fun without him. If your mom doesn't come to yours and Uncle J's, that's okay. G-Ma and *Mormor* always say that sometimes we get to choose our family, and that doesn't mean they're less special."

Gracie chokes on a sob, and Avery hovers a hand over her chest before rubbing the other up and down her daughter's arm. Nova doesn't appear upset in the slightest, and I think that's just a kid thing. Her advice came from the desire to help me, not from a place of her own pain.

Still, I'm jealous of this child's ability to feel so openly. When I was her age, I'd already been beat down to the point of not wanting to feel at all anymore.

Gracie expertly pushes back her overflowing emotions and reaches out with both of her hands. She hovers them palm up in the gap between our couches, waiting for me to take them. I sink my teeth into the inside of my cheek and fight past the shake in my hands as I press our palms together.

"Nova's right. There will still be plenty of family there. You won't even notice that your mother isn't in attendance. And if you change your mind on the dress, we'd love to be there for you then as well," she vows.

"I'll go dress shopping," I blurt out, hardly waiting for her to finish first. I flush from my chest to my ears. "I don't know where to go, but yeah. I'll do it."

Gracie's grin is all white teeth and pure joy. "Leave it up to me! Oh, this will be so fun. It can be just us girls. We'll make a whole day of it!"

"Maybe we can stop by the shop and check out flower arrangements too?" Avery adds.

It's a lot all at once. More involvement from strangers than I've ever allowed before. It doesn't feel wrong to want to say yes.

Especially not when Jamie comes strolling into the room, his sight set completely on me. With every inch of space he eats between us, the more at ease I become while simultaneously hyperfixating on his closeness.

His calm eyes scroll over my face, taking in every inch of my expression before he's lifting me off the couch and setting me on his lap. I don't have the chance to reject the new positioning with how quickly he's moved us, and that's actually a good thing. I'd have told him off on instinct and missed the steady weight of his arms around me.

His thighs are comfortable as hell as I relax the full weight of my body on them, trusting that he's strong enough to take it. That rich amber cologne hits me next as I turn to face him, our eyes clashing.

He strokes the outside of my thigh and grins up at me, an invisible tail wagging beneath him. His happiness encourages my mouth to tug up at the corner.

"Sorry to interrupt."

"No, you're not," I say, calling his bluff.

With a quick wink, he palms my waist and pushes up, his front flush with my back. "Nah, I'm not. With you in my lap, how could I be?"

It's an act for his family. I know that, yet it still has my heart racing and heat blossoming low in my belly.

"Well, hello to you, Jamieson. We were actually in the middle of a conversation," Gracie says.

"What, you can't continue it with me here? Were you talking about me?"

"You wish. We were discussing the wedding and how the planning was going," Avery states.

Jamie nuzzles his face into my hair, his nose bumping the back of my ear. "Oh yeah?"

I shiver against his body and avoid the curious stares around us. He's doing this shit on purpose now, and I'm not one to be played with. Alone or surrounded by his family members. At least not without a heads-up first.

Scooting back, I make sure to drag my ass over his crotch while turning into his body. With a pointed finger, I drag my nail along the underside of his jaw and up to curl in the messy blond hair behind his ear.

His eyes thunder as he presses his fingers into my waist and swallows hard. I bat my lashes and take a page from his book, tipping his head back and drifting my mouth over his cheek.

Keeping my voice too low for everyone but him to hear, I whisper, "Don't toy with me, or I'll toy back."

I'm not ready for him to call *my* bluff.

Turning his head, he brings his mouth to the corner of mine, leaving it there. When his lips part, I can almost taste his words.

"Don't tease me, wife. I like it too much."

"Should we get a room?" Gracie teases.

The question reminds me of what we're doing, and I pull back, blinking heavily. Jamie chases my gaze. I let him hold it.

He smooths his hand from my waist to the curve of my stomach and adjusts the both of us, seating me lower on his lap.

The stiffness beneath my ass follows our movements despite his efforts, only intensifying the burn in my gut.

His dick is hard because of me.

"You don't say anything when Ollie mauls Avery," he says, propping his chin on my shoulder.

Avery flushes. "He doesn't maul me."

"Hey, I'm not judging. Just pointing out the obvious."

"Let's move back to what I was saying," Gracie urges, tapping her legs excitedly. "Wedding dress and flower shopping."

I fall back into the conversation, this time with Jamie here to provide a sense of backup that I don't need but have grown to appreciate.

The same way I have him.

THE DESIGNER SWEATER dress moulded to my curves and knee-high nude boots should have me feeling like a supermodel. The vibe is more like playing dress-up instead.

I didn't even recognize myself when I saw the aftermath of hours being done up like a doll. My hair is shiny and curled elegantly down my shoulders, freshly washed and frizzless. I haven't worn this much makeup in my entire life. Not one patch of unevenness is showing beneath the expertly laid concealer and foundation, and the precise black line along my lashes makes my eyes pop. The lashes are fake, but you'd never know unless you were in the room while they were glued on.

Soft and comfortable, the high neck of the dress rubs my skin with every nervous shift of my body as I walk the rest of the way to the football field. It's silent this time, nobody here but me, Jamie, the photographer that I have yet to meet, and the security team lingering.

I was almost expecting Jamie to be waiting outside of the

lounge when I was finished getting ready. He wasn't. One of the security guards was instead. I would have told him to leave me be if I wasn't at least ninety percent sure that my husband-to-be had told him to walk with me.

Everything here looks so much bigger and intimidating without the fans and players all around. It almost feels unnatural to be here right now.

The moment my boots meet the turf, I find Jamie standing at the centre of the field. He looks completely at peace, unintimidated by the silence and emptiness.

It makes sense. This place is his second home.

Dressed in dark-wash jeans, beaming white sneakers, and a tan long-sleeve the same exact shade as my boots, he turns to face me, grinning wide.

I turn my head to tell the guard that he doesn't need to follow me anymore, but he's already gone, hanging back in the tunnel.

A wolf whistle carries through the field, and I shake my head, choking on a laugh when Jamie lowers his fingers from his mouth.

"Goddamn gorgeous," he calls, heated gaze fixed on me.

I reach him and paw at my dress, clearly fidgeting. "You don't think I look overdressed?"

"Absolutely not. You're just showing me up."

"He's not wrong. You look amazing. Both of you do. These photos are going to be incredible," a woman says, joining us.

I turn to her and smile appreciatively. She offers me her hand as I give her a quick once-over.

"I'm Kye, your photographer for the day. I hope you don't mind starting here on the field today. I've been told to focus on the importance of football in your lives," she explains.

I shake her hand and nod while my stomach pinches. It shouldn't matter where we get photos taken. We're here because of football in the first place. Photos of anything different wouldn't make sense.

Jamie moves to my side, hovering. "Thank you, Kye. We're excited to get started."

"Great. I guess we can just start with some poses using a ball and go from there. How about you two get together on the centreline, and we can mix the poses up between playful and romantic."

"Alright," I say.

Jamie breaks away to snag a football from the pile a few feet away and spreads his long fingers over the laces. His hand is so massive that it makes the ball look regular-sized when I know it would be uncomfortable for me to hold it the same way.

"What about a snap position? Surely you know how to do one of those, Jamie," Kye suggests, a slight teasing note in her tone.

Something sharp pricks my side when Jamie laughs at her joke, and she lets her eyes wander up and down his body. I ignore the entire interaction and wait for instructions.

Jamie points the ball at her and then asks, "You gonna blow a whistle for me, Coach?"

"I don't have one. You could teach me how to use my fingers, though."

My back snaps straight as I pause, stretching out my fingers when they try to curl.

"We'll just use our imaginations," I bite out, trapping a growl in my throat. "How do you want us to stand?"

Kye lifts the camera in her hands and points to a spot on the field. "Let's start with you throwing the ball back to Jamie, and then we'll move into a second shot. We'll pose as though you're tackling him while grabbing the ball. After that, we can do a few more fun poses."

"Great."

Silence.

"Here, Bandit," Jamie murmurs before tossing me the ball.

I barely catch it and push past the embarrassment of that

while turning my back to him and waiting for confirmation that he's gotten in position before doing anything else.

"Yeah, *just* like that, Jamie. Maybe bend a bit more. Don't be afraid to stick your butt out," Kye instructs.

Clearly, her teasing remarks have begun to fray on my nerves because every word she speaks has me debating throwing the ball at her face.

Jamie laughs again.

Again.

It's so incredibly innocent. His friendly nature shouldn't piss me off, but I'm silently encouraging him to tell her to go away.

I attempt to replicate the stance I watched the player from last night's game do and shove the ball down into the turf. The entire pose feels ridiculous in my dress and boots, but I'm not in the mood to question it.

With the whole fan-meets-player thing, it makes sense. Even if Jamie doesn't even play this position in football.

"Blakely, maybe don't push on the ball so hard. We need the ball to look natural," Kye says.

It would look natural flying through the air on its way to hit you—

A hot palm grabs my waist, and I jump, nearly falling forward on my face. Jamie's cologne hits me before he's catching me, steadying me with his body.

"You're killing me right now," he mutters, slowly easing back.

His arm stays wrapped around my middle like an anchor that I didn't know I needed. Too bad I'm feeling incredibly pissy right now and don't want it there.

"Would you prefer cremation or a burial?"

"There won't be anything left of me to bury. I'll already be up in flames by the time we're done in this position."

I peel his arm off and grit my teeth, letting up on the ball. "I don't need help right now."

"Alright. But you don't have to lean so far forward. Just enough that you can touch the ball to the ground."

"I've got it."

I refuse to look back at him. Not when I'm clearly feeling off. Maybe it's just Kye's lack of professionalism. This isn't something I'd be choosing to do today if it weren't for our contract, so the least she could do is focus and stop flirting with an engaged man.

Jamie moves back, and a moment later, Kye is clapping.

"Smile and laugh, guys. Here we go. Throw the ball back in three . . . two . . . one!"

I use more force than necessary as I paste on a smile and glance behind my shoulder. Jamie grunts, his grin wobbly as he cradles the ball I've just launched in his hands.

"Great! Now, Blakely, run at him and jump into his arms," Kye instructs, her camera in her face.

Jamie recovers quickly enough to shoot me a wink and hold the ball above his head. I narrow my eyes and palm my waist.

"Stop looking at me like that," I demand.

"Nope. Come here, wife. The ball is all yours. You know you want to send me on my ass."

"And why would I want that?"

"You tell me," he coos, waving the ball.

There isn't much distance between us, but I make the most of it. Clutching onto my frustration, I barrel toward him, the heels of my boots digging into the turf.

Excitement makes his eyes sparkle, the blue becoming lighter with every inch I erase between us. By the time I'm jumping, he's so, so close.

I know he won't drop me. The trust that erupts in my chest is almost as startling as the act of him abandoning the ball and expertly gripping my thighs, guiding them around his waist.

The strong expanse of his chest and hips keeps me steady as I engage my thigh muscles to hold myself up. His arms shift, one coiling around my back while the other holds my cheek in a lovers' embrace.

Kye's camera flashes and clicks with every photo she snaps.

She doesn't speak, doesn't give instructions, so I continue going with the flow.

"You're beautiful when you're jealous, Bandit," Jamie muses, his thumb learning the shape of my bottom lip.

"I wasn't jealous."

"I'm thinking of getting these photos blown up and put on the walls at home. Maybe in the locker room here too. Thoughts?" He switches topics without a fight, letting the jealousy thing go.

It's just another way he shows his kindness.

"What if they're ugly? Do you want the entire team to see them?"

"There's no better way to make sure nobody pops a boner in the showers than forcing them to look at my ugly mug on the wall."

My laugh is genuine, yanked from my chest. I fall into our act and run my fingers through the blond curls flopping over his forehead, forcing them back.

"It's impossible for you to be ugly, Jamie."

"You say the nicest things to me. I'm spoiled."

I roll my eyes. "Keep it up and I'll hang the photos myself."

"Yeah, that's my Bandit. I missed you."

25

Jamie

It still hasn't hit me.

The reporters are outside, stalking the venue for a chance to slip inside. Security is tight, and with the few members of the team, Graham, and Coach here, it should probably be even tighter.

Mom insisted on tying my tie, and as she stands in the back room with me, rolling her lips and sighing, I prepare for the words that I know are coming.

"If you're going to tell me to pull a runaway groom, I'll have to tell you not to waste your time, Ma."

"I'm not going to say that."

"Then what's brewing up in your head? You've rubbed your lips together so many times your lipstick is gone."

She finishes looping the tie and presses it against my chest. "I just want to make sure you still don't want to tell me the truth before going out there."

"I've already told you the truth."

"Don't play me for an idiot, Jamieson. I'm more perceptive than you think I am. And I know that you wouldn't have allowed Graham Wells to be at your wedding unless you were forced to. Those reporters outside are here for a reason, and it isn't to wish you good luck with your marriage."

Heaving a sigh, I step backward and focus on cuffing my shirt sleeves.

Mom follows, too stubborn to leave it alone. "Why aren't you telling me? If you're in trouble, I'm here to help you."

"I'm not in trouble. Please, let it go. I wouldn't be getting married if I didn't want to."

"I don't believe you."

I grab her shoulders, gently keeping her in place as I speak, voice strained. "Drop it, Mom. I'm getting married any minute now. There's no changing my mind or convincing me to tell you what you want to hear. I need you to support me right now."

"You're a good man, Jamieson," she whispers, finally relenting. "Maybe too good."

Will she still be saying that in two months when I have to tell everyone that I'm getting divorced?

It doesn't matter. Right now, I need to get out there and make good on my promise to the team. Things will get easier after that. When it's just me, Blakely, and Nate.

And a mountain of public responsibilities to make good on and events to attend. Photos to post and affection to display.

Our engagement photos were posted on Kye's website and within a few hours were shown on the TV broadcast of our last game. They're really good-looking photos, even with Blakely staring at me like she wanted to skin me alive.

"I love you, Ma," I say.

She hugs me tightly, squishing her face into my chest. "I love you, my sweet boy."

"Can we let everyone else back in here now?"

"I suppose," she says, palming the doorknob.

The moment she has the door open, Dad's stepping into the room and smiling at me. It doesn't reach his eyes, but instead of fighting me the way Mom tried, he keeps his worries and questions to himself.

When he moves close, it's to pull me into a tight embrace and speak low words of encouragement.

"If this marriage is real and important to you, Jamie, I need you to listen because you're going to go through shit with Blakely that is going to test you both every day. When I married your mom, I didn't have a fucking clue what I was doing, and I wish someone would have given me some advice. So, listen.

"You have to be patient and not cut each other off in the middle of an argument. Apologize the moment you realize you've done something wrong, and don't give excuses. Don't keep score. It's not about who's right or wrong—it's about finding a way forward together. Laugh with one another. Go on dates and buy her flowers on random Tuesdays. Living in the spotlight is hard, and your schedule as a professional athlete will keep you busy. You'll need to prioritize time together because life will always try to get in the way. When she's hurting, you shut up and offer her both words and comfort. And remember that love isn't just a feeling; it's a choice you make every single day."

Jesus fucking Christ.

I clutch his shoulders, gritting my teeth through the waves of emotion.

He's never given me advice like that. The fucker has been keeping it stored up for today, for my wedding, and I've gone and used it on something that won't last.

After a final squeeze, I release him and sniff, pretending I'm not burning to ash behind my ribs.

Oliver's lingering, and I point at him. "What did he say to you on your wedding day?"

"From your dripping eyes, I'd say pretty much what he told you," he mutters, narrowing his eyes on me.

Dad huffs. "I mixed it up a bit."

"As long as I got more advice than Oliver did."

"Why would you want to have more advice? Because you need it and I don't?" my brother asks, smug as all hell.

"We should get out there, honey," Mom cuts in before we can get really into it, touching my arm.

I tip my chin, making an "I'm watching you" gesture to Oliver before letting Mom guide me out of the room and into the hallway.

Jaxon, Chase, and Zach are already in their seats in the church with Graham and Coach. My cousins, aunts, and uncles aren't here, and that doesn't sit well with me. It's what had to happen, though.

My teammates being here over my family was just another piece of the puzzle Graham wanted clicked into place. He's the one who runs this show, even if Blakely and I were given the small part of being the ones to choose a few aesthetic aspects of today.

I wish I could talk to her right now. If I'm this tense, I can't imagine how she's feeling. Nate being there with her must be helping, even a little.

Oliver's wedding was similar yet completely different than mine. It's the same walk and wait, but instead of a full bridal party at my back, it's me and Mom with my brother trickling in behind us. Nova and Avery are already sitting, and I know Nate's with Blakely, being the one to walk her down to me.

To the outside eye, this is as real of a wedding ceremony as any.

"Ready?" Mom asks, curling her arm around mine.

I nod, and the music starts on cue, a slow orchestral song filling the church. My feet move on their own, carrying me down the aisle toward where the minister waits. Nerves tingle beneath my skin, and I focus too much on pretending they're not there.

Once Mom kisses my cheek and takes her seat beside Dad in the audience, I zone out. There are so many things going on at once, each one too noticeable. The change of song, shifting of guests, and flashes from where Kye kneels off to the side of the first row.

My heart lurches into my throat, thumping offbeat when I

realize everyone's standing for Blakely. Forgoing a rehearsal was a stupid move that I make note not to repeat the next time I'm here.

That thought poofs into thin air. They all do.

One look at Blakely and my knees grow wobbly. I have half a mind to wipe my sweaty palms on my thighs and gawk unabashedly.

She's elegant, a regal goddess in a long, silky, sleeved white gown. Her hair is twisted into a braided updo, and the pale nude colour of her lips is so unlike the usual peachy shade I'm used to. I can make out every curve of her waist and hips, and the way the fabric bunches beneath her chest draws my eyes there and refuses to let them go for seconds too long.

My throat's gone dry and tight. It's impossible to cough to clear it.

She's gripping Nate's hand where it rests on her forearm, and those deep, panicked green eyes are on me, begging for help. I release a puff of air and smile, extending my hand long before she's reached the altar.

Her dress swishes on the ground and trails behind her as she closes the rest of the distance between us and grabs my hand like it's the only lifeline she has. Nate watches me for a few moments, hiding the threat in his gaze well. I don't back down from it and tip my chin in silent agreement.

Blakely moves to stand across from me and takes my other hand, gripping them both.

"You're gorgeous, Bandit," I murmur.

Her eyelids lower, a tiny smile curving her pale lips. "Thank you. Your suit isn't pink."

"Is that supposed to be a compliment?"

Some of the fear in her expression drifts just enough to be replaced with her signature annoyance.

"If I tell you how good you look, we won't get out of the church door with your inflated head," she mutters quietly.

By the choking noise coming from where my family is sitting, it seems she wasn't quiet enough.

I let loose a breathy laugh. "Do I at least look good enough to be up here with you?"

"Better than."

"Works for me, baby."

The minister clears his throat and starts to speak, welcoming everyone to the ceremony. It's hard to concentrate on the specific words when I've got Blakely in front of me. Shit, it's hard to do anything but think of how beautiful she looks in all white.

Time moves fast. Words are spoken from beside me as I lose myself in the flecks of gold and brown in her green eyes and the tiny hairs above the arch of her brow. Her lashes move up and down, so black against the dark makeup smudged across her eyelid.

I lean forward, curious how many more lashes will appear with less distance. She releases my hand and circles my wrist, tugging lightly enough to appear nonchalant about it.

It's dead silent as I look to the minister, then the crowd, and finally at my bride. She's rolling her lips, the corners of her eyes crinkled.

"You're supposed to be repeating our vows," she whispers.

Seeing her amused is more than worth making a fool out of myself.

With a glance at the minister, I ask, "Can you give me a do-over?"

He doesn't share the same sense of humour as we do, clearly. With a straight face, he repeats his words, and I don't miss a beat before saying them to Blakely.

She does the same, and then we're saying I do.

The two syllables melt off my tongue like butter. Maybe it's the nerves or the excitement that's building up inside of me out of nowhere, but I'm practically buzzing.

"You may now kiss the bride."

It's my wife who I seek approval from. And I get it when she takes a confident step into my arms.

Without another moment of hesitation, I have her face in my hands and our mouths a breath apart. She shuts her eyes softly, and I delve a hand into her hair, taking one final look at her like this before finally kissing her.

My thoughts jumble before becoming clearer than they've ever been. Kissing Blakely is a mix of all my favourite things. It fills me with excitement and adrenaline yet carries the ability to steady me before I get too carried away. Like a parachute on your back while diving out of a plane.

A safe danger.

The perfect paradox.

I trap a moan in my chest and coax her lips apart just enough to steal a small taste of her before forcing myself back. She plants a hand on my chest and releases a shuddered breath, keeping her eyes closed.

Everyone's clapping, but it's quiet where I've gotten lost in my mind. My dad's advice is right there, repeating lowly. And . . . and I think I could be content with following every piece of it with Blakely.

26

Blakely

JAMIE KEEPS AN ARM ANCHORED AROUND ME AS WE FOLLOW HIS parents to the exit of the church. A group of men in black suits and earpieces have formed a circle around all of us. It seems like a bit much, honestly.

Being with Jamie hasn't been nearly as media frenzied as I expected. It's not like there haven't been headlines and the odd reporter stopping us for a quick few questions here and there, but it hasn't been scary.

My feet are already aching in my heels so badly that I lean against my new husband to try and alleviate some of the pressure on them. He hitches me up against him, muscle bulging.

"Five minutes, Bandit," he swears.

"I'll be fine. Is all this necessary?"

"All of what?"

"The bodyguards. Do people really care this much about our wedding?" It sounds more naïve out loud.

Avery leans forward from her place behind me. "I heard that they had to block off the entrance to the parking lot."

I blink, glancing up at Jamie. He shoots me a wink.

"Graham?" I whisper.

"Yes. Just stay close to me, and don't fight the guards when they try to help. It should be well managed."

It makes sense now. The more people that are here to take pictures, the more publicity we get.

I swallow. "Okay."

Tyler tucks his wife beneath his arm and turns to lay a warning glare on the guard at Gracie's other side, a dare to let anything happen to her. I don't have to look behind me to know that Oliver's doing the same thing.

Instead of threatening the guard moving stiffly at my side, Jamie simply shifts me directly in front of him and drapes both of his arms from my shoulders down my front. With Nate hovering on my left, I try and relax.

The church doors open, and I jump at the volume of the voices outside. My heart lodges itself in my throat as I flinch, and Jamie tightens his hold.

"When will the photos of the ceremony be available?"

"Where is the rest of the Pythons team?"

"Will this marriage distract you for the rest of the season?"

"Are you with Jamie for the money?"

I narrow my eyes at that question. It's impossible to pick the speaker out of the crowd.

Three SUVs are waiting up ahead, and like a well-oiled machine, the security team splits into three. Oliver, Avery, and Nova are ushered into the last car while Tyler and Gracie take the middle one.

I hold my breath when Gracie's guard shifts to open her door and a reporter slips through an opening. The words said are swallowed by the rest of the ones around us, but from Tyler's snarling lip and the way he shoves the reporter a foot back, it's clear they weren't the nicest.

He helps Gracie into the SUV, and I blow out a breath before allowing Jamie to do the same to me. I know his father was an NHL defenseman for almost two decades, which must make it hard to deal with the media. The fact they're still concerned with him goes to show how successful he was.

"Go first, Jamie," Nate pushes.

I stare at the open door from my seat. Jamie's trying to shove my brother in first, but Nate shakes his head, trying to back up but hitting the bodyguard instead.

"No. I'm the last one inside always. Never you," Jamie scolds softly.

Nate shoves into the back row while Jamie takes the seat beside me. It's too hard to hide my approving smile as he releases a breath and squeezes my knee.

He's becoming too hard to ignore, as if I'd want to in the first place.

"I'LL BE UPSTAIRS if you need me!"

Nathan takes off ahead of us and enters the code for the security alarm before swinging open the front door and strolling inside. I stare at the empty doorway for a beat too long, drawing Jamie's attention.

"Are you waiting to be carried inside, wife?"

Still in my dress, I smooth a hand down my silk-covered hip. "Are you offering?"

He bends and sweeps me into his arms without a second thought. I latch onto his shoulders, both terrified and impressed. I'm big-boned and not weightless, so it's no surprise that the ease of his movements and controlled strength he uses to carry me up the sidewalk turn my breaths shallow.

"Are you impressed yet?" he teases, taking the porch steps slowly, for my benefit, I'm sure.

I hardly jostle in his arms, only my legs swaying where they hang. The break from standing is appreciated, and the lack of throbbing in the soles of my feet while he carries me only goes to show why I didn't want to wear these damn heels in the first place.

They're the same shoes I wore while trying on dresses at the very expensive, very posh shop Gracie brought us to on Wednesday. Avery convinced me to buy them, claiming that Jamie's credit card was weeping from lack of use.

The white satin heels came home with me, and still, I debated wearing my safe pair of flats instead.

Once Jamie moves us inside the house, he shuts the door with his elbow and continues walking, showing no sign of setting me down.

I'm too tired to argue.

As he turns into the kitchen, I rest my cheek on his chest for just a second. Only to fully enjoy the princess treatment I'm getting.

"Are you hungry?" he asks softly.

I hadn't realized that we didn't have dinner. With only a wedding ceremony, it wasn't even a thought in my mind until now.

He stops walking and, with gentle movements, sets me on my feet. "I'll order pizza."

"I can make something," I argue, already bypassing him to pop open one of the fridge doors.

He's there a second later, standing so close behind me that I can feel every lift and fall of his wide chest.

"You're not cooking tonight. As much as I love your food, we just got married. I'm pretty sure it's against the law to spend our wedding night in the kitchen."

"Most weddings have catered receptions, Jamie. We didn't have one of those."

"Ordering pizza counts as catering. Or we could get something else. Anything, as long as you don't have to cook."

"Mexican, then. Tacos."

"Tacos it is. But first, we have to finish getting married."

I furrow my brows and look at him over my shoulder. "We're already married."

"Not without a first dance, we aren't."

I squeak as he takes me by the waist and spins me around. My feet ache with the movement, but the pain isn't distracting enough to keep me from laughing at his antics.

"I don't think that's how it works," I say.

He doesn't back down. "It is for us."

Fighting him feels like a waste of time. I slowly take his hand and hold his shoulder, falling into the easy dance at the slow pace he's set.

"I was being serious earlier, you know?" Jamie asks, tightening his arm where he has it wrapped around my back.

Having shed his suit jacket out in the car, he sways me around the kitchen in a white button-up with the sleeves rolled up his arms. Even his tie is loose, draping over his neck.

I focus on not tripping over my dress while following his lead. "About what? Having two left feet? Because you're clearly a better dancer than I am, liar."

"Okay, I may have exaggerated a bit there, but no, that's not what I was talking about."

"Go on."

He tugs, bringing our bodies closer while looking down at me with that stupid, sexy smirk of his.

"You look gorgeous."

"You're not sleeping in my bed tonight, even with all the compliments."

His laugh is deep and quiet, stroking invisible fingers down my neck. "I know. You'll be sleeping in mine instead."

"Oh? That's the first I'm hearing of this."

"Well, there wouldn't exactly be a lot of sleeping," he purrs, pressing his cheek to my temple, increasing how fast we move.

"Were you planning on telling me about this before we got to your bed, or am I just supposed to sharpen my weapons and have them at the ready?"

"I'd prefer no sharp weapons in bed, but for you, I'll make an exception."

Even through his teasing, I don't freak out.

Somewhere along the way, I've grown to trust him completely. If I didn't, the mere mention of being in bed with him would have had me kicking and screaming.

It's the opposite now. I might not have stolen any more midnight snoozes in his bed when he isn't home, but over the past few nights leading up to today, I've lingered with him on the couch after dinner and even invited him to Nate's football practice this coming week.

Our nightly dinners together have become a constant, and I don't see that changing anytime soon. Cooking whatever I want, whenever I want to because there are ingredients in the fridge and two men who could eat three portions of everything has sparked the flame in my chest that has grown stagnant the past five years.

There have been so many things that have made being paraded around like a show pony worth it, and every day, I'm a bit more grateful for saying yes.

A friendship with Jamie was the last thing I expected but is now the one that I'm the most scared to lose.

"How much longer do we have to dance? The fridge is going to start dinging at us for leaving its door open," I muse, palming his shoulder blade.

The cool light from inside the fridge streams through the kitchen, casting shadows of us on the walls. With the sun nearly set outside the window, the tiny light is all we've got.

Jamie hums low in his throat, making his chest vibrate with the strength of it. "Antsy to get into my bed, wife?"

"What would you do if I said yes?" I coo, dragging my hand to rest low on his back, teasing the waist of his slacks. When I tip my head to meet his gleaming blue eyes, I make a show of fluttering my lashes. "Lift me in your big, strong arms again and carry me upstairs?"

"Is that how you want to get around from now on, Blakely? In my arms?"

"What good are your muscles if you don't use them to make my life easier?"

"And your life is so hard right now? Dancing with your husband in our kitchen, knowing that I'm in awe of how stunning you are?"

"It's not *our* kitchen."

My palms are clammy, and I know he can tell. The further his smirk stretches, the more I want to prove that his win at his parents' house was a fluke. He's too confident, and being the one to bring him down a few pegs fills me with a thrilling sense of excitement.

With the knowledge that I'm entering a war that could end very badly for me, I press my chest against his, fully aware of the tight corset doing a million favours for my tits. They swell against the neckline of my dress, and with him distracted, I take control of our swaying, spinning us around. His back hits the fridge door, and it closes with a bang, casting us in darkness.

The black in his eyes swells as he drops his gaze between us and bravely cups the top curve of my ass, hitching my hips forward to meet his.

"You're playing with fire," he warns, voice low and throaty.

Pressed together like this, it's easy to feel his cock, hard and rigid in his slacks. I'd take that as a win if I wasn't positive that while lost in the need to show him up, I've grown wet in the lewd panties I put on for tonight.

"I'm not the one afraid of getting burned," I whisper, moving my touch around to his hip. "Are you scared of having to tap out?"

He's hard everywhere, firm and strong, and touching him like this only reminds me of that. It's dangerous to feel him beneath my fingers and know that if I just shifted a little further, I'd break every single barrier left between us.

Cross a line that's not meant to be crossed.

Jamie wets his lips and curls his fingers in the silk stretched around my ass. "Do you think I'm scared, Blakely? Because all I need is the slightest signal, and I'll tear this dress to shreds."

"It's expensive," I argue on a wobbly breath.

"I don't care."

He's too committed to our game. I genuinely believe that he would rip this dress off with his bare hands if I told him he could.

My chest heaves, nipples tightening to points in my corset. Desire pools between my legs, and as if he's reached inside my brain and flipped a switch, I'm debating just how far I could take this and get away with it.

With a cover in place, I'm brave, confident.

I repeat those words in my mind as I drop my hold on him and twirl the two ends of his tie around my fists. With a yank, he's leaning into me, our noses bumping.

"Tell me what you'd do once you got my dress off," I coax.

He curls a finger beneath my chin and tips it back before ghosting his lips across mine. "In how much detail?"

"All of it."

"In the kitchen?"

I pause, searching his eyes for the reason behind the question. The meaning of it is obvious, even to someone who hasn't been asked out by literally anyone in years. But if he's hinting at going upstairs with me, it doesn't fit the rules of our stupid competition. Even if we didn't exactly go over what we could and couldn't do, this doesn't fit in the imaginary guidelines.

So . . . does he want me to come with him for real? Outside of what we're doing right now and his teasing earlier?

"Pretend I didn't say that," he adds, his eyes flicking between mine, reading every question in my head without needing to hear them.

Relief rolls through me. Jamie is the only man I've ever allowed to get close enough to know me this well. And the way he trusts me to make decisions on where my boundaries are and when I'm willing to stretch one is comforting in a way I'll never be able to explain.

"Just tell me, Pretty Boy."

"Not yet."

My brow goes up at the same time I'm being lifted off the ground again. In a blink, I'm sitting on the island, and Jamie's collecting the hem of my dress in his hands, lifting it to pool in a pile at my knees.

With the tight fabric out of the way, he fits himself between my legs and grips the edge of the counter in both hands, leaning forward.

"Better?" I coo, planting my palms on the marble behind me, my head rolling to the side.

Tracing his eyes down the length of my body and then back up again, he swallows. "Much better."

"Get to it, then. I'm getting bored."

"Bored," he echoes, gliding his fingers beneath my right knee, digging them into the sensitive skin. "We can't have that."

"No, we can't."

There's no point trying to hide every visceral reaction he yanks from me. Not when my skin pebbles with goosebumps and my breath catches with the first sweep of his palm around my calf.

"What do you like, Blakely?"

"In terms of what?"

His grin is pure, filthy sin. "Do you prefer a tongue or fingers?"

Fuck, I'm light-headed.

"Nobody would choose fingers over a tongue."

"Mm, you've got a point."

I release the tension in my thighs and let them fall open, subtly inviting him closer. He cups my calf and guides it behind his back, hitching my thigh around his hip. The move opens me up further, and he fills the gap until our middles touch.

"Which do you prefer?" I ask, desperate to know more.

"Giving? That depends."

"Don't be coy." My words are sharp, impatient.

His eyes drop to where we touch. To the thick bulge of him and the strained silk dress hiding my panties.

"It depends on who I'm with," he reveals softly.

I curl my fingers, digging my nails into my palms to keep from reaching up and strangling him for his roundabout answers.

"You're with me, Jamie. It would be me."

Lightning flashes in his eyes. I attempt to prepare myself for his next statement, but it's worthless.

He pushes all the way into my space, demanding I hand over every inch of myself to him. I'd do it if I wasn't still somewhat in control of my mind.

"With my wife, I'd do both. First, I'd use my mouth. Drag kisses up your thighs to your hip bones. Have a feeling you like to use your hands, so I'd be expecting fingers in my hair, tugging as you try guiding me to your pussy. Am I right, baby? Yeah, exactly like that."

Soft curls slip between my fingers as I blink and take in the sight of my hand in his hair. I'm too high on his words to stop playing with it.

"You'd open these legs for me, wide enough that I can settle on my knees and toss them over my shoulders. I bet you moan when you're being pleasured. Not too loud at the start, but like with your hand in my hair, you like to lead. Every sound you'd make would be to encourage me, to tell me if I'm making you feel good or if I can do better," he rasps.

I roll my lips, battling letting loose one of those very sounds. He's too in tune with me to let that go, and once he starts to smirk, I push forward and grip his shirt with both hands. The buttons on a fancy shirt are sturdy, but when I yank on the fabric hard enough, they still scatter.

He stares at me and then down at his exposed chest before

bracing himself on the counter and groaning. My heart gallops, winning against him becoming a hovering possibility—

"Slap me, Blakely. Fucking slap me or kick me, but I need to touch you. Please let me touch you," he pleads, the strain in his tone breaking my resolve.

I nod frantically and shove at the shoulders of his shirt, needing it off. He helps, shrugging it down his arms before palming my inner thigh, offering me another chance to shove him off.

"Fingers, Jamie," I demand, reaching out to feel his flexing abdomen. "Give me your fingers."

The feral glint in his stare intensifies the burn in my blood as he reaches between my legs and smooths a single knuckle down my seam. Jaw clenching, he squeezes his eyes shut and rests his forehead against mine.

"Do you need it gentle?"

I scrape my nails down the middle ridge of his six-pack. "Even if I did, I wouldn't want that right now. Just fuck me with your fingers, Jamie."

He opens his eyes and watches me while he pulls my panties to the side and parts my lips with a finger. I hiss a breath and lurch off the countertop.

"Was trying to beat me what made this pussy so wet? Or has my wife just been craving her husband?"

The pressure of his finger sliding inside of me, stretching and claiming, is euphoric. I dig my nails into his stomach and whine, needing more.

I'm barely used to one finger when another pushes inside. I hold his shoulder, nodding when he pauses, seeming to realize the same thing.

"Don't stop. Don't stop. I'm good," I whimper.

He releases a choked-off noise and pushes them the rest of the way in. "Yeah, you are. You're doing so good, baby. Letting me stretch this tight pussy around my fingers."

They part inside of me, forcing me to stretch wider before

they're retreating. Jamie keeps his tempo quick but controlled as he glides them back inside and brings his thumb to my clit.

I cry out, and he covers my mouth with his palm, a smug smile curling his lips. I bare my teeth, but he can't see.

"Shh, Bandit. Your brother is upstairs," he soothes, petting my pussy in slow, taunting strokes.

His warning falls on deaf ears, so he keeps his hand in place while thrusting his fingers and curling them deep. I've lost this game of ours *so* badly. He'll never let me live it down, but at least I'll get something out of it. I'll make sure it's worth the defeat.

It's been so long since I've had a man's hands on me, let alone between my legs, that I'm already bordering on an orgasm. With every roll of his thumb around my clit and piston of his fingers inside my pussy, I'm teetering over the line. One last shove and I'll topple.

"Shit, Blakely. If you squeeze me any tighter, I won't be able to get my fingers out," he groans.

I try to speak, but my words are muffled.

A dirty laugh fans over my nose. "You wouldn't mind that, would you, filthy girl? Having my fingers stroking this pussy day in and day out? I could settle for that life."

He picks up speed, making me gush all over his knuckles, the sounds of his thrusts echoing through the kitchen. I hold my breath and tense up seconds before pleasure explodes in my groin and shoots through my limbs.

"Fuck. That's it, baby. Just like that," he coaxes.

Lungs screaming, I drop my head and ride his fingers where they remain buried deep, waiting for my comedown.

By the time I'm fully conscious again, he's pulling them free and bringing his hand to rest at his side. My immediate reaction to all of this is to lean forward against his chest and catch my breath, hoping he'll wrap me in his arms.

The second . . . the second is the stronger of the two. It's the one that sets me into motion.

Stiffening, I let go of him and slip my dress back down over my thighs. Embarrassment is hot and heavy in my chest, taking complete control of my thoughts and actions.

"Guess that means you win," I ramble, sliding off the counter and facing the opposite side of the room so he can't see how hot my cheeks are burning.

You're a desperate fool, Blakely.

My embarrassment takes a dive into mortification, and I immediately make a beeline for the exit. Jamie doesn't follow me, and I blow out a grateful breath.

He won, after all.

Why would he chase me?

27

Jamie

My dick's still harder than a steel pipe when I open the door for the delivery guy and take the bag of Mexican food to the kitchen. It's been half an hour since Blakely ran upstairs, and besides the creaking of the floors above me, I haven't heard a peep.

After dropping the bag onto the counter opposite to the one I finger fucked my wife on top of, I sort out the food on three plates.

Nate's yet to come downstairs again, but he seemed fine before disappearing. Tired and overwhelmed, sure. My family is a lot for anyone to handle, and even if there wasn't a long reception, the ceremony was still busy. The media circus outside didn't help, I'm sure.

The kid handled the cameras well. He stopped flinching at the flashes after the first few and even smiled a couple of times on the way to the SUV. Questions were thrown at all of us, and he did exactly as we were instructed by Sadie before the wedding and didn't answer any of them.

I take two of the plates in my hands and head upstairs. Nate's room is the first door at the top of the stairs, and with the door closed, I hesitate to knock.

Concerned with the lack of food he's eaten today, I push forward and rap my knuckles against the door. There's movement on the other side of it immediately before it's pulled open.

"Hey," Nate greets with a lazy smile.

"Hi, buddy. We didn't eat much today, so I ordered some food. Hope you like tacos."

He nods and takes the plate I extend to him. "I love them. Thanks."

There are low voices coming from where his phone sits propped by a pillow on his bed, and I squint to try and make out the video on the screen.

"Is that *Madden*?" I ask.

He glances back at his phone and nods. "I watch gameplays sometimes. Trying to build my knowledge for when I can buy my own Xbox to play."

My heart tugs, and without being asked to come inside, I step past him and search the room for a TV. When I don't find one anywhere, I'm spinning to face him, lips turned down.

"Let me get a TV in here for you, and we can move one of the Xboxes in here. You can take the one from my room if you want. It's only a couple months old, and I haven't had the time to download anything on it yet. For the record, you can play games downstairs or anywhere you want here. I have the last ten *Madden* games in the cabinet beneath the living room TV."

"Wait, for real? I didn't want to touch your stuff without asking first. I was going to soon, but . . ."

"There's no need to ask now, Nate. You're good to play whenever you want. At least, until your sister gives you shit for it."

He laughs gently. "Okay. Thank you, Jamie."

"No worries. You're a good kid, and I know your sister appreciates you a whole lot. You deserve a break from time to time."

"Did Lake ask you to come to practice with us this week? It's no biggy if you can't. Since the Pythons don't play till

Saturday, I was hoping you'd have the time," he rambles nervously.

"She did. Of course I'll come. Anytime you want me there and I can make it, you've got another fan in the stands. You've got my word."

Pride swells inside of me when he grins wide enough to flash both rows of his slightly crooked teeth. He's a better teenager than I was at his age, and everyone who knows him has Blakely to thank for that. I have no doubt that she's kept him on the straight and narrow throughout every hardship they've faced.

I wander a bit further into his room. "Can I ask you something?"

"About Blakely?"

My laugh comes out clunky. "How did you know?"

"I'm fifteen, not blind. I know that you're into her."

"Woah, I didn't say that."

"Like I said, I'm not blind, Jamie. Why do you think I came up here as soon as we got home?"

I pause, nerves pricking at my skin. "We're not really together. I know it might look like that to you right now, but that's because we're playing a part. Your sister wants to beat my ass more often than not."

"And? You don't look scared by that."

"Fair enough," I mutter, swiping a hand through my hair. All I do is remind myself of the way Blakely dragged her nails through it. "Your sister is incredible, kid. It's just not smart to mix pleasure with work."

Fucking idiot. I can still smell her pussy on my fingers through the soap I used to clean them. It doesn't get more mixed than that.

Nathan is smarter than I originally gave him credit for. He's not buying a word out of my mouth. I don't blame him. I've done a terrible job of selling the bullshit I'm spewing.

I was already interested in his sister, and after tonight, I'm screwed. By the end of our agreement, I'm going to be trying to keep her. I don't need a flash into the future to see that happening.

"We'll see," Nate says with a shrug, eyeing the second plate I brought. "Is that for her?"

"Yeah. Anything I should avoid giving her?"

"No, but I'd add some of those hot sauce pouches you have in the fridge. She loves spicy food."

With a clap on his shoulder, I retreat through his room. "Thanks, Nate. If you need anything, just let me know."

"Will do."

"And seriously, use the Xbox and buy yourself some games. Everything's hooked up to my card, so go crazy. This is your home too, and I'd like it if you took advantage of everything I have to offer."

He stares deeply at me for a moment, rolling around something in his mind before speaking. "Why does it matter to you so much if we view this place as our home?"

"Because I like to think of us as a family. And for as long as you're here, I want you to grow comfortable enough to view us the same way," I admit.

His expression loosens, emotion filling his eyes. "I do. I mean, it makes sense. We're a found family."

As someone who's been surrounded by both found and blood family my entire life, hearing him say that nearly takes me out at the knees. Both variations of family carry the same exact weight in my heart. They always will.

I have to leave before Nate's subjected to my ugly crying face. But I don't take another step toward the door without meeting his eyes and saying, "Damn right, we are."

And that's that. Nate takes his plate to his bed and hunkers down to finish watching his video while I leave, closing his door behind me.

Instead of going to Blakely's room like I'd planned, I go back downstairs. The hot sauce packets Nate mentioned have been in the fridge for way too long to offer his sister. So, I pour some of the bottled stuff into a small bowl and add it to her plate.

Before heading up the stairs again, I pull my Notes app up on my phone and add *loves spicy food* to the list I've been keeping titled Things Blakely Likes. It's the twin to my Things To Learn About Blakely one.

Her door is still shut when I make my way back upstairs. With two heavy plates of food in my hands, I use my foot to knock.

She isn't as quick to answer the door as her brother, almost like she's trying to punish me by making me wait. I quirk a smile at that.

When she finally peeks at me through the crack she's opened in the doorway, her eyes are bare of makeup, and only half of her hair is down out of her braided updo.

"Hey," she mutters.

I lift the plates into her line of vision. "Still hungry?"

"Is that hot sauce?"

"It sure is. If you let me in, you can have it."

She narrows her eyes. "I would have let you in without the bribe."

"Can't be too sure," I tease.

The air is fizzling with nerves, both hers and mine. There's no telling how we'll be around each other after what happened downstairs, but I really, really hope we don't lose the progress we've made.

"What kind of tacos did you get?" she asks, opening the door for me to come in.

Before Blakely moved in, there were so many empty bedrooms in this house that I stopped caring to fill them with furniture. The only person who ever slept over was Jax, and that's when we were both too drunk and fell asleep on the couch. The spare bed only collected dust.

It wasn't until I ran into Blakely at the sports shop that I put in a massive furniture order online. I'm pretty sure I blacked out while imputing my credit card info because the next thing I knew, a moving truck was at the neighbourhood gate, waiting for instructions.

Blakely hasn't added much of anything to the space. The hideous bag that she was keeping on the dresser with her clothes isn't there anymore, as if she's finally unpacked.

Hovering near the closet door, I drop my eyes to the food. "Beef, chicken, and a couple of shrimp ones, if you're into fish. If not, I'll eat them."

"I could have made tacos. You didn't need to waste money ordering them."

"Don't start with me tonight, Bandit. It's impossible to waste money on you. Just sit down and eat with me."

"Maybe I don't want dinner company," she grumbles, taking her plate.

"If you didn't, you wouldn't have let me in."

Without another pointless argument, she sits near the headboard and rests her plate on her lap. I join her and unwrap my first taco, taking a massive bite to fill the silence. Unlike Nate's room, there's a flat-screen hung on the wall opposite her bed.

"How do you feel about hearing people chew? Because if you're against it, we need to put something on in the background. A movie or something," I suggest after swallowing.

She slides a nail under the sticker keeping her taco wrapped, fixing her attention on her plate and not me.

"The remote is on the nightstand."

Narrowly avoiding pouncing on it like a weirdo desperate for the chance to weasel my way into having more time with her, I discard my taco on my plate and lean off the bed to grab the remote.

Once I've turned the TV on, I steal a look at her and ignore my growling stomach, knowing what I need to do before taking another bite.

"Do you want some help with your hair?" I ask, already setting my plate down where the remote was.

She finally looks up from her plate, meeting my gaze. "You want to take a thousand bobby pins out of my hair for me?"

"Why not? I'm sure we can make it count as our version of the groom taking the bride's dress off on their wedding night." I make a show of looking over her body and the baggy sweatpants and sweatshirt she's changed into. "Since you've already done that for me."

A crack of a smile. "Fine. But I'm eating while you do it. *And* I'm choosing the movie."

"For the record, I love a good romcom." Lowering a hand to her shoulder, I give a slight push forward. "Shift and make a bit of room for me, baby."

"You shouldn't call me that," she mutters but moves forward, opening the spot behind her for me to slip into.

The headboard is stiff against my back, but once I've got my arms wrapped around her front and her sitting between my legs, it doesn't matter. She's stiff as I straighten my legs out along hers.

"It fits you," I say, palming her knees.

"Stop talking."

I choke on a laugh and kiss the back of her ear before pulling at the first pin in her hair. It's clear we're not going to be talking about what happened in the kitchen. At least not tonight.

Maybe that's for the best.

It was only one time. There is still a long way to go in our marriage, and having things turn awkward now will only make it harder to do what we need to.

Is what we're doing right now all that bad, anyway? Maybe it's better to leave a good thing be. For now, it's not hurting anyone.

28

Blakely

"Are you sure I'm allowed to be at the stadium with you?" I ask, hovering at the entrance, Jamie at my side.

"You've got a VIP pass around your neck and one of the best players in the CFL on your arm. Yeah, I'm sure," he drawls confidently, hooking a finger beneath the black lanyard around my neck and stroking my collarbone.

"What am I even supposed to do while you're at practice? Snoop? I don't know if Graham would appreciate that very much."

He releases my lanyard and opens the door for me. I sneak a look at the two reporters chatting by the entrance to the parking lot, and he follows my eyes, spotting them. They notice our staring and turn our way.

We've gotten pretty lucky so far this week with not having any pre-scheduled outings, but it's only a matter of time before that changes. My guess is that's what I'm supposed to be doing here today. Why else would Jamie be so dead set on me joining him while he's at practice other than to parade me around?

Well, or to try and make me lose my goddamn mind by forcing me to watch him run around and get all sweaty again.

"You have such little faith in me, Bandit. I've got plans for you. Just be patient, hmm?" he purrs.

"You should know by now that I'm not patient."

The flash of desire in his bright eyes is as much of a reminder of our wedding night as I can handle.

"Oh, I know. I remember that quite well."

When I take a step past him, he's dropping his hand and ghosting the back of it across my ass.

I whip my head to stare at him, and he grins before leaning down to steal a kiss for the reporters right here in the doorway. It's the first one since our wedding, and I'm just as sucked into it this time as I was then.

His lips are so soft and patient despite the sharp hunger that passes between us. Without pushing, he encourages my lips to part and guides us backward. His tongue glides along my bottom lip at the same time my back hits the door.

It's so easy to tune out the world with Jamie. His energy is captivating, and with the bleeding heart in his chest, it's impossible not to carve a special place in your soul just for him.

I've never experienced such a draw to someone before. Such an overwhelming desire to simply give in and let him take care of me. My heart screams that I wouldn't regret it, but my mind and plain old-fashioned inability to give my heart to someone are always quick to slap me with reality.

Still, I can't physically pull myself away from him, and he's too aware of that. He knows the moment he touches me, I'm putty in his arms, yet he hasn't once used that to take advantage.

Jamie Bateman is a good man.

The reminder melts me until I'm clinging onto his arms and brushing my chest against the strong expanse of his. His ability to affect me so intensely should be studied. But the question is, if I was offered a cure, would I even take it?

The answer is glaringly obvious when I curl my fingers in the hair at his nape and tug him closer, intensifying the kiss all on my own.

His answering groan shoots right between my legs to where I'm wet and aching. I trap a noise of my own and gently dig my teeth into his bottom lip, trying like hell to gain some sort of power back here.

Before I can gain even an inch of it, we're being interrupted by a low clearing of a throat. I'm only half in my head because instead of jumping back, I relax in the arms that automatically find a place around my waist.

"Would you mind answering a few questions before practice, Jamie?"

Jamie's arms tighten around me, the air around us sharpening with his annoyance. I lean back to stare up at him when I register his emotions, so unused to seeing him bluntly showing this one.

The tick in his tight jaw is obvious without a beard to hide it. With his swollen lips parted and downturned, it's like he's making a conscious effort not to snap at whoever his guy is.

Slowly, he shelves his frustration and warms his expression. I notice every single twitch of his brow and feature that's been lifted a bit too high or pulled too tight that gives away his façade.

Meeting the antsy gaze of the singular reporter, he tips his chin. "Yeah, Bobby. What do you have for me?"

We move out of the doorway, letting the door shut with a gust of air against our backs. I interlock our fingers, and he immediately starts twirling my rings.

Ready with his recorder in his hand, the Bobby guy grins at Jamie and spares me half a glance. "I hear congratulations are in order for you two."

"Yeah, man. Blakely did us all a favour and married me before I got caught making a fool of myself begging her to agree. I've never been happier," Jamie declares, continuing to twirl my ring.

"I'm sure many people are happy to hear that. The better you play out there, the better it is for all the Pythons fans. Which, speaking of the fans, should they be nervous that you might not be completely focused on the game now that you're so freshly married? I assume you've been very busy as newlyweds."

I bristle, and Jamie's palm grows cold in my hold. His grin has a serrated edge, but he keeps it classy while I'm struggling to keep my tongue between my teeth.

"I'd say that it's actually the opposite. Blakely loves the game nearly as much as I do. Her passion is one of the first things that drew me to her when we met. For guys in this sort of career, it's almost second nature to write off ordinary fans of the sport as potential romantic partners out of fear of something unauthentic, but that's not the case at all. At least it wasn't for me. My wife is the first to lay it out straight for me when it comes to both my gameplay and any stupid thing I do or say off the field. To be honest, I think players should be less hesitant to make a move on the beautiful woman they notice in the stands during a game." He drops his chin and catches my waiting gaze. "You never know if she could be the one, and you're risking losing your one chance to have her."

My belly flutters, the reporter disappearing. A dimple in Jamie's cheek pops as he tips the corner of his mouth up high. Somehow, when he's smiling like that, he becomes even better-looking than normal.

"What do you think, Blakely? As far as I know, you haven't spoken much to the media. Is there a reason for that?" Bobby asks.

It annoys me that I have to look away from Jamie. What the fuck is that about? I seriously need to get a grip.

"I haven't felt the need to. I'm not here to prove myself to anyone," I say.

"You don't think so? What about to those who think you've chosen a great moment to hook yourself to a player whose value has skyrocketed over the past season?"

Due to my lack of time on social media, I actually didn't know that was being said about me. It doesn't surprise me, but I would think that Jamie would have told me that by now. Or Sadie, at least. Maybe they don't think it's a concern.

"Jamie could be worth nothing in this league and I would still be here beside him. So, I don't really care what anyone is saying. And I think it's pretty damaging and discouraging to other women out there to spew a narrative like that. Just because a woman likes football, or any sport for that matter, doesn't mean that she should be pushed aside because she's believed to be a gold digger or a fake," I rant, skin prickling with words I'm not allowing myself to say.

Jamie blows out a low whistle, flashing heart eyes at me in a way that makes my cheeks throb with a blush. "You see now, Bobby? How on earth was I supposed to let her turn me down?"

The reporter does seem a bit surprised that I was so blunt, but he's quick to recover. "Thank you, Blakely. Now, Jamie, the Pythons haven't been on a four-game winning streak in the past three seasons. With that special win on the horizon, is the team nervous? And if so, how are you handling that?"

"You know, Bobby, I actually don't have time for any more questions, but I look forward to seeing the ones we've answered today online soon. Especially Blakely's answers. We'll see you after the game Saturday. Now, if you'll excuse us, I need to bring my wife upstairs and then head to practice," Jamie says, his words suave but threaded with annoyance.

Without another look at Bobby, Jamie drops an arm over my shoulders and pulls the door open with another. We step inside together, and then he's grabbing my hand again, threading our fingers.

"You could have been a gold digger, you know? I still would have had you as my wife," he says once we've taken a left down the same hall I remember from my sideline-view game.

We pass the door he came out of after his interviews and show no sign of stopping.

"You would have willingly married someone who was planning on draining you dry?"

"Well, you would have only been able to drain me while we were married with all the legal crap we had to sign, but yeah. If it meant still getting to marry you, it would have been worth it."

Those stupid flutters are back. "You say that now. Maybe not after I had run off with your credit card and bought myself a fancy car."

"First off, you wouldn't have bought a car, of all things, considering you can't drive. And secondly, even if you had, I would have approved the purchase," he says, swiftly swatting another of my arguments away.

His pace slows, and with only one door left in the hallway, I follow suit.

With a roll of my eyes, I'm dropping his hand and gripping my hips. "Okay, since you know everything about me, what *would* I have bought?"

"New football gear for Nate. His is pretty old, right? I've seen you scowling at it in the laundry room a few times."

"It hardly fits," I mutter, embarrassed to have been caught so easily in the trap I set myself.

He's right. If given any large sum of money, I'd buy Nathan top-of-the-line gear that would last the rest of his high school football career.

Jamie leans a shoulder against the orange brick wall. "He hasn't mentioned anything about it."

"And he won't. He'll come home one day with his savings drained and arms full of gear, and that'll be it."

"I wonder where he got that stubbornness from."

I huff a laugh. "What's behind that door?"

"Oh, this one?" he asks, knocking his knuckles against the silver door handle. "Only a place I think you'll really like."

Intrigued, I lurch forward a step. "Let's go in."

With a push of his wrist, he has the door open. It looks like a lounge of some sort. Jamie snakes my hand again and leads us inside.

Three round tables are scattered along the wall of windows,

while a long one has been filled with empty serving containers. There are plates, silverware, sauce containers, drink pitchers—everything needed to feed a large group of people.

"Is this where you eat when you're at practice?" I ask, inspecting the variety of food options being offered.

"While I do prefer your food, yes. This is where we eat when we're at the stadium. Some of the players don't bother, but majority of us are always hungry, as you've learned."

I turn to face him. "Are you hungry right now? Is that why we're here?"

"No. We're here because there's an opening on the catering team, and I put your name in the ring."

29

Jamie

THE SHOCK RIPPLING ACROSS BLAKELY'S FACE IS EVERYTHING I hoped it would be. She shoves at my chest, surprise turning to frustration in the blink of an eye.

"Don't joke about shit like this, Jamie!"

"I'm not joking. The job is pretty much yours if you want it. Clyde is just a bit of a stickler and insisted that he meet you first before making any decisions. Plus, I figured you wouldn't want anything handed to you."

She physically reacts to the explanation, lurching backward with a hand to her throat as her bottom lip wiggles slightly. "Do you promise that you're being honest? That this isn't some elaborate hazing?"

"I'll spit shake you to prove myself, unless that's only for you and Nate."

She flies at me, and it's so much better than a spit-slicked handshake. If my reflexes weren't as sharp as they are, I'd have been too slow to catch and hold her off the ground. Her legs snap around my hips and hang on for dear life as she takes my face in her palms and kisses me smack on the mouth.

It's only a peck, but when it's followed by three more, I'm

grinning so fucking wide and deciding that this is by far the best way to be thanked.

"Thank you, Jamie. I wasn't . . ." She trails off, cheeks pinkening. "I wasn't expecting anything like this. And an interview? You got me an interview?"

"You deserve the job, Bandit. But you can prove that to Clyde the way you have me."

"I don't know what to say," she whispers, gliding her thumbs over the skin beneath my eyes.

"Nothing. You don't have to say anything. Not to me."

"Yes, I do. Thank you just doesn't feel like enough."

I smirk, bumping our noses. "Well, you could always just keep kissing me. Surely that will help."

She steals another, shutting me up. My chest expands, like it's trying to make room for me to shove her inside of it.

When she pulls back, she wiggles in my hold and drops her legs. I immediately want her back in my arms, but it would only embarrass her in front of her potential boss when he decides to join us.

Reaching out, I tuck a chunk of wavy hair behind her ear. "You deserve this."

"I want it," she declares before wincing, worrying her lip. "But I dropped out of school. I'm not a trained chef. I have some line cook experience, but that was years ago and in a small café. I'm not skilled enough for this—"

I pinch her chin between my thumb and forefinger and shake my head, leaning in close. "If anything, you're *too* skilled, baby. The fridge back home is overflowing with containers of your food and recipes stuck to the door. This job is yours."

Her doubt shakes. Some of the beaming light returns to her eyes, so I keep going.

"You're going to get this job because of who you are and your love of cooking alone. I've never met someone who gets the same joy you do from cooking. It's like you save your special smiles for when you get to watch someone take their first bite and moan at the taste. That's why you don't have to worry. If you need some extra confidence in yourself, take some from the overflowing cup I have with your name on it."

She lowers her hand to my chest and keeps it there, gazing up at me. "Are you sure it's my name on it and not yours? We all know you can be a bit too confident sometimes."

It's the perfect Blakely thank you.

"You're welcome," I murmur.

She softens, lips curling at one side. "If I get this job, does that mean I'll come here with you every day?"

"Mmhmm. You won't be able to hide from me for days after nights in the kitchen anymore."

"I wasn't hiding."

"You weren't not-hiding either."

"Don't make me take back my appreciation," she warns.

I dip my head to tease a kiss over her mouth. "I haven't forgotten about what happened, wife. And I'd bet you haven't either. We don't need to talk about it, though. It'll happen again on its own."

"And what makes you so sure of that, Pretty Boy?"

Throwing caution to the wind, I test how stretchy the boundaries are that she's set between us. "Because I haven't stopped thinking about the feeling of you coming around my fingers since. Revisited the moment several times in the shower and late at night in my bed."

She parts her lips on a long inhale, lashes fluttering. Her fingers curl into my shirt. "Not right now, Jamie."

"You're right."

I'd prefer not to stop, but with impeccable timing, Clyde saunters into the lounge. The short, balding man smiles at us, and slowly, I release my wife.

"Jamie and Blakely! Oh, my favourite wide receiver has arrived, and he brought his wife," he exclaims, clapping twice.

I rest a hand on Blakely's back. "Don't lie, Clyde. You and I both know you don't choose favourites."

"If I did, it would be you two," he argues.

"In that case, I'd like to introduce you to Blakely. Blakely, this is Clyde."

The bubbly man rushes toward us and takes Blakely's arms in his hands. He inspects her from head to toe with a smile that may as well be a declaration of acceptance.

"You're just as beautiful as Jamie said you were."

She lifts a brow at me. "Is that so?"

"As if you didn't already know I've been telling everyone I know about you. Clyde is downplaying it, to be honest."

He laughs and releases her. "I'm just happy to have a chance to meet you before I'm finished here. And to witness with my own eyes if Jamie was right about your passion and love of cooking."

Blakely straightens her shoulders, preparing for her test. "Cooking was my dream once upon a time."

"And now?"

"I've never felt more excited to get my hands dirty again."

Clyde beams. "Let's get to work, then, shall we?"

"Now?" Blakely asks, disguising her nerves with bluntness.

"Yes. While Jamie heads off for practice, we are going to prepare lunch for the team and staff. What better way to see what you're made of?"

"I'd be honoured to get such a fair shot at this. Truly," Blakely says.

Clyde claps again and then turns to me. "Off you go now, Jamie. I'll take good care of your wife, I promise."

"Yeah, you will. Or I'll make sure that you're on the menu today," I threaten.

Blakely reaches for me again before I make the first move. Excitement sparks as she kisses me on the cheek and hovers, whispering, "Thank you, husband."

My lungs fail, and I'm left waiting when she leaves with Clyde and disappears into the kitchen.

Fuck, I think I've died and gone to heaven.

WATER FLIES into the air when I give my hair a shake and adjust the band of my shorts. Chase scowls when some splatters his cheeks.

"Do you have to dry yourself like a dog, Jamie?" he asks, wiping his face with the bottom of his shirt.

"I was just double drying. You should try it sometime."

"I use a towel like a normal person."

"Your loss," I sing.

"Do you whip your wife with your hair splatter too, or is that just for us?"

I smirk, abandoning my stuff in my cubby for now. I've got lunch plans that don't involve my foul-smelling cleats.

"Nah. She's got me house-trained already."

"So, you're only like this here? Lucky woman."

"Oh, Chasey, are you jealous? You know that you're welcome to come join us for dinner whenever you want to," I coo.

"Only if you're not the one cooking."

"Blakely would kick me out of the kitchen before I got my hands on anything. She's the chef in our house, and I guarantee if she made a meal for you, you'd be trying to come over every night," I boast.

"Is that how you fell for her so quickly? Her food? Because I've got to say, Jamie, I'm still shocked you got married in the first place," he says with a grunt, slinging his duffle bag over his shoulder.

The showers are busy behind us, and Jax took off before I'd managed to rinse the soap out of my hair. I haven't bothered to keep track of anyone else. Not with Blakely on my mind.

"Shocked but proud, right?" I tease.

"Sure."

I frown and yank open the door. "My wife had a meeting

with Clyde today to be his replacement. Don't beat me up in front of her."

"She's here right now?"

"Yes, and as long as everything goes well today, she'll be at every practice day."

"You're clingy, Jamie," he deadpans.

I nearly shove him back into the locker room when we start toward the lounge. "Excuse me? That's rude."

"Zach was almost positive that you got married because you knocked Blakely up. But after seeing you at the wedding, I had a feeling that wasn't the case. It was still fucking weird that Graham was there, so something *is* going on, but maybe you do actually like this girl."

"She's my wife. There was no knocking up happening."

"You can marry someone without loving them," he declares.

"Don't tell that to Zach, or he'll give you a whole speech on how you're wrong."

"You're not going to do the same thing?"

"No. I don't have to convince anyone of anything," I say, playing it cool.

"For what it's worth, even if you're not trying, you've started winning over the fans. I was stopped twice on my way here this morning, and both occurrences were focused around you."

I wince. "I'm sorry."

"Don't be. I don't remember the last time I was stalked outside of the stadium. Let's take it as a good sign. Maybe the stands will stop looking so goddamn empty soon."

"We could go four and oh after Saturday. That will help."

Chase opens the lounge door for me and shrugs when I pass him. "Yeah, maybe. Don't get your hopes up, Bateman. Odds are the team will lose it first."

"Now that you shat all over my hopes and dreams, I'll be surprised if we do win," I scold.

"Sorry, man."

I ignore him the moment we step into the lounge and Blakely

appears at the buffet table. The white chef's coat she's wearing looks incredible on her. A perfect fit.

Chase drags a chair out from beneath one of the round tables as loudly as possible, and Blakely snaps her head our way. Curiosity blooms across her face before she finds my eyes and smiles.

It's such a delicate quirk of her mouth. Something special, just for me.

"Nice coat," I drawl, letting my legs draw me to her.

She glides a serving spoon into the pan of roasted potatoes and steals a look at her white coat. "Clyde gave it to me after I got the job."

"You got it?"

"I got it," she breathes out, pushing her way into my chest. "Today counts as my first day."

I hold her against me and squeeze her tight, kissing all over the top of her head. "I never doubted you, Bandit."

"Thank you, Jamie. I couldn't have done this without you."

"Yes, you could have. Cooking is your calling. I just helped find an opening for a chef as amazing as you."

She rubs her cheek against my chest and inhales deeply. I'm not in any hurry to end our hug, so I keep my mouth shut and keep her close.

I'm fully aware that this isn't helping me accomplish the whole "don't mess with a good thing" act. It was pointless to begin with. All practice, I was thinking about her and how she was doing in here. I've become addicted to her, and the worst part of it is I don't think she's aware of how interested I am in her.

She thinks this is all a big game when that couldn't be further from the truth. The reality of the situation is that I want Blakely in a very unfriendly way.

I want her, and I've yet to find the bottom of the list of things that I'm willing to do to win her over.

"Hi, Blakely. We didn't have much of a chance to chat at the wedding, but in case you forgot, I'm Chase."

Forcing myself away from Blakely, I eye my buddy with an obvious warning. He doesn't pay it any attention and waits until she's extracted herself from my hold before offering her a grin.

"I remember. Chase Hudson, right?"

"The one and only."

"He's the second-best wide receiver on the team," I jab.

Blakely leans a hand against the buffet table, giving my teammate her full attention. I'm tempted to toss Chase over my shoulder and drop his ass outside.

"Well, I hope you're hungry, Chase," she says.

The asshole attempts to lay it on thick. "I'm assuming you cooked this? Everything looks phenomenal."

I scoff, and Blakely glances at me with her lips rolling to hide a smile. Chase winks, purposefully stretching his arms above his head.

Maybe he has bigger biceps than me, but if he thinks that's going to win Blakely over, he's got another thing coming.

My wife doesn't fall for his bait, keeping her eyes fixed on his face and not the bulging muscles. "Clyde was showing me the ropes. We cooked together, but it's a pretty simple meal. I suppose all of them must be that way."

Chase nods. "High protein is always simple unless you have the time to make something pretty out of it."

"If anyone could make boring meals more interesting, it would be you, baby," I say, snaking an arm around her back to palm her hip.

Chase fails to hide his entertainment, watching me act like a fool. Blakely moves a hand to rub my stomach in round, soothing motions.

Tilting her head back to look at me, she says, "You should eat before everyone else gets here. I have to go talk to Clyde some more. When you're finished, you'll come get me, right?"

"Yeah, I'll get you."

She hesitates to move, darting her eyes between my eyes and my mouth. It's enough of a signal as I need.

Slanting my mouth over hers, I kiss her deeply, not giving a shit about Chase. The first taste of her has my cock stiffening and straining in my not-so-loose shorts.

"I'll see you soon," she murmurs.

I nod, chasing her mouth. "I have a gift for you in the car."

"You better not say it's your dick."

"No, it's something almost as great, though."

Her laugh is a soft, breathless sound. "Alright. I'll be back."

"Have fun."

When she escapes my arms, there's almost a skip in her step. Rays of sunshine glimmer in the air around her, and shit, it's a sight to see her so at peace. So happy.

Having even the smallest part in that makes me feel more accomplished than anything I've ever done.

30

Blakely

THE WHITE COAT DRAPED OVER MY ARM IS FAR MORE THAN WHAT IT appears to be. It's a gift, a confirmation that I'm still able to access my passion despite ignoring it these past few years. I always knew I had it in me to do great things with my love for cooking. It was never a way for me to kill time or just a means to eat every day.

It's something I've truly loved since I was a little girl. When I dropped out of school, I gave up on my dreams to be a professional chef. There are always ways to climb to the top of any ladder without a degree, but the means to do so were never available to me.

Not until Jamie.

And he doesn't even fully understand the value of what he's offered me. While I'm not going to be working at a five-star restaurant alongside decorated chefs, it's the opportunity that I've been needing to climb that first rung of the ladder to the top.

My husband did that for me. Not because he wanted something in return but to make me happy. To give me something that nobody else has before.

A genuine chance.

I don't know what to do with that right now.

"Do you think we could pick Nate up from school on our way home? We've still got an hour, but we could entertain ourselves until then," Jamie says, checking his watch.

Our hands are swinging between us as we walk through the back lot to where he has the SUV parked. There aren't many other cars left, but since we stayed late to help clean up lunch, that doesn't shock me. Everyone was already gone when we finished up.

"I'm sure he'd love that. Public buses don't have much on expensive SUVs."

He brings our hands to his mouth, kissing my knuckles before pressing them to his chest. "The parking lot is empty enough for some quick lessons if you're up for learning."

"To drive?"

"The sooner you know how, the sooner I can get you a car. Then neither of you will have to take the bus anymore."

"You'd really do that right now?"

"Why wouldn't I?"

"You've just been at practice. I'm sure you're exhausted."

He envelops the back of my hand so it's sandwiched in both of his. "I can sleep later."

Emotion swells and rocks inside of me, filling me to the point of spilling. Jamie's not making anything easy on me, and we still have a month and a half of our marriage to get through.

"Fine. You can give me a few lessons, Pretty Boy."

"That's the spirit, gorgeous."

My pulse doubles in speed. "What's the first one?"

He reaches into his pocket and pulls his keys free. With a grin, he unlinks our fingers and drops the keys into my palm.

"Unlock the doors and slide into the driver's seat."

"Shouldn't I do a walkaround of the vehicle? I saw that online once."

He huffs a laugh. "I stand corrected. A real teacher would make you do one of those, so have at it."

Maybe it's a stalling tactic. *Maybe.*

The sooner I get into the vehicle, the faster I'll want to scream at being trapped in such a close space with him. Usually, I can put up a wall between us to keep from pouncing into his lap and kissing him, but today? After everything?

I fear even my iron will isn't strong enough to withstand the draw.

Turning my attention to the SUV, I slowly make my way to the back. The entire vehicle is in pristine condition, not a dent or scratch to be seen. I drag a finger along the glossy black paint, picturing him doing this same check every night to make sure he doesn't have anything to buff out or fix before bed.

"Are you Blakely?"

I jump at the female voice, jamming my elbow into the side of the SUV.

"*Fuck*," I groan, rubbing at the bone and where it aches.

"I'm so sorry!" the stranger squeaks while Jamie comes barrelling into view.

"Blakely? What happened? Are you hurt?"

I shake my head, continuing to rub at the sore bone as he tries to take over for me. "I hit my elbow. It's fine."

"Who are you? Do I need to get security?" he barks, completely focused on the young woman gaping into her palm a few feet away.

His arm is rock-solid with strain when I place my hand over it and slide my body in front of him, chest to chest. I've never seen him angry before, but this move is almost more for me than it is him.

The protectiveness that's vibrating off his skin right now is an aphrodisiac. I'm struggling to catch my breath because I'm turned on by him, not because I'm scared he's going to unleash hell on this innocent woman. He'd never do that.

What I would like him to do, though, is spread me out on the hood of his SUV and grind the hard dick pressing against my belly between my legs.

"I hurt myself, Jamie. She surprised me, and I fell back into the SUV," I murmur, running a finger up and down his chest.

Slowly, the blue in his eyes lightens. He clears his throat, cheeks paling when he glances at the woman, embarrassed.

"I'm sorry," he tells her as I spin, resting my back against his chest.

She blinks quickly and lowers her hand. "Oh! Don't be. I get it. I can only imagine the kind of people that come up and try to talk to you. I'm the one who should be sorry."

"No, it's fine. You knew my name, so I assume you're a football fan?" I ask.

"I am. But I didn't come here to see Jamieson. No offense or anything!"

My husband chuckles. "Call me Jamie. And no offense taken. Blakely is the real star between us, anyway. I just catch the balls."

"Well, in that case, I wanted to come and see if you were still here so I could say thank you," the woman says, her words coming out so quickly I can hardly keep up with them.

"Thank me for what?"

Surprise loosens the woman's features, yet that doesn't stop her from explaining.

"The interview from earlier. There's a video online, and when I saw it, I just knew that I had to say thank you for standing up for women. I've never dated a pro athlete, but I do work with them, and I think your message was important. Women are judged on every single thing they do, and no matter how badly we try to prove ourselves, it hardly seems to make a difference. The world has become programmed against us in too many aspects of everyday life. So, thank you for being brave enough to speak up about it. I'm sure that wasn't easy."

Jamie brings his steady comfort to me with a hand to my lower back. "The interview with *Sports Weekly* is already up?"

"Yeah. It looked like it was shot from a few yards away from someone watching you," she explains.

"What's your name?" I ask her.

"Giana. Giana Mitchell."

"It's nice to meet you, Giana. I'm Blakely."

She tips her mouth into a smile. "I didn't mean to accost you in a parking lot. I always pass the stadium on my way home, and once I saw the video, I figured I'd see if you were still here. I'm apparently lucky today."

"You should stop somewhere and buy a lottery ticket while you're at it," I suggest, half joking.

She tucks the stray brown hairs blowing in her face behind her ears, exposing more of the freckles sprinkled all over her nose and cheeks.

"Maybe I will, actually."

Unsure what to say next, my anti-socialness kicks into overdrive. It's not a purposeful thing. Just a very annoying, natural one.

"*Sports Weekly* is full of sharks waiting for their next sniff of blood, Blakely. I'd keep an eye out now that you've handed Bobby his ass and the video of it has gone viral," Giana adds, reading the vibe between us.

Jamie steps in now, his interest piqued. "You have experience with them?"

"Not me, but I work with the Warriors, so . . ."

"Say no more," Jamie mutters.

"Or do say more. What does this guy have to do with the Warriors?" I ask, brows lifted.

Considering the Vancouver Warriors NHL team plays in the arena across the street, it makes sense that Giana would be passing here to go home, driving home the conclusion that she isn't a creepy stalker.

"There was a lot of shit that went down with them and my cousin Maddox a few years back. It's old news, and the reporter who was working there at the time has long since been fired," Jamie explains.

I nod, leaning against him. "So, there's still bad blood."

"For the entire team, really. But I'm going to stop myself

before I get myself fired too," she rushes out, smiling apologetically. "I should head home, anyway. Thank you for talking to me, Blakely. I meant what I said."

"It was nothing."

She shakes her head, her smile turning sad. "No, it wasn't. It was important."

"Then I guess you're welcome."

Raising a hand to wave, she starts retreating. "Maybe I'll see you around sometime."

"Yeah, maybe."

She hops over a cement barrier and walks with a strong sense of purpose out of the parking lot while I watch, a part of me wishing I'd had the nerve to ask for her number or something.

"That was interesting," Jamie notes, slipping the keys from my palm and unlocking the SUV doors. "She seemed nice, though, yeah?"

"Yeah, she was. I wasn't expecting anyone to come up to me today."

"We'll have to look for this video once we get home. I need to know what we're up against here."

"Don't you want to do that now?" I ask, brows dipping.

He holds my shoulders and turns me to face him and the now open driver's door. "We already had plans, Bandit. Hop in, and we can get started."

I do, and twenty minutes later, Jamie's clutching onto the door for dear life while shouting for me to slow down.

"This isn't Formula One! You don't have to go so fast!"

"But it's so fun to see you scared," I poke, stomping the gas so we lurch forward again.

"Blakely, I swear to Go—"

The tires squeal when I give a hard turn to the steering wheel and send us careening to the left. "What was that?"

"It's like you want me to sit you in my lap and guide you."

With my heart soaring with freedom, I can't help but tease him. "Are you offering?"

"I'm warning you, baby. If I get you in my lap, the main driving lessons are over. And there's nowhere for you to run this time."

His stare is intense, demanding, and I meet it with one of surrender. It feels so fucking good to give in to him.

My belly tightens. "Teach me some more first."

31

Jamie

BLAKELY WRINGS THE STEERING WHEEL IN HER HANDS FOR THE millionth time and makes another right turn in the parking lot. It's tight, the wheels nearly scraping on the curb, but I don't give a shit.

She can give all four of my tires curb rash as long as I get her in my lap afterward. If it meant she could hop up sooner, I'd instruct her to do it.

The SUV lurches when she presses too hard on the brake while pulling crooked into a parking stall. She puffs out a breath and jerks us to a stop before shifting into Park. The steady hum of the engine fills the cab, neither of us making a move to speak.

If I do, I'll be making demands that I'm not in any place to make. My mind may be made up when it comes to my wife, but she's not there yet. That much is obvious.

"I'm terrible at this," she admits, releasing the steering wheel.

"Terrible at what? Driving?"

Her glare is white-hot. "You know that's not what I meant."

"No, I don't. So either you tell me now, or I'll be spending the rest of the time we have before Nate's out of school guessing what you did mean."

She doesn't soften her glare. If anything, I think it gets more intense as the seconds pass. The only change is that now, I'm not the only one she's mad at.

"You're infuriating, Jamieson Bateman."

I blink, leaning back in my seat to gawk at her. "Me? I'm the infuriating one?"

"Yes! God, I'm losing my mind around you."

"I would feel sorry for you, but I've already lost mine."

"Don't start with your teasing. I can't take it right now," she snaps.

"It's not teasing. I'm being honest with you, Blakely. This is me being open."

"You're being confusing, not open."

I swipe a hand down my face and unbuckle my seat belt, not needing the restriction right now. "Confusing is the last thing I'm trying to be. If you want me to clarify something, just tell me. I've always been an open book with you."

"And what if I don't want clarity? It will only complicate things," she argues, stubborn as all hell.

"So let them get complicated. Do you think things aren't going to get that way regardless?"

Blakely lets her head fall back against the seat, groaning angrily. "I was supposed to make sure you weren't dead and then steal your Xbox. That's all."

It's impossible not to laugh. I palm her thigh, needing the contact. She focuses on where we touch and bites her inner cheek, a silent battle in her eyes.

"I'm grateful that it was more than that," I murmur.

"You have no idea what you're asking for right now."

"No, I think I have a pretty good idea, wife. It's you that doesn't know what I'm asking."

"What *are* you asking, then?"

She brings her torn gaze to my face, and I palm the back of her neck, threading my fingers through her soft hair. It's a firm, warm touch, something that I hope helps communicate how serious I am right now.

The air is thick with desire, both hers and mine. I'm greedy with my inhales, unafraid to drink it in.

"I want you, Blakely, even though I know it's messy."

"Very messy," she whispers.

Sweeping my thumb along the thin skin behind her ear, I add, "The way I see it, we have two options. Either we continue to pretend, or we don't. I'm not saying that this won't end in disaster because it probably will, but I have feelings for you, and I'm already struggling to keep that from affecting our friendship."

"You don't care if we crash and burn? It won't be pretty."

"*If* by the end of the contract, we hate each other and everything we've built burns, then I'll at least be grateful that I had the chance to have you for a brief time. It's better than the alternative."

"What exactly is the alternative, Jamie? Things are going fine right now."

"Fine isn't all that ideal for me, baby. If we continue to pretend that we're not one breath from fucking each other blind half the time, we're going to lose our minds. I only have a month and a half left with you, and I don't want to spend that time tiptoeing around each other."

"If this is an elaborate scheme to get in bed with me, Jamie, I swear—"

I lean over the console, bringing our faces close as our eyes lock. "Tell me point-blank that you think that's the kind of guy I am, Bandit. Tell me that you genuinely believe I'm telling you this to fuck you, and I'll take us up to see Graham so we can call this off right now."

She shudders, lips parting on a sigh exhale before she whispers, "Don't be so dramatic."

"If you want dramatic, I can give you dramatic," I warn, dropping my tone.

"You talk such a big game, but we both know that's all it is. *A game*. You want to win, but I'm not a ball that you can catch."

With a low laugh scraping up my throat, I drag my mouth across hers and playfully dig my teeth into her bottom lip. She blows a sigh into my mouth, and I tilt her head back just enough that I can make an example of how easily she bends for me despite her sharp words.

It might be possible for her to keep a straight face and play coy most of the time, but there's no hiding the pink on her cheeks or the quickening of her pulse. Yeah, it could be simply physical for her, but my gut tells me a different story.

She might not be as in as I am, but I've got time to get her there.

With our breaths mingling and sparks alive beneath my skin, I lay it all out for her.

"If you're a game, then I've already won. It's not about the final score with you, Blakely. It never was. All I want is to keep learning about you while having permission to touch you like this without anyone around. There's no pressure here. Just a timeline we have to follow. I'm open to riding out the weeks with no assumptions. Just have fun with me, baby. I promise I'll make sure you enjoy yourself."

"And if you fall in love with me? You'll still let me go if that's what I choose?"

The sting from her question is easily ignored by the blast of excitement that follows. It's the closest she's come to agreeing thus far, and that's a win in my book.

"Will I want to? No. But if I don't have another choice, then yes. What if you fall in love with me?"

"The only person I'm capable of loving is Nathan."

"You're wrong. There isn't a limit set on how many people you can love," I correct softly.

Her eyes soften. "We'll see."

"Is this you agreeing?"

She gingerly covers my hands with hers and holds them in place. It's a simple gesture. Something that could even be construed as friendly if coming from anyone but my wife.

From Blakely, it's acceptance.

"I have feelings for you too, Jamie. You've done more for me than anyone ever has because of the kind person that you are. Your heart is so big and accepting, and Nate and I are lucky to have you in our lives. Regardless of what comes next, I want you to know that you're appreciated and deserve a lifetime of good things."

I swallow. "If you're only agreeing because you want to pay me back, I won't accept it."

The firm press of her lips on mine is her answer to that.

I take the offering in stride and lower my hand from her neck to unbuckle her seat belt. She twists in her seat immediately, keeping our mouths parting on kisses that grow more frantic by the second. I help guide her out of her seat and over the wide console, both of us too busy staring at one another to pay attention to the things clattering to the floor.

It's a really fucking tight fit, but once she collapses on my lap, I'm delving both hands into her hair and hauling her against me. She digs her fingers into my shoulders, leaning over me with her knees on the seat.

"Is this what you meant by having fun with you?" she asks, abandoning my mouth to plant kisses along my neck.

I tip my head back to give her space and tighten my hold on her hair. The blood pooling in my groin has me hard and throbbing, half-wild at the thought of her dropping to my lap and feeling me between her legs.

"It's one of the benefits," I grit out when she sucks hard on the skin beneath my jaw.

"How do I find another?"

I shift and grab both of her round hips, enjoying the softness beneath my palms. She retreats from my neck and blinks down at me, waiting.

All it takes is one quick jerk of her hips and she's losing her balance, her ass hitting my thighs. A gasp fills the cab, but it's gone as quickly as it came. With my hold steady on her hips, I rock her forward.

The breathy moan that escapes her is nearly too much.

"You said your dick isn't the gift you had for me."

I tip the corner of my mouth in a lazy smile. "It isn't. You can have my cock anytime you want, wife. Not just in the car."

"You're such an ass."

"Is that why you're grinding down on me?" I rasp, staring at where she's rocking forward all on her own.

The press of her against my shaft is a tease more than anything else. It's too small in the SUV for anything more than that.

She hums, scraping a hand through my hair. "I'm just trying to make a guess at something."

"What's that?"

I'm not ready for the hand she drops to grip me with. It's so hot that I can feel the heat through my shorts. The widening of her eyes doesn't help calm me.

"Fuck, baby. What are you doing?" I grunt, shoving a hand up beneath her shirt to grab at her bare waist.

She watches me innocently while starting to drag her hand up and down my length. "I'm trying to see how big you are."

Her fingers curl along the edges of my cock, taking as much of a hold of it as she can through my shorts. I toss my head back and squeeze my eyes shut, thrusting into her hold as lightly as possible.

"You could have just asked," I groan, pleasure spiking up my spine.

"Where's the fun in that?"

My eyes roll back when she starts stroking me. "You won't get a good measurement through my shorts."

"Are you sure? I think I could make it work like this . . ." she mumbles, scooting an inch down my thighs. "But if you're sure."

I somehow manage to lift my hips at the same time she

reaches for my shorts and pulls them down in the front, just enough to free my cock.

Blakely gapes at it, and I throb in response, terrified that if she touches me bare, I'll come.

"This might be a problem," she says on a breath.

"Why's that?"

Cautiously, she brings her fingers to my shaft and runs a nail along the top. "It won't fit."

Her pupils expand when I take her hand and bring it to the base, encouraging her to grip it again, this time with nothing in the way.

"I'll make it fit. My wife can take her husband's thick cock, can't she?"

"I want to make you come, Jamie," she tells me, her speech becoming slurred with desire.

"Go ahead, Blakely. Make me cover the same hand that wears my ring with my cum."

It's enough motivation for her. With determination swirling around the lust in her eyes, she tightens her grip on me and starts to jack me off.

"How do you like it?" she asks, her head dropped forward to watch her work.

"Spit on it. Get it wet," I moan.

My muscles are straining so much they'll be sore by tonight. Showing restraint with Blakely is the greatest test I'll face in my lifetime. Her hand is tight and smooth, but I'd be lying if I said I wasn't imagining her mouth in its place.

She spits onto her fist and spreads it over my shaft before starting to stroke again. "What else?"

With the lube in play, I'm a few flicks of her wrist away from coming already. My balls draw up tight, and I spit a curse between us.

"Kiss me," I beg.

She doesn't make me repeat myself. In a blink, our lips are meeting, the sweet taste of her exploding in my mouth. Her tongue swipes along my bottom lip, and once I part for her, she's taking control.

The grip on my cock grows tighter, and the strokes speed up, coaxing out my orgasm. I break away from her mouth long enough to warn her.

"Coming," I grunt, sucking in a sharp breath at the force of the pleasure.

Throbbing in her hold, I come hard enough to see stars. Rope after rope of cum flies from the tip as I groan and watch her swap from her right to left hand through fuzzy vision.

She lets me come on her fingers, and once I realize that she's made an effort to get it on her ring . . . Jesus Christ. The milky gleam on the diamond and over the band is the hottest thing I've ever seen.

Scratch that.

I worry I'll pass out when she lifts her hand to her mouth and uses her tongue to swipe up the cum from the diamond before looping it beneath the band and sucking the entire ring into her mouth.

"Not bad," she murmurs, slowly bringing her eyes up to me.

"Not bad," I echo incredulously, staring at her hand again. "In that case, you've missed some."

She watches as I circle her wrist and bring the cum-slicked fingers to my mouth. One at a time, I glide them between my lips and spend too long sucking them clean.

"Jamie," she breathes out.

"Blakely."

"You just did that."

I push forward and kiss her, letting our tongues play for a few moments before pulling away. "I told you we'd have fun."

"Is this what it will be from now on?"

There's a vulnerability in her voice that sets off warning bells in my mind.

"I don't only want sex from you. What I feel for you goes far beyond the physical."

"Me too," she reveals softly.

Cupping her cheek, I bring our foreheads together. "We'll go with the flow. Listen to what we want and take it. I don't care if that's massaging your head while watching a romcom or stroking your pussy on the kitchen counter. Being with you is what I want."

"At least let me make the tacos next time," she teases lightly.

"Anything you want, just ask."

"What about the gift you taunted me with earlier? Can I have that?"

"They're in the back seat."

She curves a brow. "They're? As in multiple?"

"Just look behind me and find them, Bandit," I push, smiling at her excitement.

Without needing another push, she leans past me to get a look in the back seat. I know the minute she notices the bag because she reaches for my shoulder, needing the stability.

"When did you get these?"

"Yesterday."

"Jamie, I can't repay you for these. They must have cost a fortune."

"They're a congratulatory gift for getting the job today."

"But you didn't know I was going to get it for sure."

She sits back in my lap empty-handed. Concern spikes before I realize she probably didn't want to unroll a set of sharp-as-hell chef's knives in my lap.

Her glistening eyes choke me, and I reach for her, smoothing her hair out of her face.

"I knew, Blakely. And you deserve these. The only thing I want in return is for you to stay in my lap for a minute more, okay?"

My heart throbs so hard it's almost painful when she nods

and folds herself against my chest. Her steady breathing stabilizes me as it becomes even clearer that it won't be her falling in love with me that's the problem.

It'll be me falling in love with her.

32

Blakely

ON THURSDAY, JAMIE DRIVES US HOME FROM WORK—SPEEDING, might I add—and puts himself to work prepping for Nate's football practice. He's like a little mother hen, filling the squirting water bottles he bought in bulk from the closest sports shop and packing Nate's new gear into the tub alongside them.

"He's going to lose it when he sees that stuff, you know?"

My socks are scratchy in my sneakers as I slip them on, but I keep my complaints to myself. I've already promised myself that when my first paycheque comes in from the Pythons, I'll spend a few dollars on replacing both my socks and shoes before piling the rest away in my savings.

"You're sure he'll like them? If I didn't want it to be a surprise, I would have brought him with me and had him choose his own. My dad spent three hours in the store with me when I upgraded my gear the first time. Should I have done that instead?" Jamie rambles, pacing in the entryway.

Apart from waiting for Nate, we're ready to go. I think the hanging around doing nothing is making Jamie lose his mind a little bit.

I finish putting my jacket on and hand him the first one I see in the closet. It's a Pythons jacket similar to the one Coach was wearing on the sidelines of the last game.

Jamie takes one look at it and shakes his head, reaching around me for a plain black jacket instead.

"I don't want to draw attention away from Nate tonight," Jamie explains, shrugging the black one on.

"That's sweet."

He smirks, reaching for the bottom of my jacket before starting to zip it up. "Yeah?"

"Don't make me take it back."

"Alright, fine. Do you want a toque?"

"It's like ten degrees outside."

"Is that a no?"

"It's a no. I don't have the face shape for a toque. I just look like a pudgy toy doll."

Clunky footsteps on the staircase announce Nate's presence. He slides toward us on his socked feet and snags his coat from the hook on the wall. "She's more of a beanie girl, Jamie."

"Don't tell him all my secrets," I scold half-heartedly.

Jamie snaps his fingers and points finger guns at him. "That's right. Thanks, buddy."

He digs into the closet and pulls my purple beanie from the top shelf. After tugging it onto my head, he gently moves my hair behind my ears.

"Can't have you getting cold," he says with a wink.

"Are all of these bottles for the team?" Nate asks, staring into the tub Jamie spent too long packing.

My husband jumps at my brother and hip bumps him away from the tub. "They are. I was going to bring snacks too, but your sister reminded me that you weren't all ten-year-olds and probably wouldn't have appreciated football-shaped sandwiches."

"I'd have eaten one," Nate says with a shrug.

Jamie spins to face me. "It'll be you I'm sending a bunch of hungry fifteen-year-old boys to when they feel like complaining."

"You wouldn't."

"I would."

"Can we go now, please? I don't want to be late tonight of all nights," Nate says, his voice timid, almost like he's too afraid to show how excited he is.

Jamie realizes it, too, and doesn't hesitate to lift the tub into his arms and lead the charge out the front door. "Remember the door code, Nate?"

"Yep!"

"Lock up with your sister while I put these in the car, and then we'll go."

"Got it, Jamie!"

I stand on the porch steps and watch Nate stick his tongue out and concentrate on inputting the code on the door correctly. When the sound of the deadbolt turning comes a beat later, he tests the door before coming to my side.

"Jamie's awesome, Lake. I like him."

As I turn my head to look at Jamie as he slides the tub into the open trunk, my heart skips. It's such a simple task, and knowing that he's doing this all just to see my little brother smile only makes me feel more confident in the choice I made yesterday.

Despite the weight of what Jamie was asking me, I knew what I was going to do the moment he brought it up. Giving in to my emotions doesn't come easy to me, yet somehow, with him, I'm more open than I've ever been.

It's still too early to know whether I've made a mistake, so I guess I'm going to keep doing what I'm doing and hope for the best.

Putting my arm around Nate and being hit with a reminder of how tall he's getting, I say, "Yeah, he's pretty great. We got lucky."

"Think he'll be up to play some *Madden* with me after practice?"

"I think he'd do just about anything with you if you asked."

"Will you play too?"

"Only if you promise to go easy on me."

"Yes!" he shouts, beaming as he pulls away and jogs to the SUV.

Jamie catches my eyes when Nate crashes into him. He reaches a hand down to mess up my brother's hair and playfully shove him away.

"Don't roughhouse before practice, Nate!" I shout, hiding a smile as I join them.

"Sorry!"

He gets in the back seat while Jamie closes the trunk and moves to open the passenger door for me.

"After you, wife."

I grab his hand before getting in. "Thank you."

"Anytime," he coos, shooting me a wink.

He shuts the door and rounds the hood, his eyes not leaving mine until he's forced to slip into the vehicle and drive the half hour to the field.

Even then, he keeps a claiming hand on my thigh and fills the drive with questions for Nate. By the time we pull up along the curb, Jamie's repeating players' names back to Nate and matching each one up with their position. It's adorable, really.

Nate's the first one out of the SUV and is waiting at the back for the liftgate to rise before I even have my door open. I don't dare tease him for his excitement, though. I've been dreaming of seeing this spark back in his eyes for years.

"Hey, Nate, before we head up, I wanted to show you something," Jamie says, shutting the driver's-side door.

"Okay, cool."

I pause beside the back door, keeping myself hidden just a minute longer. This is a moment for them, and I don't want to interrupt.

"I got you a few things. Blakely did tell me that you were wanting to buy your own gear and that she wasn't going to let you, but I wanted to try and help a bit. I've got access to stores and brands that I've never been able to take advantage of before, so I figured that now was a great time for it. You can tell me if you don't like something, and we can make a trip together to swap it out for whatever else you'd prefer. Hell, you can even tell me to take it all back and that I totally overstepped here," Jamie explains.

A pause and then a sliding noise. "You got me new gear?"

"I did."

More silence. And some more.

I move out of my hiding spot and steal a look at them. My vision blurs instantly, and I cover my mouth to stop a sob from escaping.

Nathan is clutching Jamie in a bear hug and has his eyes squeezed shut so hard it seems painful. He tightens his jaw and clutches Jamie tighter, fighting his emotions.

"I've got you, kid. You keep looking out for your sister, and I'll do the same for the both of you. We're family," Jamie says quietly, rubbing Nate's back.

"Family," Nate swears.

I don't say a word as they finish their hug, and Jamie ruffles Nate's hair again, lightening the mood.

"Come on, we'll haul everything to the field, and then you can swap out your old stuff in the locker room."

Stepping into their line of vision, I reach for Nate's hand and squeeze while meeting Jamie's waiting stare. His heart bleeds in his eyes, so open and raw. I don't need to speak a word, and neither does he. Everything we want to say passes through the way we look at each other.

Thank you.

I'd do anything for you and your brother.

"You even colour matched to our jerseys!" Nate exclaims.

I step into Jamie's arms and touch my fingers to his jaw

before kissing him softly. He holds me close for a beat, as if reminding himself how it feels to have me pressed against his body. I know that because I'm doing the exact same thing.

Slowly, we separate and turn to Nate. He has the tub in his arms and is waving a foot beneath the SUV to trigger the liftgate to close.

"I'm going to make sure everyone tries extra hard tonight," he notes, nudging us to head to the field now. "I want to make sure you come to another practice."

Jamie locks the doors and drapes an arm over my shoulders as we follow Nate. I slide my hand into the back pocket of his jeans.

"I don't care how well practice goes. I'll come back as many times as I can regardless," Jamie says.

Nate keeps staring straight ahead. "Really? You don't have to."

Pain lances through my chest. Our mom is responsible for this deep-rooted feeling of unworthiness that he carries. At ten years old, he was too smart to miss why she left us. We were never good enough for her, never worthy of her attention or love. And now, he's left searching for affirmation from those he loves.

I've tried my hardest, but maybe I haven't done a good enough job.

Jamie tucks me closer and drops a kiss to the top of my head. "You could warm the bench every game for the rest of your football career, and I'd still come see you, Nate. You've got my word."

My brother stumbles a step on the grass, his hunched shoulders pulling back. "Even after the *you know* is over?"

I hold my breath.

"Even then. You'll just have to remind your sister to save me a seat for the games I can make it to."

This time, Nate spins to face us, and the cheek-splitting grin on his face could light up the entire universe.

"You're awesome, Jamie."

"So are you, buddy."

"Do you think you could watch how I play and give me some pointers? Coach is great, but you're, well, *you*."

Jamie doesn't hesitate for even a half second. "Absolutely. If you're up for it, we can stay a bit tonight and work on some things."

"Don't you have a run-through in the morning?" I ask him quietly.

He simply brushes another kiss to my head. "I'll live."

It's not like practice runs that late, but Jamie's up and working out in the home gym every morning before six. I learned that the hard way.

A few players on Nate's team are already here, dressed in their gear and stretching on the field. I don't have even half the number of names memorized that Jamie already does.

When one of the kids spots Nate, he waves him over, eyeing the tub in his arms.

"Hey, Nate."

"Hi, Max."

I debate removing my hand from Jamie's pocket but hesitate. And when I catch the way one of the women on the bleachers is gawking at him, I toss the idea in the dumpster.

"Looks like you've been spotted, Pretty Boy," I muse.

He chuckles and reaches across our bodies to snag my left hand. The simple silver band on his ring finger makes my breathing turn thready.

He takes my hand and brings it to his lips, flashing me a crooked smile. "Good thing I have my wife here to keep me safe, then."

I'm too petty not to look back at the woman. The envy in her expression soothes me.

"Yeah, I think I can protect you."

33

Jamie

GAME DAY FEELS LIKE IT'S COME SOONER THAN IT USUALLY DOES.

Between practice at the stadium, extra time with Nate on the high school field, family dinners every night, followed by a traditional *Madden* competition, time is flying by too quickly for me to snatch it and force it to slow.

A week of being married has felt as easy as before I said *I do*. With Blakely, that's how everything is. Easy and fun.

"Are you listening, Jamie?"

Coach has his hand on my face mask, shaking it slightly. I clear my throat and nod as he releases me.

"Go out with the team tonight. I got it," I say.

"Graham's orders."

"Why didn't he give them to me himself?"

"He tried. I figured I could handle it. Unless you'd have preferred making an extra trip upstairs before the game?"

"Nope. This is great. I'll make sure we're there tonight."

We're in the second quarter of the game, and by a miracle, we're winning. I'm aiming for another TD to add to the tally, but I guess going home with three tonight wouldn't be too bad either.

"He's impressed with Blakely's interview video. It's sparked a bit of a buzz on social media."

"We were stopped by someone working for the Warriors the other day. It's made it over there too. Fucking *Sports Weekly*."

Coach nods, tugging at the sleeves of his jacket. "Just keep it up. Mingle tonight and stop to answer some questions."

"Be a show monkey," I muse.

"That should be easy for you."

"Ouch. That's no way to speak to your star player."

"When did he get here?"

I laugh and yank my helmet off. I'm sweaty and tired as I look out at the stands in search of my family. While I wish they could be on the sidelines again, I was given regular seats to hand out to everyone tonight.

Still, I spot them close to the field, only three rows up. Dad's seated on the aisle, sharing a massive bucket of popcorn with Mom while Oliver helps Nova shake up her slushie. Avery's fixing the back of Blakely's beanie, but my wife isn't paying attention to her. She's staring straight at me instead.

My Pythons jacket hanging off her shoulders is a far better claim than a jersey. It swallows her up and should still be layered in my cologne. Nate's on her other side, a wall between her and the group of men filling the rest of the row.

I make a mental note to get him something as a thank you for that.

"Head in the game, Bateman," Coach scolds.

"Oh, it's in the game. I can't have her embarrassed to be married to me."

He scoffs. "That's the spirit."

I kiss my palm before blowing it at the stands. Blakely doesn't react at first, but when Nate gives her a shove, she rolls her eyes and blows one back. I'm a big enough goof to make a show of jumping to snatch it out of the air.

"Christ," Coach blows out, stalking to the group of players awaiting his orders.

He acts like he hates the showboating stuff. I know he's just projecting.

Nate waves at me, and the guys beside him laugh, making a show of judging him. The one seated right beside Nate, wearing a Hayes jersey, leans over to say something to him, and it snuffs the excitement from his eyes.

My hackles rise, a hot streak of protectiveness climbing my spine. I make my way to the bench and kick Jaxon's foot. He looks up from the tablet in his hands and lifts his brows.

"What's up?"

"I need you to help me with something."

He finishes going over the plays on the tablet and passes it off. "You name it."

We walk away from the bench, and I give him a rundown of the guys beside Nate before explaining what I want him to do. His following grin drips with mischief as he snatches the blanket he was using earlier from the bench and brings it over.

When he uncaps a black marker and starts scribbling his signature on the blanket, I don't ask where he got it from, not caring for the specifics.

"Make it out for Nate, a future MVP. He's a massive Pythons fan and one of the only wide receivers I've ever met that can keep up with me," I tell him, raising my voice over the noise in the stadium.

Jax glances up at Nate and gives him a wave before continuing to write on the blanket.

"Shouldn't you sign it too, Bateman? Or maybe not since you already live with the kid. Considering he's your brother-in-law, I'd expect he has unlimited access to your signature."

The two men blanch at the information being dumped in their lap, and the one who whispered to Nate even goes so far as to lean away from him. As if that would take back what I saw him doing.

I focus solely on that guy, speaking loud enough for everyone around him to hear. "Nate's my buddy. He can have anything he wants signed at any time. I've already let him sort through my old jerseys and take any that he wants. He's family, and I'd do anything for my family."

Jax finishes with the blanket and heads to the edge of the stands, waving for Nate to come toward the railing. The kid jumps out of his seat and pushes past the guys before rushing down the stairs.

He leans against the railing and beams at us with stars in his eyes. "Hi, Jaxon! Hi, Jamie!"

"Hey, man. This is for you. Feel free to rub it all over those assholes' faces. I'm sure it's got some of my sweat in the fabric," Jax says, stretching an arm above his head to hand off the blanket.

We've drawn a crowd now, and security has started our way on the field. In the stands, a couple of people in orange jackets push past the fans taking this opportunity to snap pictures and hang their stuff over the railing for us to sign.

I take a picture with one of the younger fans and steal Jax's marker to sign the baseball cap he hangs over the railing. Coach is blowing his whistle, trying to grab our attention again as more and more fans start coming toward us, realizing what we're doing.

Nate has gone back to his seat, and I make sure he sees me lift a hand and give him a thumbs-up before Jax and I go back to the bench.

Coach scowls as we walk toward him but doesn't scold us. Instead, he shoves the tablet back in Jax's arms and points at the bench.

I sit beside Jax and bump his shoulder. "Thank you."

"It's like you said, anything for family."

I'VE NEVER MINDED NIGHTCLUBS. Obviously, being a professional athlete helps with the small nuisances like waiting in lines, but still. The music, strobing lights, and lack of personal space don't bother me.

Altitude is a club that the team goes to more often than any other. The VIP section is big enough to fit all of us, and the security is impressively vigilant. With Blakely beside me tonight, the last point is the most important.

She's a goddamn sight in a tight black dress and her worn-down flats. Her brown hair is curled, hanging free down her back. I've been tempted more than once already tonight to bury my hands in it.

Red lip gloss gleams on her mouth when she spins to face me, her back pressing against the railing we were using to watch the crowds on the lower level. She bats her long black lashes, and I grip the railing on either side of her before leaning in, trapping her with my body.

"You're gorgeous," I rasp.

The smoky makeup intensifies the green in her eyes, making it difficult to look away. If I bothered to in the first place. It's not the plan from now until I close my eyes to sleep.

She's transformed herself into the woman Graham wants her to be tonight. The wife of one of the best players in the CFL, who likes to wear the fancy dresses and spend hours on her makeup. That's not my Blakely.

It doesn't change how gorgeous she is, though. In a dress or her favourite baggy sweatpants with the bleach stain on her right ass cheek, she still makes my cock hard as steel.

"Avery brought me the dress to the game. I didn't know if I'd like it," she reveals, resting a hand on my waist.

"Why not?"

She gestures from her shoulder to leg, giving me an *are you serious* look.

The dress is tighter than anything I've seen her wear, yeah.

There are curves showing tonight that I haven't seen before. And her ass... *fuck me.*

"You're unbelievably sexy, Blakely. I've had a hard-on since you walked down the stairs earlier."

Her chest brightens with a blush, and I bite down on my tongue when a groan climbs my throat. With every quick breath she takes, her breasts strain against the fabric holding them in place.

I'm too aware of every player on my team who's eyed her for half a second too long and will be threatening them with long and painful deaths the moment we get on the field for practice Wednesday.

Keeping my hands to myself hasn't happened at all, to be honest. Sure, we're supposed to be putting on a show, but with Blakely, there's no need for a show when everything comes this naturally.

"I'm scared my boobs will fall right out of it," she says, pressing a hand to her cleavage. "It's worse than the corset in my wedding dress."

"We don't have to stay much longer if you're uncomfortable."

She pinches the material of my button-up, rubbing it between her fingers. I picked it to match her dress and left the top two buttons undone on purpose. It's only fair to tease her a bit after she nearly gave me a heart attack in her dress.

"You haven't even asked me to dance yet."

"Do you want to dance with me?"

Leaning up on her toes, she brings her glossy lips to my ear. "Your wife would love to dance."

I grab her face and glide my fingers beneath her jaw, rubbing the skin while guiding her to look at me. She smirks, knowing she's caught me.

"Who am I to deny you of what you want?"

She twirls, taking my hand from her face to rest between us. I step in front of her and guide us through the VIP section to the roped-off staircase. The two security guards nod at us and pull open the rope.

It's louder on the main floor and far more crowded with gyrating bodies and the groups of friends screaming lyrics to try and be louder than the speakers. Purple, pink, and white lights roll across the dance floor, flashing one moment and dimming the next. The music playing is dirty, with heavy bass and a quick tempo.

I swing behind Blakely and tuck her against my chest as we cut through the crowds. She grips onto my arm, holding me as we move.

Sweat breaks out on my neck from the heat on the dance floor. Blakely keeps her back firmly to my chest, even once we find a bit of space to dance, and I loop an arm around her middle, holding her there.

Resting my cheek against her temple, I breathe in her vanilla perfume and sway my hips, encouraging her to follow my lead.

It takes her a few seconds to join me, and then she's looping an arm around my neck and moving with me. I keep my hold tight around her stomach, not ready to release her just yet.

Turning her head, she brushes her cheek against my cheek and asks, "How long should we do this for?"

"Already antsy to get me home, baby?"

Her eyes twinkle in the bright lights. "Obviously."

It's impossible to hear people whispering here the way they usually do when I'm spotted somewhere. I'm observant enough to have already spotted the phones pointed at us right now, yet it still feels like I'm missing something.

The muttered "Is that him?" or "Do you think he would take a photo with us?" most likely. They're camouflaged now with EDM lyrics.

We're supposed to be here to show off our marriage, and I'm more than happy to do that. As long as Blakely's safe.

She pushes her ass back against my groin, and I hiss a breath, letting my thoughts go. A second arm moves up my body to hang from my neck as she moves with more confidence.

Dipping my head, I pepper kisses along her collarbone and up her neck. "Careful, Blakely."

She shakes with a laugh I can't hear. The slow roll of her hips becomes more purposeful, forcing my groan into the open.

I'm already tempted to haul her into the bathroom and peel her dress up her hips, and this isn't helping at all. Instead of the bathroom, I'm contemplating leaving altogether.

"Don't be quick on the trigger, Jamie," she taunts with a nip at my jaw.

There's no doubt in my mind that the first time I get inside of her, I'll be worse than quick. Try instant.

I tune out the music and cameras recording our every movement, choosing to focus only on Blakely. Her touch is blisteringly hot as it glides up and down my neck, her nails taking a detour into my hair to tug at it every few passes.

My cock throbs, too restrained in my jeans while she rubs back against me, the hem of her dress rising higher with every sway of her hips. I slide my hand from her stomach to her upper thigh, holding it there.

"Do you know how easy it would be to get to your pussy like this?" I ask, my tone so garbled and strained that I'm not sure how she makes out the words with the music around us.

She moves faster, encouraging the dress to slip higher, touching my fingertips. "Maybe that was the point."

"If you want me between your legs, all you have to do is ask, baby."

"I don't want to have to ask."

My brows shoot up. "You want spontaneous, then?"

She answers with a sassy swish of her hips before leaning forward slightly and glancing at me over her shoulder. My throat strains with a swallow as I run my palm up her spine and finally bury my fingers in her thick curls. Letting go of the part of my brain that warns me we're not alone, I fist her hair and use the hold to haul her back to me.

Her head falls against my shoulder, rolling slowly before I'm sucking at her throat. I don't pull back until I'm positive I've left a mark.

"Do you know what the headlines are going to say tomorrow?" I ask into her ear.

She shakes her head, unable to speak as she rocks back against my body, muscles loose. I hold her low on her hip and plant my cock firmly against her ass.

"Jamie Bateman was unable to keep his hands to himself at Altitude and lays a public claim on his stunning wife in front of everyone who couldn't take their eyes off her," I growl, every inch of my skin buzzing with anticipation. "They could write any headline, and I'd be proud of it. Of being the man here with you tonight and the one who gets to take you home. Every single one of them wants to be in my place, Blakely. But you're not available, are you?"

She buries her face in my throat, glossy lips spreading over every inch of me that she kisses, laying her own claim.

I shift my hold to the side of her ass and squeeze. "Are you, wife?"

"No. I'm not available," she pants, her hands drifting to my hips and then to where we're connected.

Holding steady, I ensure there's no room for her to slip through and grab my dick. That's a headline in the making that would cross the line into the Blakely freak-out category.

"We're leaving," I tell her.

I'm already collecting her hands in mine and pushing us toward the exit before she can reply. If I don't get us both out of here now, my fantasy of taking her in the bathroom will be reality.

The team is up in VIP still, probably snooping on us right now. I puff out my chest at that, proud that I've made it clear she isn't up for grabs.

Blakely doesn't fight me as I lead us past the bouncer and through the doors. It's chilly tonight, and she doesn't have a jacket, so I move even quicker. When we make it to the curb, I wave down the cab coming our way.

"I haven't seen you move that quick anywhere but the field," Blakely teases.

"I've got priorities right now."

"And where am I on that list?"

I let loose a low laugh and haul her toward me with a hand on her nape. She grins, catching herself with two hands to my chest.

"There is no list. My only priority is you," I murmur, leaning in to kiss her—

"Oh, my God. You're Jamieson Bateman."

"Can I get a photo?"

"Wait, are you Blakely?"

"It's the both of you!"

Two voices appear, forcing me to miss out on kissing my wife. She turns her head to look at the women, and I follow suit, trying to keep my grumpiness from showing.

"It's totally you! I can't believe it. See, I told you we could be a few minutes late," the incredibly tall one says to the shorter, black-haired one, already pulling her camera app open.

Our cab is crawling up the curb toward us, leaving only a few seconds before we're free.

Blakely looks at the two girls and fusses with her hair. I'm more than aware of the red lip gloss that must be all over my neck, but seeing the women notice has me drifting toward arrogantly happy.

"Yes, I'm Jamie, and this is Blakely," I tell them, already starting to pull us in the direction of the cab.

The tall woman's eyes light up. "I just want to say that I think your love is so awesome. I've had such a crush on Jaxon Hayes for, like, ever, and I never expected a fan like me to—"

"Ignore her. She doesn't get out much. We'll leave you alone," the black-haired friend says with a winced smile.

Blakely doesn't let her haul the tall woman away before saying, "If you like him, go for it. He's a really nice guy."

A really nice guy? *Excuse me?*

I don't bother hiding my scowl, and when one of the women giggles, I find her staring right at me.

"That's cute. You really are in love with each other."

It's second nature to go along with what she's said. "I'm insanely in love with her. Which is why I have to get us out of here before we draw attention and lose our chance."

"Right! I'm so sorry." The tall woman moves to pocket her phone, but Blakely shakes her head.

"I can take a picture of you with Jamie, if you want," she offers.

The woman smiles softly. "Actually, could I get one with both of you?"

"Oh. Of course," Blakely says, eyes wide as they flash up at me.

I encourage her to stand beside the woman, and then her friend takes her phone, waving at us to get close. Blakely keeps a hand on my back as I toss mine over her shoulder, taking in her nervous smile when the flash goes off.

The woman rushes off to look at the photo as our cab honks its horn, done waiting.

"Have a good night, ladies," I say, nodding at the cab driver.

The women stare at us for a beat more before the black-haired one drags her friend into the line for the club. Blakely releases a tight breath and walks in time with me to the cab.

"They love you," I say.

She dismisses me with a shake of her head. "They came for you."

"Maybe. But it was you they stayed for."

And I can't blame them. I'd do the same exact thing.

34

Blakely

I ALMOST WISH I WAS DRUNK RIGHT NOW.

Being stone-cold sober is doing nothing for me. I'm horny beyond belief, and instead of having the courage to jump on Jamie the moment we got home, I flung my shoes off down the hall and ran up to my room.

I'm sitting on my bed in the dark, head hanging and swinging side to side. The soft comforter is clutched in my fists as my arousal mixes with frustration.

Jamie did everything right. He didn't push me or try to gain any ground that wasn't his already to take. I ran, and he didn't plow down my door to get to me. He's fucking perfect, and here I am, pulling away because I'm scared to sleep with him. With *anyone* after so long of being alone.

I'm not a virgin, but I'm far from experienced. My first time was in the back of a rusted old Ford in the heat of summer when I was eighteen. I didn't know how to orgasm with a partner then, and I'm still not sure if he even knew women could orgasm.

It's been a long, long time since then. Years that Jamie would have been plowing his way through Vancouver with suave grins and sweet talk.

Spikes of envy push through my stomach. It's uncomfortable enough that I stand and shove my hair back, suddenly hating the feeling of it touching my face.

Nate's already tucked in his bed, dead to the world. Even if I stomp down the hall toward Jamie's room, he won't wake up. I could slam a fist to the door, and my brother would still be fast asleep, none the wiser.

In a blink, I'm clutching my doorknob, my teeth gritted and nerves popping beneath my skin. I yank open the door and shove myself into the hallway before I can change my mind.

It's not like we have to have sex just because I'm going to his room. Jamie would never pressure me into that. Maybe I just want to sleep in his bed tonight. After our dancing at the club, I'm feeling unusually clingy. Like I don't think I could fall asleep alone.

God, that doesn't mean I don't want to bang the daylights out of him, though. Even just thinking of having him above me, or behind . . . or beside . . . *fuck*. I'm going to lose my damn mind.

His bedroom door is cracked open, and when I knock, it nudges forward another inch.

"Jamie?"

There's no reply, so I push the door open completely. Swiping my hands down my bare legs, I glance down at my nightshirt and cringe. It's unbelievably sad that this is the sexiest bed outfit that I own.

Stepping into his room, I notice the sound of running water and look toward the ensuite door. It's slightly ajar the same way his bedroom door was, and now I'm thinking back to every time I've ever passed his room at night. The door has always been shut completely. Except for tonight.

I suck in a long inhale before letting it out fast. Assumptions are for idiots. I know better than to read into something like this, but would I be an even bigger idiot not to assume he left both doors open for me?

Fuck it.

He wants me just as much as I want him. And it's not like the worst-case scenario here is that he freaks out seeing me in the bathroom while he showers and kicks me out of his house.

Yeah, no pressure.

Steam billows out from the bathroom, curling around me when I push the door open and take a cautious step inside. The vanity mirror is fogged up, and the heat from the shower is blistering. Or maybe that's just me.

I could combust into flames when I make out the figure in the shower. Glass doors do nothing to hide him, even with the mix of steam and fog. His bulk is too recognizable, every bulging muscle making the arousal in my belly start to burn.

Drifting closer, I toy with the hem of my shirt, contemplating taking it off and joining him beneath the water. That's why I'm in here, right?

I hold my breath and take it off. It's like peeling off a layer of my skin as fear and insecurity fling doubts around in my head. Cautiously, I add the shirt to the pile of his clothes on the floor and hover a hand over the shower door.

Jamie's not standing still beneath the water. Even with his back to me, this close up, I can see his arm moving at an even, quick pace.

My eyes grow wide. I throb between my legs when he groans long and low and shifts his body enough that I can see the thick shaft of his cock gripped in his fist. I gasp, my nipples tightening and becoming sensitive to the cool air that's following me from the open door.

Jamie plants a hand to the shower wall and thrusts into his fist. I peel the glass door open and blink through the fog, refusing to take my eyes from him as I step inside. The stone floor is wet and slippery as I make my way to him, careful not to fall.

Without the fogged glass in the way, I can make out every bunch of muscles straining in his back, the wet hair hanging down into his eyes, and the round ass that clenches with every stroke of his fist. He has two dimples at the bottom of his back and freckles along his spine that I can't help but want to sit and count. Thighs thick and strong and peppered with dark hair keep him steady.

My heart is in my throat when I step up behind him and press my naked breasts against his back. I wrap my arms around his body and gingerly cover the hand stroking his shaft with mine.

He doesn't flinch at my touch. It's a moan that slips from him instead of a command for me to leave.

"You came."

"I'm sorry I ran."

Releasing himself, he moves his hand aside and uses it to encourage me to take over for him. I do, not wanting to waste another moment.

Similar to the first time I had him in my hand, my pussy tightens, reminding me that there's a better place for us to stroke him. I shut my eyes and lean my cheek to his shoulder, stretching my fingers around his cock. He's so thick that my fingers hardly brush and long enough that I have to move around to his side just to touch it from base to tip.

"Don't apologize for that. I didn't expect anything," he mutters, voice shaky.

I drag my thumb over the wet tip of him to collect the slick liquid before jerking him again. He throbs in my grip, and I think he's going to come. But then he's spinning us.

The showerhead is directly above me as he steps back and rests against the wall, letting the water rush down over me. My hair is soaked in seconds, and the warm spray hits my heavy breasts next, dripping off my nipples onto the floor.

His eyes follow the stream of water, growing dark and edged with something almost feral. I feel the effects of that look with every pulse of my clit and drip of arousal that runs down my thigh.

It's the first time we've been naked in front of one another, and he takes his time inspecting every inch of my skin. First, my shoulders and breasts, then the roundness of my belly and stretch marks that span over my hips and thighs. Every wrinkle of cellulite on my thighs feels more obvious under his gaze, like they've been marked in permanent ink for him to see.

His cock doesn't get softer with every piece of me that he sees, though. With every movement of his eyes, it throbs, reddening at the tip and glistening with precum.

"It doesn't bother you?" I whisper, forcing myself not to eye-fuck his dripping wet abs.

"What do you mean?"

I push past the lump in my throat. "The way I look. My body."

He licks his lips and moves his hands to my belly. They spread outward to my soft waist and then down to my love handles. I'm completely unprepared for him to lower himself onto his knees and kiss everywhere his hands have been.

"I haven't been as attracted to another person as I am to you, Blakely. Women, men, you've trumped them all. I could spend hours standing right here just looking at you and your curves."

It's everything I've been needing to hear.

I'm weak to the pull of my impulses. With his words making me confident, I help him to his feet and then lower a hand to his balls, rolling them gently.

His entire body shudders as he struggles to hold my stare. "Baby. I'm barely holding on here."

"You're beautiful too, Jamie," I declare softly, resting my other hand between his defined pecs.

"Fuck," he blows out.

"I want you to show me what you were doing before I came in here. Show me what you do when you're in bed alone thinking of me."

He grabs his cock and squeezes, nodding to the opposite side of the shower where the water won't drown us.

"Only if you do it too."

I settle in front of him with my back to the wall and guide my fingers between my legs, parting my pussy and exposing how wet and swollen I am to him. He moves his fist in a long, slow stroke and stares between my legs.

"So perfect," he whispers, expertly collecting his cum to lube his shaft. "Don't leave it empty, baby."

My clit is so sensitive that I jerk against the wall when I roll it beneath my thumb. I'm wet enough that I fit a finger inside of myself without struggle.

"When I lay in bed and think of you, I dream of spreading you out on my bed and teasing that tight hole with my cock. Just the tip to start, but fuck, even with you dripping onto the sheets, it hardly fits," he hisses.

I thrust my finger in and out, my breasts swaying with the movement. "You said we'd make it fit."

"We will. You'll suck the tip inside after a few seconds, and I'll slip in another inch as you claw at my arms and stare down between us, begging for another."

Suddenly, one finger isn't enough. A second adds a hint of the stretch I know he's describing.

"How does it feel?" he asks roughly.

I push down harder on my clit. "Could be better."

"Mm, not yet."

"Keep talking. Please," I murmur.

His eyes flare as he increases his pace, stroking with a finish line in his mind.

"Once I can work the rest of my cock inside, I'll be deep enough for you to feel me in your belly. You'll try to suck me back in when I pull out, teasing you with just the tip again before thrusting hard, making my balls smack your perfect ass. Those pretty tits will be in my mouth, your nipples beneath my teeth as I suck on them."

There's an intense, full pressure building in my core, growing hotter with every stroke of my fingers in my pussy. The hard press of my thumb to my clit is ramping it higher, and my toes curl painfully into the shower tile.

"Oh, fuck, baby. That's it. Work that pussy for your husband, and I'll reward it with my cum. Coat that pretty clit before I lick it clean," he spits out, brows knitting together tightly as pleasure loosens his jaw.

I come hard. My knees shake when I yank my hand away from my pussy, watching in disbelief as I squirt across the distance between us. Jamie moves quickly, lowering himself to his knees again and covering me with his mouth.

Aftershocks mix with the wet sensation of his swiping tongue, and I fall forward, using his shoulders for balance. I cry out, and my legs shake as he buries his fingers inside of me and sucks at my clit. There's no time for disbelief when another climax rips through me, and he groans, staying right where he is.

When he stands, his arm is anchored around my back, carrying my weight. I melt against the wall and watch with parted lips as he brutally fucks his fists and releases a growl-like noise.

"Watch me claim you, Blakely. You're fucking mine."

He comes, and thick ropes of cum shoot from the tip, aimed directly at my pussy. Heat smothers the swollen, sensitive skin, and I whimper at the relief it brings.

"I want to taste," I whisper.

His features relax, adoration glowing in his stare as he scoops his cum onto his fingers and brings it to my mouth, spreading it across my lips.

"Open, wife."

I follow his order and moan when he glides his messy fingers across my tongue. Sucking them clean, I nip at his fingertip before he pulls them free.

"Your turn," he says, circling my wrist and bringing it between my legs.

I dip two fingers into my pussy and then push them into his mouth. Everything about this is intimate in a way I didn't expect but maybe should have. A man like Jamie is going to teach me things about myself that I've never thought to look for.

"Was that too much?" he asks after releasing my fingers and leading us back beneath the water.

It's still hot, and I close my eyes as it runs down my face.

"No. It was perfect."

His relief is obvious. "You're perfect."

"Is this when I say, 'No, you're perfecter'?"

"Only if I can say that you're perfectest."

He laughs and shifts us while digging his fingers into my hair. When they start to scrub, I smell the shampoo I always use. But I know I didn't bring it in here.

"Did you sneak into my bathroom and take my shampoo bottle?" I half mumble, half moan, distracted by the soothing sensation of his massaging my scalp.

"No. I just bought extras for my bathroom."

"Just in case I found myself needing to shower in here?"

He drags the extra shampoo through the ends of my hair before leaning my head back beneath the water. "Exactly. And right now, I'm glad I snooped."

"You're good at washing hair."

He finishes rinsing the soap out and drops down to squirt conditioner into his palm. When his fingers start brushing through the knots in my hair, he's incredibly gentle, making sure not to yank on any.

"I'll do it whenever you want," he murmurs.

"Do I get to wash yours?"

"Go for it, Bandit."

While my conditioner sits in my hair, I search for his shampoo and blow out an impressed breath when I see two separate bottles.

"No two-in-one?" I tease.

"My mom would have a stroke if she heard you ask me that.

She made sure both me and my brother used proper shampoo and body wash. I've used conditioner too. I'd bet Oliver uses three-in-one now, though, that grumpy shit."

I squirt some of the blue gel into my hands and lather it before gesturing for him to come out of the water. Leaning on my toes, I start scrubbing his head.

"You keep getting better and better."

"If all it took for you to say that was explaining my hygiene routine, I'd have shown you my shower weeks ago."

My mouth quirks as I lean him back into the water and rinse the soap out. He beats me to the bottle of body wash and uses it on me first, spending extra time on my chest.

"I haven't had a chance to introduce myself to these yet," he defends himself while I stand beneath the water.

"Oh, my apologies."

He beams up at me and pops a nipple into his mouth before retreating. "You taste like my body wash."

"Yum," I deadpan.

"Fuck, I'm so into you, Blakely. Keep saying stuff like that and I'm going to keep you."

It sounds perfect. But I refuse to get my hopes up.

We finish up in the shower, and Jamie uses his towel to bundle me up before sneaking out to grab another. When he returns, there's a towel around his waist and my hairbrush and moisturizer in his hands.

"Am I moving in?" I ask before thinking.

He blinks in surprise. "Do you want to?"

"That's not what I meant. I just blurted something out. I'm already in your house—"

With a soft kiss, he shuts me up. I let my eyes close and kiss him back, breathing in the manly body wash that lingers on both of us.

"Sleep here tonight and decide tomorrow if you want to move in. I want you here, just so you know," he says.

And that's that.

I already know this will be where I stay from tonight until the day I'm forced to leave.

35

Blakely

I WAS RIGHT.

Every night for the past week, I've been sleeping in Jamie's bed with him. I've fallen asleep still hot and sweaty from an orgasm or halfway through a movie that I've let him choose, knowing damn well I'm too tired to finish.

I wake up every morning to the black curtains still drawn over the tall windows and patio door and his pillow tucked beneath my arm from where he's slipped it before heading down to the gym.

It's become routine to throw one of his sweatshirts on and bring coffee down. At first, I didn't want to disturb him. I quickly changed my mind once I realized that sitting on the padded floor and watching him sweat and grunt every morning with a hot coffee in my hand was a damn good time.

We've spent so much time in the shower together after he's finished that I've used the rest of my body lotion just to keep from turning into a dry-skinned monster.

I ran out of it this morning and have a refill on the top of my grocery list. Because yeah, I can have a real list now. My first paycheque from the Pythons was deposited on Friday. The first of many, I hope.

Most of it went away in my savings, set aside for what I know Jamie won't take from me willingly but I'll somehow sneak into his house once we leave. The rest . . . well, the rest is mine.

Jamie has taken such good care of us. I'm grateful I can save most of what I earn. When reality hits in a month, it's going to be hard to fall back into what we used to be.

"Do you like pumpkin, Blakely?" Gracie asks, holding a tart up in front of me.

I blink, focusing on Jamie's mom and the women seated beside her at the table. The brunette on her right with silver streaks through her hair and emerald-green eyes is Ava Hutton, Jamie's aunt and Gracie's sister-in-law. Her daughter, Adalyn, is beside her, and after learning we're the same age, she has made me feel incredibly self-conscious, considering she's the definition of a blonde bombshell.

With a successful career in modelling, she's somehow not even the most famous person in this family. It seems Ava birthed and raised a top NHL player, a model, and Noah Hutton himself. I don't know how she did it and am honestly grateful for that. Having kids isn't even on my radar, let alone three who have the entire world eating out of their palms.

Gracie and Tyler seem to have the most normal family, and even that is a stretch. Oliver chose a career in firefighting, and Jamie is . . . Jamie. Labelling him as just a football player would be insulting.

"I don't mind it," I answer Gracie, taking the tart.

It's still a weird concept to me to have family get-togethers without a special occasion or planned dinner. We're not at the Batemans' house for a birthday or Thanksgiving dinner but just because they wanted to sit and visit with everyone.

"The berry tarts you brought us were delicious, and I wanted to try and make something festive for the season as a thank you. I'm not the best at them yet, though. Maybe you can give me lessons sometime."

"I'd love that," I say with a soft smile.

Braxton, Maddox's wife, snakes a pumpkin tart from the plate and sinks her teeth into it. I cover my mouth with my hand when I laugh and look back at Gracie, searching for her reaction.

"I see baby likes pumpkin. I'll make note of that for the baby shower," Ava muses.

Gracie is quick to unwrap another tart and hand it to Braxton. She snatches it instantly and, with her mouth still full of the first one, glances at me and mumbles, "I'm sorry. We skipped lunch, and I'm tempted to eat my own arm."

"Oh, it's fine. Congratulations on the pregnancy," I tell her, offering a sincere smile.

She huffs and tucks a bundle of tight black curls behind her ear. "Thank you. Apparently, the plan of only one wasn't good enough for my husband. The Huttons have magic sperm, I swear. Soon enough, I'll have to get one of those long leashes for my million babies."

"Another reason I'm glad to be a Hutton woman instead of married to a man," Adalyn cheers, taking a heavy swig of the cocktail Gracie made for us all earlier.

Braxton glares at the cocktail and sips from her massive jug of water. "As if you didn't give birth to a baby literally six months ago."

"I *let* myself get pregnant. If I hadn't, Cooper would have been trying for years with no result. You're a sucker who has to either become celibate or make Maddox triple-wrap it in a grocery bag or something."

It was easy to tell that the adorable toddler with the big, floppy pink bow in her blonde hair and a matching outfit to Adalyn was her daughter. Jamie made a beeline for her where she was playing on a fancy play mat the moment we got inside today, leaving me to figure myself out amongst his giant family.

Gracie was the perfect host and made sure I was introduced to everyone I hadn't met before. There must have been some sort of warning issued before our arrival because I've yet to be faced with even one person who doesn't approve of my being here.

I thought there would at least be one person who was obvious with their distrust and disbelief in a group this big. That hasn't been the case at all.

If Nate were here, I'd be clinging onto him for comfort, but he's at an extra practice, leaving me on my own.

Ava shakes her head at her daughter. "Can we please not talk about wrapping anything in a grocery bag, Addie? I'd like not to scare Blakely away so soon."

The weight of each one of them staring at me is hard to bear. I do my best to pretend I'm not feeling it.

Lifting my left hand, I wiggle my ring finger. "I'm afraid that there's no scaring me away now."

"That ring is gorgeous," Braxton says between bites of her desserts.

Addie leans over the table to get a closer look. "Did you help Jamie pick it out, or does he just actually have great taste?"

"I didn't help him at all."

"That's my boy," Gracie says, chin high.

"At least you don't have anything to worry about with Bateman sperm. You'll most likely end up with two boys. That seems to be their tradition," Addie sings.

Gracie hums. "That's not technically right. Tyler has two brothers."

"He does?" I ask before slamming my mouth shut with a wince.

There isn't time to worry about overstepping before Gracie's reaching across the table to pat my hand.

"Yes. His older brother isn't welcome in our family, so we forget about him more often than not. However, he is still blood," she explains.

Ava drinks some of her cocktail before adding, "Half-blood."

"If we're being that specific, yes. Both of Tyler's brothers are only half related to him. But in the same way his older brother isn't, his mother was never welcomed in our family."

My confusion must be obvious because Gracie offers me a sad smile and squeezes my hand.

"His mother was an addict for a long, long time. She didn't want help, and nobody had seen her in years to ask her to try again. A few years back, she overdosed. It was all a big hurdle to work past, but what's life without a little turbulence?"

It's a sucker punch to the gut. Emotion blurs my vision before I blink past it and gently push away from the table, smiling past the sudden pain in my chest.

"Excuse me, I just need to use the bathroom." I force the words up before retracing my steps out of the kitchen and down the hall to where I remember the bathroom being.

Taking the first left, I struggle to keep my gait slow and controlled when what I want is to run. I come to a dead end in front of a window and stop so fast I almost trip. The Bateman house isn't huge, but it's not all that easy to navigate when you've only been here once before.

"Fuck," I whisper, rubbing my palms against my forehead.

"I'm going to guess you're not in this hallway to stare out that specific window?" a deep voice asks from behind me.

It's like the universe is out to get me today because there's no other reason as to why it would be Jamie's father who found me.

"I was looking for the bathroom. It must have been right instead of left."

"Coming from the dining room, it actually would have been straight."

I blow out a tight breath. "Even better."

"Jamie's in the basement if you want to talk to him."

"Do I sound that bad?" I ask, letting my mask slip an inch.

"No. You sound fine."

I risk turning around. Tyler's leaning against the wall, his arms crossed and dark eyes peeling my skin back layer by layer in an attempt to see inside my head.

"In that case, I don't need Jamie to help me go to the bathroom," I say.

"I said that you sounded fine. Not that you were."

"Did he tell you about my mom, or does everyone only know about her from when Nate mentioned her to Gracie?" I blurt out, assuming he knows without having to be explicitly told.

He shakes his head, not giving away a single one of his thoughts with his blank expression.

"Neither. But I can tell there's a whole lot of grey in your past."

I fight past my every reaction and strain to speak without screaming. "Your wife told me about your mom."

"And it affected you," he states, not asks.

"My mom took off five years ago. She turned to drugs after my dad died. Once she couldn't stand seeing me and my brother anymore, that's when she left."

"I'm sorry, Blakely."

"Jamie knows my mom is gone. Do you think that's why he was interested in me? Because he felt bad and had some sort of epiphany that he could help me because you'd been through something similar?"

It was my first thought after hearing those words come out of Gracie's mouth. That Jamie chose me out of everyone else because he felt bad for me. That due to his father's traumas, he was doing me what he thought was a favour. If that's the case, I don't know what I'll do.

Tyler uncrosses his arms and takes a cautious step toward me. "While my son might be big-hearted, he's never let that cloud his judgment. He wouldn't have married you because of your past."

"So it's just a coincidence?" I scoff.

"Listen, Blakely, you can either let your past play into your present and make you jaded and unable to trust those who want to be in your life, or you can seek happiness in spite of it. To me, it looks like you've chosen the latter, so don't change course now.

Everyone has scars, whether externally or internally, but if you're ashamed of them, you'll never learn how to be proud of everything you've overcome.

"I went through hell for twenty years of my life, and I'll carry that with me to the grave. But with so much love in my life, it's easy to see the light ahead instead of the darkness behind me. Gracie was always my guiding light. Then my boys found me, and while I haven't forgotten my past, it's just that. My past. Jamie didn't fall in love with you because of something that happened to you but because of the person you became because of it. It will help to tell him about your past. All of it."

My eyes burn like I've just dumped hot sauce in them. I look away, putting all my focus into not crying in front of my husband's father. It's pointless when he sets a light hand on my shoulder.

"Do you hug?" he asks gruffly. I wipe beneath my eyes and nod once. "Alright."

Having him pull me into a tight, strong hug has every emotion inside of me intensifying. It's been years since I've gotten a hug like this.

Since before my dad died.

God, I know that the moment we break apart, I'm going to be mortified. Who in their right mind sobs in the arms of their husband's father after only their third time meeting? Add in my childhood trauma dump, and I'll have to use every excuse in the book to get out of coming here for the rest of our marriage.

"Bandit?"

I sniff, and with a firm pat on my back, Tyler releases me. Jamie's at my side in a flash, bundling me up in his arms. Comfort drapes over me, soothing some of the raging waters inside of my head and chest.

"What did you say to her, Dad?" he accuses, kissing the side of my head.

I part my lips, but Tyler beats me to speaking. "I'm proud of you, Jamie. Remember my advice, and come downstairs together when you're done."

Advice? Whatever it is, Jamie seems to understand. He nods at his dad, and we watch the older man walk away, not getting lost in the halls the way I did.

"What happened?" Jamie asks, voice soft.

"Your mom told me about your grandma."

He frowns. "She's not really my grandma."

"My mom is the same as her, Jamie. She's an addict who hated me and Nate. It wasn't even my father dying that made her hate us. She did from the moment we were born. I was an accident, and Nate was a mistake that she tried to correct but didn't succeed with. I'm broken and bruised and damaged. But you help. You don't even have to do anything, and you somehow smooth my scars.

"And now, I need you to promise me that you didn't choose me because you felt bad about my mom. Because if you did, I . . . I don't know what I'll do."

A thousand emotions flicker across his face, but it's affection that shines through them all. Affection that appears too much like love.

He takes my face in his hands and kisses my nose, then both of my cheeks. "You may be bruised, but you're not broken. And I didn't choose you because of your mom. Your pain and the struggle you've faced has never affected how I view you. For the good or bad. Not once."

"I'm sorry," I whisper brokenly.

Stroking my cheekbones, he asks, "For what? Being human?"

"For letting my emotions get the better of me. Especially here with your entire family around."

"Nobody knows but you, me, and my dad. Even if everyone did, they wouldn't view you any differently."

Without uttering another word, I shut my eyes and soak up the strength in the hands holding my face. Jamie ghosts his lips over my forehead and sighs, making no move to let me go.

It should be fear that strikes when I realize why Jamie's become my comfort in every terrifying situation or how he's the only one who seems to see through the walls I'm too afraid to let down.

Yet, somehow, accepting that I'm in love with this man brings me nothing but the steady calm I've been searching my entire life for.

36

Jamie

The basement game room is overflowing with members of my family, yet it's the woman sitting beside me that I care most about. She hasn't left my side since I found her in the hallway with my dad, and fuck, I don't want to let her go.

Not right now or ever.

She's sitting half on the cushion and half on my thigh, holding my hand in a tight grip that shows no sign of loosening. I'm not sure what's happening in her head, but I'm looking forward to finding out as soon as she wants to tell me.

My dad and uncle are perched at the small bar, staring over at us. The kids are upstairs, and while Mom would have usually opted out of hanging down here with us, she's hovering near Blakely. Her eyes are soft as she watches my wife, curious but silent, like she doesn't want to make anything worse.

It would be alarming to see how quickly my family fell for her if I wasn't so happy to see it. Blakely may not have told me all the specifics of her childhood and the past she's trying so hard not to let control her, but I don't need to know them. When she's ready to tell me everything, I'll be here ready to listen.

"You guys should come to Nate's football game on Friday," I say, continuing to run my fingers through her hair.

My uncle Oakley's expression fills with intrigue before he asks Blakely, "Nate's your brother, right?"

"Yes. He's a wide receiver for the Pacific Heights Thunderhawks."

"A wide receiver, hey? You been giving him some tips, Jamie?" Maddox asks, glancing up from where he's playing with toy cars on the floor with his son, Liam.

"He doesn't need them, but yeah, I've been helping. There's a future for him in football, and I'm not just saying that."

Blakely plays with my fingers, shifting even closer. "They've been practicing at the field nearly every night."

"I'd love to come to the game. It's been five years since we've been to a high school game, Ty. I miss the bad popcorn and foam fingers," Mom says with an airy tone.

Oliver enters the room from who knows where and sinks onto the opposite side of the L couch beside Mom. "You can still get bad popcorn and foam fingers at a Pythons game."

"You'll come too, won't you?" Mom asks.

"When?"

"Friday night. Nate's game," I say.

Oliver thinks for a second, pulling up his work schedule in his head, most likely. "Yeah, we'll come."

It's still weird to think that he has a whole-ass family of his own now. There's no more I for him. Only us or we.

"We'll be back home because the team plays Friday, but wish him luck for us," Maddox says.

He's constantly flying between Ottawa and here whenever he and Braxton have a chance. I've always wondered how much longer they'll do that. Once Braxton has the baby, will they choose to stay in Ottawa full-time until Dox's contract with the Beavertails is over?

Blakely nods. "I will."

"How's married life, J?" Oliver asks, his stare narrowed slightly.

I don't let his scrutiny affect me. Things are so different from when I came to talk to him the morning after his wedding. I was terrified then, and now I'm just lovesick.

"I'm happier than I've ever been," I admit, holding his stare and letting him see every bit of the truth in my words.

He sits back against the couch a few seconds later, seemingly happy with what he saw. I love my brother, but even if he hated Blakely, I don't think I'd be able to let her go.

We'd end up in a fistfight instead, and those have never ended well between us. If I win one round, he wins the next, and by the time we're calling a truce, we're bloody and bruised, and Mom is having a panic attack.

"Did I tell you that Blakely's working with the Pythons now? She's the team's caterer," I tell everyone, pride puffing my chest.

Mom gasps, grinning wide. "That's incredible. How are you liking it? Has Jamie been able to leave you alone long enough to get any work done?"

"Coach has had to come grab him a few times, but I don't mind his company. It's been great having so many people enjoy my food. Although, I wouldn't be surprised if they're all just too hungry after practice to taste what they're eating before swallowing it."

"Oh, we've been tasting it. Jax has asked approximately five thousand times if he could be invited to dinner just so you'd feed him," I say, twirling her hair around my finger.

She twists to look at me, her cheeks flushed. "Did you tell him yes?"

"Absolutely not. He sees you enough at work."

"Awe, are you jealous, Jamie?" Maddox teases with a stupidly smug smirk.

Uncle O scoffs a laugh. "Don't throw stones, Dox."

"I remember watching all of you losing your minds over anyone so much as looking at your wives, so yeah, be careful with your glass houses," I say.

"I think it's adorable," Mom sighs, touching her chest. "Jealousy keeps the spark alive."

Pointing at Dad, Oliver pokes at him, "Hear that, old man? Mom wants you to get jealous more often."

"Oh, he was jealous enough when we were your age," Mom says, winking at her husband.

"He nearly beat the shit out of your mom's neighbour because he saw him in her apartment handing her their mixed-up mail," Uncle O explains. "Seems more like anger management issues than jealousy."

Dad scowls at his brother-in-law. "He could have slipped it under the door. Didn't need to be in her place alone. And watch it. I can still beat your ass now just as well as I did back then, Oakley."

"I absolutely invited him inside on purpose. You were a real jerk back then. Don't be mean to my brother," Mom chirps.

Uncle O swirls the whiskey in his glass and huffs. "As if he stopped being an asshole just because he's old now. Why did I give you permission to marry my sister again?"

"When did this turn into a beat on Tyler fest? Pay attention to my son and his wife instead," Dad grunts.

"Speaking of sons and wives," Oliver starts, stretching his legs out in front of the couch. "When's Noah marrying Tinsley?"

Blakely brings her mouth to my ear and keeps her voice soft, just for me to hear. "I still can't believe Noah Hutton is your cousin."

I nip at her jaw. "Are you trying to make me jealous now?"

"That depends."

"On what?"

"What will you do to me if I say yes?" she purrs.

Fingers still in her hair, I tug just enough for her to feel it. "If I get hard right now, I'll be taking you out of here thrown over my shoulder."

Her body shakes with a silent laugh as she shifts forward again. I drape my arm over her shoulders and spread my legs, knocking her knee as we tune back in to the conversation happening around us.

"They've been busy. I say give it another year and we'll be planning another wedding," Mom says.

I clear my throat and draw patterns over Blakely's bicep. "Maybe baby Hutton is scared she'll turn him down."

"Okay, first, you can't call him a baby when he's older than you. And second, it's more likely that they simply don't think it's necessary to get married. When you're *that* connected to a person, maybe marriage just doesn't carry the same meaning as it does for us," Maddox says.

Mom nods, patting Oliver's knee. "They seem content doing what they're doing now. We've had so many weddings recently. A break wouldn't be bad."

Blakely yawns as I bite back a smile, watching her try to hide it. We've been here for long enough, and while I love seeing her getting to know my family and slowly finding her spot inside of it, I'm antsy to have her all to myself again.

It's harder to leave today than it usually is, and I blame that wholeheartedly on my mother when ten minutes later, she refuses to release Blakely's hand.

"She's going to come back, Ma," I say, pulling at Blakely's shoulders again.

We're on the driveway, the SUV already running and the heater blasting. I should have known when Mom followed us outside that we'd be here. What happened earlier has sparked the momma bear inside of her.

She holds Blakely's hand and stares fiercely into her eyes. "If you need anything, call me. I can bring snacks to Nate's game or swing by and visit you at work—"

"You're not bothering her at work, Ma," I tell her, sighing.

My wife squeezes Mom's hand right back. "I appreciate your offer, Gracie. Really."

"Alright. Well, I'll see you Friday night, then."

I rest my hand low on Blakely's back and open the passenger door. "Yes, Ma."

"I'll let you know about the snacks," Blakely adds.

Mom reluctantly releases her hand and quickly kisses my cheek before stepping away. "Okay, you two. Drive safe."

"We will. Love you, Mom."

"Love you, honey."

Blakely gets in the SUV and waves at Mom while I shut the door and linger. Mom waits expectantly for me to speak.

"Don't freak her out," I murmur, shifting away from the door.

"She doesn't look freaked out, Jamie."

"Whatever you saw earlier, just don't be so obvious with how it made you feel. If she thinks anyone pities her . . ."

"I know. I'm sorry."

I pull her in for a quick hug, saying, "She's strong, and I know she'd appreciate it if everyone treated her like it."

"Of course she's strong. That's why you were drawn to her."

"Oh, is that it?"

"One of the reasons, smartass."

I let loose a soft laugh and start rounding the hood. "We'll talk about the game this week."

"Alright. I love you, Jamie."

"Love you too, Ma."

She stands on the driveway and watches us until we turn out of view. Blakely drops a hand to my thigh and holds me for every minute of our drive home, and yeah, I might have driven a bit under the speed limit to get a few extra minutes of her touch.

I'm a simp for my wife. Sue me.

"Ready?" I shout, the wind carrying my voice down the field.

Nate claps his hands above his head and bends his knees, ready to take off. He's tired from practice but didn't hesitate to take me up on my offer of doing a few more drills.

"Go!"

He starts running down the field, his pace a bit slower than usual. I'm a shit shot compared to Jax, but I still manage to send the football piercing through the air quick enough for him to start tracking it over his shoulder.

"Faster, Nate!"

The kid pumps his arms harder, tearing his cleats into the grass as he pushes himself. Blakely blows on her hands to warm them and watches her brother speed down the field yard by yard. Nate jumps into the air and catches the ball in his right hand before landing perfectly.

"Touchdown! Take it all the way!" I yell, clapping louder with every yard he passes.

"He's really fast," Blakely whispers, in awe.

"Crazy fast, baby. Faster than I was in high school."

She loops her arm through mine. "You think he'll make it?"

Nate sails into the end zone and spins, throwing the ball up into the air. He shouts something, but the wind carries it away from us.

"CFL or NFL, yeah, he'll make it," I say.

He swipes the ball off the ground and starts jogging toward us as Blakely claps and rests her cheek against my bicep.

"I never asked why you chose the CFL. I doubt it was because you didn't have interest from the NFL."

"Most of the interest I had was actually from NFL teams, but moving away from my family never would have worked for me. Playing in the Canadian league meant I could stay close."

"You went to university, then?"

"UBC like my dad. I was a kinesiology student, but my grades were terrible. The only thing I remember is that it's important to stretch both before and after working out."

She laughs. "So, when Nate asks what he should do in university, I shouldn't tell him to ask you for ideas?"

It's clear that she doesn't know what she just insinuated. There was no chance of me missing it. Not when I've been searching for a sign for weeks that she might not want to leave after all.

"We've got two more years before that conversation comes up," I muse.

"It'll be hard to convince him to focus on anything besides football."

"I can be pretty persuasive," I drawl, kissing her temple.

She pinches the underside of my arm, and Nate slows his job, closing in on us while I grunt at the sting.

"That was awesome," he pants. "I didn't think I was going to get there."

Blakely rubs his sweaty hair. "We never doubted you."

"Want to go again?" he asks me, swatting at his sister's hand.

"You need to cool down. Overworking yourself sounds like a great idea until you run out of steam. Let's head home."

He frowns, holding in his argument in exchange for a tip of his chin. "Alright."

"I'm making burgers for dinner. Does that help?" Blakely asks.

I snag his duffle bag from the grass and toss it over my shoulder before the three of us head back to the car.

"It doesn't hurt," Nate answers.

No, it doesn't. But I'm sure we'd eat anything Blakely made.

37

Blakely

The heavy blue blanket draped over Jamie's and my shoulders is scratchy, but with the chill tonight, it's better than nothing. Plus, it's a great way to hide from the groups of moms crowding around us and gossiping without a care, as if I'm deaf and unable to hear their judgmental comments.

Nate's been playing better than every single one of their kids, and I think it's making them dislike me that much more. It's a shame I don't give a shit about them.

"Get 'em, Nate! Kick some ass!" Jamie shouts, unbothered by the stares and gasps coming from the bleachers.

I shouldn't laugh, but it's impossible not to. "Jamie."

"Yes, gorgeous wife of mine?" he sings innocently.

Nate puts his helmet on and waves at us before heading onto the field with the offense. I scoot closer to Jamie and tuck myself beneath his arm, trying to steal his warmth.

"The moms are already out for my blood without you reminding them that you're here," I mutter.

"It's just jealousy, Bandit."

"Oh, I know it is. Not only is Nate the best player on the team by far, but we're both here with you."

He kisses my head twice, his favourite way to show affection to me. I've grown to love it more every time he does it.

"It's too bad for them that I'm here with my family and not them, then, isn't it?" he asks softly.

My stomach flips, and my mouth curls into a smile. "Yeah, I guess so."

"Uncle J!"

Nova comes barrelling down the bleachers toward us, followed by her parents and grandparents. Avery wiggles her fingers at us and pulls her daughter's toque down over her braids when it starts slipping off.

"Hey, Nova-Bug. Loving the stripes," Jamie says, pointing at the two blue stripes on her cheeks.

She beams at him. "Thanks. I did them like you do sometimes when you play. It's good luck for Nate."

I pull my purse from the empty space beside me and tuck it between my legs so she can sit. When she flops down, she calls her mom's name.

Avery takes the spot beside her. "Yeah, baby?"

"Blakely has a purse just like I do."

It's Oliver who replies, staring at Jamie with a smug smile. "I figured that's who you ended up giving it to."

"My purse has flowers on it. Handprints too," Nova exclaims, bending forward to get a closer look at mine. "Why does yours have masks? And splotches."

"They're not splotches, Nova-Bug. They're Xbox controllers," Jamie says.

"They don't look like it. No offense."

Gracie meets my eyes from the end of the row where she sits sandwiched between Tyler and Oliver. "Sorry we're late. Did we miss much? Are you cold? I have some extra gloves with me if you want them."

"I'm okay. Thank you. And it's been a slow start. Nate's got two touchdowns so far."

"So exciting! Just let me know if you need to warm up."

Jamie chuckles, rubbing a hand up and down my jacketed arm. "She likes you."

"She's just being nice."

"No, I mean it. She loves you."

I don't know what to say, so I focus on the game instead. The offense gets into position for a second down, and Nate shifts over a few paces as soon as the QB has the ball, looking around. It's hard to see everything that's going on. I don't know much more than the basics and what I've picked up from Jamie. What I do know is that when the QB throws the ball, it's to Nate.

My brother is already sprinting down the field, players diving at him the entire way but never making contact. Not until one grabs the back of his jersey and pulls hard enough to send him stumbling backward. Jamie shoots up, taking the blanket with him as the defenseman reaches for Nate's face mask and uses it to force his head to the side.

Nate tumbles to the ground, and I go still, suddenly frozen solid. The crowd goes silent while the ball hits the field a few feet away from him. Jamie doesn't say a word before he's excusing himself through the people on the stands below us and heading for the field.

I wait for something to follow the bad play, like a flag or a whistle, but when the whistle does blow, it's only to mark the play dead. The defenseman who took down Nate steps over him and takes the ball with a smirk.

Jamie's voice is so loud I can hear his words as clearly as if he were still sitting beside me. "What the fuck was that? You're not going to call that? Are you being serious? This is high school ball!"

The referee in front of him shakes his head and replies, but apparently, he doesn't care enough about this to be loud.

I'm suddenly standing, and when a small hand takes mine, I look down to see Nova smiling supportively. Gracie is moving past Oliver and Avery, coming to sit in Jamie's spot.

My husband takes a menacing step in front of the ref and points at the field. His anger is potent, and despite his laid-back attire of jeans, a light-coloured jacket, and a backward hat, he's not someone who should be taken lightly right now.

The ref extends a hand in front of him, motioning for Jamie to take a step back. Jamie laughs, reaching beside the ref to grab a yellow flag from his back pocket.

I glance between where Nate's pushing himself up onto his feet and where Jamie moves close to him and drops the flag on the field.

"That's how you do your fucking job. Since you forgot," he snaps before moving to Nate's side and easing his helmet off.

I bite down on my cheek and watch him cup the back of Nate's head and ask him a question. Nate says no, then nods.

"He's most likely asking him if he hit his head," Gracie tells me.

"Because he could have a concussion," I whisper.

"Jamie had two when he was in high school. I used to have nightmares about them."

"Nate hasn't had one. Not yet."

Nova squeezes my hand. "He will be okay. Uncle J will make sure of it."

Oliver reaches behind his wife to rub at Nova's back before standing. "I'm going to go down and make sure he doesn't go back for that ref."

"Thank you," I mumble, starting to feel guilty for not being the one taking care of this. "Maybe I'll go too. Nate's my brother."

Usually, I'd be the one threatening a ref for missing that call. It's my responsibility to take care of him.

"Jamie's got this one, sweetheart," Gracie soothes.

I know he does. With every second he's down there talking to my brother and his coach, the harder I fall in love with him. I trust him to take care of this, and that's the scariest part.

"How about you go get a drink? I can come with you if that would help," Gracie offers, trying so damn hard to comfort me.

"A drink is good. I'll be quick."

"Alright, sweetheart. Jamie's got your brother."

I give a shaky nod in response and start making my way past everyone else and then down the bleachers. The concession stand is close, and the line is short with everyone too busy with watching Jamie Bateman beat a referee's ass at a high school football game.

It will be a good headline tomorrow. Graham will be happy with it, at least. As far as I know, while they aren't selling out of seats every night, the buzz we've managed to create so far has helped with more than just filling a few rows at the stadium. The online traction has been building, and jersey sales are up.

It's almost hard to believe that I was able to help with that. Plain Jane Blakely Monroe has made a difference in the sports world. I wouldn't have bought it three months ago.

The line at the concession clears out, and I step up, ready to order when the air shifts. A rock settles in my stomach like a bad omen, and I flash an apologetic smile at the concession worker before stepping aside. It's almost like I know who I'm going to see before I turn around.

"Blakely?"

Pain steals my breath. Her voice is the same as it was five years ago, only lighter, like without the weight of us, she's happier.

Hiding my emotions behind a blank mask, I turn around to face my mother.

"What the fuck are you doing here?" I ask before she has a chance to open her mouth.

She looks as terrible as she did the day she left, with her hollowed cheekbones, thin brows, and pale green eyes. Her jacket is puffy, missing a zipper, and most likely stolen.

The resemblance she has to me is uncanny. It's enough to piss me off all on its own, as if I don't have a million other things to be mad about first.

"Is that really how you want to greet me after five years apart?" she asks.

"I don't want to greet you at all, so I'd take what I've offered if I were you."

"Alright, fine."

I lift my brows pointedly. "So? What are you doing here? How did you even know about the game?"

"I've been around. And this is where you went to school. Nathan was always playing football. Figured this was a good place to look for you."

"I'm surprised you even remember any of that. You were high so often that you spent weeks calling him Nathanial."

She purses her lips and glances away. "It's there. In bits and pieces."

"Good for you."

"Well, I see there's no love lost here," she jokes gruffly, looking at me again.

"Does it really matter to you? What do you want? Money?"

"You always were the smart one out of you and your brother."

Anger bubbles beneath my skin. "I don't have any money to give you."

"I don't believe you."

Scoffing, I steal a look toward the field to make sure there isn't anyone coming toward us. There isn't anyone.

"Do you think you left me with a trust fund when you took off? I've been raising your son on my own. Sorry that money's a bit tight right now."

"That was before, Blakely. Things have changed for you now."

My hackles rise as I piece together what she's hinting at. "No, they haven't."

She slides her hands into her jacket pockets and sighs. "I saw the video of you, honey. All it took was one Google search to learn everything. You're not being truthful with me right now."

The video of me telling off the reporter, most likely.

"My husband's money is not my money. And it certainly isn't anything that I would give to you. So, if that's what you came for, you can leave now."

"Nathan is only fifteen, sweetie."

"You don't have to remind *me* of his age," I spit, my restraint starting to slip.

"I do. Because until he's eighteen, he's mine to care for. And maybe I'm starting to feel a little homesick."

She's not my mother right now. The only thing she is right now is a danger to my brother. That's what I tell myself when I lunge for her.

"If you're going to threaten me, do it outright," I demand, taking a fistful of her jacket and using the hold to haul her toward me. "Try taking him from me. I dare you."

"What's going on here?" Jamie asks, appearing at my side. With a steady hand, he peels my fingers from my mother's coat and shifts me ever so slightly behind him, his eyes finding mine. "What did she do to you?"

My mother guffaws, straightening her jacket. "What did I do to *her*? Did you not see the way she was touching me?"

"I did, and my question stands," he snaps.

I take a deep breath and press my hand to his back. "Let's just go, Jamie."

He doesn't immediately agree. Concern pulls his features taut as he hesitates, searching my eyes for answers, knowing he won't find any on my face.

"Please. I want to see Nate," I whisper.

Interlocking our fingers, he nods stiffly and moves me to his other side, the one furthest away from my mother.

"You don't want to stay and chat? It's rude not to introduce your mother to your husband, Blakely," she calls as we start to leave.

Jamie tightens his hold. I'm too scared to look up and see if he's embarrassed or upset. Instead, I keep my mouth shut and hope that he knows me well enough to keep from asking me to open up about this right now.

It'll happen as soon as we get home. But for now, I just want to play pretend.

38

Jamie

I shut and lock the front door before joining Nate and Blakely in the kitchen. The kid is bouncing off the walls, his shakedown during the first half of the game long forgotten in the excitement of a win. He played amazingly and deserves to feel proud.

It's a shame that I'm struggling to share his excitement. One look at where Blakely's leaning back against the countertop with her arms crossed and expression closed off and I know she shares the same feelings.

There's a conversation brewing. It has been since I caught her one second away from catching a charge by the concession stand. In the months that I've known her, I haven't seen her that angry before. Not even when I poke and poke at her just to get her attention.

Their mother is exactly who and what I pictured. Someone with more concern for themselves than they've ever shown to another person and who would sacrifice you for their own benefit every single time.

What else do you expect from someone who abandons both of their kids?

"Did you see my last catch? I totally thought I wasn't going to get it!" Nate shouts, spinning around and shooting his arms into the air.

Blakely forces a smile. "I knew you were going to catch it. You never miss."

"Well, I did tonight. But it was a dirty play, so I won't count it."

"You shouldn't. That kid is a little shit. He keeps that up and he'll find himself playing soccer instead," I say, reminded of exactly what happened.

Teenager or not, I should have kicked that shithead in the ass. You don't make plays like that. Not anywhere. I don't care if you're a pro in the NFL or some six-year-old just learning. Football comes with enough risks without adding dirty players out to cause harm into the mix.

If anything had happened to Nate, I don't know what I'd have done.

Oliver would have had to do a lot more than just take my arm and pull me off the field, that's for sure.

"Ew," Nate says, shuddering.

Blakely sighs. "Soccer isn't that bad. You wanted to play it before you started with football. It's safer, at least."

"Please don't start with the safety stuff now, Lake. I'm fine. It didn't even hurt. You saw how quickly I shook it off."

My wife brings her eyes to me, the question in them obvious.

"He was cleared, Bandit. There are no signs of a concussion," I promise.

She holds my stare for a beat longer before letting it go. "Alright. In that case, you don't need me to linger and baby you. I'm going to head to bed."

"Already? It's only nine. I was hoping we could play some *Madden* or something for a bit," Nate says.

I squeeze his shoulder, stepping in. "How about you get some sleep tonight, and we'll play in the morning before I head to the stadium?"

"Are we invited to your game tomorrow?" he asks, almost nervously.

"You're invited to every one of my games, buddy. We'll talk about it tomorrow. I think we're all just tired. Tonight was big."

Nate nods, half of his mouth tugging up. "Yeah, okay. We'll play tomorrow. Good night, Lake. Night, Jamie."

"Good night. Love you," Blakely murmurs, lingering.

I ruffle Nate's hair and move to Blakely's side. "Night, Nate. Don't forget to take a shower. You reek."

He laughs, waving me off. "Whatever."

Blakely pulls away once I get to her and starts down the hall. I follow, slowing my pace to give her some room to breathe. Now that we're alone, I expect her to finally allow herself the chance to feel and register everything that's happened tonight.

She was expertly closed off once we got back to my family and watched the game as if nothing was wrong. I saw right through her and knew we'd face it once we got home.

Not just her. But us. Together.

I trail after her, bypassing her old bedroom and going into the one we share. She collapses on the bed, staring blankly at the wall. The air goes taut as I shut the door and peel off my jacket. I sit beside her, preparing for the building storm to erupt.

"Talk to me, baby," I coax, risking having my hand bitten off when I reach for her thigh.

"What do you want me to say? Surprise! That was my mom, and yes, she is as terrible as she seems. Worse than. That was only a preview of what I dealt with my entire life. If we hadn't been in public, I guarantee she'd have said far worse things. It wouldn't have mattered that you were there to hear."

"Yeah, Blakely. That is what I want you to say. I want you to say whatever you need to so that you don't bottle it up. You're safe here. Scream, shout, cry. Punch the wall or me, even. Just let it out."

She shoots onto her feet and shakes her head, jaw straining. My sweatshirt hangs off her shoulders, falling to cover her thighs. It's a common outfit for her to wear now, and I've been enjoying watching my sweatshirts disappear from the closet one by one. Slowly, she's fully integrated herself into my life and my space, and I can't get enough.

I'm so completely head over heels in love with this woman, and all that's left now is for her to accept that and let me see the parts of her she hasn't yet.

Starting here.

"That's the thing, Jamie. This house is my safe place. This room is sacred to me. Why should I have to stain the walls with talks of her?"

"They won't be stained because I'll help you repaint them."

Staring down at me, she blows out a long breath and curls her fists. Rage morphs into pain, and then her shoulders drop. I push back on the bed and motion for her to come closer, knowing that drop was heavy.

She moves in front of me and gently braces her hands on my shoulders before crawling onto my lap and closing her eyes to hide the devastation there. I pull her further up my body and hold her thighs, keeping her in place.

"Talk to me, Blakely. Please," I beg.

There's a heavy pause as she brings her hands up to play in my hair, searching for comfort. "My dad was a scaffolder. He worked long hours every day of the week besides Sunday to make sure we were taken care of. Mom didn't work at the time and was more interested in pretending that she was a good mother than helping contribute to the family. She was a great actress in front of Dad, and I think he saw through her but never outright said anything about it because of me and Nate."

Her swallow is loud, and I palm her back, encouraging her to lean forward against me. When her face moves to the curve of my shoulder, I prepare for the worst of her story.

"He had a stroke eight years ago. It wouldn't have killed him had he been at home and not on the side of a building without being properly hooked up."

"Fuck. I'm sorry, Blakely."

She pushes forward. "Mom left three years later. And honestly, it's a miracle she stayed that long. Without Dad's job, she pulled in some money here and there while I got a job anyplace that would illegally hire a thirteen-year-old and tried to make up for what was lacking. When she left, things just got worse. I couldn't keep up with the bills she left behind, and, well, you know what happened next."

"You did the best you could. Tell me you know that."

"Did I though, Jamie? Because I went days without eating more than stale crackers, peanut butter, and whatever scraps were left after I made sure Nate was fed. I let the bills lap over for months at a time and spent so much time working that I missed out on moments with Nate that I can't ever get back. Not to mention that we were a few weeks away from being kicked out of our apartment and out on the street. For God's sake, you paid Nate's football fees, got him new gear, took care of the piles of overdue bills, and welcomed us into your home. If you hadn't done that..."

I shake my head, leaning my cheek to her temple. "Don't paint me out to be some kind of hero because of that. I wasn't a guy on the street looking for a family in need of saving. You agreed to be my wife, baby, and all of those bills and fees I paid were part of our agreement. It wasn't an easy decision or sacrifice for you to make letting me do that for you, but you did it anyway. Just like you made every other thousand sacrifices over the last eight years. It was you and you alone that kept your family in the place it is now," I declare, needing her to hear me. "Nate is beyond lucky to have you in his life. We both are."

She leans back in my arms and stares down at me, her fingers travelling along the edge of my jaw. It's like she's discovering who I am for the first time all over again with every stroke along my brow or down my nose. I let her touch me without speaking another word, giving her full control here.

"You have no idea how happy I am that it was your house I wandered into," she whispers, tracing the shape of my lips.

"Yeah, Bandit, I think I do."

"It's not just this place that feels safe to me, Jamie," she breathes out.

Gently, I hold her cheek and guide her close, our noses brushing. "It isn't?"

"No."

"So tell me what does," I murmur.

"It's not a what but a who."

She drifts her hand down to my chest and softly pushes me until I lie on my back. I look up at her as she curls her fingers into the comforter beside my head and hovers close, still too far away.

"You're my safe place, Jamie. It doesn't matter where I am. If you're there, I know nothing bad can happen to me. To us. I trust you to protect not only me but my brother. I've never trusted anyone but myself with Nate before."

My chest tightens, my heart thrashing in encouragement. I take her cheeks in my hands and stroke my thumbs across her pink-tinted skin. When I bring her close enough for her hair to create a curtain over both of our faces, it's easy to say my next words.

"I love you, Bandit. Loved you from the moment you called me Pretty Boy and left me that chicken pot pie in the fridge. I'll *always* take care of you."

She bites down on her lip to stifle the raw noise clawing up her throat. I ghost a kiss over her mouth, and she releases her lip, pressing both firmly against mine.

Her hands find my stomach as she pushes up and snares my eyes, refusing to let them go. "Show me, Jamie."

"Are you sure?"

"So sure," she whispers.

I smooth my hands down her body and cradle her waist. "There won't be any going back."

"Are you trying to scare me away?"

"It's a little too late for that, isn't it?"

She smiles softly, moving her finger in an S down my stomach before starting to make the same movement between each set of abdominal muscles.

"Yeah, husband. It is."

39

Blakely

I love you too, Jamie.

It should be easy to say the words back, yet my tongue won't form them. The feelings are there, so obnoxiously obvious that I've drawn the conclusion that there's just something wrong with me.

I'm ready to hand myself over to him completely, yet his declaration goes unreciprocated. If he were a lesser man, he'd have grown too offended to still look into my eyes with unguarded, piercing love, regardless of my inability to repeat the words.

Jamie is far from a lesser man. Instead, he's the one-of-a-kind type that you don't stumble upon out of nowhere. It was nothing short of a miracle that I found him, some sort of guiding hand from the universe itself leading me to his house.

Whatever it was doesn't matter now that I have him.

"I haven't been with anyone in a long time," I admit, keeping him pinned beneath my body.

"Good. You're mine."

It's a blunt, claiming statement.

His hips shift, and I feel the hard length of him between my legs. Sparks of pleasure ignite where we touch, and I roll my lip between my teeth, seating more of my weight over his shaft.

Eyes darkening, he presses his fingers harder into my waist and encourages me to grind down. The pressure draws a moan from my chest. I'm tempted to say fuck it and drop to my knees right now. I haven't had him in my mouth yet, but I've been trying to for days.

Jamie's usually too focused on pleasuring me to pay much attention to the way I reach for his cock and attempt to blow him damn near every night.

Maybe I should change that.

When I shrug his hands off my body, he simply quirks a brow and watches me slide to the floor. The cold, hard floor bites into my knees through my thin leggings, but that doesn't stop me from reaching for his hips.

His eyes don't sway while I pop open the button and unzip his jeans. When I tug at the waistband, he lifts his hips and lets me pull them down his legs. Doubt wiggles through my brain once I toss the jeans out of the way, reminding me that I've never done this before and will probably be shit at it.

We've been taking things slow, and yeah, I've jerked him off more than a few times, but this is . . . this is far more intimate. My lack of experience wouldn't have been such a big hitter if he wasn't who he is.

The guy who's probably had his fair share of women in this exact position. Women who didn't need any guidance or instructions.

In only his tight, black boxer briefs, I can make out every inch of his length as it stretches the material. And when Jamie lifts his shirt an inch up his stomach, I rub my thighs together and stare at the glistening tip peeking out of the waistband.

Callused fingers curl beneath my chin, tipping it back so I'm forced to stare up at his face. "What do you need from me?"

"I don't know," I say, hating how hot my cheeks feel.

"You won't do anything wrong. If you breathe on my dick, I'll be ready to come."

I roll my eyes, the corner of my mouth tipping up. "What if I hurt you by accident?"

"Don't use your teeth and you won't hurt me."

To make things easier for me, he pulls down his briefs and chucks them across the room. I swallow the excess spit in my mouth as the full, bare length of him comes into view, and he spreads his legs at the edge of the bed.

"Come here," he soothes, taking his cock into his hand and giving it a long, slow jerk.

I sway forward, sliding my hands from his knees to his thighs. Cautiously, I reach for him, replacing his hand with mine.

"You know what I like. Now, use your mouth."

The dark tip is wet with his arousal, and I act without letting myself think. With him hot and hard in my palm, I drop my head and lap at the pearl of liquid.

He hisses a breath and bucks forward, reaching for me but only sliding a gentle hand through my hair.

I moan at the pressure of him threading his fingers through the strands and pulling gently.

"Good girl, Blakely. Do that again."

There's more cum waiting the second time I swipe my tongue over the slit. And when I open my jaw and take the whole head into my mouth, it continues to flow.

Batting my lashes, I keep him pressed against my tongue and look up, searching for approval in his burning gaze.

"Take a bit more. Get it nice and wet—*fuuuck*. Yeah, fill that pretty mouth with your husband's cock," he groans, thighs spasming beneath my elbows.

My gag reflex has me stopping with only half of him inside before I'm forced to retreat. Thick ringlets of spit drip down the few inches I couldn't fit, and I use my hand to spread them along the shaft.

"You're doing so good, baby," he praises, dropping a hand behind him to rest on the bed while the other remains buried in my hair. "Just a little more. I won't last if you keep going."

I suck the tip into my mouth, then release it with a pop. "What if I don't want you to last?"

"Then take what you want."

It's good enough for me.

Determined, I keep my fingers wrapped around the base of him and drop my head, taking him as deep into my mouth as I can. The salty flavour of him is familiar, and I can only blame our feeding habit for that. It's a kink that I didn't know I had but have grown to really, really love.

I'm hot beneath his heavy sweatshirt, and with only a sports bra on, my nipples are stimulated in the tight material with every rise of my chest. The centre of my leggings is damp, my panties sodden. Every inch of me is sensitive and aching, but I'm too focused on him to search for relief.

Every bob of my head and jerk of my wrist has him fidgeting above me and my hair wrapped another time around his knuckles. I whimper when he pulls on my hair harder than before.

The sharp bite of pain travels down my spine and spasms in my core, an invisible finger flicking my clit.

"Last chance to pull back," he grunts, voice cracking.

I suck him harder, too focused on succeeding at this to heed his warning.

The veins along his shaft rub against my palm, the muscles throbbing as he sucks in a breath and releases my hair so he can hold my head in place. Gagging when he thrusts deep enough to hit the back of my throat, I don't try to pull away.

"Fuck. Swallow it for me, Blakely. All of it," he grunts before heat slashes my throat.

I press my tongue to the bottom of my mouth and swallow. His shaft slips further down my throat, and my eyes water and burn while he comes.

It goes on until tears drip down my cheeks and he's swiping them away, pulling out to haul me over his body. He drops me onto the mattress beside him, hardly breaking a sweat after tossing me around like I'm a hundred pounds soaking wet.

I don't have time to move from my splayed-out position before he's hovering above me and yanking his shirt over his head. My eyes cross at the sight of his naked, tanned skin and muscles for fucking days. It's been two months of being around him, and I've yet to not get tongue-tied because of how good-looking he is.

He's the type of guy you see acting on a TV show and fangirl over for the next six months. Only I'm planning on fangirling over him for far longer than that.

"When you look at me like that, I do feel like a pretty boy," he teases.

"You're far more than a pretty boy."

His grin is as sexy as it is nerve-racking. "Thank you, wife. Now, as much as I love seeing you in my clothes, I need you naked."

"Have at it, then."

I expect him to simply pull them off. I'm so, so very wrong.

My squeal gets swallowed in the mattress when he spins me onto my front and hikes my ass into the air. I'm a willing rag doll, and my silly fucking grin is freeing.

Jamie slowly peels my leggings and ruined panties down past my ass and thighs before maneuvering me to get them the rest of the way off. His sweatshirt hangs over my mouth, his cologne strong on the fabric as I breathe in quickly.

A grumble fills the air behind me, and two thick, callused fingers rub between my legs, feeling just how wet I am.

"Yeah, I knew I'd find you like this. Flushed pink and dripping," he murmurs, sinking those two fingers inside without hesitation. "You'll be able to take my cock tonight, won't you, wife?"

"You'll make it fit," I moan, pushing my ass back into him.

"Of course I will. I always take care of this pretty pussy."

The bed dips behind me, and I hold my breath, half expecting him to take me like this. I'd let him fuck me any way he wanted whenever he chose to, and that's because of the unwavering trust I have in him.

It's not his cock that breaches me, though. A long, wet tongue glides through my lips, replacing his fingers, seeking the same destination.

He paws at my ass and spreads the cheeks while burying his tongue inside of me, not caring about the filthy noises that explode in the room.

"Jamie," I mewl, arching further to try and open myself up more for him. "*So* good. You're—That's . . . Yes!"

He moans into my pussy and brings his thumb to my clit, rubbing hard circles around it the way I like. The stimulation is intense, but the pleasure is stronger. I rock my hips faster, riding his face while my fingers curl into the comforter.

"More. More, baby. I'm close," I plead, my forehead rubbing against the bed.

With a deep, guttural noise, Jamie sucks at my pussy and moves his thumb faster, the pressure growing firmer with every pass. My thighs shake, and I gasp, pushing myself back into his mouth as my climax crests.

His groan is loud, almost angry, and he stays where he is, continuing to pleasure me until I can't take any more and pull forward away from his face.

I've hardly caught my breath by the time he's spinning me onto my back and staring down at me, a blinding sense of devotion in his eyes. He drags his palm down his face and licks his lips before crawling on top of me and hitching my thigh around his hip.

"That's the best meal I've ever had," he muses, bringing his mouth to my neck. His kisses are hot and wet, making my core clench in anticipation. "You're the best everything I've ever had.

And when you smile at me like that?" With a hand to his chest, he blows out a hard breath. "I feel like I can fly."

"Stop it," I whisper, unable to shake the smile he's talking about.

The head of his cock slides through my pussy, painting me in his precum but never slipping inside. He takes the bottom of his sweatshirt and slides it up my stomach, kissing the skin revealed inch by inch.

"I'm not stopping. You'll have to make me."

Not happening.

When the sweatshirt gets pushed over my sports bra, he abandons it long enough to tug my breasts free of the tight fabric. As if he genuinely can't get enough of me and my body, he takes my breasts into his hands and presses them together before pulling a nipple between his lips and sucking.

I moan, dragging my nails down his scalp. Everything turns me on when I'm with Jamie, but having him feast on my breasts with no sign of coming up for air is one of the sexiest things I've ever seen in my life.

He rolls my nipple between his teeth before shifting to the other one and giving it the same love. By the time he's releasing my breasts and working my clothes the rest of the way off, I'm shaking with need.

Feeling that, Jamie kisses me. He softly coaxes my lips open and snakes his tongue into my mouth. I can taste myself, but it doesn't matter. Nothing does but him.

"I'm on birth control," I whisper, holding his sides.

"I haven't been with anyone in at least six months."

I drag my nails along his skin, holding his gaze. "Don't use a condom."

"Tell me if it's too much or you want to stop. You set the pace, baby," he says, running his fingers through my pussy before filling me with two. "I'm going to try three fingers now."

I nod, lost in the way he looks at me like I'm his one and only forever.

The stretch of his fingers is uncomfortable but not painful. By the third glide of them inside, I'm relaxing again. A beat later, he's pulling them free and holding the thigh still hitched on his hip.

"I love you, Blakely," he murmurs as his cock breaches me.

My eyes roll back as he slowly sinks inside, stalling after a few moments. A shaky, strained exhale, and then he's retreating and pushing back inside, deeper this time.

"Relax for me, baby. It's a tight fit, but we're halfway there. You're doing so good for me," he coos.

I try to relax, but it feels too good.

My clit sings when he plays with it, giving me what I need. The pleasure blooms, and a heartbeat later, he's sliding so deep I cry out, so, so full.

"Fucking Christ, you're still so tight," he hisses, squeezing his eyes shut as his expression tightens.

The roughness in his voice has me involuntarily clenching around him, growing even more turned on. His stomach muscles ripple as he falls back onto his knees and uses his hold on my thigh to lift my ass off the bed.

Somehow, he goes even deeper.

"Jamie," I whimper, wanting him to open his eyes and look at me again. "I need you . . . I need you to move."

He gives me a crooked grin before his breath hitches, and it falls. "If I move, I'm going to come."

"Then come. Just please. Please move," I plead.

My other thigh finds a home around his hip, and I grip onto the smooth wooden slats on the headboard. His stare is hot enough to set me on fire as he drags it from my head to rest between my legs, taking in the sight of me stuffed full of him.

"I'm going to need you to come for me first, Blakely. Don't let go of that headboard, and remember that I love you. It won't feel like it in five seconds."

I shiver and nod. He grips both of my hips and keeps my ass off the bed before thrusting hard. My breath flies out of my lungs at the impact. Another thrust has the headboard smacking into the wall, but my grip stays firm.

His jaw pulses as he fucks into me with a strength that doesn't surprise me. It's always buried beneath his skin, only coming out on the field and now, in bed with me.

"Keep going," I moan, my breasts shaking with every jerk of my body.

"You're my match, Blakely. The half of me I didn't know was missing," he rasps, filling me with a ferocity that could bring the ceiling down on top of us. "My *wife*."

Another climax is riding toward me on a wave that I fear will take me under. Maybe I'd like if it did. It's not like Jamie would let me drown.

He lifts me higher off the bed, his balls slapping my ass as my vision narrows, the edges growing black. Fuzz fills my ears, and a throat-scraping cry trips free of my chest as I come.

"I'm right here, baby. Right fucking here. Filling your pussy so full—Jesus *Christ*."

A low, dominating growl follows, and Jamie's hips stutter as warmth fills me. I stay in the air for what feels like minutes until slowly, I'm falling back, now bundled in strong, familiar arms.

"You did so good. I love you," Jamie whispers, stroking my neck and chest and cheeks.

I close my eyes and smile, blindly reaching for his face. "I don't know what you were talking about. You could never treat me like you felt anything but love for me."

"I'll have to try harder next time." He chuckles and pushes my sweaty hair from my forehead. "Come shower with me."

"I don't want to. I'm tired."

"Just hold on to my neck, and I'll take care of you."

I wrap my arms around him and cling like a koala as he carries me out of bed. The sheen of sweat on his chest doesn't bother me, so I rest my cheek against him and keep my eyes shut.

"You always take care of me, Jamie."

"'Course I do. If I don't, someone else will."

Even half-asleep and sex drunk, I can't stop asking stupid questions. "What about at the end of our contract?"

His hold on me tightens, becoming ironclad.

"I'll offer you another one. A contract that keeps you with me forever. For real this time."

40

Blakely

IT'S ODD BEING IN THE PYTHONS STADIUM WITHOUT JAMIE. The cleaning staff is here, waxing the floors and disinfecting all of the bathrooms. I offer the few of them smiles on my way out.

I'm hot and sweaty from a Monday afternoon spent prepping for tomorrow, but I feel good. Really, really good.

I've never been so excited to see calluses and tiny nicks on my hands and have sore shoulders and feet. Every change to my body over the past couple of weeks I've spent working in the kitchen again has made me confident in a way I haven't been in a long time. I'm excited for every shift, and even though I know it's not smart of me to get my hopes up, I've started looking into university classes again.

Going back to finish my degree is a far-fetched dream, yet I can't get myself to dismiss it completely.

One of the many security guards lurking around the stadium turns to look at me when I exit the hallway and close the gap between us by the entrance doors. He's a familiar face yet still a nameless stranger.

I wave at him and pull out my phone to check if Jamie's here yet. He's insisted on neither me nor Nate taking the bus anymore and instead has started chauffeuring us everywhere. Our driving lessons have been going well, and I think I could pass my test soon. *Maybe.*

The contact name he chose for himself has me rolling my eyes as I scroll through our messages.

> The Prettiest Husband Ever: Nate's too good at this game. He's making me self-conscious.

> The Prettiest Husband Ever: I need you to be done soon so I can be saved.

> Me: I'm moving extra slow now.

> The Prettiest Husband Ever: See, now you've distracted me and he just got another touchdown.

> Me: Poor baby. I'll be done in half an hour. Beat him and I'll give you a kiss.

> The Prettiest Husband Ever: Consider it done. See you then 😊

With it still being above zero outside, I head for the doors to wait for him. A bit of a cooldown will be nice. I've never quite understood why we have to wear a heavy coat in the kitchen when it's ten billion degrees in there. I'm sure I could get away without it, at least during prep days. It's just me back there now that Clyde has officially moved to his new job.

I almost wish I'd have gotten a bit more time with him. It's no wonder he was hired as a head chef at a boujie restaurant downtown. He made the kitchen his bitch every time he stepped foot inside of it. Not to mention how patient he was with me. Obviously, I was a bit out of practice, and he didn't mind at all as I adjusted to the work.

The security guard opens the door for me and holds it as I step outside. "Have a great day, Mrs. Bateman."

My stomach flutters as I reach for my wedding ring and rub

the band. While I love both Bandit and wife, Mrs. Bateman is my favourite.

"Thank you," I say, heading out before stalling and looking back at him. "You've never actually told me your name."

"Jake."

"It's nice to meet you, Jake."

With a soft smile, I nod and move out of the doorway. It's a couple of minutes' walk from the doors to the player and employee-only lot. There's another one underground that Jamie uses during game days, but I have something against wandering around dark underground parking lots by myself.

At least while it's not freezing outside.

Jamie's not here yet, so I lean against the light pole illuminating the parking lot and wait. Despite being early evening, it's loud outside with construction equipment groaning, people chatting as they walk to and from work, and car engines sputtering. I'm close enough to the Warriors arena to make out the tall green column at the front and the domed roof, and I wonder if Giana's there.

I've only seen her the one single time, but there was something about her that I really connected with. She felt genuine, and that's hard to come by. Especially when you're someone who doesn't go out of their way to make friends.

Letting that thought go, I check my phone for the time and frown. Jamie's never usually late. Although, it wouldn't surprise me if Nate convinced him to play one more game first.

"You have no idea how many times I've been to this place looking for you."

I turn into a statue when I register my mother's voice. Her shoes scuff the pavement on my right, and slowly, I force my neck to turn so I can look at her.

Wearing the same jacket with the broken zipper and her hair up in a bun, she stares expectantly at me. I almost wish she had forgotten me when she left five years ago just so I wouldn't have to be forced to see her ever again.

"Why bother? That sounds like an incredible waste of time," I deadpan.

"You know why. And I've grown really impatient."

"That's not my problem."

"Yes, it is. If you want me to leave you alone, you'll give me what I want."

I blow out a laugh. "You've been gone for half a decade. I don't care about what you want."

"Maybe not. But you do care about your brother."

"That's the last time you bring up Nate," I warn, pushing off the pole. "I'm not playing games with you. You're nobody to me, and you're sure as hell nobody to him."

She cocks her head, trying to read me with little success. Her sigh is exasperated. "I'm not interested in playing games, Blakely. I was just hoping that you would still feel some loyalty to your mother and be open to helping if I came to you."

"Loyalty?" I spit the word and sneak a look around us before pinning her with a glare. "You wouldn't know loyalty if it bit you in your ass, *Mother*. The fact you thought for even one second that you'd be able to just show up out of nowhere and try to get anything from me shows how little you paid attention to me when you were still around."

"I really wish you weren't being this way," she grumbles.

I blink, staring at her in disbelief. "Do you want an apology?"

"No. But, you've left me no other choice but to remind you again that you need to remember who you are and who I am to your brother."

"Don't."

"You love him, don't you?"

"I love him more than you've ever loved anyone in your life," I declare, throat tightening as my fear starts multiplying.

"He was always a good boy. A bit dim, but quiet. Talented too. Like your husband. I'm sure he'll go far in his football career."

I keep looking for Jamie, but he's still not here. And now, I don't want him to be. Not if he has Nate with him.

I'd take a million more conversations with this woman before allowing her to see him and for him to be reminded of who she is and why she didn't stay.

"Get on with it, then. Tell me what it is you want so I can get you out of our lives and keep you there," I snap.

Her eyes light up, assuming she's won. "I need money. My rent is due at my place, and I can't get away without paying it another month."

"How much?"

"Ten thousand."

I suck in a breath, jaw hanging open. "What do you mean, ten thousand?"

"It's been six months."

Rubbing my mouth, I shake my head. "You can't expect me to have ten thousand dollars to just give you."

"I searched your husband up online, Blakely. Have you been unaware that he makes three million dollars a year this entire time you've been together?"

It's hard to keep from visibly showing my surprise because no, I wasn't aware of that. I never cared. The money he makes has never mattered to me. He could be broker than I was when we met, and I would have fallen in love with him had I still gotten the chance to get to know him the way I have.

"I'm going to be honest, Blakely. I need that money. Without it, I'm going to be on the street, and I won't survive a winter out here. If you're not going to get it for me, then I'll have better luck trying to convince my landlord for another break with my son with me."

"And if that didn't work? You'd make him live on the street with you? Why? To prove a point to me? No one in their right mind would allow you to have custody over Nathan with the way you abandoned us," I push, having trouble pulling in a full breath with the terror seizing my throat and lungs.

"You wouldn't have a choice but to agree. In the eyes of the law, he's still my son, sweetie," she drawls, pushing her lips out in a demeaning pout. "I'm his mother, *not* you."

I can no longer breathe. My reply is wheezed, hardly audible. "I have a few hundred dollars."

"What is that going to do for me?"

"It's all I have. If you can wait until—"

"I can't, Blakely. Don't you get it? I've pushed it too far to wait. If you had done an interview and grabbed my attention earlier, maybe we could have found a better solution. But now, I'm too short on time," she says, annoyed.

Tears drip down my cheeks too quickly to dry them all. I've faced a lot in my life, including my fair share of back-against-the-wall situations, but I've never had anything like that thrown at me. Nathan might not be my son, but he's still mine. He's my brother and the other half of me. I've done everything for him, and I'll continue to do that every day for the rest of my life.

"It's impossible for me to give you more money than what I have."

She shakes her head, scoffing loudly. "Do you think I'm stupid? Your husband—"

"He's not really my husband!" I scream, angrily swiping at my face, ashamed of the tears. "Jamie's not my husband, you evil bitch. Now, leave me alone. Leave my entire family alone."

"Don't tell me this was all a fucking joke, Blakely. What have you gotten yourself into?" she hisses, stomping toward me and grabbing my shoulder, shaking it hard.

"I don't have the money to give you."

"Yes. You do. I saw the wedding photos. You signed the certificate. You're married to that man, and you're going to give me what I need."

"You're not listening to me! It's not our money. It's his. Everything is his. I don't own any of it!"

She shakes me harder, like maybe I'll give her what she wants if she rattles me around a little bit more.

"Let me make this even clearer for you. Either you give me the money I need, or I'll make sure everyone knows that you're not Jamieson Bateman's wife. Because what? This was for publicity? You were so desperate to feel wanted that you sold yourself to a man? We are not that different, sweetie," she hisses. "And unless you want the entire world to know that, then you will do as I say!"

I choke on a sob before stumbling back from her. "You have no idea what you're asking for."

"Yes, I do. I know too well."

"Why did you even have children? You could have made it impossible to have Nate."

"Your father was adamant about having a big family."

My hands and knees shake. Any minute now, I'm going to collapse. And Jamie can't see me like this. Neither can Nate.

"Dad would have hated you. He's rolling in his grave right now," I whisper.

She swallows, features tightening. "He lost his right to feel one way or another when he left us."

"At least he got away from you."

The sound of footsteps approaches us, and I whip my head toward the guy heading our way. Jake, the security guard from earlier, glances between me and my mother, a silent question in his eyes.

Despite how weak it makes me, I nod, taking the opportunity to leave. I'm grateful for the saving. I don't know if I'd have been able to extract myself before Jamie got here.

"This is private property. You need to leave before I call the police."

She guffaws. "Tomorrow, Blakely. You have until tomorrow."

I don't have the energy to turn to look at her as she speaks. A day isn't enough for me to find enough money for her. Not even with my job now.

One step after the other, I go back to the stadium, needing to collect myself before going home. I'm almost there when the guard catches up to me.

"Should I put her on the list?" he asks, hanging back a bit.

"What list?"

"If she shows up here again, we'll notify the authorities."

"Don't bother. It's fine," I mutter.

"Do you want me to stay out here and wait for Jamie?" he asks.

"You've already gone above and beyond your job description. I appreciate you stepping in, but I can take care of myself."

"You're a member of the Pythons family," he argues.

"So, you didn't hear what we were screaming about, then?"

A pause. "I was working the door at your wedding. Nothing about your marriage is new information to me."

Maybe later, I'll wish I'd have grilled this guy more. But for now, his answer is good enough. Plus, if he was at our wedding, Graham must trust him enough.

"I'm going to the bathroom. If Jamie shows up—"

"I'll let him know."

"My brother can't see that woman. If she comes back while I'm inside, I need her gone."

"You've got my word."

I stop walking long enough to look at him. He's not smiling or frowning, but even with a straight face, there's nothing scary about him. If I were to stick around forever, I think I could be friends with him.

Too bad my time here is approaching its end faster than I originally thought.

41

Jamie

ALL IT TOOK WAS ONE LOOK AT BLAKELY AS SHE SLID INTO THE SUV outside the stadium to know something was wrong.

I've never seen her eyes so red and puffy, not once. She tries to hide her face behind a curtain of hair, and I think that worries me more than anything. Every day we spend together, we grow closer, and I happily fall more in love with her. We've made so much progress, and her not letting me see her upset has me thinking back over the last week to see if I fucked up somewhere.

"I'm sorry we were late," I murmur, waiting for the neighbourhood gate to open.

Nate leans forward in his seat behind me. "Don't be mad, please. It was my fault. The st—"

"The stubborn game wouldn't save, so we had to finish another round," I finish for him before he blurts out our surprise.

Blakely keeps her head turned and eyes out the window. Her fingers fidget in her lap, alternating between plucking at the lint on her leggings and tapping her knee.

"It's okay."

I meet Nate's stare in the rear-view mirror and frown when he appears just as worried as I know I do.

The gate swings open, and I drive through while rubbing a hand down her thigh. "We put in an order for dinner before we left. Tacos with extra hot sauce and churros. I even convinced the cook to add extra spice into the meat for you."

"Thank you."

My worry shifts into alarm at her expressionless tone.

"We figured you deserved a break after prepping food all day."

"It wasn't that bad. I like prepping."

"Jamie brought me to the thrift shop so I could donate my old gear too. And we ran a few drills at the field. I even caught a thirty-yard pass," Nate boasts.

"It would have been longer than that, but my arm doesn't compare to Jax's," I add.

Nate shrugs. "It's pretty good for a receiver, I think."

"Thanks, buddy."

Blakely remains silent for a beat longer, and only when I pull into the driveway does she tuck her hair behind her ear and offer Nate a phony smile.

"I'm proud of you, Nate."

Her brother's smile is as real as ever. "Thanks, Lake."

A chasm opens in my chest the longer she avoids my eyes and steps outside. Nate lingers, eyeing me funny in the mirror.

"Did you do something wrong?"

"I don't think so. She was fine earlier."

Her texts sure made it seem like it, anyway. Maybe I misread her teasing and pissed her off with mine.

"I'm not an expert in women or anything, but it sure seems like you did something wrong."

"Is your sister the type of woman not to tell you when you've done something to upset her, though?"

"Fair point. Maybe she just had a bad day."

"Yeah, you could be right. Let's see if we can make it better, then, yeah?"

He all but dives out of the car. I chuckle, following and

locking the doors. Blakely's left the house door cracked open. Nate slips in first.

"Don't go in your room yet!" he shouts, quickly kicking his shoes off.

Blakely's shoes are perfectly tucked on the rack, like always. It's such a simple thing, but having her stuff out and next to mine is so satisfying. It reiterates that she feels comfortable here.

"Better hurry, then," she calls from upstairs.

Nate and I haul ass after her. We've been planning this surprise since his last football game, and I don't want to risk everything not going perfectly.

Blakely's waiting at our bedroom door with her eyes closed and arms hanging limply at her sides. When I reach her, I'm immediately sliding an arm around her waist and kissing her temple.

"Missed you today, baby."

She keeps her eyes closed but leans into my hold, inhaling deeply. "I missed you too."

"Did you also miss me?" Nate asks, slipping past us to open the door.

Finally, she shows me those pretty green eyes. "I missed you both."

Nate puffs his chest and helps himself to our bedroom. I can't do anything but grin at both his eagerness and comfortableness. Two months ago, he never would have been so confident walking inside my bedroom without explicit permission. Hell, he wouldn't have even sat on the couch unless I asked him to.

"Come on! I'm dying here. You guys can cuddle and kiss and whatever after," he groans.

"After what?" Blakely asks, intrigue sparking.

I tap the underside of her chin, and she tips it back on instinct so I can steal a kiss. Only taking one feels like a crime, but I'll fix that later. Nate will wind up grabbing the surprises off the bed and shoving them at her if we don't get a move on.

"I've got something to ask you," I whisper, keeping her close. "To ask both of you."

"Just come here, Lake!"

She tears her eyes from mine, and I release her. Nate's already bounding in place beside the bed. He waves at the jerseys on the mattress and grins.

"What are those?" she asks, her voice so brittle it cracks.

I stand behind her and hold her hips, propping my chin on her head. "We're a family, Blakely."

"There's one for each of us. And look, they're all Bateman jerseys. Number one is obviously for you, then two is for Jamie, and three is me. Get it? One, two, three Batemans," Nate explains excitedly, snagging the jersey with the number three above the Bateman and shoving it over his head. "Put yours on, Lake."

I gently turn Blakely in my arms, my heart thudding as her face comes into view. The sheen in her eyes threatens to choke me up.

"Just hold on a sec, bud. I've got to ask you both something first," I murmur, moving forward with the plan I didn't discuss with him first.

Blakely doesn't say a word, but I don't expect her to. The emotion in her expression speaks for itself. Nate comes closer and lingers at her side, touching her arm.

"I want you to live here for real. Not just because you're supposed to. This has become a home for you as much as it has for me, and it should be official. I don't want to wake up one morning and know that either one of you is leaving," I say, relieved I haven't butchered the speech I spent all morning memorizing. "As far as I'm concerned, the contract is null and void. Once it ends, nothing is going to change. Not unless you decide otherwise."

Blakely stares at me, a tear leaking from the corner of her eye. Disbelief ripples across her features, but before I have a chance to convince her, a body is hitting mine with the force of a bus.

Nate hugs me tight, burying his face in my shoulder. I hold him back, keeping my eyes on Blakely. Something shifts in her eyes as she takes in the image in front of her. I'm unable to tell if it's devastation or just a mega load of emotions hitting her at all at once, and that sets off mental alarms.

"You'd really keep us for real?" Nate asks softly.

I rub the top of his head. "Yeah, buddy. That's my plan."

"This is incredible!" He pulls out of my arms and rushes toward his sister. "Thank you, Lake."

Her lip wobbles as she bundles him close and rests her cheek against his ear. "For what?"

"For everything. You did so much for us, and now look what we have."

"I wish I had done more," she whispers, squeezing her eyes shut.

Tears track down her cheeks, and I have to force myself not to move to her and wipe them away.

"You did *everything*," he says firmly.

It's what she deserves to hear. The one thing I know she's been needing to have confirmed by him.

They hug for a few more moments until Nate drops his arms and grins at the both of us. He tugs at the shoulders of his jersey and spins to show the back.

"What do you think?"

I clap his arm. "You look like a Bateman."

Blakely stares at me, eyes wide and lips pursed. Her cheeks flush, and when she squishes her features, almost in pain, I freeze.

Nate stares at her, having the same reaction as I am. He's quicker to push past it. "Uh . . . do you want to talk to Jamie? Alone, maybe?"

"That's a good idea," I blurt out. "How about you watch for dinner?"

"Alright. Yeah, I'll do that. See ya!"

He's gone in a blink, closing the door behind him. Once it's just me and Blakely, all I have to do is open my arms, and she's taking her place inside of them.

The first sob that escapes her rattles my ribs, but the second rips them straight from my chest and plunges one into my heart. I lift her off the floor, and she wraps her legs around my waist immediately, clutching my back.

Carrying her to the bed, I rub along her spine, softly shushing her. "I'm sorry. I shouldn't have said that. I'm sorry, baby."

"Don't," she whimpers, shaking her head where it lies against my shoulder. "Don't take it back."

"Okay. Okay, I won't."

"I wish I could give you more."

I sit us on the mattress and lean against the headboard. She stays on my lap, hiding her face as her words sink in. It wouldn't be acceptable to tell her that she's talking crazy, so instead, I try and rework my thoughts.

"There is nothing I need from you that I haven't already gotten. I have you, don't I? I have another brother who feels a lot like he was always supposed to be in my life. Both of you do. It took less than two months for me to know that I want you for keeps. Shouldn't that say something?"

"Nate loves you, Jamie. If you ended up changing your mind, he'd never get over it. After losing so many people . . . I worry he wouldn't let anyone in ever again. And that would *break* me."

Gently, I press my hands to her cheeks and pull her from where she's hidden in my chest. Even with her eyes red and cheeks wet, she's the most beautiful person I've ever seen. Toss in a sniffling nose, and she's something out of a dream.

"I will never break you," I swear, pressing our noses together. "I've jumped in with two feet and am ready to either sink or swim. Of course, I'd prefer to swim, but that's up to you."

"What if I did something that hurt you? Something that broke your trust? Would you break me then?"

I push past my initial confusion and brush my mouth across

hers. "Crush me beneath your boot, and I'll find a way to glue myself back together and fight for you. I'm your husband, Blakely. I don't fucking care that it wasn't real in the beginning. It is now."

She doesn't reply with words.

When her lips meet mine, pushing with a fierceness I feel all the way in my bones, words are useless, anyway. I'm more than okay with communicating like this for the rest of time.

42

Blakely

I TRY NOT TO THINK ABOUT MY CHILDHOOD TOO MUCH. NOT THE bad memories or the good ones, because reminding yourself of what isn't here anymore hasn't ever helped anyone.

With Jamie, it became easier not to stray to that blocked-off section in my mind. He keeps me busy, distracted. Happier than I've ever been, past and present. I was in a fairy-tale world the past few weeks where for the first time in forever, I was content with only looking forward, excited about what was to come.

Maybe that was my first mistake.

If I had paid more attention to my past instead of writing it off, I wouldn't have let my mom surprise me. I'd have been expecting her to pull herself out of the gutter and show up again once things had finally changed for us. It was only a matter of time before she found something in my life worth ruining.

The one thing I could have happily kept forever.

Jamie, with his winks and booming laugh, the heart of gold that could break the world's largest scale, and arms that I could have stayed in for decades, is the first person besides Nate that I'm willing to sacrifice everything for.

Even if it's my happiness hanging in the balance.

He kisses me with an eagerness that makes me feel cherished, like I'm someone to him that he can't stand thinking about not having in his life. That almost makes everything worse.

Almost. Because right now, I'm not prepared to focus on anything but giving my heart what it wants, and that's him soul-deep inside of me.

Jamie holds me with a firm but gentle touch while encouraging me to seat myself on his lap. He's hard beneath me, and I moan at the first brush of him between my legs.

"I didn't do this for sex, Bandit," he whispers, stilling me when I buck against him.

"I know."

"You're everything to me."

Emotion tries to claw its way up my throat, but I swallow it down. "You're everything to me too."

He kisses me again, and his tongue meets mine with a soft stroke. I lean up on my knees, forcing his head back to keep our mouths fused. It's only in this position that I'm above him, and I think he likes it. The groan that rattles his chest intensifies the throb in my centre.

With a slow drag of his fingers, he guides my shirt up my body. I lift my arms while he pulls it over my head, and then it's gone, tossed out of sight. The clasps of my bra are plucked, and the straps droop down my arms before he tugs them both off.

My breasts hang free, nipples already hard but stiffening further as he lowers his eyes, staring at them. With me leaning above him, all it takes is a dip of his chin to drag his lips across one and suck it into my mouth.

I close my eyes, sighing at the swell of arousal in my belly. Jamie lashes my nipple with his tongue while I palm the back of his head, keeping him in place.

When my nipple grows too sensitive, I guide him to the other, encouraging him to give it the same love and attention. He doesn't leave me wanting. His enthusiasm is electric, confidence building. It makes me feel sexy and desired in the way I'd always dreamed of.

"I need you," I whisper, pulling lightly on his hair.

He releases my nipple and looks up at me, nodding while his hands find the backs of my thighs. I reach behind his neck and fist his shirt before pulling it up and over his head.

Chest bare and heaving, he doesn't move, waiting for my next move. I rest my hands on his abdomen and splay my fingers out over his muscles, taking in the hot, firm feel of them.

When he hisses, they flex, quaking beneath my touch. I push them up his body and move them outward, holding the wide expanse of his thick shoulders.

"You're beautiful, Jamie," I murmur.

The corner of his mouth tips up before he pulls on my thighs, forcing me to sit flat on my ass again. I keep my tongue caged beneath my teeth when he leans forward and reaches past me. He moves the orange Bateman jersey between us and then guides it over my head.

My heart flutters like it's grown wings. I slip my arms through the sleeves, and he tugs the thin material down my body. His pupils flare, eating the vibrant blue while he takes a long look at me and pulls my hair out from where it's become trapped beneath the jersey.

"How does it look?" I ask.

"Like it was made for you."

It feels that way too.

Quicker than I'm expecting, he has me on my back and my pants off. I roll my lip between my teeth and watch when he rolls off the bed and works his jeans and briefs down his legs.

He doesn't waste time. The moment he's naked, I'm yanked beneath him, the heat from his body forming a cocoon around us.

"How do you want it, wife?" he asks, starting to kiss down my stomach.

I spread my legs wide, trying to encourage him to skip the teasing. Like always, it doesn't work. Jamie is a firm believer in foreplay, and while I love his desire to make sure I'm always ready for him, I'm also horny after a single look from him. The prep isn't necessary. I'm already dripping between my legs, probably leaving a wet spot on the duvet.

"Surprise me," I tell him, wiggling beneath his weight.

He drags his tongue from my belly button to my pubic bone, humming deeply. His teeth scrape my skin. "There's one position I've been wanting to try."

"Do it, then."

"You don't want to know what it is first?"

My eyes cross when he glides his tongue further between my legs until finally, it swipes at my clit. I snap my legs shut, thighs pressing into his cheeks as he reaches a hand around to spear me with two fingers. My clit is sucked hard at the same time he curves his fingers, and I slap a hand to the mattress, moaning.

"Answer me, Blakely," he coos.

I squeeze my thighs tighter in punishment. "I don't care what it is as long as you give me your cock."

Lips glossy with my arousal, he pries my legs away and pulls back. His tongue sweeps over his mouth as a smirk appears.

"Hold on to me and try not to scream. Nate's awake downstairs," he warns coyly.

I simply nod, trusting him not to do anything I won't like.

With a tug, he has me sliding down the bed and bundled in his arms. I wrap my legs around his waist and cling onto him as he lifts me in his arms and carries me across the room.

His hair is long, curling at his neck as I drag my nails up and down his scalp, leaning in close to inhale his scent. When I bring my mouth to his skin and press wet, open-mouthed kisses along his skin, goosebumps rise beneath my lips.

My back hits the wall as he lines us up, the broad head of his cock slowly breaching me. I'm so slick he glides in with a thick stretch but no resistance. The pleasure is instant, stealing my breath as he continues to work himself deep.

"Every time I feel you around me, it gets better," he admits breathlessly.

I nod quickly, gasping for air as my nails prick at his shoulders.

Once he bottoms out, he stills, his fingers digging into my thighs. "Such a snug little pussy, wife."

"Yours," I say on a tight exhale.

"My snug little pussy? That's what this is?" He glides out, leaving just the tip inside before thrusting forward, working it inside again. "That makes this your cock, then, right?"

My eyes roll backward when he hits my G-spot, sending sparks racing up my spine. Grinding forward still buried deep, he applies pressure to my clit with his groin, ramping up the pleasure.

"Yes," I moan, wiggling my hips in search of more. "Yes, my cock. My husband. My . . ."

His thrusts become harder, pointed. Every grind against my clit intensifies the pressure blooming in my core. His cock glides against that hidden spot inside of me with every jerk of his hips, threatening to steal my vision.

"Your what, Blakely?"

I shake my head and bite down on my lip to stifle the noise trying to escape me. If he keeps pushing, I'll tell him how deep my feelings really run, and with what's coming, I won't do that to him.

Won't do that to me.

His expression shifts, anger lighting his dark eyes. Every thrust comes quicker than the last, but I refuse to speak. He parts his lips on a deep groan, but it's reluctant, like his pleasure forced it free.

"Your. What?"

While his fingers dig harder into my ass, they don't hurt. He keeps his anger and frustration in check, only allowing his emotions to slip through his staccato words and searing stare.

I'm seconds away from an orgasm. The constant pressure against my clit and strong jab against my G-spot are taking me too high. A balloon expands in my groin, and it's fear I feel now.

"Jamie—" I cry, shaking my head, pawing at his chest. "I'm going to—"

He holds me tighter against the wall, bending his head to nip at my mouth in punishment. I suck in a breath and watch when he pulls back as his eyes gain a feral, possessive gleam.

"Soak me, Blakely. I'm proud to be yours."

Tears burn my eyes as I come. The balloon pops, and I'm helpless to the spray of liquid that soaks into his groin, creating a slippery mess between us. Jamie somehow thrusts harder, faster, and grunts while grinding against me.

"I love you," he hisses while filling me with hot cum.

"I love . . ." Bliss loosens my tongue, but I'm quick to correct myself with a soft moan.

I'm grateful that Jamie's too blissed-out to catch my mistake, if anything I said at all. With a soft kiss to my brow, he carries me through to the ensuite and starts the shower. I wiggle in his hold, but he only tightens it, not saying a word.

The room gets hot with steam, and I keep my arms around him, waiting for the moment he can't hold me any longer. That moment never comes.

Not as he moves us under the water and soaks us completely or when he gingerly rests my back against the wall and slips out of me before washing between my legs. The scent of my body wash fills the shower when he uses the bottle on the shelf to scrub the both of us.

Suddenly, my tears mix with the stream of water down my face. He doesn't look away from me, and I don't bother hiding the ache in my chest. There would be no point.

Jamie's always been the one who can read me no matter how many walls I try and reinforce between us. Every emotion bubbling inside of me is his to see.

The most surprising part of all, though, is that not once does he ask for me to tell him what they all mean.

43

Blakely

I WAKE UP THE NEXT MORNING WITH MY CHEEK SMUSHED AGAINST Jamie's chest, an arm python-wrapped around my middle, and my hand in his briefs. Despite the heaviness hanging over me, I hesitate for a moment longer before loosening my hold on his very hard dick and extracting myself from his hold.

I'm never up before him, but with how hard it was for me to sleep last night, I'm not surprised by the change. Last night was awkward. Dinner was silent besides Nate's rambling, and Jamie stared at me in silence for hours until I escaped upstairs and went to bed early.

In reality, I lay in bed and stared at the ceiling until he joined me a bit later and kissed me good night the same way he always does. Other than his silence, he didn't seem upset by anything. It was all confusing beyond belief.

My heart aches, nausea creeping up as I slip out of bed and turn his phone alarm off, not wanting him to wake up before I'm gone. I can't guarantee that his silence will last if he catches me.

As quietly as possible, I grab the clothes I set out last night and get dressed. Once I'm ready, I risk brushing my teeth before hovering by the bed.

Jamie's going to hate me when I get home and he learns what

I've done. Our last night together was ruined by my inability to open up, and now . . . now, I won't have a chance to tell him how I really feel.

Before I break down and wake him up, I leave the room. With gritted teeth, I keep from crying again.

Nate's bedroom door is shut. I shove down the guilt of waking him this early before entering his space. He's sprawled on the bed, the blankets hanging off the foot dangling over the edge of the mattress. Soft snores escape him, and I clench the fabric over my sternum, needing to hold something as I sit beside him.

He doesn't stir when the bed dips beneath my weight or when I brush the shaggy hair out of his eyes. I take advantage of that, continuing to stroke his head and cheeks the way I used to when he was ten years old and heartbroken.

When I kiss the top of his head, he finally wakes up, sleepily blinking up at me in the darkness.

"Lake?" he croaks.

"Hey."

"Did I miss my alarm?"

"No. You don't have to get up for school yet."

He nods, confusion bunching his brows. "So, why are you here?"

"I just wanted to tell you that I love you and that we're going to be okay. No matter what happens, I'll look out for you."

"I know. You've always done that."

Releasing a tight breath, I continue smoothing his hair. "Have I done a good job here, Nate? Or do you only say that because I'm your sister?"

"Of course you've done a good job. Are you kidding me?"

"I'm not."

He pushes himself up on his arm and frowns at me. "You're the best sister out there. I've always known that I'll be okay as long as I have you. And one day, you're going to stop doubting yourself so much and just accept that you did everything right.

I'm far from a kid now, Lake. I don't need your protection all the time anymore. You need to stop worrying so much about me and start thinking about yourself and what you want."

"You'll always be a kid to me," I argue.

"We're good now. *I'm* good. Look where we live and the life we have. Jamie's awesome, and you're smiling so much it's almost creepy. He's family now, isn't he? He loves us, and I love him too. I love the both of you."

"You love him?" I whisper, my heart throbbing in my chest.

Nate nods, an open honesty in his eyes. "Yeah. He's like a brother. Or a dad, I guess. In the same way that you're like my mom. In a halfsies kind of way, you know?"

It's the last thing I expected him to say.

"Yeah, I know. And I love you, Nate. I love you so much. All I want is to give you a good life."

"You've done that. I think this is where we're supposed to be. We had to go through what we did so that we could find our place here. You took a big risk marrying him, Lake, but look what happened. We completed our family," he says confidently.

I lean forward and pull him into my arms before I break. He hugs me instantly, rubbing my back up and down. It's such a grown-up way to comfort someone and another damn sign that he's smarter and more mature than I've been giving him credit for.

There's only one person I've ever met who wears his heart as loose on his sleeve for everyone to see as my baby brother, and he's in the other room. Nate having a man in this life at his current age and stage of maturity, let alone one as amazing as Jamie, is something I will never take for granted. The things he's learning from him are going to help nurture him into an even better man than he's already on his way to becoming.

I know I've made a mistake immediately.

My current plan crumbles in my mind and is quickly replaced by a new one. One that I hope won't blow up in my face as fast as the first one would have.

I'm not ready to give up on our little family yet. Not by a long shot.

Jamie

THE FIRST THING I see when I open my eyes is Nate towering over me. I blink a few times to see if he disappears, but when he folds his arms across his chest, I realize he's not a figment of my imagination.

"Good morning, sunshine," I grumble.

"Good morning, Jamieson."

"Woah, what's with the full name? You sound like my mom."

He drops to a crouch and pokes me in the forehead. "What happened with Blakely?"

"What?"

The sun shining through the cracks in the curtains has me flipping over to check the other side of the bed. The lack of weight on my chest should have been the first thing I noticed, but I guess finding someone hovering over you first thing in the morning can distract a guy.

Blakely's spot is empty. A first since she started sleeping in my room. There's a reason I slide my pillow beneath her arm every morning, and it isn't just because she looks so adorable squeezing it to death.

"Where is she?" I ask, already shoving the blankets off.

Nate steps to the side so I can get up and grab the jeans lying on the floor. The pile of clothes that were on the dresser when I came upstairs last night is gone, and I rip open the first dresser drawer as fear claws at my chest.

"Fuck," I curse, staring down her clothes still mixed in with mine. The sight of her clothes only relaxes me so much. "What's going on, Nate?"

"That's what I'm asking you. She woke me up this morning way too early and was asking me weird questions."

"Like what? How long ago was this?"

He frowns. "Like twenty minutes. She asked if I thought she did a good job looking out for me. I think she was trying not to cry the entire time."

"Something must have happened yesterday."

It was obvious last night. She wasn't the same from the moment we picked her up from the stadium. Her behaviour was off, but I thought it was because of me. That I'd annoyed her by texting her too often at work and then overstepped with the jerseys. I assumed us having sex instead of talking about everything was her way of telling me that she still wanted me, but not quite that much yet. I let her shut down and close me out without a fight because I assumed she needed some time to collect her thoughts without me breathing down her neck.

That was the wrong move. One I won't make again.

She cut herself off before telling me she loved me, and it hurt. Still, I was serious when I told her I wanted her for keeps. Whatever she's gone off to do now is something we'll handle together. Those tears in her eyes in the shower weren't enough to push me away. All they did was make me surer that I want to be the only one to dry them from now on.

My gut reaction is that all of this has something to do with her mother. Blakely might have been able to do a great job of pretending the run-in with her didn't happen, but I doubt it was a coincidence that the woman who abandoned her kids just so happened to show up after I'd dragged her daughter into the public eye.

"I think she took the bus too," Nate says.

I bite back a smile. "Of course she did."

"Do you know where she went?"

"I've got a spot to check, but you're going to school. She wouldn't want you to miss class for this."

His groan is oh so very teenager. "Actually?"

"Yeah, actually. I can't be the cool guy right now."

"Well, if you don't find her, can you come get me so I can help?"

"Fine. If I don't find her by lunchtime, then I'll come get you. But you've got to have my back if we get her together and she yells at me for letting you skip school," I barter.

"Deal."

"Alright. Go finish getting ready. We leave in—" I check my watch and nearly crap my pants at the time. "Ten minutes."

He's quick to jog out of the room and stomp down the stairs. I get dressed and join him. Half an hour later, he's at school with money for lunch in his backpack, and I'm turning into the player and employee lot at the stadium.

It's empty this early, with only the same few cars that are always here, most of which belong to security. The place is guarded like a fortress, and today, that plays in my favour. One of the guards must have noticed something going on yesterday.

I park quickly and head up to the stadium doors. The construction happening a couple of blocks over hides any voices nearby, but noises don't disguise the sight of a security guard lingering at the doors with a rigid jaw and his hands cupped in front of him.

My instincts have me abandoning the doors and going to the guard. I recognize him the second he turns, noticing me.

"What's going on, Jake?" I ask stiffly.

"Mrs. Bateman is—"

I'm moving before he finishes.

Hidden out of view from the street behind the wall painted with the Pythons mascot, I find Blakely and her mother. The small black pouch in my wife's hand sparks alarms, but I slow my pace, taking in every aspect of what's in front of me.

The older version of Blakely has her back to the wall while

her daughter is shaking the bag between them. I force myself not to run over and drag them apart, choosing to listen instead.

"Take the money. It's all you're getting," Blakely pleads.

Her mom shakes her head, scoffing. "It's worthless. He'll laugh and haul me out of the apartment himself."

"Use it as a down payment or a show of good faith. Use it for *anything*, just please take it and leave me alone."

"The only way I'm leaving you alone is if I get every dollar that I asked for. Not this pathetic attempt of a savings fund. Don't you see? We're the same, sweetie. We'll chase and chase forever without getting to the top. You might as well accept it now."

Blakely's lip wobbles before it pulls flat, and she sniffs, collecting herself. "Take. The. Money. Let me have this one good thing, Mom. Don't take him from me. If you want me to beg, I'll get on my knees and do that. All I want in return is to never see you again."

"I'm not taking anyone or anything from you unless it's the ten thousand I need. All you need to do is bring me the money, and I'll take your secret to the grave."

I run through her words, trying to make sense of them. From the way Blakely's mask is slipping further and further by the second, her fear so sharp it pricks my chest from a distance, my first guess is that this is about Nate.

"If you're trying to punish me for something, this isn't the way to do it. This won't ruin my life. It will ruin Jamie's. He doesn't deserve that. Please, don't make me do that to him," she begs, voice cracking as it drops. "I love him."

I may as well have taken a football directly to the chest.

It's the wrong place and the worst timing, but her statement rams right into me, knocking the air from my lungs. I want to scoop her up and kiss the fuck her until our lips are too swollen to keep going.

It's not time for that yet.

Blakely's mom laughs at her while swiping the pouch out of

her hands. She peels it open and pulls out a handful of colourful bills.

"Did you even try to take his money? Or did you hand him your backbone when you sold yourself for a nice place to live and a bit of publicity? It doesn't matter now. At least if you'd taken his money, he wouldn't suffer the consequences. Money means nothing to those who have too much of it."

"I did think about it, but it was your son who changed my mind. He reminded me that there is always a second option," Blakely says, voice low and sharp. "I used to wonder how you could be so cold-hearted. How there could be no affection or love in your entire body when it came to us. It turns out that the answer has always been right in front of me. We stole it from you. Nate and I are nothing like you because we have double the ability to love and desire to care for others. He wears his heart on his sleeve and, despite everything we've gone through, doesn't fear love. And me . . ."

She rips the pouch and cash from her mom's hands and zips it up, gaze hot with fury. "I have never been afraid to protect those I love. I'll kick and scream and fight every day to keep my family safe and taken care of. I was prepared to steal from my husband and lose him if it meant he didn't have the chance of losing his career after you told the world about us. It was a sacrifice that I would have made if it weren't for Nate being so open with his love and reminding me that the best rewards come after taking a risk. We're everything you've never known how to be, and despite our struggles, I'm so happy that you left when you did. We've always been better off without you."

Pride explodes inside of me as I start walking toward her, done with watching. Staying away any longer may just kill me when all I want to do is tell her how incredible she is.

How incredible she's *always* been.

Blakely's mom stares at her, stunned, and I use her surprise to interrupt. My wife looks at me before I even open my mouth to speak, as if she's as in tune with me as I am with her.

I hold her stare, pushing every ounce of the love I have for her into a single look. "I've been waiting for you to say that for weeks."

"Jamie," she whispers, biting at her cheek.

"You cut yourself off last night, Bandit. I thought I'd have to wait months to hear those words for real."

"I'm sorry."

"Don't be. Just say them again. To me this time."

She shakes her head, visibly overthinking. "How much of that did you hear?"

I step in front of her, guarding her with my body while taking her face in my hands. She releases a shaky breath and carefully rests a hand on my chest.

"I'd have given you every dollar in my bank account if you needed it. I could lose football tomorrow, and it would be fine because I have you."

"Don't—"

"No. You don't. Not yet. I've been telling you for weeks that you're my wife. I told you that I love you, and I don't take that lightly. My parents have been married for nearly thirty years, and I've always known that when I find my person, I'm going to take after their example.

"My love doesn't come with strings. There are no conditions in this relationship. I want to be your safe place, the person you know won't ever run, no matter what. We don't have secrets, and we don't self-sacrifice for one another. You can have my family, my name, everything I've ever had and will ever find. Do you get it now?"

Wonder streaks through her gaze as she slowly nods and reaches up to hold both of my wrists, her thumbs stroking my pulse.

"I love you, Jamie Bateman," she declares, a smile forming on her pretty pink lips. "I'm sorry it took me so long to catch up."

"I'd have waited years."

"It won't last. Once the truth comes out, he'll leave, Blakely. Be smart," her mom snarks behind me.

I distract my wife, bringing our mouths together in a gentle caress. A soft sight escapes her while she squeezes my wrists.

I steal a second kiss before pulling my hands away from her face and linking our fingers together instead. It's an anchor for the both of us but also a promise that I meant what I said. I'm not going anywhere, regardless of what comes next.

When I turn around, Blakely's mom is watching from a few feet away. The security guard lingers closer now, watching me like he's ready to take the woman away from here. I'm not ready for her to go quite yet.

"You should have come to me instead of Blakely," I tell her mom. "I'd have done anything to keep you out of my wife's life. Including giving you your money. I probably would have given you more than what you needed to keep her safe from you. Now, though? You get nothing."

She glares at me before flicking her eyes to where her daughter stands at my side. "You won't feel that way when I tell everyone that you've been lying."

I wet my lips and flash a crooked grin. "Do you really think anyone will believe you? Without any proof? You can try it, but I'm not concerned. There's always someone trying to break a story for a quick buck. You won't be anyone memorable."

I'd never have expected Blakely to share my confidence. Not with her back up against the wall and fear driving her decisions. Though I do wish that she would have brought this to me the night her mom showed up at Nate's game or last night when she was upset. I could have saved her a lot of stress and worry.

I'm not shocked in the slightest that she considered taking the money to pay her mom off so she wouldn't talk. My Blakely would rather be miserable for the rest of her life than see someone she cares about struggle.

At least we'll have time to talk about everything that's happened once her mom is dealt with.

"I'm taking my wife home now. So, if you'll excuse us," I say, tugging at Blakely's hand.

Her mom reaches for us, but Jake is there in a flash, smacking her hand out of the way.

"I told you if you came here again that I'd call the authorities," he says bluntly.

"Don't bother, Jake. She's leaving." I keep my wife tucked into my side, not wanting even an inch of space between us after waking up without her. Her mom has frozen in place when I shift my gaze toward her. "The Pythons have a legal team that I wouldn't suggest pissing off. If you come near my family again, a public jail cell is going to be the least of your problems. I'll be looking forward to seeing what you decide to do next."

I give Blakely the opportunity to add anything, but she simply glides an arm across my front and holds me, staring in the direction of the parking lot.

It's good enough for me.

Now, it'll be just us. And I'm not letting her out of my arms again until I know every single thought in her beautiful head.

44

Blakely

"I'm sorry," I mutter, embarrassed beyond belief at this entire situation.

Jamie smooths his hand over my knee and glances at me over the centre console. "I don't want you to be sorry."

"I should have done things differently."

"What would you have changed?"

Heaving a sigh, I rub at my forehead. We've finally gotten out of traffic, but we're still too far from home. I hate not being closer to him. Our conversation feels too important to be having it in the car. I need to be outside. Somewhere we can be face to face.

"Can you pull over somewhere?" I ask.

"Yes."

His spot of choice is the front of an empty, abandoned Taco Bell parking lot. The boarded-up windows and peeling sign form a perfect backdrop behind his luxury SUV. I'd laugh if I had it in me.

Once we've parked, I rush outside and suck in a long breath. My heart races with the unknown of what's going to happen, but I try and steady myself with the reminder of what he said to me in front of my mother.

My love doesn't come with strings. There are no conditions in this relationship. I want to be your safe place, the person you know won't ever run, no matter what.

It's everything I've ever wanted and needed to hear from someone. And for him to say it so openly and confidently? There isn't a man alive who could compare to him.

"I love you, Bandit. In case you somehow forgot in the past few minutes that we've been driving," he teases, rounding the hood to stand in front of me.

His expression is open and honest. So very Jamie-like that it grounds me.

"I haven't forgotten."

"Good. Myself, on the other hand, I think I need to be reminded how you feel."

A soft laugh escapes me. "You're that needy, huh?"

"The neediest. I'm outright desperate when it comes to you," he coos, gliding a hand down my arm.

His fingers are warm and strong as they curl around my elbow and guide me forward until we're standing toe to toe. He takes my hand and brings it to rest against his chest, twirling my wedding ring.

I stare down at where we touch, almost in disbelief. "I love you, Jamie. So much that it doesn't feel like it should be possible."

"Yeah, that's what I was waiting for," he murmurs, eyes twinkling.

"Was it worth it?"

"Worth what? Every day I've spent with you? Because if that's what you're asking, then abso-fucking-lutely."

My face heats as I flex my fingers against his chest. "How did you know where I was?"

"I followed my gut."

"Is Nate okay?"

"He's just fine. Studying like a little brainiac at school," he soothes.

I nod, swaying forward. "There's a lot to tell you."

"I've got all day."

"Are you planning on skipping practice, then, Pretty Boy?"

"I was hoping you'd just forget about that, actually."

"Kind of hard to when I work with you."

He dips his head and drawls, "We could play hooky together."

With a quirk of my brow, I push forward on my toes and tease a kiss over his lips. He tries to chase me when I pull back, but I wink and fall to my heels before he can make contact.

"Not happening."

With a pout, he drags a knuckle along the edge of my jaw. "Fine. You better get talking, then."

"No pressure," I mutter.

He shakes his head and kisses the back of my hand, drifting them over the rock on my finger.

"It's just us, Bandit. You can talk to me."

Holding his gaze, I grab onto the affection and support he's offering and let it lead me.

"You saw my mom at the game. She watched the interview video of us and after some research figured that I'd finally be of some use to her. She brought up money then and tried threatening me with Nate. I should have known that she wasn't serious about taking him from me, considering she abandoned him in the first place, but I let it get to me. Then, she showed up at the stadium yesterday. It was the same thing. She needed money for her backlogged rent, and when she kept threatening me with Nate . . . I snapped. It just exploded out of my mouth before I could stop it. I told her our marriage wasn't real, and she took it and ran."

If I could go back and change one thing, it would be not letting her affect me to the point of blurting out the truth. It was exactly what she was looking for. A bloody steak held above a starving lion.

Regret shackles me, shame chasing its coattails.

"It doesn't matter what she does with that information.

Anyone who believes what she says will only do so because they already believe exactly what she'll be preaching. It won't change anything," Jamie swears.

"It didn't feel like that before. I was scared Graham would find out, and yeah, he could have sued me for breaking the NDA, but I would have dealt with that. What I couldn't have dealt with is you being punished because of me. Not only with the team but the fans, and then your parents! They would have been so hurt, and I know how much they mean to you. I'd have preferred they just hated me for taking your money instead."

"I want to make something very clear to you," he states, creating an anchor between us with his hold on my hand. "You are more important to me than football. If you had taken money from me to pay off your mom, there wouldn't have been a chance in hell that I would have considered not having you in my life. I know why you contemplated making that choice, and I love you even more for it. I'm aware of all your quirks and personality traits. From your fierce heart, protective nature, and inability to put yourself first in any situation, I know and accept them all. I'm not surprised that your first instinct was to put my career and my family first. But that's going to stop right here, right now."

He takes a step back before lowering himself to one knee in the dirty parking lot, keeping our hands together.

I gasp, eyes burning with tears. The setting around us doesn't match the beauty of the moment, but . . . I think that might make it even more beautiful.

"I don't need money or a successful football career as long as I have you and Nate. You're my family, Bandit. The only two people I see and need in a crowded stadium where tens of thousands of people are watching. I love our quiet nights at home after a home-cooked meal when you pretend to be awake enough to watch a movie but fall asleep five minutes in. I love waking up before you every morning and taking my time looking at how beautiful you are while slipping my pillow beneath your arm because you sleep better holding something. I love the way you still try to pretend that my flirting doesn't affect you when we both know that your pink cheeks don't lie.

"And I really, really love sitting in the hard bleachers beside you watching Nate play ball, knowing that you worked your ass off to make sure that he could do what he loves. That's just who you are. The woman who's going to make sure everyone you care about is happy and taken care of before sitting down and checking in on yourself. You have no idea how special you are, Blakely, and I'm going to spend the rest of forever telling you and proving that I'm here to take care of you when you forget to. So, I want to do this for real this time."

Here, in an abandoned parking lot in the middle of nowhere Vancouver, with tears streaming down my face and splattering on the filthy pavement, Jamie slips my ring off and holds it in the space between us.

"There isn't anything I want more than to have you be my wife, Blakely. Will you marry me?"

I reach out and palm his cheeks, my thumbs tracing the shape of his lips, nose, and jaw. His stare doesn't stray from where it's become locked on mine. Every second that passes between us is another that I repeat every single one of his words in my mind, trying to form a few of my own.

"I never considered myself a damsel in distress. The only man I needed in my life was Nate, and I thought I was content with that. It turns out that I was wrong.

"I didn't need a miracle to wake me up from the slumbered life I'd found myself in. Instead, all I needed to find was you and the love that you've offered me but also that you've evoked from inside of me. You showed me parts of myself that I had forgotten existed, and with every door you helped yank open, you slipped through and made a home for yourself. It only took you a handful of weeks to convince the woman who thought she was content being alone forever that she could have everything she's ever wanted and then some without losing herself in the process.

I fell in love with your devious smirks, sunray personality, and the heart that you hang on your sleeve with pride. You're the most incredible man I've ever known and will ever meet. So, fuck yeah, I'll marry you, husband."

He pounces off the pavement and bulldozes into me. I squeal as he picks me clean off my feet and spins me in a circle.

"You have no idea how happy I am right now," he murmurs in my ear.

"Actually, I think I do."

When my feet touch the ground again, I'm quick to grab him by the shirt and drag him toward me before planting a hard kiss on his mouth. He grins against my lips, and I copy him. Our kiss is sloppy, our teeth clacking and hands wandering frantically, and it's perfect.

The cool band of my ring slides back on my finger when I bring my hand to his neck and hold him, loving every thump of his pulse against my palm.

"Will you marry me again, this time in front of my entire family? Our family?" he asks, tucking my hair behind my ear.

I lean against his body, resting my face in the hollow of his throat as my stomach soars. "You want a redo?"

"Not a full redo. Just something for us. Not for the team, or Graham, but you and me and the people who love us. The wedding I wish I could have given you in the first place."

"You just want a chance to have a reception this time so you can show off your dance moves," I tease, grinning into his skin.

"Well, that, and as much as I loved our kitchen first dance, I want to give you more than that. Another memory for us to hold forever."

"I would love to marry you again, Jamie."

He releases a heavy breath and folds me into his chest. "Thank God."

"As if you thought I'd say no."

"Hey, a man can't ever be too confident."

"Coming from you."

"Don't start a war that you're not prepared to finish, baby," he warns lightly, dropping a hand to grab my ass.

"It never works properly in a vehicle, Jamie."

A smirk is so obvious in his voice he might as well be staring down at me with one right now. "What never works?"

"You're too big for car sex, and you know it."

"This sounds like the perfect chance to test that theory. We have yet to try in the back seat, isn't that right, wife?"

With an exaggerated sigh, I bite back a smile and ask, "What do I get if I'm right?"

"Anything."

"Then yeah, I think I could entertain you for a bit, husband."

45

Jamie

Jaxon leans over and pats my shoulder once we've taken our seats at the table. Both in encouragement and acceptance.

We lost terribly tonight. Our first loss in five games, but I genuinely don't care. It's hard to feel bad about losing when I've got every person who's ever mattered to me smiling up in the stands as we got destroyed.

Coach is a grumpy ass about it, and I had to focus a bit too hard on not racing out of the locker room when he started laying into us. All I wanted to do was get out here, knowing who was waiting.

Tonight's media coverage is special. For the first time in my history on the Pythons and in football in general, I have my family in the room.

"We can go ahead with questions whenever you're ready," Sadie announces, nodding at the group of reporters sitting in front of the stage.

Similar to the first time I answered questions after announcing my proposal, Graham's invited a mix of different people who, during normal circumstances, wouldn't be here. Non-sports sites and social media accounts don't usually care about a win or a loss, but they do love a dramatic life update.

Anything to gain a few followers or subscribers.

I narrow my eyes on the same guy from *Sports Weekly* who's responsible for Blakely's viral video and brace my elbows on the table.

He's not the first to ask a question tonight, though. It's a woman instead, and she smiles kindly before speaking.

"Tough loss tonight after going on your second four-game win streak of the season. Neither of you look too devastated. Is there a reason for that?"

I chuckle while Jax leans into his microphone. "Any loss hurts. We'll have a rough few days at practice after this if Coach has anything to do with it, I'm sure."

"Of course. As is expected. Jamie, can you walk us through what went wrong out there?"

"Sometimes you make the right plays, but the other team makes them better. We'll regroup, fix what needs fixing, and come back stronger. That's all there is to it." Mouth quirking into a smile, I glance to the wall where my beautiful wife stands twirling her wedding ring nervously. "But hey, tonight's not all bad. I've got my family here with me."

Nate beams from his place at Blakely's side. He doesn't seem anxious at all being surrounded by the media, even when they all turn to stare at the pair of them. Shoulders squaring up, he waves at me.

The next question comes from a guy near the back of the room. "Jamie, speaking of that, it's not every day we see family in the media room after a game. What's it like having your wife here tonight? And how are you two handling the circulating talks of relationships and sports?"

"I love having her here. I'd keep her with me every second of every day if I could. As far as everything else, I think Blakely can answer better than I can. What do you think, Bandit?" I ask, handing things over to her the way we'd agreed to earlier.

Truthfully, it was Graham's suggestion. He's enjoying the uptick of gossip, even after learning that her mother could potentially be an issue. Like me, he wasn't concerned with her threat, and considering how helpful Blakely has been, there was a quick discussion, and that was that.

I gained more respect for him during that conversation than in my entire career playing for the Pythons. Yeah, the only thing he cares about is himself and his team per the owner title, but for now, that serves us just fine.

Including Nate and Blakely in tonight's interviews was just another way for us to cover our asses just in case anything potentially damaging ever did come out.

Blakely holds my stare, and I nod encouragingly, showing that I have full trust in her.

"We're just here to support Jamie tonight—win or lose. That's what we'll always do. And as far as the stigma regarding women and sports, I think we need to be focusing on why my statements took off the way they did in the first place. There shouldn't need to be a discourse on why women can watch and love sports without having ulterior motives and being judged for it. It's sexism leading this conversation, and those who can recognize that and stand up against it are the ones who created this buzz. I was just the person who had the luck of saying those things at the right time to the right person.

"And for handling the gossip? There isn't anything for us to handle. I'm happy to see the swell of women here every night and the encouraging conversations being had. But that's all there is. Jamie is who he is, and I am who I am. The media doesn't play a part in our relationship."

Fucking hell, she's perfect.

I blow out a happy sigh, and the microphone carries it through the room. Jaxon chokes on a laugh beside me, cocking a rare half-grin.

"Yeah, safe to say our boy approves of that statement. The hearts in his eyes are a constant occurrence," he announces.

Laughs break out as Blakely blushes and rolls her eyes, playing everything off.

"So, for those people out there who are still doubtful, do you have anything to say?" The question comes from one of the few gossip reporters invited today.

With warmth in my chest and love pouring out of my eyes, I take a bit of a detour, ditching the official plan.

"You know what? I think it's time I introduce my brother-in-law and future football MVP. Nate, come here for a minute."

The kid's eyes widen in shock before he slowly starts my way. Another chair is added up on the stage, and then he's excitedly jumping onto the platform. Jax shuffles down a chair, leaving the middle one open, and offers him his fist. Nate pounds it while sitting between us.

"Nate has not only trusted me with his sister, but he's also given me a little brother. This guy is the real deal both on the field and off it. I consider myself lucky as hell to get to be a part of his life, and that's why I don't care what people believe about us. The most important parts of my life have never been publicly shown, and that's because I respect my privacy, and I'll do the same for Nate and my wife. If we're speaking to anyone in public, it's because we've all agreed to do so. My marriage and family are the most important things to me, and that will never change," I declare proudly, making eye contact with every reporter in the room.

"And one final thing. This kid is going to go pro one day. You've got my word on that. I'd recommend you get pretty familiar with his name because you'll be hearing it often in the coming years."

There's a stunned silence that fills the room. I hold in a laugh and blow a kiss at Blakely before waving her to come up. She's wearing her own Pythons jacket tonight and tight-fitted jeans that I've been dreaming of peeling off since this morning. If I had it my way, she'd be in a Bateman jersey, but according to her, she needs to change it up from time to time.

Who was I to argue?

I reach for her the moment she appears onstage and

encourage her to stay close. She sets a hand on my shoulder and winces at the lights shining down on us before relaxing.

"Tonight didn't go our way on the field, but what matters most isn't just the game. It's the people you fight for on and off the turf. I've got a team I trust and love, a family I'd do anything for, and a future that I'm excited about. Anyone who has anything to say about that doesn't know me. That's the last thing I'm going to say about it," I say, staring up at Blakely and letting her smile draw neon hearts in my soul.

The rest of the interview moves quickly, and the reporters seem content with what they've received from me. I'm more focused on Blakely and Nate than much else, so once we're finally finished, I have them up and out of the room in a blink.

The first thing I do when we're in the family room is kiss my wife. It's been hours since I've tasted her lips, and if I'm going to go home with one loss already tonight, I don't want another.

"You were feeling really loud tonight," she whispers against my lips.

"Mm, is that a bad thing?"

"Your love is never a bad thing. Having you be proud of us is more than I could have ever asked for."

"Do you think they got a good pic of me? I don't want my debut in the league to be of me scrunching my nose or squinting," Nate says, inspecting the room and the memorabilia hung on the walls.

I laugh under my breath and tuck him beneath my arm, hauling him close to us.

"Even if they got a picture of you picking your nose, you'd be fine. Your last name might legally be Monroe, but you're still a Bateman. Once you show them how you play, you'll have scouts stuck to you like glue," I boast.

"Yeah, you're right. Plus, I'm super good-looking."

Blakely snorts, arching a brow as we both eye him. "You're also very, very subtle."

"I fear this is all my influence. I take responsibility for his humility. Or lack thereof," I tease.

"How am I going to handle the two of you?" Blakely asks, flicking her eyes between me and Nate. She runs a hand down my chest before ruffling his hair.

I smooth the hair she has sticking up, and Nate flashes me a grateful grin.

"That's a question I hope you ask yourself forever," I murmur.

She kisses the curve of my jaw. "Well, I'd consider that a given. I am married to you, after all."

It's more than enough confirmation. And a promise.

"Still don't know how I managed that."

"By being yourself, Jamie. I never stood a chance."

Yeah, well, neither did I.

EPILOGUE
SIX MONTHS LATER

Jamie

THE FIRST TIME I MARRIED BLAKELY, I KNEW THE WEDDING WASN'T for us. It was for the Pythons, Graham, and the news outlets stalking the edges of the building.

This time, it's for me as much as it is her.

We chose everything together, the way we should have the first time. Avery supplied and arranged the flowers, the groomsmen's suits were chosen on a day out with all of my cousins, and the bridesmaids, along with my ma, took a trip to Ottawa to shop for their dresses at a boutique Braxton recommended.

I spent hours with Blakely tasting cake flavours and touring venues. We planned the playlist song by song and begged and convinced Noah to perform a song at the reception. He was the one who convinced Brody Steele, Braxton's sister's fiancé and one of the biggest names in country music, to sing our first-dance song.

It was an exhaustive experience, but I wouldn't change a thing if it meant that I could give her the best and last wedding she'll ever have.

Standing at the altar as every important person in Blakely's and my life walks toward me, I know that this is right. This life, this love, and the future I've always wanted for myself are aligned.

Oliver, Nova, and Avery are first, their family of soon-to-be four leading the pack down the aisle toward where I wait for my wife. My brother was here the first time, but not like this. His full support has come through, and with every day that passes, all three of them fall a little bit more for Blakely.

He releases his girls with quick kisses on their cheeks and shifts to stand beside me, a hand squeezing mine. I sniff past the emotion already swelling inside of me, and he blinks his away at the same time.

Dad catches my eye from the first row before he nods, keeping his grip on Mom's hand unbreakable. Everything he spoke to me before I was here the first time still stands.

My wife and I have been floating these past few months, but there have still been times where I've had to think back to his advice a time or two. Loving a woman as headstrong as Blakely doesn't come without some learning, and loving a man like me has pushed her in the same ways. But what we have together is and will always be worth every challenge.

Maddox and Braxton are next, and as expected, my cousin keeps a hand on her swelling belly like the proud dad he has always been. He was the first to find his happy ending, and when they had Liam, I knew he was always meant to be a father. Watching him have a second child, a girl this time, is incredible.

Adalyn and Cooper walk down the aisle like I'd expect they would a runway. The woman who's seen the most incredible year of her life with not only the birth of their baby girl but also walking in one of the biggest fashion shows in the entire world clutches onto her husband with a beaming smile and a wiggle of her fingers in my direction.

Noah and Tinsley are a sight to see. They've always been that way, yet somehow, it's like they grow closer and more attached by the day. Instead of linking arms like every other couple before them, Noah has his wrapped around her waist while she grips his front, leaning into him like she knows he could carry both of their weight if he needed to.

Their love story has so much still to be written. I feel that in my gut.

When the youngest members of my life come out with their arms reluctantly linked and fake enjoyment straining their features, everything feels complete. Amelia and Easton will have their story to tell soon, and I feel lucky that I'll be able to witness it one day.

Finally, the music changes, and I turn my full focus to the end of the aisle. I'm nearly crawling out of my skin in anticipation of seeing her. My wife from the moment she stumbled into my house that night.

The full rows of guests stand. My eyes burn before she's even turned the corner. I sniff and straighten my shoulders, my fingers sweaty where they're clasped in front of me.

Nate appears first, grinning wide and bright as I catch his eyes and huff a wet laugh. He tips his chin in a soft nod, and it's the only approval I need.

In a swishing white dress similar to the one she wore the first time we were in this position, Blakely finds my eyes and smiles. The ground shakes beneath my feet at that smile.

A veil drapes down her back and over the material of the dress that follows behind her. Lace sleeves, the same corseted top, and the same silk that I remember feeling beneath my fingertips are all in front of me, but it's her brown-flecked green eyes that gleam with emotion that matter.

Slowly, she reaches me, and Nate places her hand in mine before taking his spot beside my brother. Blakely reaches for my other hand and releases a heavy breath, clutching onto me for support.

"You're breathtaking, Bandit," I whisper.

Her bottom lip wobbles. "So are you."

It feels like déjà vu, but better. Real. Every word we speak and the vows we make. We've been here before, only this time, I'm so incredibly in love with her.

And when the officiant declares us Mr. and Mrs. Bateman for the final time, I make a show of kissing my wife like I wish I had the first.

She giggles against my lips as I take her in my arms and tip her back. Her leg kicks out as I cup her thigh and seal our mouths. Cheers and clapping follow, but I take my time right here, shoving every ounce of my love and pride into our kiss.

Only when she puts her leg down and gives a playful shove at my chest do I release her and guide her upward.

"I love the fuck out of you, Blakely Bateman," I declare.

She leans against my chest and gazes up at me. "I love the fuck out of you, Jamie Bateman."

"You feel smaller, Ma. Are you shrinking?"

She scoffs as I lead us through our dance. "That's not what you should say to your mother on one of the most emotional days of my life."

"When should I mention it, then?" I tease.

"Never. It's not polite."

"I just want to make sure you don't suddenly shrink so small you're a speck of dust that I won't be able to see. What would I tell my future children when their grandma becomes dust?"

"I'm not that old, Jamison!" she scolds.

Chuckling, I twirl her outward. Her dance skills are far better than mine, as they should be after a lifetime of ballet.

"Thank you for being here, Mom. And for everything you've done for me and Blakely."

"I love her for you, sweetheart. And I love her for our family. Both of my daughters are incredible. We're very lucky."

There's a soft pat on my back, and I swing us around to find my dad dancing with Blakely a few steps away. He must have heard some of our conversation because he nods in agreement, swaying her in his arms.

My wife smiles shyly as I consider stealing her back already. It hasn't even been the full length of the song being sung, but I've missed her since the second I gave her over to my dad.

"Life is changing so quickly," I murmur, watching them sway away from us.

Mom leans her cheek on my chest and hugs me as we finish our dance. "And it's nowhere near stopping, Jamie. You have to cherish every moment of what's coming because each one will be here and gone in a flash. It feels like just yesterday I was hauling you and your brother to dance practices and bribing you with animal crackers so you didn't climb onto the barre. You were both so, so little then. Now look at you. Oliver's married and a soon-to-be father of two beautiful babies, and you've just made your soulmate your wife and are preparing to enter into a new life together. I feel like I only blinked, and everything changed."

Tears sting my eyes and tighten my throat. "We couldn't have had better parents."

"We tried our best."

"Why do you think we grew up to be so amazing? I mean, Oliver's grumpy as hell, but I think I turned out pretty perfect."

She laughs, pulling back to look up at me and palm my cheek for a moment. "It was only fitting that one of you took after your father and one took after me. I always teased your dad that Oliver would be his karma."

"Are you finally admitting that I'm the better son?"

"Oh, don't start. I'll never choose favourites."

"But if you did . . ." I drawl.

"Stop talking and just dance with your mom, Jamieson."

With a smirk, I do exactly that.

Blakely

My father-in-law is an even worse dancer than I am. It's honestly quite adorable, considering how intimidating he is. Flaws make him a bit less scary.

"Gracie's right, you know? We did get very lucky with the women our sons chose to have in our lives forever," he says.

I almost trip on my dress as his words register. "Thank you. That's really nice of you to say."

"I'm not in the business of being nice for no reason. I mean it. We're happy to have you be a member of our family."

"It's an incredible family to be a part of. You've made me feel welcome, but also Nate, and that's important to me."

Tyler offers me a small but incredibly sincere smile. "You did well with him. He'll be a good man one day."

I roll my lips and look away, those statements hitting home. The confirmation from a man who raised two incredible men, one of whom is the best one I've ever met, is almost too much to handle.

"Coming from you, that means a lot," I croak, trying to hide the crack in my voice.

"My father was a man I didn't meet until I was a teenager. I raised myself on my own before and after that, and I wish I'd have had someone who cared about me as much as you care about your brother. He'll remember everything you've done for him for the rest of his life. I admire how strong you are. Nothing worthwhile ever comes easy, and I know that you've fought harder than you ever should have had to for the good you've found."

There are no words that would do justice to my appreciation. But I hope that as I let go of my fears and hug him, he can tell how much what he's said has meant to me.

I squeeze my eyes shut and trap the tears that try to escape and ruin my makeup as he adjusts his arms to hold me right back. It's the second hug I've received from him, and it's even more special than the first one.

"How come every time I find you hugging my wife, she's crying, Dad?" Jamie asks, his voice soft.

He peels me out of his father's arms and takes me into his instead. It feels like coming back home after a night spent lost in the woods. My head clears, and my heart races.

I smile at Tyler in a final show of thanks that he doesn't hesitate to return before patting Jamie's arm.

"Go dance with your wife, son."

My husband nods firmly, and then they share an intense look that I glance away from, giving them as much space as I can.

A moment later, Jamie's twirling me dramatically, a proud laugh escaping him. Several other couples join us on the dance floor, but it's impossible to pay attention to a single one of them.

"Have you had a good wedding night, wife?" he asks once I've landed back in his hold.

I set my hands on his shoulder and waist and hum, undecided. "I'm not sure."

"In that case, how can I make it better?"

"Will you let me feed you cake and splatter it on your face?"

"Is that a trick question? Obviously, you can rub my face with cake. But only if I can do the same to yours."

"What about a compromise?" I ask, my chest flaming when his hand finds a new home low on my back.

His head dips, words kissing my cheek. "What do you have in mind?"

"When we get home, you can rub cake anywhere you want."

"Let's skip the cake altogether, and I'll make dessert out of you instead."

A tingle rushes down my spine. "Wouldn't that look bad? The bride and groom skipping out on their wedding reception?"

"Not if you were only gone a few minutes. Look at you, Blakely. My wife is a goddess."

"So, you're suggesting we sneak off and have a wedding quickie?"

He laughs lowly. "Yeah, I guess I am. What do you say, Mrs. Bateman?"

In the last eight months, Jamie has changed my life. There's no more stress or fear. I wake up feeling cherished and excited and fall asleep settled, at peace. My life is exactly the way it was always meant to be.

This wedding was for more than the typical certificate and an exchange of rings. We already had both. Instead, we got married for nothing more than a reminder to ourselves that despite the reason behind our paperwork, what we have is real.

This is my forever guy. My greatest strength on my weakest day.

"I say lead the way."

EXTENDED EPILOGUE
SIX MONTHS AFTER THAT

Blakely

I've taken to hockey more than I have football.

It's the rules! Hockey rules are much easier to understand than football ones, and I'm pretty sure there's not even half of the number of them. Sure, I don't know what an icing is, and I always call for goalie interference, even when Jamie laughs and tells me there wasn't any, but still.

I think it's given my husband a bit of a complex. As of three months ago, I've started finding little notes around the house with football terms and their definitions. They've been on the bathroom mirror, his pillow when I woke up last week, and even inside of the kettle. Yes, *inside*. I ended up drowning it in water before I realized it was there.

He's even got the team in on it. For no apparent reason, Chase and Jax showed up for dinner last week with a CFL dictionary and ten of their favourite football movies. And it doesn't stop there. They turned Nate against me too.

This morning, he hid my limited-edition Warriors/Pythons Bateman hockey jersey that Jamie surprised his dad with a few weeks back and replaced it with the new alternate Pythons jersey. Even now, as I pull up the sleeves of the backup Ottawa

Beavertails jersey Braxton lent me, my brother smirks at me like he's an evil genius.

Sixteen years old and confident, he's grown so much in the last six months. Not only is he thriving at football, but his grades are incredible, and he's made friends. Lots of them.

Jamie's his best friend, though. The two of them are pretty much glued at the hip, and their relationship has helped Nate start to grow into the man I know he'll be one day. The brotherly role Jamie plays in his life has given him the confidence and guidance that I couldn't have on my own.

"I can't believe they're picking on you like this," Braxton says, coming up to me with a baby girl in one arm and a little boy clutching the other from the ground.

I cock my head. "You can't? Jamie won't ever let me live this one down."

"Okay, that's fair. Maddox would probably cry if I told him that I liked football more than hockey."

"It's not even that I said that! All I said was that hockey's simpler and easier to watch," I clarify helplessly.

She sucks in a breath. "Oh, Blakely."

"Oh, come on. You know he's being dramatic."

"You and I married the two most dramatic men in this entire family. This is only par for the course."

I groan. "You're right. So, what do you suggest I do? Pretend I was just lying?"

"Absolutely not," Gracie guffaws, joining us. "Twist it to your benefit. Make him jealous enough that he doesn't care which sport you prefer as long as you don't make a show out of it again."

Braxton nods excitedly. "That's brilliant."

"All done talking, Mom. I wanna see Daddy now. He's skating!" Liam whines, tugging at Braxton.

He's adorable in his Hutton Ottawa jersey, joggers, and sneakers. If you swap the joggers for jeans, he matches Braxton and Annie. That was probably the point.

"Go see him, then, baby. Look, Grandpa and Uncle Noah are already over there. You can sit with them and watch," she suggests, removing her hand from his grip to give him a light push.

He doesn't bother replying before taking off across the suite. I laugh and listen as Braxton sighs and leans her head against my shoulder.

"Sorry, I swear he doesn't stop moving," she says with a sigh, adjusting Annie on her hip.

Ava comes swooping in. "Oh, let me help. She's getting so big. I can imagine how sore your arm's getting. Maddox was so heavy as a baby that I had to wear him in a carrier on my back or my arms would ache."

She waits for a nod of permission from Braxton before slowly easing the little girl out of her arms.

"Thank you, Ava," Braxton says, stretching her arm out.

"Always, sweetheart."

I take a look around the giant suite and, of course, get drawn to the bar, where Jamie's leaning back on a barstool, legs spread wide. His Ottawa jersey is loose on his upper body, but his jeans are tight enough to squeeze his thighs and ass just right. The backward cap he's wearing is old and frayed, and as he takes it off to flip it around, my core tightens desperately.

He's sinfully sexy. Every day that we're together, I seem to grow more and more attracted to everything about him, inside and out.

"How do you suggest I start making Jamie jealous?" I ask, only half-aware of what I'm saying.

The other half of my brain is too busy eye-fucking my husband to comprehend normal thinking.

"Addie," Gracie whisper hisses in the direction of where her niece is lounging on Cooper's lap by the ice-facing windows.

The bombshell blonde looks at us past her husband's shoulder and smacks a kiss on his cheek before rushing over to us.

"You called?"

Her daughter is distracted, too busy smacking the windows beside Liam to notice that her mom has snuck away.

Gracie curls her open arm around her niece and ushers her close. "You're the only one of us who has no loyalty to a sport, and we need your help."

"Avery doesn't either," Addie points out.

Gracie snorts out a laugh. "Sure, but Oliver will be just as bad as Jamie if Avery starts fawning over a hockey player."

"Does this have to do with Jamie scowling at the team during warm-ups?"

"Yes. Apparently, I've done the unthinkable and chosen hockey over football, and now he's being a big baby," I tell Addie.

She smirks, the devious streak in her that everyone always talks about shining through. "Alright. I'm in. Come with me, Blakely. Let's make some men jealous."

"I take it you enjoy this particular game?" I ask once we leave the group of women and move to the windows.

"More like I love what comes after. There's truly nothing like jealous sex."

Over a year into my relationship with Jamie, and after all the time I've spent with his family, it's still Adalyn who takes me by surprise most often. She has absolutely no filter, and it fits her personality perfectly.

"That is if he's still jealous by the time we get home tonight," I say.

"Oh, he will be. Staying here and being forced to watch the rest of this game will only make it worse."

"That's a good point."

She winks. "I know. Now, follow my lead."

I nod and steal a look in Jamie's direction, finding Oliver and Tinsley talking to him. My stomach flutters in anticipation.

Addie clutches my arm and gasps dramatically, purposefully

drawing attention. "Look at that one! God, he's so flexible. Do you think that's just for the ice or off it too?"

"I've seen videos online, and I don't think it's just on the ice," I sigh dreamily, focusing on the towering figure in the net below us.

It's absolutely a lie. Hopefully, Jamie will be too flustered to think too much about the details of what I'm saying.

Adalyn groans and brings a hand to touch the window. "Ooh! Look, he's taking his helmet off. Oh, my God. Spraying water on your face shouldn't be so hot."

"Do you think he does *that* off the ice?"

"I sure hope so. Damn, that's sexy."

It's hard not to laugh at how terrible of a job we're doing. This sounds like the opening of a porno more than an attempt at making a grown man jealous, but—

A large, hot palm presses to my spine before travelling up and toying with my hair. With a look over my shoulder, Jamie's scowl appears. His eyes are a deeper shade of blue than usual, and my breath skips as arousal warms my belly.

"What an interesting conversation you're having, Bandit. It's almost like you were admiring the men down there."

"That's because she was, Jam Jam. Considering how stubborn football players are, maybe she was right about preferring hockey after all," Adalyn taunts, shooting me a wink that Jamie's too busy staring at me to catch.

He curves me to his side and brushes a kiss across my temple. "Blakely knows very well that being stubborn is one of my best qualities but not the strongest."

"I can only imagine that you're referring to being thick-skulled. You always could take hits to the head better than anyone else."

"Adalyn," Cooper drawls, joining us with an amused crook of his lips.

The man with the whole dirty-professor thing going on keeps

one hand tucked into his slacks while the other holds his wife's hip.

Adalyn grins at his presence and bats her eyes up at him. "Yes?"

"You're causing mischief again."

"Oh no. Am I?"

He chuckles and glances at me, offering a sympathetic look that has my brows lifting. When he only darts his eyes to Jamie, I put the pieces together.

Addie pats me on the arm and then yanks her husband's hand out of his pocket so she can hold it. "Well, have fun. My job is complete."

Jamie grunts in response, not so much as blinking while he watches me. I nip at my cheek and try to ignore him as the other couple leaves us here alone. The hockey game is in full swing, and while I can't make out who's who from up here, I know that Maddox is in one of the red-and-black jerseys.

Warm breath tickles my ear when Jamie flattens his hand to the window and leans close, making sure I feel every inch of his chest against my arm. "If you wanted to make me jealous, you didn't need to bother with Addie. Seeing you standing here looking down on the ice is more than enough."

"You're being ridiculous, Jamie," I declare breathlessly.

"Maybe. I tend to get this way when it comes to you."

"I can prefer hockey over football but love you most of all."

"If you want me to spray water into my face, that can be arranged. The only thing I can't do for you is the splits. I prefer to spend my time spreading your legs instead."

I gulp, my lashes fluttering. "I get your point."

"No, I don't think you do. Not yet."

"What do you mean?"

"We're leaving in ten minutes. I don't feel like lingering."

I turn my head, bringing my cheek to where his lips are waiting. "And if I wanted to stay?"

"Oh, I bet you fucking do, baby. I'll make it up to you."

"What do I do the ten minutes, then?"

He kisses my flaming cheek and curls his finger beneath my chin before taking my mouth in a slow, teasing caress.

"Keep looking out the window. I'll be punishing you regardless of how much longer you stare at the men on the ice. Might as well get as much time as you can."

I know the minute Jamie closes the bedroom door behind us that I'm in trouble.

My grin is cheek-pinching as I linger at the end of the bed and wait. His steps are heavy and slow, and I coil my muscles tighter, half leaning over the bed by the time he's behind me.

"I've been rock fucking solid since you put on that show for me. I'm trying not to push your face into the bed and spank your ass raw, Blakely."

I quickly unsnap my jeans and wiggle them down to my ankles while his gaze burns into me. Inch by inch, I free myself of the denim before leaving them on the floor. My ass is cold and bare besides the tiny string between my cheeks.

"Christ," he curses, his thighs pressing against me. "Nate's home."

"He'll have his headphones on by now."

I jerk forward with a gasp when he brings both hands down on my ass with synchronized claps. His fingers dip into the flesh and pull before retreating. He pulls at the top of my thong and releases it, forcing it to snap against my skin.

"You've been driving me out of my mind ever since you made that comment about hockey months ago. I know it's possessive and overbearing. *I'm* possessive and overbearing."

I reach a hand out for him and grab his knee, holding it

firmly. "Possessive, yes. Overbearing, no. I like that you get jealous. It makes me feel wanted."

"Fuck, baby. I want you all the time. Always."

"Prove it," I provoke, wiggling my hips.

"Only if you tell me that you forgive me for being jealous."

"There was nothing to forgive," I murmur.

That's enough for him.

In a blink, he has the rest of our clothes off and my thighs spread at the edge of the bed. I press my chest into the mattress and hand over control to him, knowing that I'm going to be floating on a wave of pleasure any second now.

"You're perfect, wife," he hisses while dipping a finger through my slit and guiding it inside of me. "Tight, wet, and mine."

"Yours," I echo, pushing back, needing more.

He's one step ahead, adding a second and third finger before I have to ask. Usually, that would have been enough to make me come right here and now, but tonight, I want more than his fingers.

"Fuck me, Jamie. I can't wait," I whimper.

"Okay, baby. It's going to be snug."

"I want it that way."

He groans long and low, and then the head of his cock is breaching me, splitting me in half. My hips dig into the mattress while my nipples drag across the comforter, and I whine at the fullness.

"That's it. That's it, Blakely. Your pussy takes me so well, so good," he praises, reaching along my body to take my hand as I push it across the mattress. "Almost there. You nearly have . . . *Fuck*."

"Make me stretch. I can take it. I'm ready," I gasp, already close enough to taste the explosion of pleasure on my tongue.

He shoves himself the rest of the way. My cry is silent, nothing but hot air escaping my parted lips. Then he's moving, and I feel him deep enough to wonder if he's in my stomach. A shift of his hips, and he's expertly prodding my G-spot.

My eyes roll back. His hips smack my ass as he picks up speed, driving into me harder and harder. It's not enough to just feel the pleasure from his movements, but when he folds himself over me and covers my back in kisses, the added love is what tips me over.

"I love you," I whine before burying my face into the bed and crying out with the power of my orgasm.

He powers into me, grunting as I squeeze him tight, my pussy spasming with my pleasure. "That's it, wife. Take my cum and keep it deep all fucking night."

Heat lashes at my walls, and I go limp, smiling sleepily. By the time he's finished, I'm as loopy as I am happy. He bundles me in his arms and carries me to my side of the bed.

"I need to clean up," I mumble, lying on my back once he's tucked me in.

"Sure. If you're awake enough to get up and do that. I was serious about you keeping my cum inside of you all night."

"I'm on birth control."

He laughs softly, pushing my hair out of my face and kissing my forehead. "We have a lifetime together to worry about kids. For now, I just want to fall asleep knowing you're marked as mine."

"Alright, weirdo," I tease.

"Your weirdo."

Blinking up at him, I reach for his hand and interlock our fingers. "I do want kids with you one day."

His features soften, eyes brightening. "I want kids with you too, Bandit."

"Maybe only two max. I'm not sure yet."

"We don't have to know that number quite yet."

"You're right. But I want you to know that I do want that. Especially after seeing your cousins' kids and the way you interact with them. You'll be a good dad. The best one."

"I've already seen you be a mother to Nate. You'll be incredible to our children one day."

I tug at his hand and bring it to my lips. "I fall more in love with you every day."

"And I'll continue to do the same for the rest of forever."

I've never looked forward to the future more.

Thank you for reading *Their Greatest Strength*! If you enjoyed it, please leave a review on Amazon and Goodreads.

This is the "official" end of the Greatest Love series, but not the final book of the universe. There are still stories to be told for characters that just didn't *quite* fit in this series.

To make sure you don't miss a single update + to snag some bonus chapters including one for TGS, make sure you're subscribed to my newsletter and a member of my Facebook group!

www.hannahcowanauthor.com
Hannah's Hotties on FB

(Second generation) - Greatest Love series:

Her Greatest Mistake – Maddox and Braxton (Hockey romance)
Her Greatest Adventure – Adalyn and Cooper (Brothers bff, age gap romance)
His Greatest Muse – Noah and Tinsley (Rockstar x boxer romance)
His Greatest Treasure – Oliver and Avery (Single mom, firefighter romance)
Their Greatest Strength – Jamieson and Blakely

Acknowledgements

I don't know how I got here. Somehow, just like that, the world that started everything has come to a very unofficial ending. The Swift Hat-Trick trilogy was the beginning, but the Greatest Love series changed my life. It made my dream of being an author a reality. These characters are my comfort, and losing them after five years feels like I've chopped off a limb. But if I'm going to have to say goodbye, these are the characters and the story I want to leave this series and universe with.

Jamie and Blakely are everything to me. I feel like I always say that, but there's just something different this time. I truly feel so incredibly proud of them and their love and the story they've told, and I am so beyond excited to have everyone finally meet them to see what I do. Jamie is the book man of my dreams, and Blakely is so much like me it's almost uncanny. Their love is one I'll cherish forever.

I have so many thank yous like I always do, but they hit a bit harder knowing that this is the last time I'll ever write a thank you in this universe.

To my best friends, you hold me together when my pieces are dropping one by one. I've lost track of the number of voice memos I've sent or SOS texts too late at night. Nicole, Becci, Hayley, thank you for listening to my rants, offering your hands for me to take when I'm tipping off the edge, and for helping me brainstorm when my pantsing habits take over. I love you more than words.

Thank you to the phenomenal team of creative masterminds

who have been here with me for such a giant chunk of my career. Mary + Julie at Books and Moods, Sandra with One Love Editing, Cassie at Cassie's Creative, and Maddy and Tori with The Bubbly Bookshelf, thank you for helping me turn my words into something beautiful.

Thank you to my fiancé/husband/best friend, for being my BIGGEST cheerleader. Because of you, I took the leap to put words to paper in the first place, and hearing you shout about my achievements, regardless of how big or small, every chance you can get is an incredible thing to witness. I love you.

Thank you to LB, my friend and powerhouse PA. I've lost track of the number of times you've texted me reminding me of the million things that I've forgotten about because you know better than anyone that I have the memory of a fish. I'm so grateful that I get to call you not only my friend but a crucial part of my team. You have a heart of gold, and you'll never get rid of me now.

To Sierra, Courtney, Glav, Jenine, Elin—I SEE YOU. I see you, and I love you, and I just . . . you blow my mind. You've helped me accomplish so much in the last year, and I truly hope you know how much I appreciate everything you do.

Thank you to Hannah at Penguin Michael Joseph for seeing something in me way back while reading Lucky Hit. You offered me an opportunity to live out my dream as a traditionally published author, and I'm so grateful for that.

Thank you to my incredible influencer team, who continue to show up for me with every book I write. To this day, I still can't believe you read my books and love them enough to constantly show up for me. I don't say thank you enough, but even if I said it every day, it wouldn't feel like enough. You truly have no idea how much it means to me to have you share my books and offer me such love and support.

And finally, thank you to everyone who has ever picked up one of my books, whether it was my very first, tenth, or if this is your first time meeting me. Your ability to shock me every single day is incredible. I owe this all to you.

Here's to many more years of storytelling to come. Thank you.

He just wanted a decent book to read ...

Not too much to ask, is it? It was in 1935 when Allen Lane, Managing Director of Bodley Head Publishers, stood on a platform at Exeter railway station looking for something good to read on his journey back to London. His choice was limited to popular magazines and poor-quality paperbacks – the same choice faced every day by the vast majority of readers, few of whom could afford hardbacks. Lane's disappointment and subsequent anger at the range of books generally available led him to found a company – and change the world.

'We believed in the existence in this country of a vast reading public for intelligent books at a low price, and staked everything on it'
Sir Allen Lane, 1902–1970, founder of Penguin Books

The quality paperback had arrived – and not just in bookshops. Lane was adamant that his Penguins should appear in chain stores and tobacconists, and should cost no more than a packet of cigarettes.

Reading habits (and cigarette prices) have changed since 1935, but Penguin still believes in publishing the best books for everybody to enjoy. We still believe that good design costs no more than bad design, and we still believe that quality books published passionately and responsibly make the world a better place.

So wherever you see the little bird – whether it's on a piece of prize-winning literary fiction or a celebrity autobiography, political tour de force or historical masterpiece, a serial-killer thriller, reference book, world classic or a piece of pure escapism – you can bet that it represents the very best that the genre has to offer.

Whatever you like to read – trust Penguin.

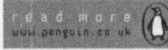